FAKING IT

or
The
Wrong
Hungarian

Gerald Green

FAKING IT

or

The

Wrong

Hungarian

TRIDENT PRESS

NEW YORK

SBN: 671–27073–7

LIBRARY OF CONGRESS CATALOG CARD NUMBER: 70–138430

PUBLISHED SIMULTANEOUSLY IN THE UNITED STATES AND
CANADA BY TRIDENT PRESS, A DIVISION OF SIMON & SCHUSTER,
INC., 630 FIFTH AVENUE, NEW YORK, N.Y. 10020

PRINTED IN THE UNITED STATES OF AMERICA

And Moses sent them to spy out the land of Canaan.

—Numbers 13:17

Intelligence is probably the least understood and most misrepresented of the professions.

—Allen Dulles

FAKING IT
or
The
Wrong
Hungarian

I

"Sorry, sir. First-class passengers only."

"But the economy toilets are full up," I lied. "I think there are a couple of Arabs planting bombs in them. Occupied for the last ten minutes."

She giggled. But she didn't budge her firm *tochis* from the closed curtain that separated the plebs from the patricians. Blonde white hair, black eyes, muddy skin: Miss Donnizetti from the Bronx in an albino's wig.

"Ask the stewardess to knock on the doors," she said.

"But I got to wee-wee."

"Sorry. The whole first-class section is full of VIP's. Nobody allowed in."

I peeked through the slightly parted gray curtain, and I saw Arno Flackman's Brillo-head bobbing and nodding—the old athlete himself, the old counter-puncher. He was talking to James Warfield Keen, seated across the aisle. I managed to catch Keen's breathy voice.

"Yes . . . yes . . . Arno . . . an incredible sensation . . . killing a man with your own hands . . ."

"Miss Donnizetti," I said. "Those are not VIP's. Those are literary people. I saw them skulk on at Kennedy. Two famous novelists and two critics. They rate several rungs below the Aqua Velva After-Shave Club and I think I have the right to use their john."

"I know, I know, Jack," Arno Flackman was muttering. "I once strangled a guy with my mitts . . ."

Oh, Hemingway. Oh, Papa. What you did to a generation of writers! All that ballsy-gutsy, *machismo*. See, I'm an intellectual type fellah, I write books, but I'm also all muscle, all heart, with a killer instinct, a slit-eyed, cool-headed assassin, *'fraid of nothing,* like Ernest said when he was five.

There was a flash of burnished gold in first class: Lila Metrick, the Juno of the Bigdomes, the Little Iodine of Academia. She was gorgeous, a tall, great-rumped Boston blonde, all WASP dignity and Far-out lefto opinions, and I had hungered for her a long, long time.

"Ah, that would be Miss Metrick," I said, standing on tippy-toes. "I, ah, I would like to get in there."

Miss Donnizetti guffawed. "Not on Pan-Am, you don't. And you can't fly United unless you're married. Oh, gee, I just saw one of your Arabs come out of the potty."

Did she shove me gently? It was clear in any case that I was not welcome in first class. Flackman was a king, a despot, a celebrity as gleaming and iridescent as any Kennedy, any actor. Old J. W. Keen was passé, a hoarse voice from the past, and Lila Metrick was not really Big Dubs. But if Flackman wanted privacy, he got it. I had wanted to ask him about the conference we were all going to attend in Paris, and to argue with Metrick about her article in the little magazine *Spasm*, but all that would have to wait.

I am an indifferent and untalented liar, and I had the feeling that Miss Donnizetti was watching me to see if I really had to urinate. So I ambled back to the john. The passenger exiting the head grinned at me. A dark, satiny, thin young fellow, hawk nose, sharp cheekbones, and gold teeth.

"*Salaam aleikum,*" I said.

Yes, an Arab. But not the terrorist type. He smiled cheerfully and spoke excellent English. "Very good, very good. *Aleikum salaam.*"

Back at my aisle seat, I tried *Time, Newsweek,* and *US*

News—the latter ran its semimonthly article proving that more American Negroes drove Chryslers than all the Bulgarians in the world—and then turned to the young couple seated next to me. Rejected by the Literary Giants, I tried them, although normally kids decked out in headbands, beads, fringed vests, and faded bell-bottoms scare me.

"Quite a group up front," I said to the boy.

"Hah?"

"Delegates to the big conference in Paris. All the heavies are in first class. The State Department is probably paying."

He squinted at me with dull contempt—a chubby, white-skinned boy in his early twenties, fleshy nose and blubbery lips, brown hair down to his shoulders, scraggly beard, his eyes darting about like cockroaches. His girl friend—or wife—was small and smudged, pretty in a bleached, bloodless way. I admired her dusty pink pantyhose, which may have been a sign of growth on my part. An old-fashioned fetishist, I normally am stirred by long garters, stocking tops, the edge of the girdle, and a darting flash of white thigh.

"Screw 'em all," the young man mumbled. "Establishment finks."

"Well, yes and no. James Warfield Keen has won a Nobel Prize and three Pulitzers, even though he turned a little right-wing in his old age. And I thought young people regarded Arno Flackman as your *guru*, your leader and inspiration."

The little girl crossed her pink legs. What there was of the miniskirt moved up to her navel. No pants. "Flackman is out of it," she said. "He's irrelevant."

"Ah, I can see how you'd feel that way," I said lamely. Frankly, I can't stand Flackman either. But still—customs of the service and so on. Fellow novelists. Fellow delegates to the conference.

"What the frig is this conference anyway?" the young man muttered. "Anything worth seeing?"

I inhaled. "Why, yes, I think it would interest involved young folks like yourself. It's the first World Conference on

11

the Arts and Sciences, with delegates from seventy-two countries. You know, C. P. Snow's old dictum—the two cultures, the two worlds of the humanities and the scientists, getting together in meaningful dialogue."

"Like you believe all that shitman?"

"My name isn't Shitman. It's Bloodworth."

He grinned mockingly. The girl leaned forward, her hand sliding into her companion's denim'd crotch. "Jesus, he's outa sight," she muttered.

"Out of his tree. Shitman, the only thing we got to do with conferences like that is destroy them. Glad we found out, so's we can get the brothers together to picket you."

"You have the wrong people. These are all intellectuals, scientists, artists. All the way from liberals to Maoists. It's a chance for them to exchange ideas, extend the frontiers."

"Shitman, it's a goddamn bourgeois diversion." He put his hand on his lady's thigh. "Vannie baby, we got to change the scenario. This bash the fellow is talking about is too good to lose." He winked at me, and now, when he spoke, I heard the drawled preppie accents of Scarsdale, Great Neck, or Red Bank. This bearded punk, this bomb-throwing excrescence, was threatening to disrupt *our* conference. "Cold water is better than Vaseline for Mace," he sneered. "You see a bottle in the air, lay flat and turn your head to the wall." He turned his back on me. The children embraced.

We had six more hours to Paris. I enjoy flying, but not next to these rebel children of the suburbs. Let them abuse their own parents, those muscled Met fans, fresh from the country club.

"Ah, *salaam*, sir, I am attending the conference, yes."

My Arab friend from the toilet was standing in the aisle. "Oh, I'm glad. I'm Benjamin Bloodworth. An American novelist."

"Yes, yes. I suspect I may have heard of you. I am told Mr. Flackman is on the plane."

I wasn't insulted. After all, Flackman is Flackman. He is a

force of nature, a presence, a face that stares at you from *Paris Match* and *Esquire*. "He's up front with the elite," I said. "Are you a writer?"

"Oh, goodness no. I am a soil chemist. An occupation, sir, that is more important to my countrymen in Jordan than writing, with all due respect to you, sir."

The fellow was seated on the arm of the vacant seat on the aisle. He wanted to talk, I gathered. A Jordanian. I had made my joke about bombs, and I was sorry. Israelis have told me that Arabs, individually, are the sweetest, nicest people, the warmest of friends. Why not?

"Here is my card, sir, and I do hope we shall have a chance to dine together in Paris."

I read it:

DAOUD JABALI
Director of Agronomy
Khalil Institute,
Amman, Jordan

For some reason, I was studying his shoes. They were odd-looking high sneakers—brown canvas, with thick rubber soles, a rubber toe, round patches on the ankles.

"You admire them?" Jabali said. "Marvelous for the deserts and the mountains, where I spend a good deal of time."

Where had I seen crazy high sneaks like that? An Abercrombie & Fitch advertisement?

At dusk I smelled the young couple next to me—B.O., grass, and something like incense. His name was Harvey; hers was Vannie. At nightfall, winging over the Atlantic, lulled by the drone of Messrs. Pratt and Whitney's mighty engines, I was awakened by a rhythmic pumping noise. They were making love. Right next to me. They'd yanked out the arm rest between their seats. Young Harvey was on his side, playing at the beast with two backs, thrusting and withdrawing in short, determined strokes. In deference to me, I gathered, they were doing it under a gray airline blanket. The girl's

13

pantyhose were wadded into the elastic pocket on the back of the seat.

Was I outraged? Embarrassed? No, I was not. When young Harve, that Westchester County Trotsky, exhaled fiercely in climactic frenzy, and his mate moaned breathily, I experienced only a wasting jealousy. They were only fifteen years or so younger than me, but they seemed to have solved all the problems that rattle my fragile soul and starved body. In a million years, owning a million dollars, I could never do what they had just done, and I felt the poorer for it.

Of course Flackman and his party did not bother claiming luggage. Flunkies from the conference had done it for them. So I did not see them until after I'd passed through French customs. The mob of French reporters—irritable small men in dark blue raincoats, Mod photographers, newsreel men in leather windbreakers—told me that Arno, Numero Uno himself, was being interviewed. He is Big News anywhere in the world—Burton, Taylor, Kennedy, Ari. And Arno Flackman, the toughest, meanest, most brilliant novelist of our age; all balls and a yard wide.

"Oh, hell, Jack. They've cornered Arn."

This was a new voice, but I knew it. From another of the customs exits, two Americans emerged—Don Quixote and Sancho Panza.

The voice I'd heard was that of Warren Cooperage, the male half of the party-giving Cooperages, the rulers of New York's with-it, inside, turned-on literary crowd. How to describe Warren Cooperage? Professional conferencier, critic, friend to Nobel laureates, a man summoned to the White House by three Presidents for his views on the intellectual Mafia *vis-à-vis* the government, he is almost too much to take. Like Flackman, he is everywhere at once.

"Fa Chrissake, let's get Arno away before he starts swinging," Cooperage muttered, as he and the Quixote of this duo—old James Warfield Keen—brushed by me.

I knew what he was afraid of. Flackman had a vile temper. Foreign journalists brought out the worst in him. It would be a dreadful prelude to the World Conference on the Arts and Sciences, if Arno, El Lider, El Supremo, of the American Literary Contingent, started things off by belting the man from *Paris Soir*, or urinating on the floor of the Orly terminal.

They loped past me—old Keen swaying, reedy, his arms in the attitude of a praying mantis, his gray spade beard fluttering, truly a knight of mournful countenance. Poor old guy! Once he'd picketed the governor's mansion in Boston for Sacco and Vanzetti. Today, in paranoid right-wing sheets like *Manifest Destiny*, he informed his readers that "those two Wops were guilty as charged"—when he wasn't reviewing Eleanor Roosevelt's wicked life, and concluding that she was a paid agent of the Kremlin.

Cooperage was short, ruddy, and ruggedly handsome, gaudy with his shock of golden hair, his twig-tweedy green suit. Shuffling along in tan suede Wallabees, he seemed to have his nose shoved up Keen's lean buttocks.

"Ah, Mr. Flackman," a French reporter was calling out, "ze burning down of ze New York University last week. You favor zis?"

The mob was huge, and I could only see the top of Flackman's black Brillo, his creased brow. He was a big bastard, Arno, tall, thick in the shoulders, forever ducking punches, cocking his right. Oh, he was full of manly crap, telling the world he feared no one, ate nails, screwed around the clock, and favored bloodshed.

"Yup, yup," Flackman mumbled. "Yup, I liked the way the kids did it. An existential act."

"What does zat mean?"

"Means what I say, pal. An existential act, an act of will."

I elbowed my way forward. "Did NYU deserve it, Mr. Flackman?" I shouted. "What was their big crime? Are universities the real enemies of society?"

"Part of the system," Flackman mumbled, tossing a few left jabs.

"The murder of the old couple in Harlem last week, Mr. Flackman," an English lady journalist pursued. "Feinstein, I believe their name was, owners of a newsstand. Were you correctly quoted in saying that you understood the murderers better than you did the victims, and felt closer to them?"

Arno Flackman's black brows conjoined over his snub nose. He hunched his massive shoulders—El Toro, Zeus, the greatest cocksman of them all. I noticed he'd abandoned his standard black turtleneck (to signify his sympathy for Black militants) and was wearing an elegant Mod suit, a bright olive-brown plaid job, with emerald shirt and a knitted tie the color of dried dog turds. "Lady, what's your name, hah? Lady, I said that, and English intellectuals wouldn't understand. Yes, I am with the blacks, all the way. Let the Feinsteins move, get out——"

"Pretty hard when they're dead," I shouted.

Cooperage and Keen had gotten in back of America's Greatest Living Young Writer and were trying to pull him away. It was odd how everyone ignored James Warfield Keen—Nobel Prize winner, three Pulitzers, the best-read author in the Soviet Union and Japan—and were hypnotized by Flackman. The man had that power. He gathered in all the electricity. Everyone else was short-circuited, switched-off, when he was around.

"Let's go, Arn," Cooperage pleaded. "They got a limousine coming for us."

The mob surged and billowed around Flackman. Sound cameras whirred; microphones were thrust under his head. I'd seen Flackman a few times, but he didn't know me. What surprised me was his white, soft skin, his vague features. No wonder he grew that black mop of steel wool, and the thick black beard. Without them, he'd have been a large, unformed, overfed Jewish boy from Cleveland. Maybe a spare parts jobber, a dental technician.

"Explain that more fully, sir," another reporter asked. "You approve of universities being bombed and burned, of elderly storekeepers being murdered? Are they not innocent victims, as much as are the aggrieved blacks——"

"Listen. Listen. You all misread me." Flackman was shaking his head: the old punch-drunk act. "It's all clear in boxing terms. We, society, whites, the elite, we're like old heavyweights on the way down, slow to counter-punch, leather-catchers. The legs go first. The blacks. They're Sugar Ray on the way up—fast combinations and the left to the gut. A body puncher always comes out ahead. Is that clear?"

"No," I said. "How can you make that analogy? Boxing is a sport, a game. There are no moral issues involved. Tell that to the children saying *Kaddish* for the Feinsteins."

Flackman squinted at me. Cooperage was whispering in his ear; identifying me. They'd handle me on their own time. Warren Cooperage knew me slightly. We'd tangled at a seminar at the 92nd Street YMHA a few years ago.

"Mr. Flackman regrets to inform you that the press conference is over," Cooperage said. He placed his stumpy form in front of Arno, shoved the microphones away, and then he, Flackman, and Keen began to walk off. But the conference was by no means over.

"Flackman, you eat shit."

We all turned. The purveyor of this delicate sentiment was my companion on the flight over, Harvey. His concubine, the pink-hosed Vannie, was at his side, and they had been joined by a half-dozen young French galoots in army field jackets. God knows I want to love these rebellious children, to sympathize with their idealism, but something impedes me. It's their odor of sanctity, I suppose.

"Who said that?" Flackman said. Numero Uno spun about. His fists were up, and he was ready. The cameramen cocked their Rolleis and Pentaxes; a man carrying a sound Auricon braced himself against a confederate bearing a French Eclair.

17

"Harvey Ungerleider, Flackman," the long-haired boy cried out. "Chairman of the Deadfall Committee. We don't need your lousy bourgeois diversions here. You and your conference won't last a day when we get through with you! The scenario's been changed, Flackman."

"Arn, let's go," Cooperage begged.

"No, no, the boy deserves an answer." The combatants faced one another—Flackman, forty-ish, fat, a menacing man, and Ungerleider, hairy, chubby, backed up by his soiled goons. I thought of the gentle liberal middle-class Jewish homes that had spawned these egomaniacs, and I sorrowed for my people.

"Flackman, admit that you suck for the Establishment," young Ungerleider shouted. How would they edit *that* on the French TV that night?

"Fuck you," Flackman riposted. "Yes, fuck you. I was advocating revolution when you were crapping in your diapers. I'm the only revolutionary in America, the only writer with the guts and the brains and the know-how to make a revolution. You squirts——"

"Tell it to your press agent, Flackman," Ungerleider cried. "You start revolutions whenever you want to sell a book."

"Fuck you. Fuck you. Let me get this straight for you gentlemen from the press, not that any of you have ever gotten anything I say right, but anyway, I make my stand here as an Old Left Visionary, a Prophet, a Witness to my Age, perhaps the Only Witness, because as far and away the greatest writer of my time, the only man gifted enough to see things clearly, I——"

"Up your royalties, Flackman."

"As I was saying—fuck you. And fuck you, too. I was saying that I——"

"Good God, Arn, let's split," Warren Cooperage whispered at him—and started to tug him away. The nasty kids were screaming at him now: *motherfucker, racist, imperialist, Zionist lackey*. None of it applied. At heart, Flackman is a spoiled Talmudic scholar, ruled not by philosophy but by a need to demonstrate to the world, *ad nauseam*, that he has huge balls, huge muscles, massive talent, and fears no man. At least Hemingway's lunacy had deep American roots: he shot hyenas in the ass the way his ancestors killed deer and Indians. But *Arno Flackman?* A painter's son from Cleveland? A *yeshiva* student raised in a kosher home?

"Admit you're part of the conspiracy, Flackman," screamed the little girl named Vannie.

"Fuck you, too. And fuck you also."

The brilliance! The elegant turns of phrase!

Flackman could stand no more goading. He broke loose from Cooperage's restraints and hurled himself at young Ungerleider. The kid seemed surprised; he would have been no match for an alley-fighter like Flackman. The reporters spread apart to let them have an arena; the cameramen slicked and whirred away.

"Stop them! Stop them!" Vannie screamed. Cooperage and old Keen and I each grabbed for Flackman's flailing arms. I caught his right knuckles on my cheek and felt the bruise blossom. Then I realized he wasn't trying very hard. It dawned on me what was wrong with him. His brown plaid J. Press suit, sharply tailored, wasp-waisted, tight-vested, was holding him back. The poor jerk couldn't throw a proper punch in that $200 rig!

"Kill the bastard," Arno mumbled.

"Flackman eats shit!" the kids chanted.

I noticed that my sweet-faced Arab agronomist, Dr. Jabali, appeared to have joined the swarm of long-haired children. He lingered at the edge of the mob, smiling enigmatically, enjoying it. Cooperage maneuvered Flackman toward the glass exit doors of the Orly terminal. I followed.

"Flackman is a fink for the fascist power structure," someone called after him.

"And fuck you, too," the novelist shouted over his shoulder. He was, I noticed, affecting a hoarse tone, an old club fighter whose tonsils have been calloused by too many left jabs to the throat.

"Is this customary?" my Arab acquaintance asked.

19

"For high-priced novelists, yes, Dr. Jabali. I hope you, as a representative of an emerging nation, enjoyed the choice of words, the elegance of style. It's not quite the Koran, I'm afraid."

"Ah yes, yes. Extremely entertaining."

Outside the doors, a tall Englishman with a red-splotched face and thickly waved blond hair was flapping his arms like an insulted cassowary. He evidently knew Keen, Cooperage, and Flackman, and was obviously connected with the conference.

"The French, the bloody French!" he shouted. And he stamped his foot. As he shrilled out his indignation, he pointed to a departing bus, its metal flank bearing a banner reading:

CONFERENCE MONDIALE DES ARTS ET SCIENCE

"The bloody French *always* do this! Hahlf of the bahstards aren't even dewegates, and they gwabbed our pwivate bus and dwove away!"

I knew the type: part faggot, part RAF hero, part free verse. His lean cheeks were multihued—purple, scarlet, peach—suggesting Cotswold cottages, the northern reaches of Hadrian's Wall, Tintagel.

"Der baby! Ole Derek!" Cooperage was hugging the raging Englishman. "Der, you know Arno Flackman. And Jimmy Keen. And you met Lila at the conference we co-chaired at Cuernavaca last year."

Derek. Of course. It was Derek Venables, the perennial boy poet of the British Isles. The modishly waved hair, the baggy Daks, the shrill nasalities should have told me. But as I studied the lank, lisping limey, I observed one thing that struck me as crazy. He was wearing, dangling around his corded neck, a large gold crucifix. My knowledge of British poets is limited; in my muddled mind I'd also thought of Venables as some kind of lefty. He was the editor of an obscure but influential English magazine, *The Discoverist Re-*

20

view, a butcher paper affair, widely quoted but rarely read. In a way, he was an Anglo-Saxon counterpart of Warren Cooperage, and I was wary of him at once.

Yes, it was quite a collection of nice customers. I studied them standing at the curb, awaiting transportation, and I realized they had *command presence*. All of these people— old James Warfield Keen in his cream-colored linen suit and 1934 cake-eater shoes (brown and white wing-tips) and floppy Panama, Cooperage, tossing his mane out of his darting eyes, jabbing ribs, grabbing elbows, Flackman, muttering his drunken "fuck you's" at the taunting youngsters, Lila Metrick holding high her proud ass, so firm and perfect that a martini glass could have stood on its upper plane, all of them had a firm grasp on the world and its bounties.

"Irwin might show up," Cooperage babbled. "And Jimmy promised. Also Norman. What about André, Der? Any chance?"

But Venables was so enraged over the French commandeering his bus that he barely answered. Flackman was tossing short punches, snorting noisily through his nose. Keen and Lila Metrick wandered arm-in-arm along the platform. It was rumored he had once been a great swordsman. I doubted he'd get anywhere with Metrick, for all his fame. She detested and dismissed all proletarian writers of the past. Keen, to her, was a relic. Her tastes ran to young fags who used no punctuation.

"Is Red here?" Cooperage prattled on. "What about Artie? Bill promised me he might show. Gadge tol' me he'd give a talk on film."

Names, names, names. Warren Cooperage (and his rich wife, the legendary Tookie) was a multiple-choice name-dropper. You got only a first name or nickname, and you had to guess the rest. In my lumpish, outdated way, I thought that "Red" meant Sinclair Lewis, a novelist to whom I'd once been compared. But of course, Lewis was long dead, and Cooperage meant Robert Penn Warren. This was explained to me later by a fellow from the Paris *Tribune*.

"Hi, Warren," I said shyly, *shlepping* my Grasshopper scotch-plaid valises from Korvette's Carle Place. "I'm Benny Bloodworth."

"Hah?"

"Ben Bloodworth. We met at the 92nd Street Y a few years ago. I'm, ah, a writer. Novelist."

"Oh yeah. That book about the druggist in the Bronx."

Pegged, pigeonholed, filed and forgotten. Cooperage turned his back on me and began to harangue Venables. "Der, you as co-chairman with Imre, and me, as chief conferencier, we got to arrange a schedule that'll give all the big wheels a chance. The East Europeans are sending an all-star cast—heavy on scientists and economists, short on artists."

"Yew know something?" Venables asked the world-at-large. He was such an Upper Echelon Snob that he could ignore Cooperage, and even snub Flackman.

"Whazzat, Der?"

"Frahnce. Bloody Frahnce. It always seems to be at war."

"Yeah at war, Der. Great." Cooperage shaded his eyes. "How in hell do we get to Paris? I'll ream out that crowd at the *Review* for not sending the limousine they promised me and Arno."

From the corner of one eye I saw a bus approaching. It was smaller than the one the French had hijacked—one of those Citroën minibuses—but it had the same cloth streamer on its side, and was chugging toward us.

"Hey, there it is, a bus, a bus!" Cooperage called. He gathered up his group—old Keen, the callipygean Miss Metrick, a fluttering Venables, and a growling Arno Flackman. ("Where the fuck is my limousine, Warren? This is the shits, I mean, the real shits." Arno Flackman would not ride to his October Revolution in a sealed train; he'd be squatting in the air-conditioned rear compartment of a Carey Cadillac, nibbling some rich WASP society broad, some Southampton tart hungering for a short course in American fiction.)

With typical French wrong-headedness, the bus parked at the distant end of the loading platform. It was every man for himself. I sprinted in my thonged sandals, wobbling under the weight of my matched Korvette bags. Having lived in France, I knew what was about to happen as soon as the bus stopped. From hiding places inside the terminal, a garlicky, winey swarm of French came roaring out—cranky middle-aged women, Algerian sweepers, surly blue-overalled mechanics, and those elderly semidapper men in black hats and dark coats, their faces forever buried in *Le Figaro* or *Le Monde*. They lifted me off the ground, shoved me aboard, and in seconds, the bus was jam-packed—thick with the stale weariness of France at three in the afternoon, flatulent, wine-bloated, sleepy, irritable.

But I had a seat, which is more than the conference wheels had. I was wedged between a moustachioed woman who glared at me with Gallic contempt, and an Algerian workman, a furnaceman or street cleaner, grinning gold teeth at my pale face.

"*C'est le bus seulement pour le conférence!*" the driver called out. "*Si vous n'êtes pas de la conférence, dehors, dehors!*"

No one budged. Naturally, everyone was with the conference. Try to get a Frenchman out of a seat, anywhere. Cooperage was hurling his body through the clotted forms, angrily demanding seats. Behind him trailed Flackman, scowling, muttering, and then Venables, and then Metrick, holding up James Warfield Keen.

"Outa here! Outa here! Git off the bus, goddammit, this our bus! Hey, driver, get these people offa the bus!" Cooperage was raging.

Lila Metrick—she was an awesome intellect, slick in seven languages including Urdu—tried it in French, and with the help of the sodden driver, they actually cleared some seats. Only Cooperage was standing. And it was now evident that no more French could be budged. I heard grumbles about *sales cons* and *chien-lits Américains*, and the driver started to move off.

"Waita minute!" Cooperage bawled. "I ain't gotta seat!"

The bus stopped. And with that, Warren Cooperage, editor, essayist, party-giver, party-goer, conference-holder, came toward me. "Whaddya say, Ben. Lemme have your seat."

"My seat? Why?"

"I mean, look, I'm an official delegate, chairman of the conference committees, how will it look if I have to ride into Paris standing? What if Lennie finds out?"

"Ah . . . Bernstein?"

"Lyons. He'd have the laugh on me. Come on, Ben, lemme siddown."

"No. Goddammit, no."

"Look, kid. I know all about your books. Three pretty good genre novels, New York City *shtick*, the forties. They should sell better. You deserve better notices." He leaned forward and I was inundated with his cologne, essence distilled from the musk pouches of kangaroo rats. "Kid, I'll stick ya in my next survey of young Jewish-American novelists in *Esquire*. I get to do the March list."

A hot rage brought moisture to my eyes. "And you left me off the last three!" I cried. "But included all your fag friends! Including one creep who never wrote a book, but goes to your house for cocktails and grab-ass! No, Cooperage, I won't——"

"Come on, come on, Ben. We're a coupla old pals. I'll take care of you at the conference. You can sit on the journalism-as-art workshop."

"*Allons! Allons!*"

"*A Paris, à Paris!*"

Mutiny, always close to the skin in France, was erupting. How did Cooperage do it? Before I realized it, I was on my feet, reaching for my bags. It was the word *workshop*, I understood later. Everyone wants to be on a *literary workshop* at some time in his life.

"Stay on, kid," Coop said, resting his butt on my surrendered place. "It isn't a long ride."

But I wanted to wallow in my shame. *I had been thrown out of my seat by Warren Cooperage.* In the irrational way in which justice operates in France, the other passengers shoved me out the door, as if I had been the *cause* of the delay. They act the same way toward victims of hit-and-run drivers, expressing no sympathy for the mangled wretches in the street, but avoiding them as pariahs.

I had asked for it. Running away—not deserting them, but sort of ditching them—from my wife and kids in Hicksville, Nassau County, Long Island, to make a name for myself at the biggest world conference of intellectuals, eager to rub elbows and behinds with the elite. . . . And how had it begun? *Thrown off a bus by Warren Cooperage!*

A dusty green Peugeot 404 sedan pulled up to the curb. "Want a lift, young man?"

An elderly white-haired American in shirt-sleeves was at the wheel. A middle-aged woman was seated next to him. I had the vague notion that I had seen them looking on during Flackman's press conference, standing in the background, a puzzled, bemused older couple, rather like the onlookers Kafka introduces into his scenes.

I tossed my luggage onto the back seat and climbed in. The car moved on, and the driver, talking to the woman, suddenly said in a low voice: "Look, look. One of *Them*."

I looked also, and I saw my friendly Jordanian soil chemist with the high-top brown canvas shoes.

"He was on the flight with me. Dr. Jabali, an agronomist."

"Yeh, yeh."

"He showed me his card."

The white-haired man—he was a barrel-chested fellow, his eyes almost closed behind smoked glasses, his nose a smashed lump, reminiscent of Victor McLaglen—dropped the subject of my Arab co-passenger. "Been in Paris before?" he asked.

"I worked here ten years ago. World News Association. That's a wire service like the Associated Press, only much smaller. Now defunct. We had an office on Rue de Lafayette."

"Oh, you're a writer," the woman said. She had a pleasant accent. Polish? Czech? She turned to smile at me—a pretty,

25

perky woman in her early fifties, reddish hair, snub nose, attractive crinkles around her eyes. Both she and her husband—I assumed the white-haired driver was her husband—were richly tanned. Miami Beach?

"Well, yes. My name is Ben Bloodworth. And you . . . ?"

"We're the Blooms. Mr. and Mrs."

"Ah. New Yorkers?"

"Yes and no. We travel a lot."

Mr. Bloom swung the Peugeot onto the *autoroute de sud* and we charged toward Paris, passing the busload of celebrities. I was tempted to lean out of the window and razz Cooperage, but I settled for telling the Blooms about the way they'd eased me out of my seat.

"Cooperage? Cooperage?" Mr. Bloom asked. "Never heard of him. But Flackman, yeh. Everybody heard of him. Dirtymouth fellah, for a smart Jewish boy, with all the education he's had. I heard the kind of filth he was muttering at the airport there. He should be ashamed of such talk in public."

"My husband is old-fashioned," Mrs. Bloom said.

Bloom then asked whether I was on vacation, and I told him a little about the conference. As a member of the American PEN Club (he looked blank when I mentioned it, so I explained about the Poets, Essayists, and Novelists Club) I was entitled to attend this gathering of artists, writers, intellectuals, and scientists.

Mrs. Bloom was impressed. "Imagine that, Moe. All those famous people in Paris at once. It might be worth visiting."

Her husband wheeled the car off the last exit on the *autoroute* in St. Cloud, and turned into the street leading to Boulogne. He seemed to know his way around Paris.

"Nah, nah, no time for that sort of thing," he muttered.

Again, I had the odd sensation that somebody was trying to deceive me. Oh, I am a sucker, a mark; I believe in fairies and the law of averages. At a stoplight in the Bois, Mrs. Bloom rested her tanned arm on the back of the seat, and I saw the faint blue tattoo above her wrist: 324567.

"You were in a camp," I said.

"Yes. Theresienstadt."

There is something about these dreadful memories that demand nothing more than silence, contemplation. I never know what to say. "I'm sorry."

"Well, I am alive," she said cheerfully.

My memory is an excellent one. I might have made a good policeman. Not walking a beat, or frisking suspects, because I am a physical coward. But I am good at casing people, putting clues together. "I beg your pardon, Mrs. Bloom, did you address your husband as Moe?" I asked politely.

"That's right." She patted Bloom's iron forearm: a tough old guy. "My Moe. My liberator."

"Moe for Moses?" I asked. "Moses Bloom?"

"That's me, sonny boy."

"Moses Bloom who wrote *The Pickets? And We Accuse? And Report from Dachau?*"

From the white-haired driver I got only an enigmatic grin. From his wife, a proud: "That's my Moe. Did you ever read *Terezin Diary?* How he found me there?"

"I don't think so. Look, I have to be candid. Mr. Bloom is one of the heroes of my youth. I once did an article for my college literary magazine, the *Columbia Literary Review,* and I said you were the greatest realistic novelist of the thirties, that *The Pickets* . . ."

". . . was the finest labor novel every written in America, maybe the finest ever written anywhere." Bloom turned and winked at me, then waved—in an oddly familiar manner—to a gendarme, as we moved down the Rue de Passy, thick with shoppers, pushcarts, the ineffable odors and colors of French foods.

"You know it," I said stupidly. "Then you knew who *I* was."

"Yeah, in a way," he said.

"Moe, stop fooling with the boy. Of course he knew who you were, Benny. Can I call you Benny? I'm Sophie."

"But . . . how . . . who . . . ? Listen, I saw you at the edge of the mob of reporters when Flackman had his press conference. Why didn't you break in? You must know him. And old man Keen, heck, he's of your generation isn't he, Moe? I'm sorry. I keep making it sound like you're older than the first Moses."

"Flackman. I've known him since he was a *pisherkeh* in short pants. Used to write me fan letters. Today . . . he's a rich famous writer, a real celebrity. And me . . ."

"No, no. You inspired a whole generation of us, Moe! Even if, if——" No matter what I said, I was making it worse. Bloom must have been close to seventy. He'd been out of circulation for years, vanished, out of the book columns, many of his works out of print. Where had he been? What had he been doing? I looked at the creases on his burned neck, the white bristly hairs, like bits of steel filings, the corded brown arms, the deep chest beneath the white shirt.

"You can say it, sonny boy. The novels, the articles, the literary crap, the luncheons, I gave that up."

"Why?" I asked.

"Hmmmm . . . different interests . . . you know maybe a little about what I did from 1947 on . . ."

"Moe, please stop *fonfering*," Sophie Bloom said, as he double-parked the Peugeot outside the Hotel Bavard on the Avenue d'Iena, headquarters for the conference.

"Wait a minute, I remember," I said. "Israel. You've been in and out. Gun-running? The Second Aliyah?"

"Yeh, yeh, a little bit of that. Soph and I go back there all the time. I'm western European correspondent for the *Israel Express*, a weekly bilingual paper. It keeps me in motion. No money, but a lot of action."

"But where are you based? Here?"

We were standing in the street, my grasshopper bags at my feet. Bloom was staring up at the banner across the facade of the hotel.

"Hah? Based? No, not in Paris. I move around a lot."

"Well this should be pretty good duty. Covering the conference."

"What?" Bloom looked offended. He had pale blue eyes, almost invisible against the walnut-juice stain on his furrowed face. "What? I should cover this nonsense? No thanks. Soph and I have some business in Budapest tonight, a story to cover. We're leaving in a few hours."

"I'm sorry I took you out of your way. I assumed you were going to Paris also."

"My pleasure, boychick. Any man who remembers *The Pickets* and *Report from Dachau*. Old Zionists never forget a favor. Marxists will screw you every way you turn."

"I apologize for being such a jerk. I thought you were retired schoolteachers from Brooklyn. Can I do anything for you while I'm in Paris?"

Bloom appeared to have been waiting for my query. He nodded at his wife, and she bent forward—an agility, I gathered, stemming from long hikes through the burning Negev —and fetched a small wooden box with a screened top from beneath the seat. She handed it to Bloom through the car window and he in turn gave it to me. At once a rank animal odor assailed me. There was something alive in the box.

"There's a Hungarian at the conference, Ben," Bloom said.

"There are lots of them. The co-chairman is a Hungarian. Imre Somebody."

"Imre Malar. No, not him. He's the wrong Hungarian. I want you to look up Dr. Veg. Easy name. V, e, g. Laszlo Veg. Tall, skinny man, a professor from the Lenin Institute in Budapest."

"How do I find him?"

"If you have trouble, find Malar first. You find Malar, Veg will show up."

A pink snout followed by a furry white body emerged from the shredded newspaper in the box. "Rat?" I asked.

"Yeah, a rat."

The animal sniffed the air of Paris, its white whiskers twitching, then retreated to its pile of reading matter. It had a kidney-shaped black saddle of fur on its white back.

"Any message for Professor Veg?"

Bloom frowned at the banner across the Hotel Bavard's *fin-du-siècle* facade. "Tell him this rat doesn't work."

"Doesn't work at what?"

Sophie Bloom rolled her eyes. "Moe, stop with your games. The boy is confused."

"Just doesn't work. Like a busted watch."

"A mechanical rat?" I asked. "He looks like the real thing to me."

"Never mind. It doesn't work. And give him this." He reached into the breast pocket of his drip-dry white shirt and gave me a sealed envelope. There was no name on it.

"Okay, a rat that doesn't work, and a letter for Professor Ludwig Veg."

"Laszlo, Laszlo. And after you've delivered them, stay away from him. Don't get too close to Malar. He'll get your ear and you won't be able to stop listening. On Tuesday he'll tell you he *started* the Hungarian Revolution in 1956, but on Wednesday he'll claim he *ended* it. He'll charm you crazy, and you'll forget why you came here."

"To tell the truth, Moe, I don't know."

"Better yet." He grabbed my free right hand—the cage and its tenant rat were tucked under my left arm—and pumped it hard. A tough old kibbutznik, a hard old gunrunner. Dimly remembered stories of Israel's birth came back to me as I looked into his bronzed face with the busted nose and iron chin. Bloom landing on secret airfields in Italy to pick up Czech machine guns . . . Bloom disguised as a Jesuit priest shepherding concentration camp children across Europe . . .

"*Shalom*, boychick."

"*Shalom*, Moe. So long, Sophie."

The dusty Peugeot pulled away. I was left with a white rat, a letter, and a heightened sense of importance. Cooperage and his Beautiful Writers had kicked me off the bus, but I had a mission.

The Hotel Bavard, conference headquarters, had that resigned, beaten look of old elegance, long surrendered to the ineptitude, laziness and vengeful slovenliness of French workmen. It sagged and drooped. Its old carved stones were cracked and soot-stained. Malraux's sand-blasters hadn't gotten around to it, or had decided it wasn't worth the effort. It appeared to be the sort of gloomy pile reserved for group tours from Des Moines—Iowa Association of Registered Chiropractors. No wonder the World Conference had chosen it. (To be fair, it had one advantage: walking distance to the Palais de Chaillot, where the sessions would take place.)

The lobby reflected the French national urge to decay, the revenge of the underpaid French artisan. Plaster cracked, ceilings crumbled, long gray stains decorated the vomitous green walls. In his heart, the French blue-collar worker would like to murder all those rich, arrogant snobs driving sports cars; lacking the nerve and organization to rebel, he gratifies these urges to kill by sabotaging anything he is called upon to repair. Half-stewed on *vin ordinaire* (the wine is part of a national plot to keep the working classes incapable of rebellion) he gets his jollies by screwing up the plumbing, the carpentry, the electricity, the masonry.

The *Force Ouvrière* had done a superb job on the Hotel Bavard. Maroon drapes sagged dismally. The marble columns were chipped. The rugs were of an indeterminate gray-blue, spotted, threadbare. Withal, the place had a sullen defiance about it, rather like the French themselves. Distantly, a shivering wrought-iron elevator, a narrow cage traveling on creaky cables, disgorged a batch of frightened delegates—a kerchiefed Burmese, a black man in a yellow robe, a few loud

31

Italians. It was my first look at what advance literature had called "the world's first meeting of artistic and scientific minds, to further mankind's progress, save the earth itself, end war, and promote the essential dialogues."

Against one peeling wall there was a long table laden with handouts. Behind the table a dozen girls in pale blue smocks —an Oriental, an Arab, but most of them French—were registering delegates. They looked underpaid and constipated. Yes, let us demolish that myth right now, the one about the beauty and chic of Frenchwomen. I'll take the Italians any day, especially those Romans with their wiggly *culos* and curved beaks.

There was a grievous shortage of personnel—not a porter in sight. They knew, I imagined, that artistic and scientific types were deadbeats, not guilt-ridden American tourists, lavish with tips. I wrestled my bags to the long table, still carrying Bloom's rat under my arm. The black man in the yellow robe stared into my face. "*Américain?*" he asked, in fine French. An ID card pinned to his flowing garment read:

AUGUSTIN KAKIMBO
Haute Volta
Rédacteur

"*Mais certainement,*" I responded.

"*Vous êtes le Nobel lauréate, James Warfield Keen?*"

"*Ah, malheureusement, non. Je suis Benjamin Bloodworth, romancier.*" I smiled my people-to-people smile and offered my hand, the hand of friendship and brotherhood. This Food Parcel is a Gift of the People of the United States.

"*Merde,*" said my editor from Upper Volta, and turned his back on me. He scanned the lobby for someone famous—a Keen or a Flackman.

A frowning girl with short blonde hair asked for my credentials, and I showed her the letter of acceptance I'd gotten a month ago from conference headquarters in Paris.

"Ah, you air nut offeeshul delegate."

My French was better than her English, so I said: "*Alors, quel espèce de délégat suis-je?*"

"*Simplement délégat.*"

I asked what that meant, but she scowled and began to type an ID card for me. Ah, the French. What joy they experience in turning you down, refusing information, canceling your pass, screwing up your hopes! The opening lines of the *Marseillaise* should be "*Je ne sais pas de tout,*"—I don't know a goddamn thing at all.

She handed me the card in its plastic folder, with a safety pin attached to its back, and then stopped and reread the words she'd just typed.

BENJAMIN BLOODWORTH

U.S.A.

Novelist

"Ah, moment," she said. "Please. Wait."

That was more like it. I was certain—as she got up and walked across the crowded lobby—that my publisher, or maybe Lennie Lyons, had tipped them off. *Yes, yes, Bloodworth, wonderful speaker and wit, by all means put him on the panel on World Directions.* . . . I'd be an "official delegate" after all; I'd have my innings. Of course. It was Cooperage who'd done it. He'd tipped them already (but wasn't he still in the minibus?) that I was worthy of special attention. Good old Coop!

A pudgy, sweating man with lank brown hair that fell to either side of his lumpish face returned with the French blonde. She made no formal introductions, but in a rude way pointed to me. The man—his mud-brown suit sagged and his shoes were scuffed—walked up to me.

"Hi fellah," he said cheerily. "How goes it?"

"Fair. Ah, you're with the conference? Mr. Cooperage spoke to you about . . . ?"

"You betcha. You have something for me, right?"

"Beg pardon?"

33

He pointed to the cage with Bloom's rat, under my arm. "Oh. Heck, you're not Professor Veg, are you?"

"Sure am."

"But . . . but . . . he's a Hungarian . . . he . . ."

"Oh, my lingo set you off? Four years in the states. Berlitz courses. And the Voice of America every night. My friends kid me a lot, the way I use American slang, the New York accent. Could have fooled you, right?" He reached for the cage, and I moved back. I didn't want to be rushed. The potato-nose, the fat cheeks, the ill-favored figure. Ten minutes ago, Moe Bloom had told me that Laszlo Veg was a tall skinny man.

"Ah, Professor Veg . . . is Mr. Malar here?"

"Imre? Sure. Right over there." He gestured with a thumb —a very American gesture—to a dark, solemn man with a melting nose and sad drooping eyes, who stood a few yards away, his back to a marble pillar.

"That's Imre Malar?" I asked.

"You betcha." As I studied the sallow fellow—his suit didn't fit either—the lumpy man firmly took the cage away from me. "Thanks, fellah. Thank Mr. Bloom also."

"Wait a minute, wait a minute," I cried. "Professor Veg is tall and thin . . ."

Potato-nose approached the man with the long face. Both turned their backs on me and started to the doorway.

From behind the long table, a red-headed girl—a willowy beauty—ran out as I trailed the two, and asked me: "What is this about Mr. Malar?"

"That's him there——" I pointed to the dark fellow with the bloodhound face.

"He is *not*," she said—in a delightful accent. "Malar is my father. I know my father. I know *them* also. They are not even Hungarians."

As the two fakers exited, a mob of robed Africans, shouting at each other in liquid French, filled the sidewalk, and the girl and I darted around them, confronting the baggy-suited team.

"Why, Mr. Pochastny!" she cried at the heavy man. "And Mr. Keramoulian! I didn't know you were in Paris already!"

Veg? Malar? They spoke to each other: *Russian.*

"Your English is great, Mr. Pochastny," I said to the thick man. He was clutching the cage tightly; and his eyes darted left and right. "But you shouldn't imitate Hungarians. Professor Veg is tall and slender. And I think his suits fit a little better."

"Excuse me, guy," Pochastny said. He spoke in Russian to his friend, smiled gallantly at the girl. "Explain to your father, dear girl, that we just saved him a lot of bother. This young fellah was just going to get him involved. A silly business, and I figured your dad didn't want another headache."

The red-headed girl looked at me: I saw the appeal. She was confused; so was I. I would be damned if these Russian goons would steal Bloom's rat.

"Give me my rat," I said.

"Cool it, fellah," Pochastny said.

"You're a cop. I'm an old journalist, Mr. Pochastny. I should have known you were a cop when you walked up to me. I don't care how good your English is, you're a cop."

The swarthy man—his skin was darker than an Arab's, his hair a curly gray-black, like dyed caracul—edged toward me.

"You too, whoever you are. A pair of cops. I'll take my rat back, please. It's for Professor Veg. You aren't Veg, and you aren't Malar. She's Malar's daughter, and she should know."

The dark man shoved me roughly: I'm skinny and not too strong, and I wobbled back. Both moved toward the street.

"Rat . . . ?" Miss Malar asked me.

"Yes. And it's Bloom's. Or Veg's. In any case, not theirs."

"Settle down, guy," Pochastny said. When he grinned, he displayed handsome steel incisors. Were the real choppers yanked out in Lubianka by one of Stalin's hoods? Keramoulian was trying to hail a cab, waving frantically. I could have told him about Parisian hackies. The Bavard's doorman came to his help and began tootling.

"Who are you anyway, fellah?" Pochastny asked, getting a firmer grip on the cage.

"You might say I'm that *Cosmopolitan* girl."

"Not bad, not bad, buster."

I shaded my eyes and looked up the Avenue d'Iena. It was a kid's trick, one my son Eddie and I worked all the time. ("Gosh, Eddie, there's Joe Namath coming down the street," I'd say. And when Eddie turned, I'd smack his behind.)

"Holy smoke, look who's in town!" I shouted, pointing toward the Place d'Iena. "It's Trotsky! Hey, Lev! Leon!"

God knows what the Russian thought. But he turned, and I smashed one fist as hard as I could against the wooden box. Keramoulian saw me and came running. The box smashed to the *trottoir*. I beat Pochastny to the splintered wreckage, retrieved a quivering, squeaking rat, and stuffed it in the side pocket of my brown suede jacket.

"As Chairman Mao would say," I said, "it is the rat who survives that makes history, not the rats who are tempted by poisoned bean curd. *Adios, muchachos.*"

"Give it back, fellah," Pochastny said. He held a pudgy hand out. "Be a good guy. We're all working together. Veg, Malar, all of us. Miss Malar, am I leveling with this creep or not?"

A fearful look clouded the girl's delicate face. God, she was a beauty—creamy white skin, red curls cut short, narrow green eyes. A bit of the old Asian Magyar strain in her—high sharp cheekbones slanting the eyes.

"I shall find Professor Veg for you," she said to me.

The bloodhound—Keramoulian—started to move toward me, but Pochastny, the diplomat of the group, barred his way. "No sweat, buddy. We'll get what we want soon enough. On your way, kids." He sounded almost relieved. But when he turned away, I heard his voice turn rough and angry; he was bawling the hell out of his chum.

Miss Malar and I walked back to the lobby. I kept a firm but gentle hand on the rat, feeling his furry form trembling

36

with life. Poor little creature! Years ago, in P.S. 176 in the Bronx, I had taken care of the white mice, feeding them stale white bread and lettuce, cleaning up their little turds.

The lobby of the Bavard was jam-packed. It was registration day, and the world's finest minds passed in review. A pale Eurasian woman with a spatulate nose, hidden eyes and a pair of bazooms that defied gravity, two Ming Dynasties in black watered silk, stared at me, and I stared back.

SOO HAN MING
Malaysia
Poet

Rhyme me this, Lotus Blossom. Around me were surly Slavs, Black Africans, Arabs in Kaffiyehs, and elderly gray-haired ladies in space shoes. There were nuns, priests, and pipe-puffing Englishmen. Oh, they were all there—failed poets, cocky economists, shrewd biologists, a mixed grill, a true *fritto misto* of nonentities, the famous, and the awesome (like Flackman, who was not in sight) and the legendary Malar. I recalled that the conference had had its origins in a famous "East-West" exchange of letters between the British critic Derek Venables (the blond tweedy bloke wearing the crucifix) and the father of the adorable girl at my side, Imre Malar, last of the great eastern European radical intellectuals, an independent and brave voice in the arid wastes of Stalin's Europe. . . .

"You knew those two men?" I asked her. She had stopped at a table full of brochures and bearing a placard: BRIDGE BUILDING—*East-West Meetings Arranged.* She had moved to the rear of the table. Apparently she worked there.

"Slightly. They are with the Soviet delegation. Mr. Pochastny, the fat one who speaks good English, is the editor of an agricultural magazine. Mr. Keramoulian is an expert on external trade."

"Why did they want Veg's rat?"

"I haven't the faintest idea, Mr. . . ." She studied my ID card. "Bloodworth."

"Ben."

"How do you do, Ben. I am Judy Malar."

A Siamese ethnomusicologist stopped to ask how he could meet with *both* East and West, and Judy excused herself, relieving a German girl with yellow braids who had been manning the table. "In an hour or so, Papa will be here," she called to me as I headed for the elevator. "And Mr. Veg also."

I shoved my bags toward the creaky lift and waited. With a bumpity-bump, it settled into place, and a dozen terrified passengers, including my young Arab soil chemist, grinning, waving fingers at me, lurched out. Someone belted me in the kidneys, and I was shoved forward, spun about and wedged into place.

"Golly, I'm sorry, sir. Didn't mean to hit you that hard."

Next to me was an Eagle Scout and a grossly fat woman in a soiled sweatshirt. The kid looked to be about seventeen, skinny, bespectacled, with an innocent vulnerable look on his face. An old Eagle Scout myself, former senior patrol organizer of Morris Weinberg Troop, East Bronx, meeting Thursday nights in the B'nai Jeshurun Synagogue, I saw that he had earned merit badges for life-saving, conservation, journalism, and wrestling. He seemed to be holding up the fat woman, whose splotchy puffy face said to me: *alcoholic.*

"That's all right, son," I said, as the *ascenseur* rose with a neurotic lurch. "I'm an old scouting man myself." I gave him the old salute, two fingers up.

"Jesus, thassa namerican, Chipper, a friggin' American," the lady belched. "Shake hand, American." Drunk she may have been, but she was quick and strong. Her right paw leaped out and grabbed my suede lapels, pulling me close to her doughy cheeks. "Americans gotta stick together in this friggin' place, right, American?"

Oh, how her breath stank. It parted my hair and cleared my

sinuses, a true bourbon stench, rising from her soiled guts.

I leaned back and read her white card.

LOUISE LATOUR

U.S.A.

Novelist

Who else? Only the richest woman writer in America, the author of *Manderby Corners,* ten million copies in eighteen languages. Yes, it was our Louise, the fat homely girl from Nebraska, who got back at all the small-town bullies and gossips who had mocked her, by writing, in painful longhand on yellow pads, on cold prairie nights, the sex-and-violence story of her neighbors that made her rich, rich, rich.

"Miss Latour, this is a pleasure," I said, and I said it honestly. I am in favor of wealthy writers. "I'm a fellow novelist, but not in your class. Ben Bloodworth."

"Betcherass, Benny. This my nephew, Chipper. Ole Chipper comes along keep an eye on Louise, right, Chipper?"

The Eagle Scout beamed. "Golly, I've never been out of Nebraska. Aunt Louise was sure nice to ask me to come along."

"Bullshit, kiddo. Publisher forced him on me, but Chipper's a good kid. Let's Louise drink alla booze she wants."

I shook the boy's hand, surprised when he did not immediately respond to the Scout's two-fingered shake. He grinned sheepishly, and shoved the rimless specs up his snub nose. "Hope we see more of you, sir. Aunt Louise gets lonely when she's away from home."

The fat woman moaned and collapsed against her nephew. "Hate foreigners," she muttered. "Hate 'em all. Spics. Wops. Frogs. All hate Americans, 'n' I'm a namerican."

She wore a dirty gray sweatshirt, blue culottes and white basketball sneakers. A tall Englishman was looking at her in horror; two small Orientals recoiled from her venomous breath. We stopped at the next floor, and the lift this time rattled upward more pronouncedly. Louise Latour yawned,

39

then announced to her fellow passengers: "Jesus. Gotta barf."

"Try holding it back, Aunt Louise," Chipper said. "We're almost there."

I edged away, trying to place myself out of the line of fire. Ten million copies! A movie, a sequel, a TV series. Lawyers had cheated her, agents had done her dirt, three husbands had guzzled in the great trough of greenbacks replenished by her novel. Leeches and parasites had sucked her dry, and she'd turned to the booze. Pity drowned me; I wanted her to be slim and beautiful and happy and sober.

I moved back an inch or so, into the huge round breasts of

KATJE WESTERDOOP
Netherlands
Ceramicist

—a pneumatic blonde with sad eyes. Her round pale face appeared to be permanently engloomed by the huge Rubens melons she had to carry around. Ah, Saskia, my love. Lusting for Katje Westerdoop and her Flemish frontage, I had the feeling that Louise Latour would be my only conquest.

"Lemme outa here, Chipper," she moaned. "Gonna upchuck."

"Ew, this is revolting, really," the Englishman piped.

Katje Westerdoop covered her dolorous face. The Orientals giggled nervously. "Everybody stand back," I said. "The lady may be sick. *Sauve qui peut*."

"You okay, Auntie Louise?" The Eagle Scout asked. He held her firmly as she belched—loud, clear, and fruitily.

The *ascenseur* bounced into place at the next floor. Jiggling, settling, it surely played hell with Miss Latour's fluttering duodenum. Chipper opened the scrollwork doors, one of Hector Guimard's *art nouveau* creations. Nervous bodies parted; Louise squirted from Chipper's strong arms and stumbled into the dark corridor. The Eagle Scout and I flew after her.

40

All over the Bavard's faded maroon hall runner and marble floor it burst. A chambermaid witnessed it, and cursed, "*Sales gens, ces artistes.*" Well, she had a point. Louise was an artist, one of the richest in the world, and she was surely a loser in the neatness sweepstakes. There is a myth that these orthodox boozers don't eat. Don't believe it. What gushed, exploded, streamed, out of Miss Latour's gaping maw was surely the *prix fixe* ten-course luncheon from Le Grand Véfour.

"You okay, Aunt Louise?" Chipper was asking. "You okay?" He was holding her spreading midsection tenderly. She was bent double, like a semi-inflated beach mattress. Chipper took off his green-and-gold scouting scarf and was wiping her forehead.

"There, you're swell now."

Reduced to convulsive dry heaves, the lady novelist slowly straightened up. "Watcha lookin' at, friggin' foreigners?" she muttered at the staring passengers in the lift. "Watcha lookin' at? Fat lady gettin' sick?"

The elevator moved on. They'd stared at her with too much pleasure. Her regurgitation gave them joy, a sensation I had to fight. How good it was to see this rich, famous woman vomiting all over herself! Losers are forever sustained by this myth—money makes misery. (Don't believe it.)

I helped Chipper Latour guide his dehydrated aunt to their room. She seemed to have gone into a semicomatose state, breathing heavily through her fishy mouth.

"It must have been those funny dark clams we had at lunch," the nephew said to me. "She ate an awful lot."

"Mussels," I said. "*Moules.*"

"Right! Auntie drank a whole bottle of white wine with them. That darn wine alone was five dollars."

I held her upright as he opened the door. "Money well spent, Chipper. The white wine came up with the shellfish."

In my room I was momentarily disoriented by Louise Latour and her faithful nephew. The sour odor of her barf lingered in my nostrils like two small cylinders jammed into my sinuses. I'm hypersensitive to odors. Most migraineurs—I get some of the all-time record headaches—are. Aromas, good and bad, are magnified and tend to linger.

The room was no help. It appeared to have been unoccupied since the Paris Commune. The walls were a latrine-brown, the drapes a darker brown. It stank of dust, cheap soap, and rotting damask. It was so narrow that I could barely open the hall door and the closet at the same time. There was no john, no bath, no shower—just a small canted sink, with disturbing iodine-colored stains around the drain.

In the stale and stationary air, I rested on the coarse coverlet. Then I felt a gentle wiggling in my coat pocket. It was Bloom's rat, asking for freedom. I took him out carefully and held him in my palm. White rats tend to be sweet-tempered and shy, not like the gray monsters who frequent garbage dumps.

"Hi fellah," I said, holding him in the palm of my hand. He sat up and rubbed his pink paws in front of his pink nose. A cute little guy. Having smashed the box in rescuing him from the fat Russian—Pochastny?—I had to find some place to keep him. There was a wire trash basket under the sink. I up-ended it and put Bloom's animal under it. He seemed happy enough, although every now and then he would rise on his haunches and poke his muzzle out of the mesh.

He was lonely, and so was I. Here I was in Paris, a delegate to the world's biggest intellectual bash in years, and I was lonely—for my wife, my kids, my split-level house on a 76-by-100 plot of crabgrass in Nassau County, Long Island. *I wanted my wife with me.* God, I'm a middle-class man, a stodgy, straight nonentity! We go wild in hotel rooms. It's nobody's business but ours. But it's the truth. Suddenly guilt, or something like it, impelled me to write to her. I found some yellowing hotel stationery in an ancient table, sat down, and began to scribble, first opening the drapes to let the grand view of the Paris rooftops, those Utrillo mansards, inspire me. I had a panorama of a gray airshaft.

How is this for an opening number [I wrote to Felicia], a first act? I was on the same plane with Arno Flackman, Numero Uno himself, also James Warfield Keen, the great voice of social protest of the thirties, Lila Metrick, Lady Blue-Stocking, and Warren Cooperage. They're a pretty decent bunch, all of them, and were quite friendly.

Having written these lies, I felt queasy. Friendly? Decent? Cooperage had thrown me off the bus. Flackman had told me to go screw myself. Keen was half-asleep all the time, and Lila Metrick, she of the great blonde *tochis*, would not acknowledge my existence. But I had to lie to Felicia. I'd convinced the poor girl of the absolute urgency of my trip to Paris. I was sick of being an outsider. I had to get in the literary swim. We'd had it out at breakfast about two weeks ago, when I'd reviewed for her the way my career was sliding downhill. Finally, she agreed; I could go off to the conference and establish my bona-fides, slowly work my way into Lennie's column, Truman's parties and maybe a few choice beds.

You may catch some TV news clips of Flackman's hilarious press conference at Orly. I was on the edge of the group and you might see a glimpse of your dear husband, tossing queries at Arno. I must say he's a great guy. Really tossed off some great cracks.

And it was a thrill to be near a noble man like James Warfield Keen. A gentle, reserved old fellow, tall, thin, aristocratic. I didn't have the heart to ask him about that last article of his in *Manifest Destiny*, "I Remember Eleanor," the one in which he called her the greatest menace to the American social order since Eugene V. Debs. . . .

Now the crazy thing was, as I wrote these lies, I began to believe them. I was in Paris, at a cultural conference, surrounded by intellectual *machers* of an exalted order. What good would it do me to be bitter? Better than that, I'd get to be *like* them—witty, worshiped my words worth noting.

Honey, do you remember my giving you a marvelous novel called *The Pickets* to read, by an old Midwestern social realist named Moses Bloom? I'd thought Bloom was dead, or out of commission, or retired, but he turned up in Paris, not as a delegate, but on some private business, and he and his wife drove me to the hotel! For reasons that elude me, he gave me a white rat to return to a friend of his, a Hungarian scientist. . . .

I left out the business of the Russians trying to steal my rat. Why worry my good, kind Felicia? She is a wonderful broad, a good mother, a sharp and devoted person. Since she is not Jewish, but an Italo-American, daughter of a Bronx fireman, she can espouse radical causes in Nassau County with great humor and vigor and no guilt feelings and stun the opposition. Bear with me for a story about Felicia. We had a bad scene at a Hicksville school board meeting last year about censoring the library. The usual ball-breakers were there—Birchers, Minutemen, Concerned Patriotic Mothers—denouncing Henry Steele Commager and Dr. Spock and their works, and Felicia took as much as she could, then stood up and said: "You people are fascist idiots, no better than Nazi book-burners." Well, the chief Bircher, a foreman at Grumman, a good old union man, got to his feet and leveled a hand at my wife and said: "If we are, you better watch out, lady, we know your kind of kike and we have you in the cross-hairs." I suppose I should have leaped to Felicia's defense, but my black-haired, black-eyed, 105-pound mother of two got to her feet and burned him to a crisp with: "Just try it, you fat bastard, and see what you get! My maiden name is Amalfitano, my old man is a retired fireman, and I'm not afraid of you or fifty like you!" You see why I love her, even if her idea of a wild time is standing around the kids' birthday cakes?

Sweetheart, we—I—made the right decision in coming here. I know my reasons were idiotic—that night when Suzy Parker dipped my tie in her gin-and-tonic and called me square, the time Arlene Francis turned away from me in the middle of an anecdote, the night the other actress fell asleep while I was holding forth on James Joyce. We agreed, dear, that none of these things ever happen to people like Warren Cooperage or Arno Flackman. Never. A history of the world could be written in terms of snubs, envy, and spite, and I admit I want some *respect*. But when Leonard Lyons walked away from me on 44th Street and Broadway just as I was getting to the punchline of a funny story about my new book, that was the last straw. And why did he say, as he turned downtown, "Remember me to your wife"? He's never met you. That convinced me I had to do something about my public image. So here I am, and I shall prevail. What is most important is that I have sworn off self-pity now and forever. I promise you, dear wife, when I get home there will be no more brooding, jealousy, and hatred, the natural state of unrecognized novelists. Already I am clearheaded, optimistic, and vigorous. Warren Cooperage, not a bad guy at all, has promised to place me on a few important "workshops" and I swear they'll remember me when I'm finished with them. . . .

Und so weiter. Most of it was harmless distortion. But the part I meant was when I said I would stop bathing myself in pity. I'd be a *mensch*, like my late father, Aaron Bloodworth, the impoverished East Bronx pharmacist, whose ravaged, comic, embattled, outraged life had been the basis of my best-known book (a modest sale), *Shake Before Using*. Old Aaron, old socialist, old humanist, would be proud of me before I was through.

I sent my love to the kids, my twelve-year-old Eddie, clean-up hitter and catcher for his Little League team, and ranking tennis player in the Nassau Public Courts League, and to seven-year-old Rosa—named for my mother-in-law—and sealed the letter. These bonds reaffirmed, I felt better. Apologies again. I am, after all, a fumbling, sentimental middle-class fellow. My kids are no better or worse than other kids, but they are mine.

45

Washed and shaved, I put on a cobalt-blue turtleneck sweater, and studied my lean, hollow-cheeked face in the cracked mirror. Not bad. Nothing too strong or assertive, the nose a fraction long, but a passable Bronx face. The small dark beard on my chin was just right—a concession to individualism.

I started to leave, looked at Moe Bloom's rat—the little bugger was snoozing—and decided not to bother him. If I found Laszlo Veg, I'd bring him to the rat, and try to pry something out of him. Yes, I'd use the rat as bait. *Ah, Professor Veg, I have something for you, but you must come to my room for it. . . .*

Female voices filtered through, and as I exited, I saw two women at the adjacent door. Evidently they were having trouble opening it. I recognized Lila Metrick, tall, high-rumped, golden, jamming a key into the hole. A slender young girl was standing next to her, and after a moment I recognized her as the kid named Vannie who had sat next to me on the plane, the little *tsatske* who'd been *shtupped* by Harvey Ungerleider, the fat radical from Larchmont or Great Neck.

"May I be of assistance?" I asked.

"I doubt it," Lila Metrick drawled.

"I'm good at this sort of thing. I've had long experience in second-class European hotels."

They ignored me. You have to tread carefully with people like Lila Metrick. She is not only highborn and fiercely erudite, she is a multi-level snob. But she mattered; she had clout. Already the critics who review critics were hailing her as the successor to McCarthy, Sontag, Hartwick, and Huxtable. And she was certainly better-looking than any of them—blonde-gold, high forehead, proud nose, and a thin, hard waist, blooming into the most awesome round, wide, arched ass ever designed.

"Miss Metrick, I'm Ben Bloodworth," I blurted out. "We met last year at the Hunter College Forum on New Trends in the Novel."

She fiddled with the key. I knew she was doing it all wrong, but I'd been spurned. "You were *not* there," she said in flat New England tones. "The panel consisted of Warren Cooperage, Harlan St. James, Makamba Indaba, and Velvel Katznelson."

"No, but I was in the audience. I'm the fellow who referred to you as the Fair Frictionist, in honor of that article you wrote for *The Discoverist Review* that got you so much notoriety, 'Friction or Fiction'."

"Who is this creep, Lila?" Vannie asked.

"I have no idea. I wish he'd leave."

"Gosh, Miss Metrick, don't you recall the question I asked you? I mean, you maintained in that article that Art was relevant only insofar as it concerned itself with the rubbing of skin against skin. You went further than Flackman did in his cries for more orgasms, you called for an art in which rubbing, frottage, fondling, and groping replaced thought."

"Shit, he knows you by heart, Lila," Vannie said.

"I have no recollection of you or anything you ahsked," Lila said.

"I'm impelled to remind you, because you never responded to my question that night. I asked you, Miss Metrick, that, if as you wished, we developed an art, and by extension a *society*, in which everyone was going down on everyone else, in which all that mattered was cooze and cock and come, who, who in heaven's name, would deliver the mail or pick up the garbage?"

She raised her proud Bostonian head (even her nostrils excited me) and I took the key from her shaking hand. "I know something about old keyholes, Miss Metrick. There's a trick to it. You only shove it in halfway, and sort of probe or feel around, like a sly proctologist. Never jam the key all the way in."

So saying, I fiddled and tickled the inside of the keyhole, as Metrick and her devotee studied me with bland contempt. Frankly, I had trouble keeping my eyes off the Lady Critic. She was wearing a lemon-yellow shirtwaist dress, and the wide, flounced skirt did a poor job of hiding that magnificent behind. What made it so delicious was that the rest of her was aloof, cold, disdainful, unreachable. Her long, large-featured tanned face combined High Goy Breeding and Unassailable Intellect, a combination hard to beat. You felt that the woman was icy, unresponsive, downright antagonistic. That is, until your eyes followed the line from her modest breasts and slender waist to that feast of passion, that globous, glorious *derrière*.

Click. Knack. The door opened. I gave Lila Metrick the key.

"Thanks, in any case," she said nasally.

"My pleasure. I hope we get a chance to pursue that argument. I was hurt, Miss Metrick, when you didn't respond to my question. You see, these clarion calls for a life-style based on stroking and grabbing and coming are okay on paper. I like that sort of thing as much as the next man. But you get the whole United States thrashing and coupling, and no one will want to grease cars or wash clothes. Not to mention cleaning up the slums and saving the environment. In short, your advocacy of Dionysian excess can lead only to social decay and repressive tyranny."

"I'm in no mood to argue. I must unpack."

Impulsively I grabbed her wrist. "But you must answer me," I cried. "You and Flackman and those kids who keep telling us to *feel*, to *screw*, to *grab*, to *grope*, to *explore* the limits, you'd be doing nothing but ensure the triumph of people worse than George Wallace, much worse. You see, Americans won't respond. The last fellow who came on strong about blood and emotions and wanted to throw out reason and the intellect was named A. Hitler. Turn the beasts loose on this binge of passion you are urging on the world and you end up with monsters in charge. I mean it, Miss Metrick. It's the old argument. Hebraicism versus Hellenism. I'm all for the Greeks with their Bacchic and Priapic feasts, but for God's sake, temper it with a little Talmud."

48

"Jesus, what a freak," Vannie said, and walked into the room. She was making herself at home. "Wow. What a neat room. Boy, a bidet."

"I have no desire to discuss this with you," Metrick said.

"Maybe in the workshops. Is there a panel on Friction?"

"Derek Venables and Warren Cooperage are making up the list of conferenciers. Speak to them." The grand ass moved by me, beauty on ball bearings, oiled, mobile, a mountain to be climbed because it was there. The door slammed on my quivering nose. Losing no time, I bent to the keyhole. No luck.

Sneak that I am, I unlocked my own door and utilized an old FBI trick I'd read about, or rather a trick used by the old union boss Harry Bridges, for listening in on FBI finks in the next room, sent to spy on *him*. I placed a glass tumbler, mouth against the connecting bolted door, bottom to my sensitive ear. A few mashed words trickled through.

"Bloody room is a disgrace," I heard Metrick saying. "Wait till I tell off those bastards in State . . ."

State? Ohio State? Penn State? Metrick was much in demand at university seminars, colloquia, workshops, and other hoo-hoo levitations.

". . . damned busybody next door, putting him near me. These conferences turn up all kinds of low animal life . . ."

"Whassis name? Bloodhound?"

"Bloodworth. A third-rate novelist. Cooperage should have warned me about him. Damned cretin. Why I let the State Department talk me into this . . ."

Ah, State *Department*. Are you listening Senator McClellan? You hear that Congressman Rooney? Is this what you vote funds for, so this lady can come to Paris, and announce to our allies in the free world—as she had recently in an interview in *Time*—that "America is a great suppurating sore, a malignancy, an infectious exudate in the body politic of the world"?

Weary of eavesdropping, I tickled my rat—the little guy roused himself and greeted me—and wandered to the lobby in search of Malar's daughter, the little redhead who'd helped me in my *mano-a-mano* with the Russian cops. She was at the Bridge Building desk, dispensing brochures and applications to two smiling Congolese. I glanced at one of the leaflets and stopped after the first sentence: *Science and art recognize no national boundaries* . . .

"Ben, I was waiting for you," Judy Malar said. Lovely, lovely—a joyful, innocent girl. There is something about these East European kids, the Czechs, the Hungarians, the Romanians. They are so reassuringly optimistic. "And here is my papa."

A gray-haired man in a rumpled dark gray suit walked over to the table. Judy introduced us. He gave me a damp handshake and a vague smile.

"Delighted, Mr. Bloodworth. I am glad the conference has attracted some younger Americans. The old voices are perhaps ready for retirement. Indeed, my old voice will barely be able to make itself heard here, and perhaps that is all to the good."

Malar appeared to be in his early sixties, stooped, weary-looking, stains on his lapels, the collar of his cheap shirt frayed. He was, altogether, a gray man—hair, suit, manner.

"You will, I am sure, help an old radical build bridges?" he asked. His English was formal, the words carefully spaced; he spoke with a disarming accent.

"If your daughter is going to be your assistant, how can I refuse? How can any normal male refuse?"

"You must be part Hungarian, Mr. Bloodworth. Why not? I am a pragmatist. Juditka does not mind helping the old man." He turned to wave to a regal Ceylonese woman in a white sari, and as he did, I noticed that he had a white plaster patch on the back of his head. Part of the gray hair had been shaved to accommodate it.

"What happened to your head?"

"A stupid fall in my bathroom. The day before we left

50

Budapest. It is a scalp laceration, but it bled quite a bit."

"I hope it doesn't bother you . . . with all your jobs here . . . co-chairman . . . building bridges . . ."

"No, it is nothing." As he said this, he patted the plaster patch tenderly. "Ah, I forgot, I forgot what Juditka told me. You are the young writer who has something for me."

"Do I?"

His gray eyes, mangled behind distorting lenses, glinted with sly Hungarian humor. Was this the great voice of independent Marxist thought in eastern Europe? The man who defied the Stalinists and led the students in 1956? Malar was markedly unprepossessing: soft features, pitted and creased skin with a jail-house pallor, a matted mouse-colored moustache.

"Something from Moses."

"Moses? Sorry, Mr. Malar. No stone tablets."

"Ah? Oh, very good, very good. Moses of the Old Testament, I see. I meant Mr. Bloom."

"I have something for your friend Professor Veg." Bloom would have been proud of my caution. He'd warned me: Malar is the wrong Hungarian.

"So, we shall find him. Like all Hungarians he is probably sitting down in an outdoor café and drinking coffee at this hour. Come along, my boy."

Judy Malar was on the phone talking Italian. Then she switched to French to give information to a Gabonnais who wandered by. Then, a bit of shouted German to a girl helping out at the Bridge Building table. Finally, she used a language I did not understand to a second girl who arrived to relieve her.

"Finnish," Malar said proudly. "My daughter speaks seven languages."

The three of us walked toward the street. "How many do you speak, Mr. Malar?"

He patted the white dressing on his skull. "Mr. Bloodworth, as many as I find necessary."

"That patch seems to be bothering you."

"The stitches are too tight. A minor annoyance." A wise Marxist smile shut his mangled eyes. "If you know anything about me, Mr. Bloodworth, you will understand that I am an old hand at surviving—shall we say—discomforts? Horthy's police cracked my skull. Szalasi's fascists relieved me of my fingernails. Rakosi's hoodlums ruined my digestion. But——"

Judy Malar shivered. "Papa, please . . ."

"Oh, my darling, I am optimistic, I am in fine fettle. I was about to say that when I am in Paris, when I can walk the boulevards of this heavenly city, all those ancient terrors vanish, like the flimsy arguments of old social democrats."

I knew little about Imre Malar. Bloom's warning was too cryptic—was he, or wasn't he? Communist? Socialist? Generalized Marxist? One thing I was sure of. He was a survivor, a witness. With agility and wit and courage he had passed through the fiery furnaces of the century—wars, revolutions, tyrannies, political lunacies—and he was still able to smile and joke.

The street was flooded with late afternoon sunlight. It danced on the bright green leaves of chestnut trees and sycamores. I knew all about the ineffable joy of merely walking down a Paris street. I'd lived and worked here. If it meant so much to me, thirty-three, free, American, footloose—what could it mean to Malar, that veteran of cold prison cells, rubber truncheons, electrical prods, and a diet of watery soup and stale black bread? Paris, for all its cranky inhabitants, is one of man's great sensual creations, a monumental work of beauty, as mysterious as it is satisfying. Who built it? Surely not the French. Not that irritable race of plaster-manglers and short-circuiters.

"Latzi said he would meet us here, did he not, Juditka?" Malar shaded his eyes and surveyed the Café de Lussac, the sidewalk gathering place which the delegates had taken over. It was on the Place d'Iena, not far from the Palais de Chaillot. The writers and artists were identifiable because they made the most noise. Engineers, scientists, and medical people spent a lot of time stacking Perrier bottles. Waiters hurried about peevishly, serving *veesky*, pale French beer, espresso, mineral water, ice cream.

"Europe at rest," Malar said. "This is how we avoid worrying about heart disease, bad schools, inequities."

"How?" I asked.

"Sitting down and drinking *eau minérale*. Wasting time in cafés."

"It sounds as if you approve. That isn't very Marxist."

"No, but it is very human. Europe has already built Chartres and St. Mark's and given the world Giotto and Shakespeare and Einstein. As one of your theater critics once told me, those are extremely hard acts to follow. Is it so important for the French or the English or even Hungarians to create a better computer or automatic rifle than the Americans can make?"

"Or the Russians can make."

"Absolutely. You both suffer the curse of bigness. National sprawl. Obesity of the intellect. A glandular, unnatural, and sickly enlargement of the limbs. Acromegalic industrial plants and giantism of the will."

"There is Uncle Latzi," Judy said. She pointed to a distant, tree-shaded corner of the bustling café.

"Oh, good. I can give him his letter."

I stepped off smartly, halting as old Malar grabbed my arm. "Not at this moment, young man." Once again his eyes vanished behind wrinkled pouches, and this time, it seemed less a smile than a grimace brought on by sudden pain. He steered me to a table some distance from where Veg—whom I had yet to recognize—was seated. Some old revolutionary's sixth sense was at work. But Malar's gray features, the thick gray moustache, brought to my mind the face of my Uncle Moishe, a long-dead garment worker, ILGWU stalwart, born victim and loser, a gentle, mumbling, sweet, eccentric fellow, known to my parents as "Moishe Kapoyr"—*Moses Back-*

wards—because of his circuitous and wrong-headed attitudes.

"Which one is Veg?" I asked, and turned around as soon as we were seated.

There was no response from father or daughter. "Hey, there are those two Russian galoots who tried to steal my mouse! Why the nerve of those guys! Showing their faces here after they pulled that trick. I have a good mind to tell 'em off——"

Pochastny, the fat man with the tuberous nose, and the long-faced Keramoulian, were at one of the rear tables, seated on either side of a slender man, whose back was to me. It was Veg. It had to be.

"Well, this is too good," I said. "I can tell those cops off right in front of Veg. I'll have a few choice comments to make——"

Rising, I felt Malar's restraining hand. For an old man who'd spent years on prison food, he was remarkably strong. "Please, Benjamin. Never transmit messages or opinions or anything other than a good morning in front of Big Brother. As you have guessed, Mr. Pochastny is more than an editor, and Mr. Keramoulian, while indeed an expert on trade, specializes in some unusual varieties of exports. Ah, my café filtre has arrived."

"They're cops," I said. "I'm not afraid of cops. I'm a Bronx boy, Mr. Malar, which means we are brought up to sass them."

"I do not question your courage, or your desire for justice. What Moses Bloom gave you is, in a sense, a trust, and you are angered by the attempt to steal the mouse, or rat, or whatever it is. And the letter."

I blinked. I had said nothing about Bloom's letter.

"You don't want beer? Or an aperitif?" Judy Malar's pale green eyes were smiling at me.

"I can't drink alcohol. I get migraine headaches. Even a sniff of Scotch can bring one on."

Malar stretched. The seam under his left armpit was unraveled. Poor Uncle Moishe. "I, too, have no capacity for

54

strong drink. My digestive system is a remnant."

"Papa can tolerate only bland foods. He has an enzyme imbalance due to prolonged starvation and lack of protein."

Malar patted the patch on his head. "A dreadful fate for a Hungarian, when you consider that paprika is our national vice. Benjamin, dear boy, please stop looking at our friends. You will meet Laszlo Veg soon enough."

I sipped my Perrier. "Who ruined your stomach?" I asked.

"The national leaders of my fatherland."

"Papa, please. I don't like you to joke about, or to talk about it."

I touched Judy's slender hand. "I'm sorry. I shouldn't have asked."

Malar chuckled. "Oh, not at all. It is all a matter of record. My internal organs have been ravaged by politicians. Admiral Horthy's secret police gave me gastritis. I never see a policeman, to this day, that I am not forced to suppress a belch. Do you remember Szalasi, our native fascist leader, Hitler's puppet in Budapest? He escalated my ailment—a bleeding ulcer. Then came Matyas Rakosi, that engaging Stalinoid. Rakosi's secret police endowed me with colitis. I had several operations, including one while in a communist prison. The revisionists who followed, more humane men, worked their way down the alimentary canal, and left me with a spastic rectum. So you see, my digestive system has survived Europe's political wars, but in modified form."

"But you joke about it," I said.

"Papa's jokes do not make me laugh." Judy's eyes were moist. She and her father engaged in a short, sharp Hungarian entr'acte, of which I understood nothing. He kissed her cheek, and I was jealous. They chatted a bit more, and laughed, and I was glad to be with them, in a Paris street café. Even the noisy arrival of a group of young long-hairs did not upset my good humor. Harvey Ungerleider, the bearded boy who had baited Flackman, his girl friend, the nubile Vannie, my Arab chemist, Dr. Jabali, and four or five bell-bottomed young folks were in the group. They took over a front table. Ungerleider opened a large carton. It was filled with handbills, which the others began to study.

"Forgive my ignorance of Hungarian history, Mr. Malar," I said. "But just where do you fit in?"

"Papa was one of six Marxist intellectuals who started the revolution in 1956. The students bore him on their shoulders across the Erszebet Bridge after he called for the liberalization of the Stalinist regime."

"Judy is my greatest advocate," he beamed. "But she is telling the truth." For a man with eroded guts, he appeared to be in bouncy good health. Sipping coffee, he waved to a turbanned Sikh, shook hands warmly with two Africans in orange dashikis, and exchanged a few words in Portuguese with a Brazilian economist.

"You look puzzled, Benjamin," the old radical said. "In brief, I have always been my own kind of Marxist, an artistic Marxist, I suppose. Let me sum it up this way. The Hungarian Revolution of 1956 was a Marxist and intellectual uprising, led by dissident communists, socialists, and others of the left. The Church did not come in until the end, the aristocracy had long vanished, the military stayed back. It was a revolt of the anti-Stalinist left, led by the intellectuals, writers, and critics like myself, with workers forming our frontline soldiers."

"I'm lost," I said. "As the late Senator Joe McCarthy might have said, are you now or have you ever been a member of the Communist Party?"

"Hmmm . . . not really."

I recalled Bloom's warning: Malar was a slippery old fox, an unpeggable man. "But you worked *with* them, *for* them?"

"Of course. As an intellectual, what choice did I have? There is no intellectual right in Europe any more, and I daresay, anywhere in the world."

A hawkish starved face was staring at me: Laszlo Veg. The cadaverous head on its spindly neck had turned, and I looked into a pair of cold, contemptuous eyes. As Veg glared at me, Pochastny whispered in his ear.

"During the Horthy era, when I was a young teacher, I served as secretary to Vajda, our great socialist leader. He was assassinated in the steam bath in the Gellert Hotel. I was seated next to him, and a second bullet, intended for me, missed my head by an inch.

"When Szalasi and his murderers ruled Hungary, I worked in the underground, as aide to Zoltan Bartha. The fascists stabbed Bartha to death, but I escaped. A long story. This brings us to postwar Hungary, when I served as press secretary to Laszlo Rajk."

"Wait a minute. He was hanged by the Stalinists. For being too liberal, a Titoist."

"I was under sentence of death also. I was in the cell next to Rajk, but I was pardoned at the last minute—too minor a figure to be executed." He turned his head to the warming sun and stared into the lovely foliage of the *marroniers*. "Ah, life is full of small pleasures, my children."

"What happened after Rajk was executed?"

"Old Rakosi, Potato-Head as we called him, a charming man when he wasn't sentencing you to be shot, thought I could be useful, and I went to work as a speechwriter for him. Of course, the Russians removed him in 1956, under pressure from us . . ."

"And by then, you were leading the revolution *against* him," I said. "And while he was shipped off to the Soviet Union, you landed on your feet again."

Judy Malar looked annoyed. Sly old cat her daddy may have been, but she didn't like it put so crudely.

"Ah, my daughter is sensitive. You phrase it correctly, Benjamin, but it was not that simple. Perhaps you recall that after the fall of Rakosi, a coalition government was established under my friend Imre Nagy. Nagy was a liberal communist, a humanitarian. Naturally, the Russians shot him, after deceiving him and trapping him."

"But you were let off?"

"This time it was not so easy. Another eight months in jail, and then Comrade Kadar decided I could be trusted."

I nodded. "I think I understand. Janos Kadar knew all about communist prisons. He'd had his own fingernails trimmed very short in one of them, didn't he? So he saw you as a sort of spiritual brother."

"A generous man, Comrade Kadar. I am now a semiofficial cultural ambassador to the West. No politics, of course. I am happy to be nonpolitical."

The old nine-lived cat, the original slippery article. You had to stand in awe of the man. For all the tortures his guts and his brain had endured, he appeared at peace with a horrid world, a world he'd tried to change and that had repaid him with blows in the kidneys.

I looked down the sunny street and saw Warren Cooperage, the Perle Mesta of American Literary Life, waddling along, having burst from the Hotel Bavard with a group of the anointed. He was wearing a double-breasted yellow suit, and he seemed fatter, blonder, more ruddily handsome than when he threw me off the bus that morning. With him were some conference All-Stars—ancient Keen, leaning on Lila Metrick's strong right arm, and a few talkative foreigners. One I recognized as the Italian Nobel laureate, Vito Anzaletti, and another was Derek Venables.

"Question, Mr. Malar," I said. "Why does your co-chairman Mr. Venables wear that crucifix around his neck? Wasn't he a Marxist also, and not too long ago?"

"Ah, dear Derek, dear sweet Derek. Yes, a Marxist of sorts. Actually, a strong supporter of Comrade Stalin. He once wrote an article defending the purge trials."

"And you co-chair a conference with him? I'd ask him to return your fingernails."

"Oh, very good, Benjamin, very good! No, Derek is a critic, a poet, a man of letters. He does not understand anything about Marxist dialectic or the imperatives of history. The cross he wears signifies his conversion to a rarefied kind of

Anglo-Catholicism. It is quite recent. These late-in-life mystics can be wonderfully charming, as you shall see."

I withheld judgment. Venables was, to me, a long-legged snob, a putter-down, a lavender foot-stamper.

"Mr. Malar." I said, "lots of people here seem to have been acrobats, quick-change artists. Anzaletti was also a communist once, but now they hate him. And you. I can't figure out where you stand. Don't you sometimes awaken in the middle of the night and wonder whose side you're on, or if you made the right speech that afternoon?"

A prison cough convulsed him. Phlegm clotted his throat, and Judy patted his hunched back gently.

"Splendid, splendid!" Malar guffawed. "That is part of the fun! And if it permits me trips to Paris and New York, why not?"

"Don't ever ask me for a job. All your employers come to lousy ends. You remind me of an old comic-strip character—Hairbreath Harry. He was always getting by, by the skin of his teeth."

Malar tapped at his poreclain choppers. "A feat I manage even with these East German imitations."

Yes, he was something. Like a scrambling quarterback he'd dodged and faked and backtracked and bounced all over East Europe for fifty years, a step ahead of the firing squad, waiting for the next pardon, conning his jailers and sweet-talking the hangmen.

"You and Papa are going to get along," Judy said, with a mocking smile. "You both have a bloody sense of humor. I find nothing funny about his being under sentence of death five times. Or the fact that he led our revolution."

"*Counter*revolution, dear Juditka, *counter*revolution."

We all looked up. Laszlo Veg, gaunt, birdlike, his eyebrows arched and protruding, resembling dingy feathers, was looming over our table. He spoke with a contemptuous intonation, and his eyes had a fixed harshness about them.

He sat down, and he and Malar exchanged some swift Hungarian comments. Then I was introduced.

59

"What was that about a counterrevolution?" I asked Laszlo Veg.

Malar held up a hand. "Latzi made a poor joke. The re-writers of history in our dear land refer to our uprising as a *counter*revolution, to deprive us of the honor and historical truths due us. We are converted into fascists, landowners, anti-Semites, archbishops, and criminals."

"But . . . but . . . you and Professor Veg can't be ene-mies of the state . . . they let you come to conferences like these . . ."

Malar made a short lateral movement of his right palm—Uncle Moishe, Moishe Kapoyr, telling my father that the ILGWU was a "no guteh union."

"Benjamin, it is nonsense. We live, we die, we make ar-rangements. Nothing is ever the way one wants it. There are degrees of evil and of good. Much better what we have now than Rakosi. Enough."

Veg stretched a bony hand across the table. He was offering me a cigarette.

"No thanks, Professor. I don't smoke."

"Kossuths. Strong and aromatic. Named for our national hero."

"I know all about him. There's a statue of him in New York."

"Then I insist you try one."

"Sorry, Professor Veg. I can't inhale. The smoke makes me sneeze."

Veg shrugged, as if to say it was my loss, then lit his weed with a huge chrome-colored lighter, the kind sold in Army PX's. Probably a gift from a relative or friend in Munich. The Kossuth stank immoderately, as if a GI blanket were being burned.

"Ai, Latzi, these stitches," Malar complained. "They are too tight." He touched his skull lightly.

"I shall remove them soon."

A blank look must have clouded my face. "Professor Veg is a physician, a neurologist to be precise," Judy Malar said. "He

60

took care of Papa, when Papa fell in the bathroom."

My head swiveled: I saw Warren Cooperage and the conference wheels bearing down on us. Coop was waving to Malar. Then they stopped to talk to Arno Flackman, who was seated with three gorgeous girls, the pneumatic Malaysian in black silk, the Dutch girl with the enormous boobies, and the Ceylonese lady in the white silk sari. I tried to drown the envy in my bowels, consoling myself with Judy's sweet aroma, her bobbing red curls. Flackman was ahead three to one; he was always ahead.

"You may give me the letter now, Mr. Bloodworth," Veg said softly. As he did, he half-turned and looked at the Russians. Pochastny and Keramoulian were on their feet.

Helpless, I looked to Malar for guidance. It was a foolish move. Imre Malar was guided by one standard: *survival*. Whether I gave Veg Moses Bloom's communiqué or not would not bother him in the least.

"The letter from Mr. Bloom," Veg persisted.

"Yes, of course. It's for you, no one else." I reached into the inner right pocket of my jacket. No letter. I tried the outside pockets, stood up, searched my denim bell-bottoms, searched the jacket again, and then smiled stupidly at the neurologist. "Looks like I left it in my room."

Did those two old Hungarian fakers smile at one another?

"Mr. Bloom will be unhappy," Veg said. "I don't think the letter is important. The other gift from the gentleman is. The rat is in your room still?"

"Ah, yes. Yes, I left it there."

Warren Cooperage materialized. "Imre baby!" he shouted. "C'mon over where the action is! Jimmy Keen wantsa say hello, and Lila, and the whole crowd!" With coarse familiarity, he began to stroke Judy Malar's neck. "You too, sweetie." He pointed to Veg. "And your friend." I was not included in the invitation.

Malar touched his patch. "I don't think so, Warren dear boy. I am rather tired."

"Ah, we'll cheer ya up, Imre. Tookie and me got some great

61

ideas for some magazine pieces you can do on the conference."

Malar mumbled his appreciation. Veg lit up another malodorous cigarette with his blowtorch lighter. They chatted in Hungarian.

Cooperage pulled up a chair. He pushed his rufous face close to Malar's and practically yelled in the poor man's ear. "Imre, the word is out. I hear you are really gonna blast the Russkies this time. The gloves are off. The speech that the world has been waiting for since 1956, right, Imre?"

"Dear boy, you know so much . . ." Malar was not smiling.

"Derek clued me in. Leave it to old Venables and the crowd of ex-Bolshies and ex-Trotskyites over at *The Discoverist Review*. They know everything, Imre. No secrets. Imre, you make that speech, you give the Russians what-for, and I'll guarantee you page one of *The New York Times*, and a spot on the Cronkite show."

"We shall have to wait until . . . until . . . the speech is made."

"Oh, don't play coy, Imre. I hear you are gonna really sock it to them." Cooperage was grinning.

Pochastny and Keramoulian had moved two tables closer and were listening, heads cocked, like attentive Dobermanns.

Veg got up, moving jerkily. "Enough of this political nonsense. For me anyway. Mr. Bloodworth, shall we go?" His cigarette must have gone out, because he was lighting up again.

"No, really, Warren," Malar muttered. "You should not make conclusions based on what Derek Venables or anyone else says . . . I . . ."

"Papa, are you feeling ill?" Judy had her arm around the old radical. He yawned mightily, yawned again, and shook his gray head.

"I am all right, quite all right."

Veg patted him assuringly on the shoulder, and we left, Cooperage braying in Malar's ear about the blockbusting speech he was going to make, the fierce attack on Moscow and the new Stalinism.

Moving through the café, past Indonesian sociologists, Finnish physicists, and editors from the Ivory Coast, I passed the table of the young radicals, and helped myself to one of the mimeographed sheets.

"Fink," Harvey Ungerleider sneered at me. "Whyncha join us, ya Establishment creep?"

"I don't know who you are," I said.

Daoud waved a smooth brown hand. *"Salaam aleikum,* friend."* He seemed too sweet a young man to be in such low company.

With Veg at my side, I glanced at the paper, copies of which Ungerleider and his troop were evidently going to distribute.

CONFERENCE A ZIONIST FASCIST PLOT

Who are the leaders of this purported conference on the arts and sciences? They are a mixed bag, but the prevailing influences are ZIONIST, FASCIST, and NEO-IMPERIALIST. Make no mistake about it, the tenor of resolutions and debate will all be in favor of the Zionist-fascist state of Israel and her international fascist supporters, chief among them the United States, determined to suppress the legitimate demands of the freedom fighters of Palestine, the Al Fatah guerrilla heroes . . .

"You make any sense out of this?" I asked Laszlo Veg. "I mean, that kid Ungerleider and a lot of his gang are Jews. Healthy, safe, secure American Jews. What the hell do they know about Auschwitz? What is this fascist crap?" .

My blood was boiling, my ears pounded. I'm no two-fisted money-raising Zionist, but I know who I am, and I have read a great deal of recent history. My library at home is filled with works on Treblinka, Theresienstadt, Dachau, Auschwitz, and those other interesting places. And the best single history book I have ever read, one to which I have returned dozens of times to clear my mind and give some direction to my haphazard life is called *The Destruction of the European Jews,* by a man named Hilberg.

"I am not a political man," Veg said.

"But your friend Malar is. It sounds as if he's going to blow the lid off the conference. This was supposed to be the East-West love feast. If he makes a speech denouncing the Russians, the way Cooperage said he would . . ."

"Mr. Malar will make his own speech. He does not need hints or assistance from American busybodies."

We walked past Arno Flackman. Already he was King of the Conference. The three women at his table had been joined by three more, and there was a group of a half-dozen assorted delegates standing around, listening to the pearls of wisdom from El Lider's lips. As we passed him, I saw his head bob and duck, and he threw two left jabs. "I'm a swarmer," he was mumbling, "I swarm and throw leather from the bell, like Henry Armstrong . . . I'm all fists and arms . . . and I never let the other guy get inside . . . like Sugar Ray."

"One of your countrymen?" Veg asked. We walked toward the Bavard.

"*Primus inter pares,* Professor. The most important person here. Arno Flackman, a writer so famous they bottle his sweat and sell it to make sterile women fertile."

He did not smile. "I have no interest in literary people. They are bores, preening peacocks. Inflated egos and twisted sex lives."

We were alone in the creaking elevator. The wading bird, the starved stork folded his wings. "So. You are in Moses Bloom's employ. Two innocent Americans, eh, Mr. Bloodworth?"

The lift settled with a noisy shiver at my floor. "I am no man's servant, Dr. Veg. I am a writer, a fierce and independent spirit. Mr. Bloom and I are colleagues only in that we both belong to that ancient fraternity."

"Yes. That and the Shin-Bet."

"Beg pardon?" I let him precede me out of the elevator and into the dank, gloomy corridor.

"Do not feign ignorance. We need not keep secrets from

one another. You and Bloom are agents of the Shin-Bet."

"Wrong, whatever it is. Moe is a *landsman*, that's all. I once wrote an article praising his books."

At the door, I paused. "There is a verbal message to go with the rat."

Veg grinned wickedly. "Let us see if your memory is better than your talents as a bearer of letters. You realize, Mr. Bloodworth, that letter was stolen from you."

"By who? I mean, who would want a letter to you?"

He shrugged. 'The message? The verbal one?"

"Bloom says that this rat doesn't work."

"Of course. Tell Mr. Bloom that was my intention. I arranged for him to steal a nonworking rat."

"Bloom stole it?"

"Please, let us get this over with."

We entered my narrow room. Don't ask me why, but the room smelled strange. My migraineur's sensitivity told me so. A faintly rotten odor? I went to the up-turned wastebasket, lifted it, and picked up the rat. He was terribly still, and as soon as my hand grasped the furry body, I knew he was dead.

"Ah, a pity," Veg said.

"Isn't that odd. He was lively and happy when I left. I wonder why? Thirst? Too much handling?"

"You are failing your friend Bloom on every count. The letter stolen. The rat dead. With this kind of inefficiency, you could be a Hungarian."

Veg's humor eluded me. I probed the soft white fur with its black saddle to see, in my bumbling way, if I could determine what had killed the rat. At the base of the little fellow's skull was a small gouge. Equidistant between his pointy ears, a small chunk of hair and flesh, and for all I knew, skull, had been cut away. Strangely, there was little blood. It was a neat, small puncture, surgically neat, the way one of those snippers puts a hole in the end of a cigar.

"Hell of a lot of trouble to kill a rat," I said.

"This rat made enemies."

"Or knew too much?"

"Possibly. Well, he is my rat, so as next of kin I will claim the body."

Dutifully, I handed the corpse over. "I guess he doesn't work at all now. I mean, Bloom said he didn't work, like a busted watch."

The neurologist placed the dead beast in his coat pocket and turned stiffly to leave. "You will do well, if you are not in the employ of Shin-Bet, to avoid Mr. Bloom. I know nothing about you. You do not interest me in the slightest, so I offer this advice impartially. Do not get involved."

In the lobby Pochastny was sitting near the elevator reading the Paris *Trib*, peering over the logo like a dumb cop in an old Hollywood flick—Nat Pendleton or Warren Hymer. "Hi fellah," he greeted me. "Hi, Professor. Everything copacetic?"

Veg held the dead rat up by the tail and showed it to the Russian. He said nothing.

"Darn shame," said Pochastny. The two of them walked out of the hotel, and the Russian called to me over his thick shoulder. "You win a few, you lose a few, guy."

I dragged myself back to the boulevard and down to the Café Lussac again. Malar and Judy were gone. I saw Veg and the Russian get into a taxi. The café was noisier, more crowded than before. Naturally, an excited crowd had gathered around the wheels. Cooperage, Keen, and Lila Metrick had joined Flackman and his harem. A dozen onlookers had pulled chairs up close to catch the honey as it dripped from these godlike lips. Ungerleider, the Zionist-hating little *shmuck* from Scarsdale, his girl friend in pink pantyhose, and the young Arab, with *their* crowd, were at an adjacent table. I sensed a crackling in the air, an imminent outbreak of foul language and maybe fists. Quite simply, Flackman would not tolerate being upstaged, outcursed, outlefted by anyone; he had a long history of angry *confrontas* with wild kids. Professing to love and admire their "existen-

66

tial" violence, he abhorred and feared them, not because they differed much in philosophy ("The black mugger," Flackman once wrote, "is the century's true hero") but because they were a threat to his primacy in the press. If Flackman peed on the floor of Loew's Sheridan, Harvey Ungerleider would move his bowels on a professor's research. Forever topped excrementally by these wild children, he felt uneasy in their presence.

"Ah, a remarkable sensation, to kill a man with your own hands . . . as I once did . . ."

That, of course, was James Warfield Keen.

"But what . . . how . . . when, Jimmy?" a girl reporter asked.

"Ah, a long story, Depression years, way back . . . with my own hands . . ."

Flackman scowled. The curly bristles on his head seemed charged with ozone and his beard sparked. "Balls, Jimmy. Sure you did, but I have also. I don't talk about it much, but in the army, back in the zone, I once got my mitts on some MP's throat, and I squeezed . . ."

They were bragging about having *murdered* people. Lying, of course. But bragging.

"Yes, Arno, I'm sure you have," Cooperage said loudly. "Nobody ever questioned your guts, Arn."

"A man," Flackman said slowly, as all leaned forward to catch the guru's revelations, "a man has to keep his killer instincts finely honed, and be ready to go for the jugular at all times. The times demand nothing less of the writer than he put up his dukes and fight, not figuratively, not in his gassy literary efforts, but out in the world. Last week some black bastard challenged me. It was out in East Hampton, at Shappstein's big party for the Clutts. Well, we went down to the beach, and I decked him twice. The jab, then a right cross, the left hook. He shook my hand."

There were a few gasps from the crowd, some orgasmic murmurs from the women. It was a purely Flackmanian

67

speech. He not only had taken on a Negro hood, but he had let the world know that it had taken place at the East Hampton palace of Sheldon Shappstein, the world's richest dealer in tax-free bonds, and that the party was for Amy and Jack Clutt, the world's richest art collectors.

"You'll shit too, Flackman, if you eat regular." This came from young Ungerleider, a table away. His retinue applauded. I could see the youth-age conflict emerging.

Flackman rubbed a fist in a palm. Behind huge sunglasses he stared at the bearded boy. "Shall we do it right now, son? In the street? In my room?"

"Ah, fuck off."

The level of dialogue was not notably high, but the audience gasped and murmured, and, I am certain, young girls had secret spasms in their pants watching this battle of bull elephants. Why? *Why?* Hemingway, do you know what you started when you shot that hyena?

Seated at the fringe of the group, I was surprised to hear Cooperage addressing me. "Say, Bloodworth. I hear you're a pal of Moe Bloom's. Is the old guy around?"

"No. He's got better things to do than go to conferences."

Cooperage snorted. "Old has-been. The Ben-Gurion of Cleveland. Incidentally, Arn, if Bloom does decide to show, we'd better be on guard—Derek, and Imre, and all of us—to see he doesn't start one of his monomaniacal harangues. Crazy old gunrunner."

I pulled my chair closer. Moe Bloom was an old hero of mine, and I had always admired his hard-nosed Zionism. Someone had to defend him. "Coop, is it true you and your wife barred Bloom from four magazines?"

"I did not. He got himself in the bad graces of every leading editor by his intemperate remarks about me and all the people I respect."

You had to learn, early in the game that you played ball with them. Does this sound paranoid? Am I a psychotic, brimming with a persecution complex that chokes my reason? No, I am not. You watched your step with the Cooperages and Flackmans and their "people"; if you attacked one, another would strike back at you.

"And I suppose the same applies to me?" I asked. I was referring to an article I did some years ago for a Columbia alumni magazine in which I accused Cooperage, who is actually a rather soft, peaceful young man, of being "the *milchediker* Arno Flackman." Coop worships Flackman; sighs at the sight of his muscles and his bloody boasts and "existential" brutality.

"You don't matter that much," Cooperage said. "No offense, Bloodworth, but you aren't in Bloom's league as a nut. He wins all the prizes for paranoia. Israel should get itself a better historian."

"I do hope this damned thing doesn't get too political," Lila Metrick said, shaking her bell of blonde, gleaming hair. Ah, to bury my starved face in it, all that Protestant glory. "What about a workshop on erotic imperatives for the artist?"

"Sounds great," I said. "Down with Lenin, and up libido. No more politics, just friction. You get the artist out of politics, lady, and just wait till you see who takes it over, if he hasn't already. That fellow in the yellow construction helmet has a few ideas what to do with long-hairs and intellectuals. We better start reaching him before he burns us all up, and the cops stand by and applaud."

"Screw off, loudmouth," Numero Uno muttered. "I may have to deck you."

Cooperage was whispering in James Warfield Keen's ear. "Jimmy, ya gotta put up with a lot of these boobs at conferences."

"Who . . . who . . . is the fellow?" Keen asked drowsily.

"Bloodworth. Third-rate Bronx novelist. Herman Wouk without the yarmulka. Magazine pieces. Professional crank."

Harvey Ungerleider, his girl friend Vannie, Dr. Jabali, and the rest of the far-left contingent were now moving among

69

the sidewalk café-sitters, distributing their mimeographed sheet denouncing the conference as a Zionist-fascist plot. What else? Golda Meir and Moshe Dayan in cahoots with an aging Hitler, living secretly in Rehovoth.

"Tookie's driving up from Cannes," Cooperage announced —to Keen, but loud enough for all to catch a driblet of the honey. Tookie was Coop's wife—millions in a textile fortune, an Alabama accent, and high literary pretensions, which had gotten her the ownership and editorship of *Seminal,* a literary magazine which I had once referred to as *New Erections,* and for which they had not yet forgiven me.

Cannes. People like the Cooperages were always arriving from Cannes or Port Ercole or Malaga. I thought of my wife Felicia battling the Bendix washer-dryer in Hicksville in our split-level house. My son Eddie was fielding grounders, tossing his abraded Official League ball against the garage door. But I had sworn off self-pity. It was odd. My contact with Bloom; my dealings with the Hungarians; the way I'd battled the Russian fuzz for the white rat; all these endowed me with heady reckless courage. Let Tookie drive up from Cannes! Let Metrick dominate the workshops! I knew something denied them. But what?

Young Ungerleider deposited the sheets on the tables at which sat Flackman, Cooperage, Keen, and the other High Priests.

"Read it and learn something," he said. "Why not admit that this farce is a bourgeois diversion, a cover-up? We of the Third World Liberation Movement, speaking for the workers of the world——"

"New York City construction workers?" I asked. "Longshoremen? They appoint you?"

Now the only point I was trying to make was that the most offensive and extreme of these kids—the flag-burners and shouters of "motherfucker" and "pig" and "fascist" can succeed only in creating one kind of revolution in America: Hitler's kind. Yes, it's true. Shout fascist long enough and you'll create 'em. You can't move the lumpen masses of America, those honest laborers, by spitting on the flag. There must be other ways of getting the good things done.

"You're irrelevant," little Vannie said to me.

"Now, Harvey," Metrick said impatiently, crossing her goalie's legs—tan, hairless, smooth as Gucci leather. "The key to this meeting is intellectual freedom for all mankind."

"We oppose that also," the bearded boy snarled. "When we're in charge, we'll decide who is free and who isn't."

Oh, lord, the innocence of that overweight, spoiled, indulged twenty-two-year-old! Summer camps, prep schools, tennis lessons, sailing off Larchmont. As Vanzetti said—*nothing!*

I tugged at Vannie's miniskirt. "Hey, dolly, do you and your sweetie represent any organization?"

She raised her elegant head. Very *goyish*—short nose, firm chin, clear skin. "We represent the liberated spirit of man. Harvey led the burn-in at Columbia. He showed his hatred for the Establishment by shitting in Professor Volkmann's filing cabinet."

"Your scenario is corrupt," Ungerleider was telling Metrick and Flackman. They eyed him narrowly. He was, in a sense, a caricature of their own public selves, and it was disturbing them. "This whole bag of shit can be made meaningful and revolutionary if it develops the proper life-style. It can still be restructured."

"Listen, kid," Flackman growled, "I was a communist before you got your first piece. I know all about revolutions. And I can handle you or five like you, with my fists alone."

"Once killed a man with my own hands . . ." Keen was mumbling again.

"I'd love to heah what the young fewwow has in mind," Derek Venables piped. He'd glided over, fingering the cross around his neck.

"Okay, okay, I'll put you into it, but I doubt any of you will dig." Harvey stood facing the elders and orated. "You people who run this bash, this cheap bourgeois deceit, can change your image in only one way."

It bothered me that a hoo-hoo literary fellow like Venables was ready to listen to young Ungerleider. Still, crapping in a professor's files had a certain panache. It topped anything Venables or his generation had ever done.

"I'd wike veddy much to heah," Venables piped.

"Jesus, don't encourage him," I cried. "This boy's claim to fame is defecation in some poor professor's research! These kids are great at burning libraries and attacking colleges, the places that can save them. Let them go out and do missionary work with the AFL Building Trades Union and see how far they get . . ."

I was a voice crying in the wilderness.

"Shut up, Bloodworth," Cooperage snapped. "We've got to keep our lines of communication open to the young. Tell it like it is, Harvey."

Ungerleider leaned forward. His larded thighs bulged his denims. "There's only one way for you straights to rap with us, only one way to get relevant, to get out of your tree. The word *fuck* must be used freely and frequently at all sessions."

"Reaaaally," Lila Metrick drawled. She was all for wide-open sex in her essays, but that azure Boston blood recoiled from dirty words. In her writings, she was fond of fellatio, cunnilingus and all the other smarmy crap that these lofty eminences roll off their coated tongues. But I had the feeling that if you goosed Metrick she'd faint.

"You people are running things," Ungerleider said truthfully. "Make the decision. Fuck is a simple word. F, u, c, k. Give the okay, and you become a revolutionary concept. Otherwise we will have to destroy you, since you have no legitimacy and offer no options to the alienated youth of the world."

"Harvey," I said. "Try hollering dirty words in front of Local 42, Plasterers and Bricklayers Union, of Perth Amboy, and see how far you get with Vinnie Colucci and Dom Esposito."

"Ignore him, Harvey, he's a nobody," his girl friend said.

Ungerleider obliged her. "You're all uptight. You're repressed. Get it out. Right out of the mouth. It won't hurt long."

Behind her smoked glasses Lila Metrick, high priestess of abandoned screwing, all varieties, looked upset. Prudish despite the big behind and the dirty writing. People like Metrick went to parties with millionaire raincoat manufacturers with ten-room suites in United Nations Plaza, and these generous hosts are rendered uneasy by profanity.

"You people might as well get *our* message right now," Harvey Ungerleider said thickly. How old was he? Twenty-two? There was a babyish softness about him; he'd never hit back if a longshoreman, one of the noble proletariat, belted him with a lead pipe. He'd cry and hold his poor bloodied head. And this *pisherkeh* was going to create revolutions!

"What might that message be?" Derek Venables asked.

"We want the whole world and we want it now," the young man said. "And if you don't get it, we are ready to destroy you and all like you. To bring you to your knees."

There was applause from his disciples, and the agitation of arms roiled the warm air with body odor. Daoud, the House Arab, was the last to applaud, and looked a bit confused. He was so damned sweet, I was sorry he'd fallen in with this mob.

"*Arriba la revolución!*" cried Harvey's girl Vannie.

"*Votre monde est un fleuve de merde!*" cried a boy with blond curls down to his navel.

"Fuck or no fuck, Cooperage?" Ungerleider taunted.

"You're joshing me, young man. I won't play your game."

Flackman scowled. "Beat it, you lousy fruit. I was using dirty words before you knew any. I'm Flackman, and I have the biggest balls at this conference. Flackman says what he wants, where he wants."

"No answer, fink," Harvey taunted. His mob were on their feet, howling insults at the conference leaders.

"Fascists!"

"Pigs!"

"Bourgeois scum!"

Metrick, the coolest cat on the scene, got up. Regal, proud, she announced she had had enough, and was leaving. I had to hand it to that blonde goddess with her queenly rump, her heavenly haunches. But what else could I expect from a twenty-five-year-old broad, who, in a much-quoted article in *Seminal*, had written, *"This commentator regards Mesdames McCarthy, Sontag, Huxtable, and Hartwick as interesting, if conventional figures."*

This was the signal for all of them—Cooperage, James Warfield Keen, Venables—to rise and start shuffling off.

"Cowards," Vannie simpered. "Scared shitless of a confrontation."

"Hold it!" I shouted. "This kid deserves an answer!"

"Bloodworth, stay out of this," Warren Cooperage said angrily. "You'll provoke them, and they'll wreck the conference. Stay *out*."

"No, no, Coop. We owe the boy an answer. I suggest we agree. Not only the word he mentioned, but *all* dirty words are on limits."

"You have no authority to do anything, Bloodworth. You're not even an official delegate."

"Coop, you said you'd put me on the workshops, to make up for taking my seat on the bus. Please, let me handle this."

There was a hiatus, Cooperage mulling over the possibility that I might be a good sacrificial lamb, a lightning rod to draw the fire of the young radicals.

"Okay, Harve, let's get them all out. Let's get all the dirty words out, right here, so we're in agreement on what we want to say." I looked the fat boy in the eye. He was a child, an overweight sad child, the kind who never learned to hit a backhand properly, despite many hours of tennis lessons from an expensive pro.

"You're a cop," he said. "I get it. Where you from, fuzz?"

"Honest I'm not, Harvey."

74

"Fink, spy, informer. Who you sending the names to?"

"Harvey, I'm plain Benny Bloodworth, minor Jewish-American writer. I bet I learned more dirty words when I was a kid in the Bronx than you ever picked up in Great Neck or where the hell ever you were raised."

"Jesus, Bloodworth, you'll get him sore," Cooperage wailed. Yes, they were afraid of these children. Even Venables, who had encouraged them (he fancied himself an advocate of the young), looked distressed by my assault.

"For all the marbles, Harvey," I said. "This is for the Lady Byng Trophy of dirty words. Ready?"

"Good God, let's leave," Lila Metrick moaned. "Must we watch this?"

"It'll take a minute," I said.

Flackman was watching me narrowly. Actually, it should have been his job to put down the rebellion.

"I'll lead off," I said. "Fuck. Shit. Prick. Cunt. Cocksucker. Bastard. Bitch. Cooze. Gash. Quim. Quiff. Hair Pie. Poon Tang. Snatch. *Tochis.* Ass. Behind. *Merde.* Bugger. Fart. Piss. Balls. That's a partial list. For openers, you might say. Your turn, Harvey. Let's really show the gang how free and progressive we are."

"I've heard quite enough," Lila Metrick said. She wheeled her awesome behind, and the others followed it. Then, she turned and called to the little girl with Ungerleider. "Vannie, you can talk to me at the Teagues' party tonight. I'll leave the address in my letter box."

Off they went. I was left alone with the alienated young.

"Up against the wall, motherfucker," Harvey sneered at me. "You tried to put me down, but we'll have the last word here."

"Beg pardon?" I had been studying Lila Metrick's *culo,* wondering how she kept it so firm and high, and how it would feel to the touch. A Monopoly board could have rested comfortably on its upper plane.

"Up against the wall, motherfucker."

I shook my head in sorrow. "Harvey, it is no improvement over 'Workers of the World Unite.' "

"*Al paradón!*" a tiny girl shrieked.

"All pigs die," another added.

"Have your fun," I said. "When *Der Tag* comes, thanks to your foul mouths and bad manners, we'll end up in the same concentration camps. Explain it to your cellmates how you wanted to destroy fascism in America, but by mistake you burned down the universities."

Engloomed, I wandered through the café tables, along the tree-shaded street, the summery loveliness of Paris. How little they knew! There were hard-handed men with long rifles, lead pipes, honest union fellows with monkey wrenches and brass knucks, waiting for all of us, waiting for these defenseless and soft pisspots to burn one more, just one more American flag in front of them. They would never understand that you moved our great American citizenry with deceit, cajolery, fakes and appeals to patriotism. You didn't get anything done by spitting on their flag and accusing them of incest.

"Ah, sir, Mr. Bloodworth, that was a most interesting conversation, although I did not understand all of it."

Daoud Jabali was at my side, padding along in his high-topped tan sneakers.

"Oh, it wasn't really important, Daoud. A lot of crazy Americans arguing."

"Ah. Ah." How this well-mannered Jordanian agronomist had fallen in with assassins like Harvey and Vannie eluded me. I asked him why.

"Well, sir, do not take offense, but I am also an Arab patriot. I support the just aspirations of the Middle East people, my people, although I am a moderate, and recognize Israel's right to live. They told me, the young people, that they, too, were interested in Arab nationalist movements. I am the only Jordanian at the conference, and they asked my assistance."

I stared at his innocent face, and by God, I wanted to help him. Jordanian Arabs, especially the West Bank people, I had been told, are the most gracious and charming folks in the world. How easily the whole Middle East agony could be resolved if reasonable men like Daoud and myself could talk it over!

"Don't get too thick with them, Daoud," I said. "They don't matter much, and they use too much filthy language for an educated gentleman like yourself."

"You are such a funny man, Mr. Bloodworth. And so many interests."

"I'm just a novelist. Magazine writer."

"I was told you are also ah, a biologist of some kind. A fellow scientist."

"No, no."

"Ah. But the white rat. The white rat you had . . . was he not part of a demonstration . . . ah, a subject for . . . ah . . ."

"I don't have him any more."

The young Arab looked as if he were about to weep, as if I were a headwaiter who had just told him the kitchen had run out of *hummus*. "No, no more?"

"He's dead."

Daoud Jabali clapped a tan hand to his mouth, and his head jerked back.

"Oh, how terrible, how unfortunate. Surely that was a great blow to your plans . . ."

The words stopped on my tongue. Sorry, Dr. Jabali. I would not, I decided, tell him that the rat was Bloom's, or Veg's and that someone had killed it with a gouge in the skull.

"I must . . . I must join some friends . . ." Daoud, silent and swift on sneakered feet, darted away.

In the lobby, I ordered a lemon *pressé* and rested. I was off to a great start. Bloom's letter lost. Bloom's rat dead. I was in the bad graces of all the conference powers, and I had made lasting enemies of the wild hairy kids who threatened to ruin the whole affair.

I had also caught Lila Metrick's invitation to Vannie.

77

Something about a party at the Teagues. Well, I knew the Teagues, and I knew what kind of party it would be—the biggest, the wildest, the in-est, the most with-it of the conference. And I had not been invited. No, no self-pity, I told myself. I'd sworn off that. But let us be frank, are not snubs and insults among the great unrecognized causative factors in human affairs and the fate of nations?

An elderly bellhop was carrying a slate with the chalked message: *Telephone: M. Bludwart.*

"*C'est moi*," I said. He pointed to the phones at the rear of the gloomy room. I slipped into the alcove, which was not far from the bar. As in many Parisian hotels, it was not entirely shut off from the lobby, but partially separated by a frosted-glass partition.

"Bloodhound," a hoarse voice called to me as I picked up the phone. "Ole Bloodhound, thass him." Louise Latour, recovered from her digestive ailment, was squatting like a pale bullfrog in an armchair off the bar. She was in formal dress—gray sweatshirt, gray Bermudas, black sneakers. "C'mon, heist a few with Louise, Bloodhound."

"In a second, Miss Latour. Soon as I take this call."

"Betcher ass, kid." She sipped from a tall glass, savoring whatever it was, with the finesse of the true alky. Chipper, her Boy Scout chaperon, came by and sat down with a Coke.

There was some French fussing on the line. I identified myself and I heard Moses Bloom's hoarse voice.

"Ben? Did you deliver them? The letter, and the animal?"

"Moe! Where are you? You said you were going to Budapest."

"I'm at Brussels Airport. We're making a connection with Malev, Hungarian Airlines. They don't know from schedules. Based on dialectical materialism. *Nu?*"

"Somebody lifted the letter from my pocket. Or I lost it."

"You run into a Russian named Pochastny?"

"How'd you guess? I bet he took it, the big lug. He and some other creep also tried to steal the rat——"

"Keramoulian. Looks like a sick anteater. Stay away from him. From both of them."

"Why?"

"Take my word. Pochastny is KGB, but political. The other guy is with the Thirteenth Directorate. Mr. Bloody Business. If he gets smart with you, pull that on him. I got plenty on both. So, you got the rat back, and you gave it to Laszlo Veg?"

I hesitated. Chipper Latour, wearing his sash of merit badges, and his Aunt Louise were staring at me. Chipper waved his fingers. I waved back.

"Moe, you'll hate me for this. I left the rat in my room, and by the time I got back there with Veg—it was hard finding him, and I got stuck with Malar—the rat was dead. There was a little hole in its skull. Between the ears."

Bloom's voice seemed heavier. "What did he say?"

"Not much. Stuck it in his pocket. He accused me—and you—of being Shin-Bet agents. What the heck is that?"

"Nothing important."

"He also said your rat made enemies. Frankly, Moe, he didn't seem interested—in the letter, the rat, or the message about the rat not working. I remember. He said the rat wasn't supposed to work. That you stole a nonworking rat, something like that."

There was a pause. I could hear Bloom's heavy breathing.

"Got a pencil, kid? Good. Take this down. Another message for Veg. First I'll give you an address where you can find him tonight. Avenue du Général Dumont 19. It's in the thirteenth arrondissement. You know where that is?"

"Gobelins. Southeast." I scribbled on the back of my Pan-Am ticket.

"Veg stays there. So does Malar. The Wrong Hungarian. You met his cutey daughter?"

"Yes. She's great."

"Stay away from them also. Now, when you find Veg, tell him there is a seat open on the eastern wall."

"A seat open on the eastern wall. What is this? An invitation to go to synagogue?"

"He'll know. Ai, what a lousy Hungarian he is, what a *shtunk.*" Bloom laughed secretively. "Shin-Bet, he thinks we're the Shin-Bet."

"Are we? I mean, you?"

"Who do you think I'm doing this for? The German-American Bund?"

"I don't know," I said. Then, like a Hemingway hero I repeated the words. "I don't know anything at all." (See "The Killers." *You don't have to laugh. You don't have to laugh at all.*)

"*Shalom,* sonny, I'll call again."

He hung up. I was sweating slightly, and Bloom's cryptic remarks had drawn me close to the phone, as if I wanted to climb in. I barely noticed young Chipper in his Scout uniform, standing outside the open booth, Coke in hand. "Aunt Louise wants you to join us, sir."

"In a minute, Chipper." He saluted me. When he had gone, I dialed the hotel operator and asked for Malev, the Hungarian National Airlines. It took me two minutes to establish that they had only three flights a week to Budapest from Brussels, early mornings on Tuesday, Wednesday, and Saturday. This was late afternoon, Friday, so unless Malev was atrociously behind schedule, even for a socialist airline, Bloom had lied to me. I walked out of the booth convinced he was in Paris.

An odd clicking noise brought me up short. It was Louise Latour ordering a fresh drink. She did it by tapping the apple-sized diamond ring on her chubby finger against the side of the empty tumbler. *Tak-tak-tak!* It was a demand bid, a gesture I'd never seen before or since. The waiter hurried over.

"*Oui, madame?*"

"Fill 'er up, shortass. Double Scotch and ginger ale. Bet you never seen an American lady put it away the way Louise can, hey? Watcha want, Bloodhound?"

"Seven-up, please."

"You temperance? Wassa matter you don' drink?"

"Migraine from alcohol." I tapped my temple. "Never touch it."

Chipper Latour was smiling at me with shy friendliness. "Golly, Mr. Bloodworth, I wish you'd talk to Aunt Louise about her problem. She respects other writers, and they're ignoring us terribly here. Mr. Cooperage didn't even recognize Auntie Louise when she went up to him."

Fair Louise! She was doomed to be ignored, put down, snubbed. For all her millions, she would never cut the mustard with the Flackmans and Metricks.

"Hate conferences," she said, as the waiter gave her a brimming glass. "Hate foreigners. Lousy French, lousy English, stinkin' Italians. Know why I puked inna elevator, Bloodhead? Puked because I was surrounded by foreigners. I'm a namerican, thass what. Greatest li'l country inna world. Friggin' publisher sends me around to foreign countries to sell books, and I get sick alla time. Right, Chipper?"

The Boy Scout patted her hand. "That's right, Auntie."

"I don't understand, Louise. If you dislike foreigners and get ill when you're away from the States, why do you do this? Why did you come to the conference?"

It seemed hard to believe, but in two mighty gulps she had drained the glass, and once more signaled in her boozer's Morse code. *Tak-tak-tak!* The diamond tapped out its message, and this time the waiter merely nodded to the barman.

"Why? Why I'm here?" A smile turned her porcine mouth. "Shhh. Shhh, Benny. Don't tella soul. I'm a spy. Yup. I'm a goddamn spy." This notion convulsed her and she began to giggle, short explosive *hee-hee-hee's* that jiggled her puffy face.

"I don't believe that. You're too open, Louise, too honest. Like your books."

And although I had never read her sexy novels of small-

81

town life, I was glad I had lied. The praise transformed her ravaged face. For all the millions, all the sales, she wanted to be loved, to be admired. And I was her idea of an *inside* writer, a talented and successful man. I suppose the relationship was good for both of us.

"Hey, Benny, you all right," she gurgled, as the waiter gave her a fresh glass. "C'mon have dinner with us tonight. You an' me an' Chipper. Louise'll pay, pay for the works."

"Gee, please, Mr. Bloodworth," the nephew said. "You're the only person here who's been nice to Aunt Louise. I mean it, honest."

I begged off; I'd become Bloom's boy.

In my room, soaking in a sulfurous lukewarm bath which issued protestingly from the rusted spout in brown spurts, I regretted my inability to cheer Louise Latour. But in the literary life, as King Promoters like Flackman and Cooperage had shown, one's eye must always be open for opportunities. Besides, there was little I could do for Miss Latour. I had one mission to perform for Bloom—and presumably for those two and a half million beleaguered Jews in the homeland—and several for myself.

As I dressed in a casual powder-blue turtleneck, pale green slacks from Alexander's, and a navy Korvette's blazer, I had a moment's panic as I forgot the message for Veg. Ah, the eastern wall. *A seat open on the eastern wall.* I knew enough about Hebrew folklore, even though I was never barmitzvahed. (My old man was a socialist; Debs was his hero, not the Lubavitcher *rebbe*.)

Through the door that separated my cell from Lila Metrick's I heard the telephone ringing. Swiftly, I pressed my glass to the door and pressed my ear to its bottom. (I'd have preferred pressing it to Metrick's smooth bottom. But too many walls, physical, social, ideological, separated us.) Loud and clear I heard the lady's Ivy League drawl. Like Cooperage, she could dribble honey off her tongue, and it dripped now, as she discussed social events with the caller.

"Yaaas," I heard, "yaaaas. There's a party at the American Embassy for the American delegates. It's the ambassador's idea. He's standing for dinner at La Perouse, and then we're all off to the Teagues' house for the rest of the night. *Ciao, bella.*"

I had not been invited to the embassy. Or to the Teagues', people I knew rather well, and regarded as friends. There was only one solution left. I would crash the Teagues' blast, after delivering Bloom's message.

The outlying districts of Paris—Gobelins is on the Left Bank, far to the southeast, a poorer residential area—look their best at dusk on a warm day. I wandered the cluttered streets, taking my time, marveling at the pheasants and rabbits and quail in the game butchers, the mounds of redolent cheeses, the windows full of hot bread. The French are a pain, but they know all about food. I liked the grimy, lived-in, well-used look of the high narrow apartment buildings, and the blue-collar people.

Avenue du Général Dumont, which I gathered from Moe Bloom was a sort of Hungarian headquarters, was off the Rue de la Glacière. Like many such nondescript streets, the ground floors housed modest shops. There they were—the National Class of France, the pinched, starved, frustrated small shop-keepers—*papeteries, charcuteries, boulangeries, quincailleries.* Number 19 was a bit more elegant than the other gray-brown edifices, but it hardly seemed the place to house delegates to a world conference on the arts and sciences.

The lobby was dim and smelled of frying potatoes. The aroma came from the concierge's cell. I walked to thé frosted-glass door and studied the list of tenants pasted to the pane. There was no Veg, no Malar, nothing that sounded foreign.

There was no answer when I rapped at the concierge's door. It must be understood at once that the concierge population of France is recruited from asylums for the criminally insane. A committee of landlords visits the sanitaria annually and signs up the most stupid, vicious women available, giving them crash courses in rudeness and the wearing of old army shoes. Many are also supplied with rabid dogs and spitting cats, and these are trained to defecate and urinate in dark corners.

I now heard shouts and conversation from the courtyard, beyond the elevator. I walked through two doors and into a typical dark hollow square, around which rose the four rear walls of the apartments. In the crepuscular light I saw a dozen or so people standing on the winding back stairs. They were shouting, pointing to the courtyard below. On the ground, six more people were gathered around a cluster of trash cans.

I spotted the concierge at once. She was a bull-necked woman in her sixties in a flannel wrapper and felt slippers, weeping and wailing. At once I knew that something appalling was happening. Paris concierges are not given to hysteria; rather they tend to induce it in others.

"*Oh mon petit chat!*" she bawled. "*Oh mon petit Michaux! Pauvre Michaux!*"

Beside her was an Algerian in a dirty blue smock, probably the fellow who started the boiler going in the morning, a sort of general handyman. Armed with a long-handled shovel, he was poking amid the trash cans.

"*Où est le chat?*" I asked. "*Qu'est-ce qu'il a fait?*" I saw no cat, heard none.

The woman shrieked again. The Algerian, not looking at me, but concentrating on the trash bins, jabbed at them, and said: "*Il a eu attaqué par une bête, sauvage, un monstre.*"

"*Un chien?*" I asked.

No, the furnace man replied. Michaux, the concierge's huge cat, was afraid of no dog in the world. But now, some mysterious wild animal—a ferret? a weasel?—had him cornered.

A cat wailed—a long ululating wail. The concierge stuffed a handkerchief in her maw and blubbered. "*Oh, sauve-le, sauve-le!*" Others in the audience shrank back, as the trapped Michaux bawled again, and the cans shivered. A small bourgeois in pince-nez and bathrobe threatened to run upstairs, get his gun and shoot the beast.

"*Maintenant*," the Algerian said grimly, with the menace of an old FLN *plastiqueur*, "*je vais le tuer*." He moved to the rattling tins, but as he approached there was an odd hissing or spitting noise—presumably from the wild animal—and he backed away.

"Enough of this *merde*," I said. Having listened to Flackman brag about all the people he had beaten up, James Warfield Keen on the subject of manual murder, and having read too much of old Ernest and imitators like that gutsy fellow Ruark, I realized I had to prove my courage, even if it were only in a crowd of French apartment-dwellers. You write, man, you got to screw and fight and get bloody.

Feeling like Hemingway advancing on a wounded water buffalo—*watch yourself, laddy-buck, some of these native boys understand a bit of English*—I pulled the nearest can away and kicked the one next to it. Out leaped Michaux. His black back was arched like a croquet hoop covered with erect bristles and his thick black tail was like a young saguaro cactus. The jerk, not realizing he was free and could make a break for it, backed against another can and wailed louder than ever.

"*Oh la la, Michaux!*" screamed the concierge. "*Viens ici!*"

God, but he was a huge, ugly, black galoot of a cat, a born murderer of larks and killer of mice.

"All right, let's get it out," I said. "*En garde!*" I yanked away a third can, and it fell with a rolling clatter. In the dim light, the monster stood revealed.

Some monster! Sitting up on his soft white ass was a medium-sized white rat. He might have been a brother to the one Moe Bloom had given me, except that he was pure white, without the dark saddle. Snowy, furry, pink-nosed, he was rearing, snickering, waving elfin pink paws. It seemed to me that Michaux could have bitten him in half with one bite.

"*Tiens*," I said. "*C'est seulement un petit rat blanc.*"

85

"*Oh, mais il est enragé, il est rabique!*" the concierge howled.

I moved to grab the petrified cat, and the rat went for my trouser leg, hissing, nipping. Michaux flew from his protected corner and raced for his *Maman*. But the rat wasn't ready to quit. He darted across the courtyard, a white flash, a blur, scattering the French like a *flic* wading into a group of picketing students. The concierge tried to pick up Michaux as he whizzed by, the rat went under her varicosed legs, and she fell flat on her behind, screaming bloody curses.

Only the Algerian stood his ground, raising his shovel, and smashing it to the pavement, trying to squash the rat. "*Sale con! Sale rat!*" he shouted. Sparks skittered, the audience roared (from the safety of the stairs). Michaux had landed on a windowsill. He seemed to be four feet high and two inches wide, and the rat was trying to reach him, stretching his sinuous white body upward, striking out with his pink feet.

"*Bitte! Bâtard! Con!*" howled the Algerian. He went for the rat again with the shovel. I helped the concierge to her feet. But the little white terror, realizing he was in trouble, ducked, ran, turned, and came back hissing. He was threatening the Arab, daring to try again.

I stopped the furnace man. "*M'sieu, ce rat a gagné le droit de vivre avec son courage.*"

"*Non,*" the Algerian snarled. "*Le monstre doit mourir.*" Slowly, he maneuvered the rat into a corner, darting the shovel one way, then another, feinting, half-striking, keeping the rat ahead of him.

Up on his hind legs the rat was pawing the air, squeaking defiantly. He seemed to sense his number was up, but he was going out fighting, a battler all the way. High above his head the Arab raised the weapon. He aimed it, then halted at the sound of a harsh commanding voice.

"*Ne touche pas le rat. Il est le mien.*"

On the first landing, directly above us stood Professor Laszlo Veg. He was in the process of lighting a cigarette, one of those malodorous Kossuths, I assumed. Fire from his flame-throwing lighter illumined his starved face. He scared me a little, and I could see that the Algerian janitor was thoroughly shaken.

"*Pardon, M'sieu le professeur,*" the Arab said, "*mais ce rat est rabique. Il est feroce, méchant.*"

"*Non. Vous pouvez rester calme.*"

Down the steps came Veg in his rumpled socialist suit, puffing on his fag, ignoring us.

Veg spoke a few gentle Hungarian words to the beastie, and as nearly as I could gauge, he called him by name. *Tibor.* Kneeling, extending his arm, Veg kept calling him, and the rat scampered to him, allowed himself to be stroked and tickled and gently inserted in Veg's suit pocket. Once, Tibor stuck his quivery nose out to sniff the air, and then vanished. Veg turned stiffly and walked toward the lobby, past the astounded French. I followed him.

"*Vous avez un monstre, M'sieu!*" the concierge wailed. Michaux was nestling against her iron bosom. All my life I have enjoyed watching bullies get their lumps. I was a lousy fighter as a kid, skinny, nervous (as I am now), and full of fear. Once in my life I won a fistfight against Bernie Mandelbaum, and he was wasn't much of a scrapper either. Yes, I was on Tibor's side.

Veg was standing at the elevator, obscured in a cloud of noxious tobacco smoke.

"You have quite a rat there, Professor," I said.

He looked past me; no response. Odd for a Hungarian. They love to gab.

"I have a new message for you, from Mr. Bloom."

With a weary clunk, the lift settled in front of us. Veg took my arm. "Outside, please. I can give you but a few minutes."

Kids rode bikes on the sidewalks. A group of burly workmen were drinking cheap wine at an open café.

"Why is it so hard for me to talk to you?" I asked. "Someone stole the letter. Someone murdered your rat. I think there are men around here who will stop at nothing." Bloom had warned me not to talk too much to Veg, but I felt the need to "build my part" as actors are fond of saying. I babbled on. "This is a serious business, Dr. Veg."

The neurologist exhaled, inundating me in fumes. "You have no idea how serious." He squinted at me. "I am amazed that the Shin-Bet is relying on someone as—as—amateurish as you. Still . . . they are rather bright fellows on Allenby Street in Tel Aviv, and I have always respected their creativity. Several of their people have approached me, but none equaled you in ineptitude."

Most of this was lost on me. By now I realized that Shin-Bet was some Israeli intelligence operation. No mystery there. Bloom had smuggled guns and refugees years ago.

"Mr. Bloom says there is a seat open on the eastern wall," I said.

"Typical of him. I have no response for him."

"Nothing?"

"I have known Mr. Bloom a long time, and I know he is persistent. But he must stop these ridiculous games."

From the apartment house, a burly figure emerged and started toward us. "Hi, fellahs," he called. "Hey, guy." It was Pochastny. His companion, Keramoulian—whom Moe had said belonged to some special department, and was a man to be avoided—was not in sight.

"Good night," Veg said curtly. He tossed his cigarette in the street and turned from me.

I felt I owed Moe Bloom something. As a salesman, as a messenger, as a courier, I was a bust. "Well," I said, edging closer to the Hungarian, "there are only so many seats on the eastern wall, Dr. Veg."

"Hi, guys," Pochastny said. "Nice evening, hey?"

"It's of no concern to me, Mr. Bloodworth." Veg said. Was he smiling at me? I couldn't tell in the dark whether it was a scowl or a friendly curve to his bloodless mouth.

Pochastny was studying us warily—a dull, uninspired cop.

Feet spread, huge hands on hips, his entire fat figure shouting: *polizei*. "Fellah, you better go home and leave the professor alone." He said something in Russian to Veg, and they returned to the house.

There was another man standing in the lobby—hesitating, hand on the door, as if uncertain whether to come out. It was Imre Malar and he seemed to be shaking his head, as if warning me.

II

My mission for Bloom accomplished, I had time to kill until I attempted to crash the Teagues' party. Bubba and Manuela Teague were old friends of mine, from my Paris newspapering days, and I didn't imagine it would be too hard to get in. The big embassy bash that preceded it—I'd heard Metrick dribbling honey about it over the phone—was beyond me. Those shave-headed Marine guards wouldn't give me the time of day, and besides I can't stand those diplomatic types: frozen-faced, blue-eyed, wafer-assed clerks, saving us from godless communism, True Believers in NATO. Once, years ago, I'd told a first secretary at the Paris Embassy that we should trade France for Romania and a left-handed pitcher and he called me a Red.

It's odd, though, how the Metricks and Cooperages, yes, and even the wild swinging radicals like Flackman, enjoy running with these people. There's a reason, of course. The literary lords want it all—everything from *all* the politics, to all the dirty words, to all the good reviews. Cooperage, for example, with his rich and social Southern wife, envisions himself as a link between the crass worlds of commerce and government, and the delicate arts. "I informed the President," I once heard Cooperage tell the press, after a meeting with John F. Kennedy, "that he has given the creative people of America a new lease on life, coming on the scene at this seminal moment."

Let me add that this visit of Coop's to the White House is one of the few sources of friction between the young fellow and his idol, Arno Flackman. Flackman never made it to 1600 Pennsylvania Avenue during JFK's brief tenure. He was *pointedly ignored* by Jack and Jackie, and he has never gotten over it. "I need to be near the rich and famous," Flackman once wrote. "When I go to a party I immediately seek out those who have status, wealth, fame—to see if they are a match for Flackman, on any count. They fail, all the time."

For several years, Flackman and his flunkies, friends, lawyers, agents dropped hints that Arno would just love to go to one of those big White House parties and straighten the President out on a few items, to be tough and charming and witty with Jacqueline. The summons never came. Then Oswald murdered Kennedy, and Flackman's dream of glory died. There are moments, I am certain, when Arno awakens at three in the morning in a cold sweat, shivering, recalling how Styron and Baldwin and Steinbeck all made it to the White House—*but not him.*

When the metro train stopped at the Place d'Iena station, I heard sirens, claxons. I flew out of the car and up the stairs, and found myself in a shouting, pushing crowd. The station was full of *gendarmes*, herding people to one end, making them leave by a single exit.

"*Qu'est-ce que s'est passé?*" I asked a *flic*.

"*Rien,*" he snarled.

A bespectacled short man grabbed my arm. "*Une bombe. Les Arabes. Ils ont jeté une bombe dehors.*"

I was shoved and propelled upward into the street. A typical Parisian frenzy: ambulances, police vans, squads of red-faced *gendarmes*, and as many of those raincoat-clad plainclothesmen, those *barbouze* types.

Someone must have been badly injured, or perhaps killed,

but the French onlookers did not seem terribly upset. The attitude in Paris is: *better them than me.* I always carry my World News Association press card with me. Ten years old, it still gets me through lines. I waved it at two gendarmes and elbowed my way through a mob to the Café Lussac. Why anyone would throw a bomb at that place eluded me. Perhaps it was not an Arab, but a gourmet, registering his opinion of their watery ice cream.

"*Oh la la, le café est détruit.*"

"*Gardez. Est-il mort?*"

"*Non, blessé. L'autre est mort.*"

In pleasurably horrified voices, the French were discussing the outrage. Someone was dead. Someone else wounded. I worked my way to the front rank. One plate-glass window of the sidewalk café had been blown away—completely. There were not even jagged bits of glass left. It was gone—totally. Inside and outside the restaurant, chairs and tables had been knocked off their moorings. A lot of cognac and *eau minérale* had been spilled.

"Anyone killed?" I asked.

A conference delegate—a Canadian physicist puffing a peaceful pipe—pointed to the ambulance. "They got one of the Arabs. Shot him dead. There's the other."

A dark, bloodied man in a dirt-covered black suit lay on a stretcher to one side. Two police medics were standing over him. A third man, in a white coat, came running out of the ambulance. All three bent over the wounded man, and they appeared to be giving him an injection. Then they lifted the bloodstained stretcher and rushed him to the ambulance.

"Was anyone in the café killed?" I asked, my voice choking. A few hours earlier I'd sat not fifteen feet from where the café had been blown apart.

"Don't believe so," the Canadian said. "There were only a few people sitting there, and they had some kind of warning. Someone saw the damned thing—a lead pipe—and shouted, and they cleared out. Some woman was hit with glass fragments and a waiter was shaken up."

"But the guys who threw it—the Arabs—how did they get shot?"

The Canadian shook his head. "Don't know. Maybe their own bomb. Hoist on their own petard."

My small French bourgeois leaned toward me. "Ze police knew. Ze Paris police always know. Zey were here, waiting." He nodded sagely, full of inside dope.

We were ordered away. A cordon of French cops (I have learned never, never to argue with them) started moving us off in two directions—up the street toward the Hotel Bavard, or toward the Place d'Iena. There was still a metallic, nasty odor of explosive in the air—cordite, or gelignite, or whatever it is Arab terrorists favor.

I fell in step behind two men who seemed to be American newsmen.

"They were after somebody," one said.

"Nah. Not necessarily. These madmen will throw a bomb at anyone they feel like. If they have an extra one left, they'll toss it."

Shivering, I cursed Moe Bloom and his errands. Was I on some insane Bedouin's list? I wanted to question them, but they raced ahead, presumably to file their stories.

"Awful, awful, I am filled with shame." Dr. Daoud Jabali was at my elbow. Well, a friendly Arab.

"Ah, Dr. Jabali. Look what your countrymen just did." It seemed odd to me that the French hadn't grabbed him. But then, he could have been a Greek, or a Turk, or an Italian, or even Jewish. He was not wearing his white ID card.

"I am mortified, sir, mortified." The man was pained, his café mousse face contorted. He kept biting his lower lip as if trying to stem tears. "Violence begets violence. Those foolish people, those misguided children."

"Who were they?"

"I am not certain. I have no interest in politics. I am a scientist. Probably one of the Palestinian groups."

"You didn't know the fellow who was killed? Or the guy who was wounded?"

93

He looked at me in astonishment, vaguely insulted. "Why, sir? Why should I know them? There are over one hundred million Arabs in the world, sir."

I offered to buy him a drink, but he was trembling by now, a nervous, fretful young Jordanian. "Oh, the shame, the shame of it, and I suppose now the French police will want to question me, a man who is afraid of guns, a man raised in a Quaker school." He rubbed his slender, elegant hands together. "I shall take a walk along the Champs until my stomach settles, sir; thank you, in any case."

Jabali left me in front of the Bavard. The lobby was deserted: the explosion had cleared everyone out to the street. A notice on the bulletin board informed me that tomorrow's main events would be the address of welcome by the co-chairmen, Venables and Malar, and later the highlight would be "an intellectual confrontation" between Arno Flackman (Left) and Boyle Huffguard (Right) on "America's Directions." This *mano-a-mano* I did not want to miss—Dominguin and Ordonez, my homeland's two biggest politico-literary essayists fondling one another in public.

The desk clerk asked me how many Arabs the police had killed, shrugging his disappointment when he learned they'd only gotten one.

I asked for my room key and got it, together with a wrinkled white envelope. It looked familiar. It was the one Bloom had given me for Laszlo Veg. Inside was a sheet of notebook paper covered with Yiddish or Hebrew script. The page had those curious linings I recalled from my Bronx youth—alternate spacings, one wider than the other. I could not read a word of it, and I wondered if Veg would have been able to. Replacing it, I saw that someone had scrawled something under the envelope flap. It was in blue ink, scrawled with a thick felt-tip pen:

STAY AWAY FROM VEG

This seemed sensible advice. I had no more messages to deliver to him—or white rats—although I confess I was

94

curious about that tough little Tibor who scared the concierge's cat. Veg had gingered him somehow, and, at the moment, I felt the need of some wild courage myself.

Determined as I was to crash Bubba and Manuela Teague's party—it would be talked about for years to come, the Capote Thing of the conference—I now found myself walking nervously up and down the Avenue Georges Mandel, opposite their mansion. The soaring house was on a corner, protected from the mob by a high wrought-iron gate, reminiscent of the spiked fences that kept us out of Bronx schoolyards years ago. Oh, the place smelled of the big money. Eternal, undying would be those great carved blocks of limestone, the ornate cornices and balustrades. Inside the enormous windows I saw lush silver and maroon drapes, as sensual as the robes of a Rubens' goddess. Above sparkled crystal chandeliers.

The Teagues went first class, and who could blame them? They were rich, rich, rich. Bubba, that piney woods redneck, navy enlisted man, born in Bat's Balls, Georgia, was, like Louise Latour, the American Writer's Dream Incarnate. He'd dropped out of school in the eighth grade, run off to sea lying about his age, and had never read a book in his life until he stumbled on paperbounds at the Great Lakes Naval Station Library.

"Ah got me some of them itty-bitty softcover books, hyeah?" he told a misty-eyed girl from the *Paris Review*, a small bird from Radcliffe, who wet her pants every time Bubba cursed. "Ah got me thisyear book called *Huckleberry Finn*, and dang if hit didn't come on me that Ah was a writer lak that fellah Mark Twain, jes' lak him, only Ah dint rahtly know hit. Me, Hennery Pope Teague, a redneck from Jawja, Ah was a writer all mah life, raht in mah haid. So I sat me down, an Ah wrote *Down to the Sea* and y'all bought it."

We all bought it, three million copies of it, and Bubba wrote his ticket after that. I knew him, and his wife Manuela, when they had first come to Paris after the success of *Down to the Sea*, a marvelous dirty rough book, full of blowing and bungholing and jacking off (way ahead of Portnoy on that score, but because it was *goyim* abusing themselves rather than guilt-ridden Jews, no one commented about that aspect of Teague's book) and we had been reasonably good friends. And as I paced the street, waiting for a chance to make a run past the three French cops posted outside, I realized that it was a sign of my maturity that I was no longer jealous of Bubba Teague's wealth and fame and talent. He was a kind, generous, sweet man, who, despite all the bloody fighting and savage screwing in his books, and his own frightening physicality, was gentle and soft-spoken, and went out of his way to avoid combat.

Besides, his financial rewards were so staggering that it was pointless for a struggler like me to worry about them. Last year he had signed a two-million-dollar contract, cash money guaranteed, with a new publishing house, for two unwritten novels. (My last, and best book, *Shake Before Using*, had sold 3,456 copies in the trade. A meaningful sale, my agent told me. All the right people read it.) The night Bubba got the word that the contract had gone through, that he was richer by two million dollars and secure forever in his Paris castle, they were entertaining some embassy stiffs at dinner.

"Charley," Manuela said to some social-register polo-playing embassy paper-shuffler, "Charley, me and Bubba are so rich now we can tell the whole world to fuck off." And so saying, Mrs. Teague ran to the lofty windows of their palace, threw them open, and began shouting up and down the Avenue Georges Mandel: "Fuck off. Fuck off. Everybody, fuck off."

The porte cochère and driveway inside the iron gate was jammed with Jaguars and Mercedes and an ancient green Rolls Royce, owned by an eccentric Hollywood director. A few elegantly dressed people were taking a breather under the pillars of the mansion's portico.

I gathered up my courage—after all, I'd been tracking down

a Hungarian scientist and sassing Russian cops—and crossed the street. At the closed gate, a man and a woman were arguing politely with one of the gendarmes.

"*Carte d'invitation*," the *flic* said dully.

"Sir, we don't have one," the man said.

"Ah, *nous n'avons pas*," the woman tried, in appalling French. "Our daughter is inside. Our *fille*."

"*Carte d'invitation*," the cop repeated.

"Maybe I can help," I volunteered.

"You speak French? You American?" The man turned a tanned, rugged face at me. Then, curiously, he took in my powder-blue turtleneck, love-beads and sandals. He wore a cocoa-brown porkpie straw with turquoise puggaree band, and one of those starched seersucker suits that suggest Wall Street in August.

"Yes, I do, and I'm trying to get in there also," I said. "I've lost my invitation, and if I can get to Mrs. Teague, I'm sure she'll let me in."

"Well, hiya, there," the man said. A great tanned paw engulfed my hand, pumped it. "I'm Tom Bragg, and this is my wife, Evie. I gather you're with the conference, right?"

"Yes. I'm Ben Bloodworth, a writer. Of sorts."

"I'd guess that in a minute," Mrs. Bragg said. She was a quintessential tennis-court *shiksa*. Broad-beamed, high-waisted, armored in an iron corset. But she was pretty in a rugged way—close-cropped blonde hair with bangs and the blonde honest, uncomplicated features of Darien and Greenwich.

"We're hardly artistic types," Tom Bragg said, digging my ribs gently. "Just a coupla yokels. Evie's brother is a writer, and he's speaking tomorrow. Thought we'd catch his act."

Bragg had not let go of my hand. My fingers were being ground to a paste. His was the potent mitt of a tournament golfer, a server of tennis aces. Ah, I knew them. Fairfield County; he a high-level messenger at Standard Goy of New Jersey, she the president of the Garden Club. Powerboat squadron, three Bloody Marys for breakfast at Sunday brunch, and the Republican Party town committee. Yet you had to love them, because they wanted to be loved. Besides, in America we are thankful for all smiles, all hearty handshakes. Better Tom and Evie Bragg than those construction workers.

After the rarefied oxygen-poor air of the altitudes I'd been at—Cooperage and Metrick and Flackman—I welcomed Tom Bragg's snub-nose, cleft-chin, cigarette ad phiz. As for Evie, she had already given me a bad case of the dirty hots. Fetishist that I am, I kept thinking of the layers of elastic and nylon that kept her tall figure in trim.

"And who is your brother, Mrs. Bragg?" I asked.

"Boyle Huffguard. He's debating Mr. Flackman tomorrow."

"Golly, he is a clever fellow, Huffguard is," I said. "I like when he advocated having Earl Warren beaten up by a posse of longshoremen."

"Yes, Boyle is a great wit," Bragg said. "Actually we're also here to see our daughter. She's at the conference with some sort of youth group."

"And think of it," Evie Bragg said, "she was invited to this party at the Teagues! A kid like that. And here *we* are, but these police won't let us in."

Bragg peered through the fence, to the flaming house. "Haven't seen hide nor hair of Vannie."

"Vannie?" I asked. "A pretty little girl with long hair?"

"Why yes," Mrs. Bragg replied. "That's our baby."

"She was on the plane with me. Traveling with a young fellow named Harvey Ungerleider."

"Hmm, yes." Bragg smiled tolerantly. Jews, radicals, beards —his Standard Goy heart had room for all. "We haven't met the lad, but Vannie says he's a genius."

"Vannie is so much smarter than her poor parents," his wife said. "She calls Tom an economic royalist."

"You should have heard what she called me," I said.

"And to think," Mrs. Bragg said, with a puzzled lateral motion of her handsome head, "she was once ranked second in sixteen-and-under tennis in Greenwich."

"And fifth statewide, honey," Bragg added.

Ah, this was rude justice. I stared—not without sympathy —at these two pillars of High Middle-Class rectitude, awash in their martinis and private clubs, True Believers in their own Excellence. And what a reward for their virtue! A daughter who screwed for the hairy likes of H. Ungerleider—on airplanes, yet—and shouted "motherfucker" at her elders. Unbathed, undiaphragmed, pilled and petted, the world was her bed.

"I think I've heard of you," Mrs. Bragg said, wagging a ringed finger at me. "Bloodstone . . . ?"

"Bloodworth."

"Black humorist?" she asked. A whiff of Detchema wafted from her high bosom, or her firm neck, and I almost fainted.

"Not really. I'm more of a meditative neo-realist. Black humor is like trying to belch the *Emperor Concerto* on an empty stomach."

"Say, that is good," Tom Bragg said. "Ben, you have got lots of smarts, lots of smarts."

There was a commotion at the door to the Teague mansion, and I heard Manuela Teague's high-pitched, angry voice. "Getcher ass out of here! Get lost, you squirts, and don't come back!"

"Ah, don't get your bowels in an uproar, lady," Harvey Ungerleider responded.

"You kids make me want to puke. Think you can insult everyone, hah? Well, I'm the only one allowed to use dirty words in my house."

"Why, goodness," Mrs. Bragg said. "There's our Vannie."

Vannie Bragg, Harvey, and three other members of the radical youth group were being shown the gate. Mrs. Bragg's bosom rose and fell in shame, love, surprise. Three strands of discreet pearls rose and fell with it.

Her husband looked pained. "As Boyle says so often, none of this would have happened if we'd fought World War II on the right side."

A houseboy in a white coat escorted the young folks to the

99

gate and slammed it behind them. No sooner were they out than they picked up gravel and began tossing it over the fence with a few choice "motherfuckers" and "fascist pigs." The gendarmes moved quickly and shoved them away.

"It's all right, Officer," Tom Bragg said. "We'll be responsible. Vannie, honey! It's Dad! And Mom!"

The slender young girl turned and glared sullenly at her parents. "Shit. Just when I was having a ball."

"Darling, why did you write us that wicked letter?" Evie Bragg asked. "Mummy was upset."

"And called your old Dad those names," Bragg added.

"Ah, shit, why'd you have to follow me here?" she whined. And turning her tail, she ran after the three young men who had been tossed out with her.

Deep down, I felt sorry for them. They were secure, powerful, richly rewarded by the American System, but they were innocent. Besides, I had my own problems, and to resolve them, I shouted after Manuela Teague: "Hey, Manuela, it's me, Benny! Ben Bloodworth!"

"Darling," Mrs. Bragg was calling after her departing daughter, "sweetheart, all your friends at Rosemary Hall keep asking about you . . . and the riding instructor, Mr. Fess, wanted to know if you've kept up the jumping . . ."

Yes, I could have told her, but without a horse.

Manuela Teague was peering through the gate. "Benny? Where are you, Bicycle Thief?"

Don't ask me why, but Manuela had decided I was the Bicycle Thief. "Here, here, Manuela!"

"Jesus Maria, come in, Benny. Always room for one more starving Jewish writer." The houseboy opened the portals for me, and I bade good-bye to the unhappy Braggs.

"See you at the conference tomorrow, Benny," Tom Bragg called. "Awful glad we got to meet a real novelist." You cannot discourage these seersuckered Americans. The man's daughter (I heard this clearly) had just told him to "screw off" and here he was, happy that he had met me.

Manuela gave me her arm. I admired her flashing Mexican eyes, the Continental Shelf of her bosom. Her hair is black, parted in the middle, with two chignons over each edible ear. She is a great woman—kind, funny, loud, without side or jealousy. The big house loomed above me: *money, recognition, success*. I could smell it.

"Why didn't you tell me you were in town, Benny?" she asked.

"My name is on the list of delegates."

"I never saw one. Cooperage made up the guest list."

Good old Warren, old arbiter. Like the Southern delegates to a political conference, he had veto power over the guests. "Since when are you and Cooperage such Big Dubs?" I asked. "Wasn't Bubba sore at him when he left Bubba off his list of germinal American writers of the sixties?"

"*Mierda*, Benny, that was a long time ago. Coop is going to do the definitive piece on Bubba's use of regionalisms for *The Discoverist Review*."

Ring around the rosey. You review me, I'll review you. I would be generous. I had crashed the Party, thanks to Manuela's compassionate heart. I crossed the golden threshold, and Manuela, trailing Myrugia, ran off to bawl the hell out of three of their seven kids, watching the festivities from the winding marble staircase.

Entering the great salon, I realized at once I'd lusted for gold and gotten dross. Unless you work at these literary brawls full time, you are bound to be bored, disheartened, excluded. Wind, belches, marsh gas.

"Is that supposed to be a beard?" I heard a piping voice, the voice of a twelve-year-old eunuch. I realized that I was being addressed, that someone disapproved of my Van Dyke.

Turning, I saw that it was White Fag King, one of the separate powers, independent principalities, small autonomous states of the literary world. He had insulted me even before we had been introduced. Flackman I can try to handle; Cooperage is just another *shmeichler*; but White Fag King scared me stiff. What do you say to him? How approach him? Years ago, I read about him telling how he and some superannuated society broad, one of his rich admirers, had "shared a bird and bottle" before going to the theater. His choice of words filled me with deep longing. Why could he not have said "some roast chicken and red wine"?

"Yes, it's a beard," I said. My voice was strangling.

A group of tall women, Americans, including a slit-eyed flat-chested, hard-voiced TV panelist, were grinning at me. They surrounded White Fag King like a Hessian guard. The little queer was always being stroked, fondled, loved-up.

"Oh, it's such a funny little triangle, that hairy thing under your chin," he hissed.

"Funny . . . ?" I was all tongue; no lips; no powers of enunciation.

"Yes. You look like you were eating it and fell through."

Feline laughter bubbled around my crimson ears. "I was, as a matter of fact," I mumbled, "and I'm recommending that Michelin give it three stars."

"*Quel fou*," White Fag King sighed.

What infuriated me was that my French was three times as good as his. As was my Italian, and my German. But *he* was Continental, suave, elegant and desired, and I was not.

"Good Christ, the *bores* the Teagues put up with," the television woman said. They all turned their backs on me.

I call him White Fag King because there is a Black Fag King, and he was at Bubba's house also. About two years ago I'd gotten into a nasty verbal scrap with him at a Literary Evening at the Brooklyn Jewish Center, and I doubted that he wanted to see me again, ever. He'd been ranting on, threatening all those guilt-ridden middle-class store-owners and dentists with hellfire, rape, and sudden death, until I could stand it no longer. "Look, Darrell," I said, "you keep threatening us white people all the time, but you are the only black man I ever knew I wasn't afraid of, the only one I can beat up."

Needless to say this did not sit very well with either Black Fag King, the other panelists—Cooperage chaired the session, as he usually does—or even the audience. I was called a bigot and a fascist and I had to shut up. Now the odd thing is, about a year later I read an evaluation of black writers by a leading black critic and do you know what the cat had to say? Merely what I, in my clumsy, head-on way had been shouting all along. *"This man is the pet novelist among white liberals, because he is the only one among us of whom they are not physically afraid."* There you have it, Your Honor. I am guilty of being ahead of my times, saying the right things too early and too rudely.

If anything, Black Fag King had a bigger audience than White Fag King. A lot of them looked like wealthy appliance jobbers from Roslyn, or osteopaths from Beverly Hills. BFK was lolling against a white marble fireplace, sipping brandy. His eyes were half-shut, and he was intoning his standard put-down for rich honkies.

"You know nothing about *meeee*," BFK was saying. "But I know all about *yooooo*." Ritards and rubatos colored his speech.

"Now hoddya mean that, Darrell?" a thickset man in an electric-blue tuxedo asked. "Hoddya mean we don't? I mean, I'm as sympathetic as anyone to the legit demands of black persons."

"I survive, like a lean, hungry black cat," BFK said, "by knowing what goes on in your minds, whereas you know nothing at all about me."

Man, he was gorgeous. Skin the color of Schrafft's coffee ice cream, lean and trim, almond-eyed, bearded like the pard, lithe and limber in white duck bell-bottoms that made a tight white drum of his sexy little ass. Golden hoops dangled from his ears, and he had lately had some West African design tattooed on his forehead.

"I am a mystery, a lie, a false front to deceive all of your bleached-out, boiled out, fucked-out white faces. I see through your transparent skin to the pale guts and sickly blood."

"Oh my God, he's beautiful," a woman in a blonde wig festooned with red velvet bows moaned. "Oh, he is too much."

"Outa sight," a stout-hammed man of middle age, with the look of a wholesale lumber dealer from Mamaroneck, said.

"Black hides me," BFK went on. "You can never get beneath my black pelt, and so, you will never know what deep lusts for murder, rape, revenge, arson, and mutilation lurk under it."

"You left out cheating at craps, Darrell," I called, from the outer edges of the *minyan*.

"Who said that?" he cried. "Who is that?"

You would think that those pantyhose manufacturers and job printers from Old Westbury would be on my side, after the way Black Fag King had threatened to rape their daughters. Never. They live with the need to be mocked as Goldberg and abused for imagined historical crimes against blacks.

"You know you got a filthy mouth?" the woman with the red bows said to me. Her own mouth, a red gash, seemed to hang in midair, an independent but functioning part.

"Yeah, whaddya, a bigot, a racist?" the man in the blue tuxedo asked.

"Ask him," I said, "what he thinks of Goldberg. That's his generic term for us folks."

"Ah yes, Goldberg." BFK shut his eyes again. "He will be among the first to go. With his jacked-up prices and his rent-gouging and his phony liberalism. Up against the wall, Goldberg."

This was the time, I suppose, to start on how Jews have done so much for blacks, the NAACP bit, charities, and so forth, but the atmosphere was too thick. Besides, the jargon makes me ill.

"Cut the crap, Darrell," I said. "You went to Harvard on a Lefkowitz Scholarship and you have a town house in the East Sixties and a villa in Rapallo. I don't begrudge you any of the loot, but stop trying to scare me with that Mau Mau stuff."

The heavy man in the tuxedo—he was wearing a sexily ruffled pale blue shirt that suggested lace petti-pants—edged toward me. "You better beat it, Jack. Your kind is not needed around here."

"Tell him, Si," the woman in the wig cawed. "He needs a lesson."

I backed away. You have to watch these burly golf players from Deal, New Jersey. They can kill you with one karate chop.

"Oh, he is of no account," BFK said airily. "A small-time honkey scribbler. His name is Bloodworth and he makes a profession of bugging his betters."

"But never buggering them, Darrell baby."

"Get after him, Si," the blonde wig said. This time I moved faster, toward the end of the vast salon. Is it clear why people like Black Fag King—and White Fag King—make me wonder about the future of society? Nor could either of them ever lose. So long as there were "critics" like Warren Cooperage or editors like his wife Tookie to come to their rescue when they floundered, they'd be on top.

Derek Venables, looking extremely clerical in a dark sack suit that set his gleaming crucifix off, was talking to Judy Malar in one corner of the room. Both saw me retreating from BFK and his worshipful company; Judy waved to me.

"Did you see Uncle Latzi?" Judy asked. I was glad that her companion was Venables. Fruity, he presented no physical threat.

"Uncle La——? Oh, Dr. Veg." I paused a moment. No matter. What could mean anything to Venables besides his next conference? "Yes, I did catch up with him."

"Who is this Veg?" Venables chirped. He was truly a Briton, bred-in-the-bone. You could never guess his age. His hair would stay streaky blond for years, and the scarlet splotches on his sunken cheeks would never fade. He seemed to lack eyes: they were so palely blue, so close-to-colorless, that he appeared eyeless at times.

"Dr. Veg is a neurologist, I think," I said.

"Yes, but what does the chap *do?*"

"Well," I said, "he trains rats. He's got one that beat the hell out of a big tomcat a few hours ago."

"Fasc'natin'." Venables was smiling at me. "How do you know all this? Twains wats. Fancy that."

"'Oh . . .'" Careful there. Although the way it appeared, everyone at the conference knew I'd been appointed courier by Moe Bloom. "I met Judy and Mr. Malar today, and through them, Dr. Veg. You know how it is, Derek. You meet a Hungarian, you suddenly know everyone in Budapest."

"Yace, yace, vewwy good." He opened his mouth, paused, then said, "I take it you have some kind of special intewest in . . . ah . . . animal conditioning, Mr. Bloodworth?"

"No, not really. I could never even train my dogs to sit up and beg when I was a kid. I always seemed to have wobbly dogs."

Warren Cooperage, tinkling a glass full of Scotch, came by. The sight of booze made me think of poor Louise Latour dining with her Eagle Scout keeper, the two of them friendless in Paris.

"Say, Der," Cooperage said, "that bombing at the Lussac was a bad business. That second Arab died. The darn thing is, no one can figure out how they were killed. I spoke to Emile a few minutes ago——"

"Emile?" asked Venables.

"Lamoureux. Minister of the Interior. He says the cops didn't start shooting till both of those guys were on the ground, and the wounds aren't self-inflicted."

"Hmm. Bad show.'"

"Well, it can't hurt the conference," Cooperage said. "We're front page all over the world. You know, PLO tries to break up big East-West conference. I mean, it gives us some status. Emile assured me it won't happen again. They're arresting Arabs all over Paris."

"I say," Venables said. "I say, that suggests another workshop, don't you know? Wesponsibiwity of the artist vis-à-vis the Middle East. Is there anyone from Iswael attending?"

"No. The Arabs threatened to pull out if we let them come." Cooperage frowned. "Of course, we never took a position, but then the Israelis said they couldn't be bothered anyway. They were very nice about it, sort of got us off the hook."

"Moses Bloom may be in town . . . later," I said.

Cooperage shook his head. "Oh, come on, Bloodworth. That old crank?"

I wanted to come to Bloom's defense, when there was a sudden commotion at the entrance to Bubba Teague's study, which was located just beyond the double doors of the vast salon. Actually, Bubba did his creative writing on a barge anchored in the Seine. The study was just for writing checks. There was a Derain, a Vlaminck, and two Henry Moores in the room. We all moved toward it, and I said to Judy:

"It's always this way when Flackman shows up."

"How do you know he's there?"

"It's like a wind rising, or a smell of ozone or brimstone. Flackman collects all the electricity, all the power. And everyone else feels weaker, neutralized. Once he takes command, with his overcharged batteries, he becomes a generating plant, Consolidated Edison, and he deals out voltage and wattage. It's beyond belief. Look at what's happened already."

It was astounding. The salon had all but emptied. Oh, there were still small groups around the two Fag Kings (who sulked a bit now that Flackman had appeared), but the majority of the guests had surged into the study to stare at Numero Uno.

Flackman is a tall, burly man, and his black bushy hair was distinguishable above the bobbing, whispering polls of the plebs. He moved pantherlike among the guests, his bee-bee eyes looking past most people.

"Arno baby, howsa boy?" a short, horn-rimmed Great Neck type, sporting a polka-dot ascot, called out. "Howsa guy, Arno?"

Flackman ignored him. The tiny eyes did not see the

greeter. Recently Flackman had written that he regarded the prime effort of his public appearances to be the avoidance of *shlemiels*, failures, climbers, or ugly women. *Flackman had sworn an oath, he wrote, to recoil from such excrescences, indeed to refuse to acknowledge that they existed. Years of hard labor at his craft, his crowning as king of the literary nation, had convinced him that he deserved only the best— the most beautiful and desirable women, those for whom lesser men lusted but would never prong, the awesomely social, rich, lofty, talented, and in the case of a few men, those very few who could beat Flackman, man to man, in a fair fist-fight.*

Women exhaled perfumed sighs and men sneaked out jealous farts as Flackman prowled through the high-ceilinged room, padding softly, with feline grace, toward Bubba Teague's high-backed chair, a precious antique once the property of a Venetian Doge.

"He travels with a harem," I said to Judy. "Look."

Two tender young girls, Barnard or Vassar types, quintessentially American, if a bit soiled, trailed El Lider. *Au pair* girls, volunteers, trainees, graduate English students, little Bryn Mawr or Smith quims, learners, acolytes, dishwashers, they came to him free of charge, more than he could handle if he were multi-cocked and ten-balled.

"He is a handsome man," Judy said. "So . . . magnetic. He draws your eyes, like a hypnotist."

"Yes, he does." I darted a nervous look at my Hungarian doll. No, no, I would not let Arno Flackman ravish her. Then I reflected: she wasn't really his type—too demure, too foreign, no social rank. Palm Beach and Newport *shiksas* with lank hair and flattened vowels were Flackman's favorites: revenge of the intellectual lefto Jewish outsider.

"See the big man in back of him?" I asked Judy—as Flackman eased his way through the murmuring mob and settled into Bubba Teague's chair. "That's his bodyguard, his own private SS, militia."

A troglodyte with white skin, a blond crewcut, oddly scarred around the nose and eyes, trailed the writer. This was a huge man, neckless, with shoulders like slabs of granite, and a beer belly that suggested strength, not sloth. I guessed that he was Arno's newest pet jock. At the University of Miami, Flackman had played varsity football, and with each book he wrote, his skills magnified. Actually, he had been a JV tackle.

"A Greek god," Judy Malar whispered to me.

"Who? That big Polack football player?"

"No, no. Mr. Flackman. Oh, Ben, he is so exciting, just to look at. Those little black curls . . . and the way his eyes are almost closed."

"He's nearsighted without his glasses."

"You must *know* him, Ben. Can we have dinner with him one night?"

I am not alone in suffering eternal jealousy about Flackman. One writer I know did an entire book about him, a collection of serious little essays, the burden of which was that Flackman, a close friend, had prevented said writer from fulfilling what might have been a brilliant career, by doing *first and better* all the things he had always wanted to do. Mind you, this had nothing to do with *writing*, but with Flackman's colorful public behavior.

"Mr. Flackman, have you ever been to Israel?"

The questioner was a tall, straight-backed, gray-haired woman. A leader of liberal-left politics in Westchester, I gathered. To Flackman, of course, she was one more loser.

"No. And I have no intention of going."

Everyone leaned forward. A respectful hush descended over the room. "But why not, Mr. Flackman?" the tall woman persisted. "You are one of the world's leading Jewish writers."

"Madam," Arno mumbled, "that is a goddamn non sequitur."

"I respect your genius and your mind, Mr. Flackman," she went on, "and I won't even be insulted. But tell us, why, why have you never visited Israel?"

Flackman rubbed his hands. He hunched forward. "Hmm. Hmmm. You might say, madam, that the confrontation would be too overwhelming. Something would have to give. Me or them. It would be too tough on both of us."

"I'm not sure I understand," the gray-haired woman persisted.

"No Israel," Flackman mumbled. "Not for the present." He patted one of his houris on her tight ass. "Get me some booze, Mauna."

Well, I'd sworn to myself that I'd be well-mannered. But I couldn't resist. I know this sounds paranoid, but I was, at that moment, the only person in the room who deep down, truly understood why Flackman had not been to Israel, and why, in fact, he had never written a single line, in his voluminous outpourings, about our soul brothers on the edge of the Mediterranean.

"Let me toss this notion up for grabs," I said, pushing my way forward, past Cooperage and Venables. In a corner of the room, perched on an ottoman, clad in Grecian robes, I saw Tookie Cooperage, Warren's rich wife, patroness, fairy godmother, everybody's sweetheart.

"That jerk Bloodworth," I heard Flackman grumble to one of his attendant odalisques.

"Hi, Arno. You see, madam, Mr. Flackman can't go to Israel, because it's an entire nation of people tougher and braver than he is. He'd be coming in *second* all the time—to old women in Haifa, to little kids on the kibbutzim, to paratroopers with names like Ha-Cohen and Aharoni, to anyone who lives there and is ready to fight and die for what he believes in."

"Crap out, Bloodworth," Flackman called, across the burnished desk. "I don't have to defend myself against that."

"It calls for no defense, Arno," I blabbed on. "You used the word *confrontation*, and that's what your life-style is. Every person you meet has to be sized up—is he more talented? Richer? More famous? But most of all—do I have more courage? But you see, folks, in a place like Israel, where everyone has to be courageous, when this street-brawling, cockshowing bullshit is just that to people battling for survival, plain, tired, sweaty, humble Jews, trying to live, Mr. Flackman's ego-trips would be nothing more than a megalomaniac's ravings. Israelis don't go around challenging each other to Indian hand-wrestles."

"Ah, screw off, Bloodworth," Flackman said. He darted his tiny black eyes to the gold-leafed ceiling. "Two-bit no-sale novelist. One of the problems of the craft. Keeping out the sucks and the bores."

The scene reminded me of one of those early FDR press conferences at the White House, before television. You recall the photographs—a mob of reporters crushed at the edge of the President's long desk, all eagerly awaiting word, all trying to get as close as possible, yet held back by the respect due the office. And I must concede there *was* something presidential, authoritarian, kingly about Arno.

"Hey, ole Arno, you a mean ole man, takin' Bubba's chair lak that!"

Bubba Teague, our host, had entered the room. Old carnival wrestler, lumberjack, piney woods and red-dirt farmer, navy gunner: that was Bubba. Like Arno, he was a physically big man, full of muscles and quick moves. They'd never actually tangled, fist on nose, but they'd come close several times. I never could tell whether they loved or hated one another. Bubba is a kind, generous, and sweet-tempered man. A youth and young manhood full of violence has made him a pacifist. Not so Flackman, who is forever overcoming his Jewish Intellectual heritage.

"Hangin' loose, Bubba?" Arno asked. Like Nixon, the man tends to drop his final G's to prove his earthiness.

"Loose as a goose, Arno."

As this witty dialogue progressed—the guests gawked, awed, magnetized by the high level of riposte and sally—I studied Bubba's red, red face, the carroty hair, the quarter-sized freckles. He was a native American type, a son of the soil, and he carried his wealth and his fame gracefully.

"Quite a pad you got here, Bubba," Flackman said. He squinted at a huge rectangular abstract on the cream-colored wall. It looked as if four Mexicans had barfed their *chili con quieso* on a billboard for Tecate beer. "I like that, Bubba. It's got *cojones*."

"Friend of Manuela's in Corny Vacker done it, Arn."

"Hot damn. Manuela knows *cojones* when she sees 'em, Bub."

"Dang, Arno, thass why Ah married her."

"And you got big *cojones*, Bubba, two of the biggest."

"Oh God, this was worth everything," the woman with red bows in the blonde wig said, "to come to Paris, to see Flackman and Teague talking literary."

"They are a pair of goddamn geniuses," the man in the blue tuxedo added.

Black Fag King had drifted in; his savage eye betrayed his envy. They were center stage now, and he was not being listened to. "All that fake jockery, all that bragging about big organs. They know deep down it is the black man who will someday castrate them all."

"You can shove the whole Louvre you-know-where," the gray-haired man in horn-rims said triumphantly. "You can stick Notre Dame up you-know-what. Gimme this kind of intellectual stimulation, any day, and twice on Sunday."

Flackman was rolling now. In Teague's home, he had seized command. Not that Bubba minded. Bubba knew that on a verbal level, in any foray into abstract arguing, he could not match Flackman.

"Now Bubba, I got a guy here tonight, who with one hand tied behind his back, could kick the shit out of both of us, you dig?" Flackman chuckled into his fist. A curious gesture: I'd read somewhere that Hemingway, in his more incoherent displays of manliness, did the same. "Bubba, shake hands with Ronnie Buzovitch, middle linebacker for the Fort Worth

Vandals. Ron does the hundred in ten flat and weighs in at two seventy, all gristle."

"Hi dere," Buzovitch said. He grabbed Teague's proffered mitt, and was gentle about it. Like many monstrous jocks, he had a squeaky voice and a shamefaced manner.

"Yeah. Hey, Arno, I keep forgittin' you an ole Miami University tackle. Ole Bubba never got past the sixth grade."

Actually, it was the *eighth* grade, but Bubba always shaved a few years off, for status.

"Did a little boxing, too, Bub," Flackman said, with an edge of menace.

"Any time, Arno," Teague said lightly. "With or without gloves, at night or day, in a back alley or out in the woods."

The spectators gasped. This was too good. Hemingway and Morley Callaghan all over! Would they let me be timekeeper, like poor, nervous Fitzgerald?

"Fuck them both," Black Fag King simpered. "Black will prevail."

Derek Venables looked pained. He was a trembling, lacy presence; he detested violence. "I do think they should be stopped," he muttered to Judy Malar and to me. "It won't look too good if . . ."

"No, they won't belt each other around," I assured him. "They've been threatening to for years, but it's never come off."

Venables' aristocratic head rotated. "Is your father heah, my deah?" he asked Judy. "Or that fellow Veg?"

"No. Papa was too tired. Professor Veg does not go to parties of any kind."

I wondered what he wanted with old Laszlo, the cunning rat-conditioner. He was too curious to suit me. For a moment I wished Moe Bloom were around to answer questions.

"Ron, dig the rewards for writing dirty books," Flackman said cruelly. His thick hand swept around the vast hall. "You see those paintings? And the tapestry? Man, that's success. It beats red-dogging for a living."

"I got no complaints," the linebacker piped. Flackman was intrigued with muscle, with mindless strength. There was always one of these Olduvai Gorge relics in tow—a heavyweight, a pro football player, a wrestler.

"Dirty books is right," Teague laughed. "Ah got no apologies, and leastwise Ah don't go readin' out loud from mah friends' books, mockin' them, and makin' sport o' them in public."

It was getting sticky. This was a long involved story, and the insiders in the room—the Cooperages, Lila Metrick, Venables—knew what Teague was talking about. Some years ago Teague, who respected Arno's fiery intellect, and the weight he pulled with critics, had sent him galleys of his novel, *The Turpentine Fool*. One night, in front of a circle of his brown-nosing friends, Flackman proceeded to read aloud from the proofs, making wicked sport of Bubba's ridge-running locutions and barbarous grammar. A born mimic, he had convulsed all those *Partisan Review* bigdomes, who hated Teague for being so rich and so happy.

"Hey, you guys," Warren Cooperage cried. "That's Christmas Past. And not in front of the whole world."

This was Vintage Cooperage: *keep our family squabbles to ourselves.*

"Ah jes' asked." Teague was smiling ruddily. "Arno seems to enjoy mockin' folks less educated than himse'f."

"Oh, Arno, that calls for a defense!" Tookie Cooperage called. She whooped or cawed—a noise you were allowed to make in public if you were worth ten million in blue chips.

"Yoch, yoch, yoch, Bubba," Flackman gargled, "I was tanked that night, drunk as a coot. You know I'd never put the blocks to an old buddy."

"Boy, I'll second that!" Cooperage called out, as he moved to place his stubby figure between Flackman and Teague. "Bubba, he was sozzled, soused, utterly incoherent!"

"He mocked me," Teague said softly. "He made fun of ole Bubba."

"Nah, nah, never!" Cooperage cried. "Now come on, you two guys, we got lotsa big guests here, and they are here to pay tribute to you guys, so shake hands."

They did so, Cooperage braying that he'd see that "Lennie Lyons reported the whole thing," but I could see that Teague was not appeased.

"Don't believe them, Bubba. Flackman took you apart. Everyone in New York knew about it. He said you couldn't write a note to the milkman without screwing up the tenses."

Teague's rosy-red face, the blunted features, looked for me in the murk. "Who said that? Dang, who said that?"

"Me, Bubba. Benny Bloodworth."

"Hot dang. Manuela said you was hyeah. Ole Bicycle Thief. Hah yew, Benny boy?"

"Great, Bubba. Don't let these guys con you. It's a big hype. Flackman is still sore that you got invited to one of Jack Kennedy's parties and he wasn't."

"Shit, Bubba," Flackman growled. "Don't listen to that City College Jack London———"

"Columbia, Arno. And worked my way through."

"—that sentimental little *putz* writing about that warm-hearted druggist in the Bronx. He gives Jewish writers a bad name."

"And you give us bad breath, Arno. You've substituted your ego and your cock for the Talmud."

Flackman lumbered to his feet, rubbing his huge fists. "I got to handle this myself."

Suddenly I was inspired. If Flackman were looking for a fight, I'd oblige him. I'm five foot ten and weigh about one hundred and fifty, and I have never thrown a hard punch in my life. But it might be worth it; at least I'd get my name in print, and if they closed me out of the conference workshops and threw me off their buses, I'd make a name for myself in some other fashion. I'd be like Ralph Branca. Who can ever forget the home-run ball he threw to Bobby Thomson? Or those even more obscure pitchers, whom great batting stars recall as the suckers who threw them the pitch off which they blasted their five hundredth home run? "Yeah," I could hear Flackman recalling in his old age, "the hundredth man I decked was a *shmuck* Bronx novelist named Bloodworth. Poor jerk never even got his dukes up before I laid him out with a right."

Anything about Flackman made print. There was no escaping the man. Like the Blob, or the Thing, he absorbed and digested the entire American scene, and the media recorded it all. Frowning, scowling, menacing, his bird-shot eyes and bushy black hair adorned *Time, Newsweek, Show, Look, Ramparts,* and *The Menorah Journal.* God knows he was a genius, our only resident genius, but did we need so much of him?

"Lookit him," an elderly woman said. "Lookit that face. God, what an intellect. You can see it in his eyes."

I could take no more. "Arno," I called out, edging up to the desk, "Arno, tell us how you ran out on the Black Panthers last March."

He ignored me. A French critic, an older man in a black suit with a *Legion d'Honneur* rosette in one lapel, was talking to Flackman, whose French was awful.

"You know what I mean, Arno," I said. "Hell, you even wrote about it, to explain why you ran out on the Panthers' march on the Museum of Natural History to protest the African exhibits. You were invited to Ari and Jackie's party. Arno, don't you know you can't lead a revolution when your belly is full of smoked salmon and champagne?"

"Got to handle this myself," Flackman said. The two Vassar types tried to hold him back, and the mob sighed and gasped as he lowered his boots and got to his feet. They claim that getting hit only hurts a little bit at first; so I raged on.

"It's true, Arno, and you know it. For years you claimed you were the Secret Spade, a black mother, a killer deep down, and that the most violent acts by Negroes were acts you condoned and acts you could gladly participate in. So along came this invitation from the brothers to tear up the Hall of Primates, and what do you do? Why, you fink out on your black brothers, as you explained it, without shame, because of an invitation to rub elbows and asses with perfumed armpits and jeweled rumps."

"Knock it off, squirt," Flackman growled.

Rage consumed me as I recalled his explanation as to why he had not marched with the blacks.

It became apparent to Flackman, he wrote, *that he could no longer trust himself in these street brawls. His temper was too short. His fists were too quick. His outrage overcame any cautionary restraints. Only a week ago, Flackman had come terrifyingly close to killing a man with his own fists, beating him to a smear of raspberry jam, and he had decided that even if he had given his word to the blacks, his potential for murder and maiming was sound reason for demurring. Moreover, there was the matter of the Onassis reception . . .*

"Tell us, Arno, how you paced Fifth Avenue, waiting for an invitation from the doorman, hoping Jackie or Lee would see you from the window—and meanwhile Sonny Lumumba and Malcolm X-Plus-Two were being clubbed and busted!"

"Warren, shut that fool up," Tookie ordered.

"Yeah, shut up, Bloodworth," Cooperage called. "Go on, beat it. Get lost."

"The guy is a bigot, that's all," a Scarsdale type said.

And the woman with red bows: "And such a filthy mouth."

Flackman seemed to be nodding. For a moment, as the mob tried to hold him back, and a woman in a red satin pants-suit shoved me in the kidneys, I thought he was agreeing with me. But it was a signal to his trained goon, Buzovitch, the linebacker. Before I could protest, the ape was on me, gently locking a white arm around my throat and pressing me against his iron chest.

"Whaddya wan' I should do wit' him, Arn?" Buzovitch squeaked.

"Ah, throw the bum out," Flackman said.

It was an odd sensation. The football star lifted me off the ground, easing the pressure on my tortured Adam's apple by raising me from behind, his meat-hook hand dug into my wide belt. Like a gaffed bluefish I wriggled and dangled, choking, weeping, voiceless.

"Oh, please, let him down," Judy Malar cried. "You'll strangle him."

"Nah, lady, I was a bouncer oncet. He won't git hurt."

Everyone applauded. The Cooperages led the cheering.

"Where should I put him, Arn?" the linebacker asked.

"Outside. With the garbage."

It was strange, being suspended in midair, groundless, sniffing Ron Buzovitch's spicy cologne. "Be a good guy, Ron," I said. He'd eased up on my neck and was holding me in a bear hug, my waist at a level with his chest. "Flackman uses you. Part of his campaign to prove his *machismo*. All cock and a yard wide. When he's through with you, he'll get rid of you, as if you were a pet dog or a court dwarf."

"I ain't no dwarf."

"Good God, throw him out!" Tookie Cooperage cried. "Ah cain't stand another word out of him."

"He secretly hates you," I told Buzovitch, as he started carrying me toward a rear door. "He's jealous of your muscles and your lust for violence and the way you withstand pain. In his heart of hearts, Flackman is a pale scholar with soft hands, ashamed of his Jewish intellectuality, and hence this lunatic compulsion to prove to the world that he is all hard fists and bloody noses . . ."

"Out the back door," Warren Cooperage ordered. "Follow me."

Waves of laughter; more cheering. I could hear Derek Venables—oh, he'd been all faggy sweetness when he wanted to know about Laszlo Veg—sniffing: "Jolly good show, this. Jolly good show."

"Hey, Manuela! Bubba! Can't I stay?"

But I was beyond redemption. Like Lucifer, I had fallen from grace. No one could save me. I was going down like Tashtego on the *Pequod*.

"Ronnie," I cried—he'd thrown me over his shoulder like a sack of rutabagas. "Ronnie, once your knees go, and you aren't butting helmets with the Giants any more, Flackman will discard you. You might as well wise up now and go back to Texas Baptist for some graduate work."

"Don't badmouth Arno to me," the athlete said. We walked through the opened rear door of the mansion, into a small garden, surrounded by high wrought-iron fencing. "Arn is the best pal I ever had. He's gonna get my memoirs published."

At least it was a mild summer night, a good soft Paris night for my humiliation. Oh, I had blown it. I had crashed the biggest, most glittering party of the conference, and now I was being tossed out—de-pantsed, exposed, friendless. And for what? For telling the truth, for plain-speaking.

We strolled through the garden, to a side gate, Buzovitch swinging me around, so that I was now being borne in his hairless perfumed arms, like a bride across a threshold. A few merrymakers, led by Warren Cooperage, trailed us.

"Should I really believe all that charming stuff in *Paper Lion?*" I asked my brawny St. Christopher. "Are you fellows all so darned witty and kind? My impression of professional athletes, especially football players, if you don't mind my getting personal, Ron, is that they are a mob of right-wing hoodlums, spoiled, flattered, cozened, sneaked through college on fake grades, ass-kissed and otherwise exalted, so that they become stealers of sweat sox and forgers of signatures, big apes equipped with primordial brains urging them to maim and hurt. Am I right?"

This didn't go over too well. "You better cut that out," Buzovitch said. "I got my graduate degree. In sociology, urban problems."

I was abashed. There seemed little else to say.

"Right in the ash can, Ronnie," Cooperage ordered. Just inside the high gate were some emptied trash bins. Luckily, I'm very thin and limber. Buzovitch set me in one of them gently, jackknifing my undernourished form, so that my legs and head emerged.

"Attaboy, Ron!" Coop shouted.

"Serves that lousy racist right," a woman said.

"Talk about justice," the man in the blue tuxedo added.

"Sorry, guy," Buzovitch said. "But you shouldna insulted Arnie like that. The reason he had me handle you was he knew I wouldn't hurt you. If Arn was to go after you, he could kill, he has such a turrible temper."

Everyone left, except Cooperage, and a frightened Judy Malar.

"Serves you right, Bloodworth," Coop said. "I know all about that nasty mouth of yours and that damned compulsion you have to insult your betters."

"Ah, get lost, Coop. Know what you are? You're the *milchediker* Arno Flackman. You envy his balls and his bloody temper and his maniacal domination of the media—and you wish you could do it, but you can't. So you suck along and help him promote himself."

Cooperage shook his lush blond mane, more in sorrow than anger. Then, espying Judy Malar, he offered her some advice. "Judy, if I were Imre Malar's daughter, I'd stay away from troublemakers like this man."

"I don't understand any of this," Judy said. "And why don't you help him out?"

Cooperage looked a little sheepish. He isn't a violent man, and he isn't cruel. In fact, he can be rather engaging when he isn't brown-nosing. He ambled over, and he and Judy yanked me out of the can. I was ejected with a noise like the popping of a champagne cork. Apart from a layer of dust and a creakiness in my knees, I was fine.

"You know, Bloodworth, you aren't a bad sort," Cooperage said, "but you *try* too hard. When you're not wanted, why show up? And if you do, why go on provoking people like Flackman, and me, and Lila, who are impervious to your insults anyway? Look, if you'd only learn to hold your tongue, you might make it someday."

"Goddammit, Warren," I said—suddenly not angry with him, relieved to at least be offered a chance to explain myself.

"You know that everything I said about Flackman was true, true, true! All that crap about being afraid to trust his fists and his temper . . . Jesus, what cant!"

"I give up," Coop said. "You're determined to be your own worst enemy. Why did you come to Paris, anyway?"

The answer was on my tongue: *I came to be as famous, as "in," as accepted, as important as you and Flackman and all the others!* But I couldn't say it. And suddenly—old Joyce would have called it an epiphany—I realized there was a tremendous opening for me, an opportunity, that, no matter what its consequences, could not be ignored. It all had to do with Moses Bloom's messages and his rats, with Laszlo Veg, with the murderous Russians who seemed to be on his tail all the time, the one who spoke New Yorkese, and the one whom Bloom said was "Mr. Bloody Business," Derek Venables' nosiness . . . There were connivings and deceits going on at the World Conference for the Arts and Sciences; and I would thrust my own tender white body into the middle of it.

"Judy dear, will you excuse Mr. Cooperage and myself?" I asked, flicking ashes from the seat of my bell-bottom denims, and the back of my jacket. "I'll be just a minute."

Judy nodded—my only friend—and I grabbed Cooperage's arm. I walked him down the garden path. The gay, bubbly noises from the Teagues' blast filtered out to us. They were playing rock records; a lot of people were dancing. A world I never made.

"Warren," I said in a low voice, "this conference is full of CIA people."

"The hell it is."

"I know who they are, baby."

Cooperage's tanned face turned pale. He ran a hand through his hair. "You lie, Bloodworth. What do you know?" I was liking him better every minute. Yes, I had found the right person to start my grand game with. Tell him your blood type, and it would be in Lennie Lyons' column the next day.

"I know, Coop, I know."

He was hooked. I hadn't the faintest idea who was working for the CIA or anyone else. But I knew they did cover these international gropes as a matter of course. For all I knew, Cooperage himself was filing inconsequential, pointless reports on who said what. Could that explain his pique, his confused response? Outside the front gate, some of the young folks who'd been thrown out of the party by Manuela were chanting abuse at the revelers.

"*Al paradón!*"

". . . *the wall, motherfucker!*"

"*Au poiteaux, au poiteaux!*"

The *gendarmes* watched them with dull eyes, dreaming of the moment when they could smash those sullen faces with the lead weights in their gay capes.

"Listen to me, Ben," Coop said tensely. "Whatever you know, whatever you've found out, from Moe Bloom, or anyone else, about who is working for what, keep it to yourself. I want you to understand this, Ben. I'm clean. So are all my friends. We wouldn't be caught dead fooling around with the CIA or anyone else. And you could queer the whole conference if you shot your mouth off about whatever it is you've found out."

"Ah. What I suspected. You're witting." I had come across the word in a magazine exposé of CIA operations. It meant an agent who was aware he was being used, as opposed to an "unwitting" or duped spy.

"I am not. And don't you say a word to the effect that I am." He pushed his chest out. Oh, but he didn't want to be left out of anything. "But I do happen to be privy to, ah, certain aspects of the intelligence operations going on in Paris right now."

"Yes, ours."

"No. Everybody's."

"Like the Shin-Bet?"

Cooperage frowned. "That comes from hanging around Bloom. He's nothing but a low-level courier for the Israelis, that's all. A messenger boy. The Shin-Bet is too smart to use him."

"I'll tell you something you don't know. There are two men from the KGB posing as delegates, one of them a professional assassin from the Thirteenth Directorate."

He breathed deeply. Clearly, this was something he didn't know.

"And I have evidence that one of your top Arab delegates, a distinguished scientist, is an Al Fatah terrorist, who had something to do with the bombing at the Café Lussac."

This last one I had made up on the spur of the moment. Dr. Jabali, my smooth friend, my soil chemist, was the most unlikely terrorist in the world. But I didn't give his name; and I didn't intend to. It just seemed a good idea to throw in the hint.

"How . . . how . . . how in hell do you know so much?" Cooperage asked. "What is all this espionage crap . . . and . . ."

"I know a little bit about everyone here who isn't what he seems to be."

I'd had my vision on the road to Damascus. A vision of J. Edgar Hoover in glory. There was nothing easier in the world than to pretend you were a spy. And what status! Cooperage had practically encouraged me. Involved himself, with everyone, everywhere, he was quick to leap to the conclusion that I was something more than I seemed. I'd fed him just enough to keep him interested. And it soon appeared he wasn't merely interested; he was ravenous, insatiable.

"Dammit, you'd better level with me, Ben," he said. "You start spilling this stuff around you could sabotage my conference."

"That isn't my assignment."

"Assign——?"

"Think about it, Coop. Maybe now you and Flackman and Metrick and that crowd will watch their step just a little.

Maybe I'll rate a seat on one of the workshops, or even on the bus."

"Sorry about all that, Ben." He grabbed my forearm and looked deeply into my eyes. "Jesus, I should have guessed it."

"Guessed what?" Better and better.

"*You're* the CIA man."

"Maybe yes, maybe no. I won't talk."

"All that crap about knowing who they were. That was a schoolboy's trick to put me off."

I coughed into my cupped hand; old secret agent, old conspirator, on his last run. "I'll put it this way, Warren, and that's all I'll say. Yes, I'm in black. But for who, and for what purpose, I can't say."

"Black?"

I was in command. How good it felt. "Black, you jerk. I'm on a run. It's tricky business, high echelon, and they wanted someone without a record. That's all I have to say."

Cooperage's face was agleam with concentration. He turned his head and spied Judy Malar, waiting faithfully for me at the rear of the Teagues' garden. "Wait a minute . . . wait a minute," he said slowly, as a knowing smile twisted his mouth. "I'm on the right wavelength. Yes, I have it all clearly."

"Don't be too sure."

"Malar."

"Hmmm?" I tried to be offhand.

"Malar. They sent you to bring Imre Malar to the United States. To convince him to defect, and to bring him back. God, how plain it is. How perfect."

I started toward Judy. He was a step behind me, and he grabbed the vented tail of my jacket. "Not so fast, Benny. Fair's fair. If I guessed right, I have a right to know."

"I can't say anything else, Warren. You'll know soon enough."

He walked alongside me. "Yes. That's it. That's why you're

124

hanging around Judy. To get to the old man. What an idea. What a master stroke."

"I'm glad you approve."

His eyes twinkled, and I could smell the change in his attitude toward me. It was almost envy—an envious, warm admiration—that lit his eyes, turned his lips upward. "Approve? I'm stunned. I'm flabbergasted with admiration. What a brilliant gambit. Sending you—you common scold, you malcontent, you climber, the *shlemiel* of America's young Jewish writers——"

I wasn't sure if this was complimentary or not, but I took it.

"—to pull off the biggest diplomatic coup of the year! Ben Bloodworth, the man nobody takes seriously, dispatched to snatch Imre Malar, the great voice of anti-Stalinism in eastern Europe!"

"Got it all figured out, hey, Coop?"

"It all dropped in. Like the *Times* crossword puzzle. Congratulations, Bloodworth. I can't tell you how differently I regard you. And the way you've been playing it! Right down to the insults and the boorishness! When I see Malar I'll——"

"Shut up!" I was thrilled with the authority in my voice. "Who is being a boor now? Coop, keep one thing in mind. This isn't some stupid literary game I'm playing, of who reviews who, and who gets a contract. This is for a man's life."

He stopped me a few yards from Judy Malar. "Who's your contact out at Langley, at the big pickle factory? No, they're too smart for that. Probably never had you out to Plans Division. Did it all in some fake office in Westbury, Long Island. Contacted you, proposed the deal, looked you over. Perfect. You are the least likely man, the last man in the world to be entrusted with such a job. God, what genius."

"Judy," I said. "Pay no attention to anything you may hear from Mr. Cooperage's ruby lips. He goes on like this when he's drunk."

The young editor was embracing himself, chuckling, walking around me, as if admiring my physique. "Once and for all, we put down the Stalinist lies about revisionism and the thaw. And how? Why, with Malar, the leader of the revolution! Bring him to freedom, to tell the true story!"

"What are you saying about Papa?" Judy cried.

"Too good," Coop said. "All of it . . . too good."

A small prayer of thanks issued silently from my lips. Yes, rewards evened out in the long run. Somehow, I had arrived. With Cooperage's help, of course. I'd started by faking some mystery. But he, in his headlong way, had created a new identity for me, a dashing new spacesuit. No alterations please, I'll take it as it is, including the police .38 and the Minox camera.

"Spill it, Ben. Tell me I'm right."

"Only partly. That's all I can say."

"Bigger than Malar?"

Judy walked up to us. "Stop all this talk about Papa, please. What do you mean?"

"Nothing, Judy, nothing important. It has to do with the workshop on African criticism."

We walked to the rear door. I, of course, would no longer be admitted—or would I?

"Come on back in, Ben," Cooperage said warmly, putting his hand around my shoulder. "No hard feelings. I'll clue Arno in on this deal, and I swear he'll forgive and forget. Arno's big about these things."

Disdainfully, I took his arm off. "No thanks, Coop. You know too much already. I shouldn't have talked." But I hadn't told him anything: he'd invented it all himself, and I'd nodded my head and looked knowing.

"Okay, have it your way. Miss Malar?"

"Thank you, I will stay with Ben."

Cooperage left us, shaking his head in wonderment. Ten minutes. Or maybe fifteen. That's all it would take for him to spread the word at the party. He'd let it out a little at a time, keeping some of the choicest bits to himself, revealing these over the next few days, a morsel at a time to favorites like Flackman and Metrick and Keen. And I would be transformed; I would ascend the ladder of fame. From a scrambler, a hanger-on, an intruder, I'd emerge as Bloodworth, *agent*. I could almost hear the words oozing from Cooperage's sensual lips. *That guy had us all fooled . . . imagine, Derek, he's up to his navel with the CIA . . . the guy they sent to grab Malar . . . all these wild attacks on Arno and me and the conference, all a cover, a fake, a blind, to fool everyone, to let him work his deal with Malar . . . the little son-of-a-bitch even knows who the KGB people are and he's been in contact with them . . .*

I was practicing a slouch, a certain narrowing of my eyes. A trench coat was indicated; a soft rainhat.

A black Citroën parked outside the gate; then another. It was a blue zone—no parking of any kind—and I suspected police. Two slender men in dark blue raincoats got out of one car and walked through the gate.

"*Mademoiselle Malar?*" one asked.

"*Oui, c'est moi,*" Judy said.

"*Votre père est attaqué ce soir. Pas mal blessé. Dans le Rue St. Denis. Il y avait une heure.*"

Judy cried out. She put her small hand to her mouth. "*Oh! Papa! Blessé? Mais . . . ?*"

The detective explained patiently, in slow, considerate French. Malar had been taking a stroll and had been jumped. He had been unconscious a few minutes, in an alley, had gotten to his feet, found a *gendarme*, and was now resting at the Hungarian living quarters in Gobelins.

"*Allons,*" said one of the men in blue raincoats. In that unique policemanly way, he placed himself between Judy and me.

"*Je vais assister,*" I said confidently.

"*Pourquoi?*"

"*Ancien ami de la famille Malar. Je suis le protégé de M. Malar.*" My French is pretty fair, and he nodded. But that wasn't what I found so exhilarating. I had imposed my *will* on the cop; and he had believed me. It was my new role—spy, undercover man, agent, the man in the Mackintosh. It fitted me like a pair of stretchable tennis sox, soft, cozy, warm, tight.

The two detectives paused to whisper to one another and point to one of the Citroëns. I wondered: his political enemies may have ruined his digestion, but evidently there was nothing wrong with Imre Malar's glands. Rue St. Denis was the heart of the red-light district. Old goat! Was there a Mrs. Malar? These mean thoughts I kept to myself as Judy nestled against me.

"Poor Papa," she said softly. "Oh, I hope he is not hurt badly."

"He can't be if they let him go to the apartment. French cops are thorough. They must have learned he was a VIP attending the conference."

"Vous pouvez partir," one of the detectives said. He held open the door of the second Citroën. It had one of those fancy little Venetian blinds over the rear window. Judy entered; I followed.

In the darkness I smelled the Russians before I saw them. My nose, as I believe I have mentioned, is hypersensitive, a common gift of migraineurs. And the inside of the black sedan was strongly reminiscent of intermission time at the Bolshoi—potatoes and sweat and cheap soap.

"Hey, fellah," Pochastny said, turning from the wheel. "No room on this job. Blow."

"Oh, but there's plenty of room, Mr. Pochastny. That's from Alice in Wonderland. Besides, Miss Malar has insisted I come along."

Keramoulian was next to him, and he studied me with those black olive eyes, the long twitching nose appearing to sniff me out. "Go avay, plizz."

They exchanged some Russian. Judy looked terrified. "Ben . . . perhaps you should leave . . ."

I looked to the sidewalk. The French fuzz had vanished. Yes, they were a big help. An appeal to them would have been useless anyway, I realized. Keramoulian undid his seat belt—a cautious fellow for a professional assassin—and climbed out. He opened the door on my side and he reached in for me.

"Plizz, Bludward, go. I don' want to make trobble." His chest seemed twice as broad, his arms twice as long as I remembered. Apparently he and Pochastny hadn't forgiven me for recovering Bloom's white rat.

"Play it smart, fellah," Pochastny said, grinning. "No need to work up a sweat."

And then I realized, as the big ape reached for me, and I backed away, pushing Judy Malar to the far corner of the Citroën, that I had to be true to my new role. A loyalty to my grand fakery was indicated. I wasn't quite sure what *kind* of spy I was, or who I was working for, or what I was after. The important thing was I had a new existence, a new role, and just as Arno Flackman worked perpetually to maintain his role of angry artist, so I was now mandated by some higher power to perpetuate my new existence: *the man in black*.

"Hands off, Keramoulian," I said. "I don't think I'll leave. I don't think I'll leave at all." I liked the Hemingwayesque repetitions; and I hoped the Russians would catch the nuance.

Keramoulian's right hand was on my arm. Oh, he was a strong one. It seemed my destiny to be manhandled, tossed and toppled by the hoodlums of East and West. "Mr. Keramoulian," I said frostily, yanking my arm away, "you are a member of the Thirteenth Directorate of the First Department of the KGB, a department known to your countrymen as Bloody Business. And I am not afraid of you, because I represent a principal who is every bit as determined to see that justice is done."

"Hey, go easy there, fellah," Pochastny said. "We're just two friendly delegates to the conference, right, Hrant?"

Thus far I'd been tossing back information that Moe Bloom had furnished me. What could I lose? I'd throw in a few furbelows of my own. "And your name is not Hrant Keramoulian. I'll have your proper name in a day or two, at which time I may be prepared to talk privately with both of you."

Oh, this was easy, so easy. Why had I not been told before? No wonder all those young shave-heads and Ivy League failures drift into the CIA, the State Department, the FBI. It beats working. Keramoulian, after a few Russian curse words, withdrew, and at Pochastny's calm urging—he was clearly the boss—went back to the front seat. The Citroën lurched off.

They were silent for a while, acting as if I'd poured ammonia into their borscht. We roared down the Rue de la Pompe, and I gathered we'd cross the Pont de Grenelle and cut across the south of Paris to the Gobelins district.

"Have you seen my father?" Judy asked Pochastny.

"Half hour ago, kiddie. He's okay. He's fine."

For a while she was quiet, then she started to sniffle, and I put my arm around her. "Don't cry. Judy, your father is an old hand at ducking bricks. What's a *klop* on the head to a man who has cheated the firing squad six times?"

"It is different now. I warned him not to go to Paris."

"But . . . it's just for a conference . . . a lot of talk."

Pochastny laughed. "Hah! Put your finger on it, guy! Lots of talk, talk, talk. And who cares? Besides, the little lady should appreciate that we're here to take care of her dad. Listen, we're both friendly socialist states, and we'd never let any harm come to a great old Marxist like Mr. Malar."

"I bet. Like letting him get knocked down and beat up in the Rue St. Denis."

Judy touched my arm and shook her head. She didn't want me taunting them. I patted her hand, as if to say, *trust me*, although I had no idea what I was saying, or where it would lead. It simply made me feel good.

"Hah," Pochastny laughed. "That's a hot one. *We* knocked him down? Fellah, you better ask some of your own people here in Paris about that little business. Those wiseguys in CIA, that NATO crowd. They pull stunts like that, not us. No sir, we behave ourselves in friendly cities."

Pochastny knew the city. He'd whizzed down side streets in the Grenelle district, turned down the Rue Vaugirard, and came out on a street alongside the Montparnasse Cemetery. I was high, full of fight, full of wild ideas of my own powers.

"What makes you think I'm CIA, Pochastny?" I asked, with a hearty chuckle. "Or NATO? Or any of that crowd?"

"You're with them, pal. It's a mugg's game, fellah. We have too much clout in this town."

"Don't be too sure," I said airily. "As Chairman Mao says, 'All rivers can be forded, but if they are too deep, the wise man will be patient and build his own bridge.'"

This stopped the conversation. I'd given them something else to think about, and all I got was a stony Bolshevik silence in return. Once they looked at each other, Pochastny smiling, Keramoulian, the gunman, droopy and grim, but they said no more.

How easy it was! Through the painful day I had been thrown off a bus, snubbed by the conference elite, put down by people like Metrick and Venables, dismissed as an arriviste, and finally dumped in an ash can by Flackman's janissary. Now it had all changed. A few judicious lies, hints, and brags—and I was Bloodworth, secret agent. Never had I felt more exhilarated, more energized. I needed no snub-nosed automatic, no dispatch case with a secret knife and a two-way radio, no codes, no hollow nickels, no teeny-weeny cameras or mini-recorders, no covers, no contacts. I needed only my lying, faking imagination—all a writer ever needs.

The Russians voted unanimously to keep me out of the apartment house. It was the old building where, a few hours earlier, I had seen Laszlo Veg's rat terrorize the tomcat.

"Okay, fellah," Pochastny said, as he took Judy's arm. "Get lost. Fun's over."

For the moment I'd run out of ammunition. Identifying Keramoulian to his face as a killer had given me considerable status. And the invented quote by Mao wasn't bad either. But

I couldn't think of anything else to give me a small edge.

"I'll go only if Miss Malar tells me to," I tried.

"Ben, you need not come up. Mr. Pochastny is right."

"I will wait here."

Pochastny rubbed his bulbous nose. "Go on home, guy. You're in over your head."

"I intend to wait here until Miss Malar is satisfied that her father is all right, and tells me so in person."

"Don't push us, fellah. One word from us to the French police and you'll be jugged. Ever been in a French jail? You read the newspapers. You know how the French feel about racist Zionists like your buddy Bloom. All I got to do is make one phone call to the Sûreté and you're through, fellah, out of business. Now beat it."

He scared me a little, but only a little. The marvelous thing about my new life, my reincarnation as an agent, was that I wasn't anything at all. It was all in my fertile brain. My external deeds, words, relationships were meaningless, spontaneous, free-form improvisations. Except for the few silly errands I'd run for Bloom—and I hadn't the faintest idea what his rats or his messages signified—I was as innocent as Dreyfus. So there seemed absolutely no danger in pushing my advantage.

"No, I don't believe you will say a word to the French," I said firmly. I was back in the schoolyard at P.S. 176, facing down Hymie Shulman, the neighborhood bully. "I'll tell you why, Pochastny."

"You're a fake, kid. You got no clout."

"No? Suppose I got to the conference and tell them that two alleged Russian delegates, one the supposed editor of an agricultural magazine, the other an expert on trade, are actually KGB hoods, and that furthermore they are keeping co-chairman Imre Malar under surveillance. Wouldn't that look nice! I know every American correspondent in Paris, and I can get the story spread in a matter of hours."

"Who the hell would believe you?"

"Anyone who knows how you people operate. Which means any honest reporter who has ever covered these international conferences."

My advantage over them was staggering: since I was a fake and a liar, I could not be exposed, or even threatened. They were genuine operatives, killers, undercover finks. They had a good deal to lose. Oh, I was learning. The rewards of fakery and humbug, in life as in art, are richly satisfying.

"You jerk," Pochastny sneered. "What makes you think we give a darn?"

"You do, *Tovarish*," I said. "You people attend these conferences full of assurances that you're friendly, mellow, kindly. You snuggle up to Africans and Latin Americans, you grin and drink and shake hands, and you want to be loved. But you send spies, killers, KGB galoots and thugs who won't even let your own best writers and scientists open their mouths. Man, you have the worst public relations in the world. Come to think of it, I intend to make a speech commemorating Babel, Mandelstamm and all the other writers you've murdered."

"Okay, okay, knock it off, Bloodworth," Pochastny said. "I don't know who's paying you, but I sure as hell will find out. You keep your trap shut, and we won't turn you in."

"I am waiting here until Miss Malar reports to me that she is satisfied with her father's condition."

"You got a deal, guy." As he and Keramoulian, flanking Judy, walked off, I heard what must have been some choice Russian cuss words.

Fifteen minutes later—I'd settled into a hard chair in a small sidewalk café and was sipping *infusion de tilleul*—Judy joined me.

"Papa seems to be all right," she said wearily. I lit her Kossuth for her. She handled it with deft, smart movements, and when she crossed her legs she did so with an elegance that would have shamed most New York girls. Living in that deprived and constricted country, she still managed to convey

133

charm and style and joy. I suppose it was the Hungarian in her.

"What exactly happened to him?" I asked.

"He is not certain. He's confused. You know, Papa is a hard man to confuse. But he could not make any sense out of the attack."

"Were the Russians in the room when you talked to him?"

"No. They left us alone." She looked at me; her eyes glowed. "I think you had something to do with it. You see, Papa is valuable to them. He is a . . . a . . ."

"We would say a showcase, Judy. A window to display the best goods. Your father is a widely respected, old-time Marxist, one who is at home in almost any city in the world. They want to show the conference that even though he lives in a country in which there are still fifty thousand Soviet troops, and even though the revolution he helped create was crushed, he, Malar, is free to speak his mind. Proving what liberal guys the Politburo are."

"Yes. They make no secret of that."

"Okay. Why was he attacked? Robbery?"

"No. They left his wallet, his watch, just took some useless papers he had—notes for a speech, a list of stores."

"From the beginning, dear."

"He went to meet some old friends at a café near the Rue St. Denis. They had a few drinks and Papa decided to walk home because it was such a warm night, and in one of those little *passages*, two men attacked him and punched him. That's all."

I mulled this over. The offices of *l'Humanité*, the communist newspaper, were not far from Rue St. Denis. Malar kept his lines open to all the shadings on the left. But it seemed strange for him to be meeting second-rank communist hacks in a sleazy saloon. He ran with thoroughbreds—Malraux, Sartre, Silone. Reluctantly, I decided that the old nine-lived cat had gone to the *quartier* to get his valves ground. He'd been on the prowl and a couple of hoods had jumped him. Of course I didn't reveal my theory to Judy.

"Is he badly hurt?"

"Not seriously. A bruise on his arm, one on his back. When he fell in the *passage*, the patch on his head came off. The one covering the wound from his fall in the bathroom. But that isn't serious. Uncle Latzi put a new dressing on a few minutes ago."

"The stitches didn't come loose?"

"Oh, no." She frowned. "What I don't understand is . . . well, I wasn't sure what Pochastny and Keramoulian were saying exactly, because my Russian is not that good. But I think they were talking about sending someone to look for the patch. Silly for a small piece of *gesso*."

"*Gesso?*"

"Plaster."

"Ah. Plaster of Paris. Very appropriate." I ordered another *infusion de tilleul* and a Perrier for Judy. Relaxed, I was determined to pursue my role as long as I could. It was far more invigorating, heartening, than attending workshops on the mass media in Asia. "How about the men who jumped him— I assume there were two—does he remember what they looked like?"

"No. It was very dark. One was tall and had a kerchief over his face, or so Papa thinks. The other . . . this is very strange, Ben . . . and maybe Papa imagined it."

"Yes?"

"He thinks one of the men was wearing the *fleur-de-lis.*"

"A *fleur-de-lis?* That's the symbol of the French monarchy. What the devil . . . ? There is a monarchist movement of sorts here, but they're a handful of cranks. And what would they want of a socialist intellectual from Hungary like your father?"

"That's what Papa was wondering."

"There's even a royal pretender, the Count de Paris, I think. He lives out at Louveciennes. But they're a tiny group, and as far as I know, violence isn't their bag. It's possible your papa imagined it. Or maybe he saw a sign in a shop window, or something, that made him think of the *fleur-de-lis* before he was zapped."

"Ben, I know this was a political attack."

"Why? Those notes for a speech that were stolen? Oh, Judy, I like your father, and I respect his reputation, but he's no threat to anyone here. This whole conference is a grand irrelevancy. People who run things aren't going to pay any attention to it."

"You are wrong, Ben. People will listen to what Papa says."

I remembered Cooperage talking about the "blast" Malar was going to give the Russians. Perhaps he was planning something they didn't like. But why bother attacking him? He seemed to be under their wing. They'd assigned those two unbathed lumps to shadow him, and they hardly had to send a third lout to pick his pockets on a dark street.

Pochastny and Laszlo Veg came down the street.

"Dad's feeling great," Pochastny beamed. "The professor gave him a sleeping pill."

Veg's sour face managed a smile and he spoke in Hungarian to Judy, who excused herself, got up, and said good night to me.

"Professor Veg, that seat on the eastern wall is still vacant," I said.

They were a few steps away, but my taunt brought Pochastny back.

"Stay away, fellah. Last warning. You and Bloom both. We don't waste time on Zionist adventurers. Know why? You got nothing to trade. No offers. If you were CIA, I might talk to you. But I got you pegged . . . you're nothing, a zero."

"Typical Stalinist bullying," I said quietly. "But that's all obsolete, Pochastny. You should read your Chairman Mao."

"Oh yeah?"

"Yeah, fellah. Chairman Mao says 'The smallest fish is often the hardest to catch and has the biggest teeth.' Put that in your borscht."

"Don't bull me, buster. Peking is boycotting the conference."

"If you keep thinking so, you're dumber than I figured. *Shalom*, Comrade."

I watched them walk off to the gloomy apartment, waved again to Judy and looked for the nearest metro station.

It was close to midnight when I got back to the Hotel Bavard, but I wasn't sleepy. Indeed, I'd never felt better. I had an embarrassment of riches in my pale hands. What was important was to keep all the balls in the air at once—running messages for Moe Bloom, taunting the Russians, making overtures to Imre Malar, pretending to be an agent of the CIA, the Shin-Bet, Peking, or anyone else who came to mind. It was the damnedest fun I had had in years, and it was the greatest antidote in the world to the gnawing sense of snub, insult, and exclusion that had eaten at me ever since they'd kept me out of the first-class section on the Pan-Am flight.

As I asked the desk clerk—there were no messages for me—for some hotel stationery, I realized that I'd found the key to art and perhaps to life itself. There was life in the booze, after all, as Harry Hope tells us in *The Iceman Cometh*. If Flackman could play out his public part as a hard-nosed brawler, and Teague his as redneck illiterate, and old prize-winning Keen his as a murderer who used his own hands to kill, what was to keep me—a lesser figure, to be sure—from spreading the word that I was an undercover agent? I could envision the reviews of my next book:

Benjamin Bloodworth's new novel must be judged not only in terms of what it is, but in terms of the author's strange personal life. Some aspects of this life are still a secret. But it is generally known in literary and government circles that he has played an ambivalent and intriguing part in the East-West detente, having access to high persons with great power. Like Philby, Azov, and Abel, he has moved silently in curious

137

corridors of power, and there are still unanswered and baffling
gaps in his curriculum vitae . . .

The broken window at the Café Lussac had been boarded up, and the Arab terrorist assault all but forgotten. Nothing stops Europeans from sitting on their keisters and sipping mineral water. The bloodstains had been scrubbed from the *trottoir*, the glass shards swept away. I settled down at a table, ordered a Perrier and started to plot my next move. It occurred to me, that my pocket having once been picked—Bloom's message to Veg, which was returned with a warning —the same crowd might try to frisk me regularly. This presented too good an opening. I decided to give them something as a bonus, whoever they were.

But what? Suddenly I began to think of my son, Eddie. I missed the little guy terribly. He is short, fat, muscular, twelve years old, a born jock. Maybe it's because I have never been strong or agile or good at sports—I have a defeatist attitude even when I'm ahead—that I love him so much. The kid is all heart, all spirit. Plays middle linebacker for his Pop Warner League team and makes all the tackles. Catches for his Little League team, a brown, tough, wise little guy, with an arm cocked to throw out any squirt who dares try a steal of second. My Eddie, my Eddie! He cries when he loses and he laughs when he wins, but he never chokes. No, no big red delicious apple under Eddie's chin, never. Someday he'll get a football scholarship to Columbia and I'll watch him at Baker Field, playing the brave jock his father never was.

These thoughts of my son inspired me. I wrote as follows on a sheet of hotel stationery:

Dear Friend:
The figures you have requested for the month of July are as follows:

CAVATELLI	4	3
KUPPERMAN	4	3
DEEGAN	3	2

CAVATELLI	4	4
KUPPERMAN	3	1
DEEGAN	4	2

You will note that the AB's total 22 and H's total 15, making a BA of .681.

> Yours truly,
> Savino P. DiGiglio
> President,
> Oyster Bay Township Little Leagues

For those who do not understand the esoterica of baseball, what I had done was list my son Eddie's batting statistics for the first six games of the season. I knew them by heart. The figures on the left were his times at bat, the other column his hits. Computing the batting average, or BA, is the most basic kind of American schoolboy arithmetic. That .681, I might add, is pretty damned good batting for a twelve-year-old, in any league. As for Savino P. DiGiglio, I invented him. The actual Little League president is a neighbor of mine, Arnold Rainberger. I folded the letter, put it in an envelope, and stuck it in the inner pocket of my jacket.

Then I studied the conference schedule for tomorrow. There was an opening plenary session, which I would skip, a luncheon for the scientists at the Pasteur Foundation, various addresses of welcome by French officials, ad hoc committee meetings to set up workshop personnel and agendas, a cocktail party for Afro-Asian delegates at the Hotel Plaza-Athenée (leave it to them to use the grandest pad of all) and assorted minglings.

The only event that intrigued me was an afternoon "dialogue" between Boyle Huffguard, the sweetie of the New Conservatism, and Arno Flackman, self-proclaimed herald of the New Radicalism. It was entitled "American Directions." Cooperage (who else?) was to be the moderator. As soon as I envisioned these three fondling themselves in public again, paying tribute to each other's "honesty" and "sincerity" and "erudition" I felt pangs of nausea. They'd be at it tomorrow, dividing up the public the way two dishonest movie exhibitors divvy up world markets.

And as I began to simmer, I made a remarkable discovery: *I was no longer envious of them; I no longer brimmed with callow self-pity!* All I had to do was think of myself as Bloodworth, Secret Agent, and pat the phony letter in my jacket, and I was relaxed, strengthened, assured of my own importance and validity. Where had I been so long?

A miniature Frenchman, squinting at *Paris Soir* through thick distorting lenses, was seated at the next table. He wore a striped suit and spats. I leaned forward and read his ID card.

MAURICE RIGNAC
France
Historien

"Pardon, M'sieu," I said. *"Vous-êtes délégat?"*

"Mais certainement."

I asked him if he had been at the Café Lussac during the bombing. He had, and had been shaken up a little. But a few *"sales cons Arabes"* were not going to keep him from his favorite table.

"No one even knows why zey throw ze bomb," he said to me, evidently unwilling to listen to my French.

He seemed like a friendly sort, a not unusual condition in French academicians. There is a myth that they are the elite of France; not so. Intellectuals, among the French business-and-money powers, rate a step above Algerian street cleaners. Hence, your French intellectual is generally friendly and accessible to foreigners. He can use a kind word.

"You are a historian, sir," I said to M. Rignac, as he sipped his vermouth. "Perhaps you can assist me. What is the origin of the *fleur-de-lis?*"

"Ah. *Le fleur-de-lis.*"

"Yes. The symbol of the monarchy."

140

"It is an ee-reece."

"Iris?"

"*C'est ça.* Some people say a lily, but I believe that is a misconception. It is an iris."

"But what exactly does it signify? I mean—how did it come to symbolize the crown?"

M. Rignac pursed his lips. "I believe it goes back to the twelfth century. It was first used by Louis le Jeune and later appeared on a seal of Philippe Auguste. Charles V made it official, exactly as it appears on the banner of the monarchy— three *fleur-de-lis*, golden, on a field of blue."

"Why three?"

"The Trinity, I imagine."

"Does it have any other significance? I mean, is the *fleur-de-lis* used by other countries?"

"Oh, M'sieu Bloodworth, it has an ancient history. Etruscan. Egyptian. Roman. A rather common design in the classical world." He stroked his creased chin. "And more recently in the Vatican."

Now we were getting somewhere. "The Vatican?"

"There is a Papal order of the *fleur-de-lis*, not very well known, and dating to the sixteenth century."

"What kind of an order?"

A Gallic shrug: M. Rignac did not know. "I am afraid that Vatican history is not my field. Actually, the rise of socialist democracy in western Europe is my specialty. *Garçon!*"

I thanked M. Rignac, offered to buy him a drink, but he had done his café-sitting for the day, survived a bombing, given out some arcane information, and was ready for bed. He left, and I mulled over the possibility of Vatican agents attending the conference. *Opus Dei?* They were a wise and wide-ranging crew, and they'd have their reporters and experts on hand. I'd seen several fine-looking priests, Belgians or Dutchmen, the tough, intellectual progressives of the Church, registering that morning. But strong-arm men, who would jump Malar in an ally in the red-light district?

141

Tak-tak-tak..

Louise Latour's diamond rock was tapping the side of an empty glass. She was squatting three tables away, simmering in her own boozy vapors, thinking of her ten million copies in print and the way foreigners made her throw up. Chipper, her nephew, was alongside her. For dinner, he had changed to mufti.

"Hey, Benny. Bloodass. C'mon talk Louise."

She *tak-tak-tak'd* once more, and a drowsy waiter came by to take her tumbler. The signal was for my benefit too, so I obeyed. No matter how ugly, soused, and miserable you may be, I understood, you don't glom onto that kind of money without acquiring *noblesse oblige,* a bossiness that makes you a terror to editors, agents, publishers, and lesser breeds.

"Siddown, Benny."

Vaguely I wondered what her corroded organs looked like. An open can of Ken-l-Rations on a hot day?

"Louise, I have had a hard, long day. It's bedtime."

"You inna big time, aincha, Benny? Louise knows you been to Teagues' party. But not Louise. No 'vitation for old Louise."

My heart suffered for her. I was not alone. Everyone wanted a piece of the big pie. Louise hungered too, for all her wealth, all her fame. The Scotch-and-ginger-ale lasted about thirty seconds; she drained it like a Viking quaffing mead from the king's cup.

"I think that should do it for today, Aunt Louise," Chipper said. "Mr. Bloodworth, if you're retiring, perhaps you might give me a hand."

"Sure thing, kid."

I had deep respect for the editor, or agent, or analyst who had chosen young Chipper to be auntie's keeper. A reliable, bright Midwestern kid. He'd honestly earned all those merit badges. They should have awarded him one for handling drunks.

"Here we go, Aunt Louise." Chipper hooked his left arm

under hers, put his right around her padded back and yanked her from her seat. She rose, gasping, like a hooked porgy.

Derek Venables, sniffing the night air, a bearded Sikh on his left arm, passed us. I gathered he had had enough of the Teagues' blast; dirty words and displays of *machismo* were not Venables' dish of tea.

"Friggin' limey," Louise said. "Friggin' faggot. Won' even say hallo Louise. But Benny says hallo."

"Hallo, Louise."

"Ole, Benny." Ai, her breath. It parted and pomaded my hair, and hung heavy in the night mists. Little beads of sweat, each one hundred proof, dotted her low brow, and I saw her insides as a great distillery, sucking in the mixtures she imbibed, leaching out the congeners and coloring agents, and exuding pure alcohol through her wide pores.

In lockstep, the three of us marched down the Avenue d'Iena. A high-priced whore at the wheel of a new Peugeot 504 sneered at us. No business in our group, *bien entendu.*

In the lobby, she squirted from our grip, stumbled forward and hit the carpeting. Like all good drunks, she didn't really fall, but sort of bounced and rolled.

"Golly, Aunt Louise," Chipper said. "You're being naughty tonight."

The two of us rassled her upright, bumping together a few times, dragging her to the elevator. I was deathly afraid she'd barf again, and this time I was practically under her.

"Ha, sawright, Benny, Louise only throws up onceta day," she giggled. "You safe."

We manhandled her into the lift, but I refused to ride escort. "Thanks a million, Mr. Bloodworth," young Chipper said. "Auntie Louise and I don't forget friends. You're not like the rest of those people here who won't even talk to us."

Would you believe it, that I was touched? Good deeds are hard to come by; I'd done my share for Louise Latour.

As I waited for the lift to return, one of the blue-coated

policemen who'd been at the Teagues to notify Judy about Malar's accident walked up to me. He flashed a badge. It might have been a fake, but who was I to argue? Besides, I'd seen him earlier, and his bearing said: *cop.*

"Dunand, Préfecture Centrale," he said.

"Goldberg."

"*Comment?*"

"An old joke, *M'sieu l'agent.* I'm Ben Bloodworth, an American writer."

He took me away from the lift to the corner of the lobby near the phones and showed me a photograph. It was Moses Bloom, some years younger, deeply tanned, wearing a pointy kibbutz hat and a sour expression.

"You know this man?" Dunand asked.

"Yes. That's Mr. Bloom. Also an American writer."

"He has been in contact with you, correct? He gave you an animal for Dr. Veg? And messages?"

"Well . . . he . . ."

Pochastny had bragged to me: the Russians had all kinds of leverage with the French police. A hangover from de Gaulle's flirtation with Moscow. They liked the idea of trading secrets with big, mean, rotten Communists.

"You have seen Mr. Bloom since he gave you these orders?"

"How could I? He is in Budapest. With Mrs. Bloom."

Dunand sighed. "He is in Paris. Mr. Bloodworth, if you know where, or if you know what he is up to, please tell me. Not for our sake, but for Mr. Bloom's."

"Why? He can take care of himself. He's only an elderly Jewish writer, a Zionist."

The French policeman sighed again. "You need not play stupid. Mr. Bloom is working for Israeli Military Intelligence and has been for many years. We have a dossier on him that fills a drawer in our headquarters."

"Well, find him and arrest him if he's so dangerous."

"He is in danger himself. The bomb that exploded in the Café Lussac tonight—it was intended for him. To kill him."

"He wasn't even there."

144

"But he was. He left seconds before the charge exploded. It was a timed charge set in a valise underneath the table at which he was seated, disguised."

"They picked the wrong guy. Two of their assassins were killed and Bloom got away."

Dunand squinted at me. "Perhaps, perhaps. Well, I have told you all I can. Should you be in contact with Bloom, advise him to report to the police at once. If he does not want to, he must leave Paris, although we are in no position to deport him. It is simply not our desire to send men after him when he goes out."

"Look . . . have you checked out the Arabs at the conference?" I hesitated before saying anything else. "There's this Jordanian . . . a chemist . . ."

"Dr. Jabali. He is under surveillance. He is not political."

I was glad to hear it. The friendly young agronomist seemed a decent sort. I would have hated to think he was the one who tried to blow Moe apart. "Finished with me?" I asked Dunand.

"Yes. But I suggest you stay a good distance away from Dr. Jabali. *Il faut mieux l'éviter.*"

"Hmmm? Why? You said he isn't political."

Dunand shrugged again. "Who can be certain? You have run errands for Bloom, you are surely on their list. *Bon nuit.*"

In the dank corridor, I found myself slinking against the walls, looking behind me, imagining footsteps. In my pauper's room, I checked the closet, the window, and looked under the bed before falling down. To my great satisfaction, I experienced no fear, no uneasiness. I was sorry that Bloom was a moving target for the Al Fatah, and that perhaps I was also; but I was not afraid. In fact, I was fulfilled, redeemed, euphoric. All over Paris, competing intelligence teams were building files on me. I would oblige them by pursuing Imre Malar to the ends of the earth, and bring him to America, freedom, and a three-book contract with a responsible old house.

I dozed off, fully clad. A rap on the door, which sounded

like doom, the old man in the white nightgown calling, caused me to rise horizontally from the coarse bed. My role now dictated my every move. I unbolted the door but held the knob firmly and backed to one side in case someone started pumping lead.

"Who . . . who . . . ?"

"Please open up. I must talk to you." No mistaking those flattened Ivy League vowels. It was my next-door neighbor Lila Metrick. I opened the door, and there she was—tall, blonde, haughty, her erudition as exciting to me as her behind.

"Miss Metrick. Lila."

"May I speak to you?"

May you? May you, lady? All I could think of was an old James T. Farrell short story: "When Boyhood Dreams Come True." My voice came out as a strained coloratura. "Please come in, my dear."

"In my room."

Better, better. More space to run around, for grabbing, jumping, rolling. I followed her down the hall, admiring her incredible body. Let me explain—confess—that I am a butt-worshiper. Hers ranked number one. She was wearing a short, somewhat flared chartreuse dress, revealing a good deal of her hockey goalie's legs—creamy tan, touched with gold. Her waist was delicately thin and hard, not an ounce of fat. But between that prim schoolmarmish midriff and those curving iron legs there nested a great protruding blonde peach cleft for me. God knows how all that firm round *culo* got bred into her austere Bostonian body, but there it was. Her sort of background and .genes—Radcliffe, Beacon Hill, boiled dinners, Emersons in the genealogical chart—usually produce lean flanks and withered hams. There must have been some wild chromosome somewhere, a batch of DNA gone haywire.

I followed her into her room. Yes, the rewards of fakery were coming so fast I could barely handle them. Arabs were gunning for me. Russian cops were warning me. Imre Malar looked to me for salvation. Derek Venables had been friendly.

146

And now, the prize of all—Lila Metrick, the keenest, most original mind in American letters. I would hunt the white whale, and bound to its flank, like Ahab, I'd go down.

"Please sit down," she intoned.

I did so, on a Queen Anne chair, noting that her room was three times as big as mine. Feeling magnanimous, I eschewed envy. She traveled with foundation money, it was well known. Or the State Department helped out. Me, I'd paid for everything out of my savings in the First National Clam Diggers' Bank of Hicksville. There was a vast double bed, on which she now rested her case, crossed her legs and studied me. This was a good sign.

"I know why you are in Paris," she said coolly.

"Really?" Understandably, I had developed a tingling, thrusting erection. I pushed my arms between my legs and tried to be suave, indifferent to her arch perfume, the way she shook her bell-like mane.

"Warren Cooperage has told me all about you. I left the party because I felt I had to talk to you at once. A lot of things are clear to me now."

"Such as?"

"Why you were assigned the room next to mine."

"Happenstance. Personally, I'm delighted. I've always admired you from a distance. Your mind, your fresh approach to letters, and to be frank, your womanly charms."

No response. Her jaw thrust forward, her nostrils turned pale. "You are a goddamn CIA spy, Bloodworth."

"Is that a fact, my dear?" I tried to be lofty, above-it-all, but I sounded like Maria Callas in her decline, faking her way through *Casta Diva*.

"Cooperage wormed it out of you tonight. He and I agreed you were a menace to the conference and that those of us responsible for its success had better make known to you our total disgust."

I essayed a knowing smirk. "That Coop sure is a pistol. No secrets from the little gossip, are there?" I'd called the turn.

As soon as he jumped to the conclusion—led on by my lies—that I was undercover, he had spread the word to the Illuminati, to Metrick, Flackman, and all the other conference powers.

"He may have gotten his facts a bit twisted, Lila."

"I doubt it."

"Okay, Lila. You think I'm a spy, a CIA agent. But I'm still a warm, human person. I crave affection. If not that, at least some recognition of my existence by people like you, and Venables and the others. Now that we are here, alone, why don't I order some drinks and we can resume our discussion of Fiction versus Friction. Are you familiar with Levy-Bruhl's theory of *Frottage* as the basis for most primitive creation myths? Or maybe it's Levi-Strauss."

"I asked you here for one reason. I have always wanted to look at a murderer, face to face."

Light-years! I had traveled light-years since Cooperage had taken my seat on the bus. "My dear girl," I said, "I have never murdered anyone except when I have been forced to, and those who met death at my hands deserved what they got." How easy and natural it was! At last I understood all that bloody bragging that intrigues writers. Keen with his manual killings; Flackman with his celebration of violence and brutality; Hemingway shooting those hyenas in the belly and laughing as they devoured their own guts. Long hours at a typewriter, a wasting sense of being a sissy, a fag, a dainty intellectual.

"Gad, what an appalling appearance you make," Metrick said. "Pale skin and weak chin and that small arrogant beard, hiding your black reactionary soul, your inner fascism with an outward sign of protest. You are vile and corrupt."

"Lila, I think you are jumping to conclusions. Cooperage may have shot his mouth off to you, but he didn't have the whole story. There are wheels within wheels. My role, let us say, is an ambiguous one."

"Indeed?" Yes, she was on the hook also.

148

"It's difficult to explain, and obviously I can't tell you everything. You must realize that the CIA doesn't attach much importance to these cultural conferences. And they are well staffed throughout Europe. But . . . if you must know, I am on *someone's* payroll. That's all I can say."

"Oh, spare me that. You are precisely Washington's notion of a literary fellow, someone—who by their standards—would pass muster as a writer or a poet. Glib enough to fool some stupid subscriber to *Partisan Review* and middle class enough to be acceptable to the asses who read the *New Yorker*. You are a spy, a paid informer, and the only thing that concerns me is that you be exposed, and that everyone here be aware as to what you are and what you are up to."

"You are on the right track, dear girl, but you aren't quite there. No, not quite."

She lit a cigarette, as if temporarily stumped. These people know very little about anything out there in the real world. They're too busy reviewing each other's books. Metrick leaned back on the bolster and the chartreuse skirt rose six inches. She had lots of heavy, muscled thigh. The urge to rip her dress off her and swarm all over that aristocratic body ate me in great greedy gulps.

"I doubt you are working for the people's democracies——"

"*Some* people's democracies."

"—they'd be far too perceptive to hire a clod like you."

"I won't tell you. You'll have to find out."

"No, you're ours. Now let me tell you why I have asked you here."

"To look at a murderer."

"Not the real reason. It's to warn you."

"Lila, people have been doing that all day. You'd be surprised what important people, too. KGB men, the Sûreté, the Al Fatah, and now you. Golly, word gets around that a man is doing a little eavesdropping and the world beats a path to his door."

"I warn you, Bloodworth, if you file anything on me to

those fascists in Washington, I'll ruin you. I know why you were given the room next to mine. I'll be on my guard. But one single word about me—anything—to those idiots at Langley, and I'll destroy you."

This, this is what I wanted. As Mrs. Loman said, attention must be paid to B. Bloodworth. "Lila, my dear, why should I send back data on someone as lovely as you?" There was a fluty flutter in my voice; the hot tremors in my member were forcing themselves up my burning body, constricting my nose and throat.

"Human cancers like you exist on gossip, innuendo, and lies, aimed at aggrandizing your own miserable image. I had my suspicions about you from the minute you tried to barge into the first-class section of the plane——"

"At least you noticed me."

"—and that idiotic business outside my room this morning. I'm a political person, and I don't hide my beliefs. I look at you and I see burning villages and starved children. I detest the power structure and I shall fight it every chance I get."

I looked around the lavish room, easily one of the best in the old Bavard. "Well, you certainly work both sides of the street. You come here with State Department help, you go to parties at the Embassy, and you call for the overthrow of the republic. Do those congressmen know that you advocate free-style all-out screwing and sodomy and other sports as a national way of life? I might add this is some room. Your rabbis take better care of you than mine, Lila."

She studied me with a cold stare, the look she reserved for IBM execs. "Scum. Filth. Yes, I'm sure you were in on the murder of Che. In a way I'm glad to see one of you close at hand."

"That's the final judgment on me?"

"You're viler than I imagined. Let me warn you again that if you file a word about me, I'll ruin you professionally—as a writer or as an agent. I have friends of my own in Washington."

"What if I'm not in the CIA?"

"I'll have that confirmed soon enough. My contacts are better than Cooperage's."

My limbs were melting. Inside my tight denims, Master John Thursday screamed for release, the thick, hard monster. Hot juices simmered and bubbled, rattling my lid.

"And that goes for any of my friends. You are not to inform on any of us."

"Hmmm. All pals together. You people don't give a man a chance. It's always *us*."

"Quite true. Anybody who amounts to anything here knows what you are. Sneak, spy, untalented climber, *arriviste——*"

"You left out loser. Flackman's favorite."

"Spoiled and frustrated scribbler. Go ahead, bomb villages, murder the revolutionary cadres, but you cannot get the best of us."

I got up, half-bending to hide Cherubino. It wasn't much help. Sweat poured from me as if I'd gone three rounds with Willie Pep. Approaching the tawny feline figure, I spoke in a hoarse croak:

"Lila Metrick, I have the worst case of the red-hots for you. I intend to ravish you, to bend your fierce intellect to my overpowering will. Doesn't this prove I am not a high-level CIA agent? If I were, I'd be cool and correct and maybe even a little faggy. But I have lusted for your proud rump and your creamy thighs too long, baby. I shall now commit our bodies to the burning ghat."

I began to undo my belt buckle and unzip my fly.

"You are disgusting."

"Think about it, Lila. Nothing is certain in this vale of tears. Who am I? The mystery should make it all the more delectable. I could be the man from the First Directorate, a KGB killer. Or a Peking spy, on orders from Chairman Mao himself. Shin-Bet? Sûreté? M-5? Choice of two, ma'am. But one thing is certain. I am going to make love to you. We shall play at the beast with two backs, right now."

She moved slightly, and the light glancing on her long golden hair drove me to a frenzy. Light on my feet, I leaped, pinning her to the bed. I mashed my panting face into her tresses, gasping, moaning, my blubbering lips seeking her forehead, her eyes, her nose, her firm, rather prim mouth. Oh, but she was powerful. I managed one slobbering encounter with an eyebrow, a brush past her left nostril, as we backed and filed, my meager arms trying to keep her down.

"Aaaargh . . . aaargh . . . Lila, my love . . . think about it . . . I'll never send a word about you . . . to Washington or Moscow or Peking . . ."

With a mighty heave, an extraordinary bit of timing and leverage, Miss Metrick flipped me, ass over tea-kettle, tumbling me like a male nurse handling a senile alcoholic. Our positions reversed. She had me pinned like a cabbage butterfly on a drying board. Those massive thighs straddled my narrow waist and my pulsating peter went wild. Her large, corded hands, rendered potent through years of tennis and sailing, nailed my pale paws to the bed. I was neutralized. As Dryden put it, *thus ever did rebellion find rebuke.*

"So it was your intent to take me?" she mocked. "Is that so?"

"Oh, dear God, yes. I'm drawn to high round backsides. Yours is the greatest I've ever seen, a classic, a work of art. Venus Callypigea. A Hottentot virgin's dowry. Opposites attract, Lila. You, finely bred, healthy, huge, rich. Me, starveling Semite, scrambler and scribbler. So what if I'm a spy?"

"This is fantastic," she said. "Absolutely fabulous. I've got a CIA criminal in my power. I could kill him if I wanted to."

"I'm ready to die, Lila, but first, let's make love. Let's play the grand game, conjoined in ecstasy. Don't you feel the vibrations, my love? Had we but world enough and time, Lila, and all that jazz. At our backs we always hear time's winged chariot hurrying near."

She released one of my hands to tug at a brassiere strap, and I darted my free mitt under her hiked skirt. I grabbed for that great rump and felt her underpants—silken-smooth to the touch. That was all I needed. Yes, Dr. Freud, let's get it all out. I'm a mad, wild fetishist also. That's all I needed; one touch of Van Raalte Peachglo briefs, three for $3.75, marked down.

"Aaargh, oh, you must let me, Lila," I moaned.

"I'm throwing you out." She climbed off me, and as she raised her huge thigh, I reached underneath again and tweaked her. She smashed my hand away, cracking several metatarsal bones, and as she left me, I went off. Out of me it came, one endless gush of spleen, liver, lights, both kidneys and thirty feet of intestine. As Joyce reminded us, through old Leopold Bloom, warm at first, cold later. I rested there, drained, deflated, gutted, a beached dead mackerel.

"Get out. Get out and never speak to me again." She opened the door and pointed the way.

Rising awkwardly, bent at the middle like some ancient Japanese farmer doubled over after a life of toil in the rice paddies, I limped to the door. "Gosh, not even at the workshops? I was looking forward to some lively arguments with you about life and art."

In my room I whipped up a pill parfait—one tranquilizer, two aspirins, and a barbiturate—and fell into a deep, dreamless, and smug sleep. A long fruitful day it had been. Even the misfire with Lila Metrick had had its rewarding moments.

But the next morning, my head felt as if it had been worked on by Inca surgeons, trepanning the skull to release evil spirits. I stumbled into the lobby. It was chock-a-block with delegates—more Asians in dhotis and ao-dais, Africans in dashikis, and a group of grinning American nuns from Chicago.

"Which one is Arno Flackman?" a cheerful, rosy-faced sister asked me.

"Sister, just look for the biggest crowd."

I was right. Near the high front windows of the lobby, Flackman was being interviewed. A tape recorder was set on a table, and Harvey Ungerleider, of all people, was asking the questions. At least twenty people had gathered around to hear Flackman's wise words. Two photographers, a man from *Paris Match*, and a famous old fellow from *Life*, whom Flackman kept winking at and trading insider's gossip with, were snapping 35 mm. photographs.

"Don't you agree, though," Harvey was asking, as the tape reels spun busily, "that the Palestine Liberation Front is a valid aspect of the Third World Revolution and deserves the support of all progressives, no matter what their origin?"

I turned to little Vannie Bragg. "Who is Harvey interviewing for?"

"*Suck*," she replied.

"I don't think I'm familiar with it. Family-type mag?"

"New Far-Left. Harvey's really into it."

"I support all progressive Third World movements as a matter of course," Flackman said, "and while I don't hold for terrorist bombings such as we witnessed here yesterday, part of the problem is Israel's refusal to recognize the legitimate rights of the expelled Arabs."

"That's a cop-out," Ungerleider said, moving the small microphone.

Flackman's head ducked an imaginary right, bobbed as he moved away from a jab, and his words came out of the side of his mouth, New York slum fashion. "Fuck off, Jack. I don't have to give you people interviews. I'm covering the conference myself, and I save all my goodies for my own writing, dig?"

It occurred to me that he had been up all night. You had to admire the man's staying power, his bottomless energy. Two of his miniskirted *pisherkehs* dozed, arm-in-arm, on a bleak sofa nearby. As Ungerleider pursued his "interview," two film cameramen approached. One was shooting straight newsreel stuff for NBC, but the second had a fancier rig—a French Eclair camera—and he was doing a ninety-minute *cinéma vérité* film on Flackman for French television, entitled "*Le Roi.*"

It's important to visualize what was happening at ten in the morning in that bleak hotel lobby. There was Numero Uno, being interviewed and taped for a New Left rag, while two still men took photos of him, one film man took newsfilm shots, and a second recorded *everything* said and done, for ninety minutes of television spectacular! Is it clear what I mean when I say that Flackman was a small industry, a communications network of his own?

"And this conference?" Ungerleider asked. "Isn't it nothing more than a bourgeois attempt to co-opt the world revolution?"

"No. No. Not at all. I'm on the board of the conference, and I'm a revolutionary, I'm more goddamn revolutionary than fifty of you young snots . . ."

Enough. I bought a Paris *Trib* and settled into a distant corner of the lobby where I ordered a café-au-lait. The banner headline was about the bombing at the Café Lussac. But the newspaper did not report what the French cop, Dunand, had told me: that Moses Bloom had been the target of the Arab bomb-throwers. One paragraph puzzled me:

> Eyewitnesses said that the shots that killed the two terrorists seemed to have come from across the boulevard. A half dozen French gendarmes were on the scene seconds after the blast, apparently acting on a tip. The Paris prefecture would not comment, but a spokesman, who would not give his name, said it was possible that additional police had been staked out across the street in buildings opposite the Café Lussac.

Idly, I wondered if my sweet friend Dr. Jabali had been picked up for questioning. Odd, the way he ambled about the city on his brown sneakers, smiling, bowing, apologizing.

Since I was now a full-fledged agent I decided to track him down and ask him a few questions.

In type almost as big as the report on the bombing was Arno Flackman's own personal by-lined report on the World Conference of the Arts and Sciences. He was like spots before the eyes, or a plague of boils, a cloud of stinging gnats. The man could not be avoided. A puffed-up preamble read:

> We are proud to have Arno Flackman's by-line in the Paris *Herald-Tribune*. Mr. Flackman is one of the great literary voices of the century, and his fresh, original, and challenging reports on the conference will do much to dramatize this important meeting of the great minds of East, West, and the Third World. This is the first of a series of reports.

Reasonable enough. Then I began to read the piece and my heart became numb, contempt tightened the blood vessels in my head, and I had that wasting sense of inadequacy, an awareness of brilliance on the part of my betters. Flackman was writing about himself and the conference in *the third person*.

> Yes, Flackman would have to be on his guard. His footwork would have to be sharp, his wind good, his jab swift, his right cocked and cunning. There were some rugged opponents in the ring against Flackman, such as the lofty poet Venables and the old Marxist battler Malar, and he knew they could not be easily put away. Flackman understood this too well; his nose for the honest adversary was as acute as ever. There would be some bloody moments in the corners of the literary ring, and Flackman would not shrink from gouging and kneeing and heeling . . .

Translation: I am a little bit ashamed of myself for attending this conference at all, having to rub elbows with faggy poets and old burned-out European radicals. They are beneath me. So I will make the whole affair sound like a brutal, hard-fisted, rock-'em-sock-'em brawl. By making *them* sound murderous, and bragging about my superiority, I make myself even *tougher*. Moreover, there is the chance that one of them might get more publicity than me, or make a better speech, so I'd better set everybody straight right away.

It occurred to Flackman that he was the only person present, the only talent, the only revolutionary force, who could accurately report the proceedings. None of the delegates he had thus far met, from the unreachable enigmatic Keen to the beauteous if arcane Metrick, came close. He was so far ahead of the field, so obviously the only creative power equipped to tell the truth, to see the nuances, understand the plottings and achieve a synthesis of the entire complex affair, that he felt vaguely ashamed because of his overwhelming superiority.

To avoid vomiting I turned to the sports section, hoping they might have the Little League scores from Nassau County. I wanted to see how Eddie had done in his last game. No luck. Then I remembered the phony letter I had written the night before, the one with Eddie Bloodworth's batting averages. I reached inside my jacket. Success: it was missing. Some scavenger, surely the same pickpocket who had taken Bloom's letter to Veg, had sneaked his deft fingers inside and made off with it. They were pretty selective thieves. The letter to Veg, the one that was returned to me with a warning to avoid the Hungarian rat-trainer, was still in my side pocket. I opened it. The Yiddish (or Hebrew?) meant nothing to me.

Judy Malar, rosy-cheeked, as lithe as a cat in a short green dress—her legs were lovely, free of stockings, and so innocent that I could not entertain lewd thoughts—appeared at the Bridge Building table, saw me, and came over for coffee.

"How is Papa?" I asked.

"Much better, Ben. He started the day with a double cognac. He was not badly beaten, just shoved around a little."

157

"Where is he now?"

"Resting. At the apartment. Those Russians! They sent Mr. Keramoulian back to the *passage* last night. To look for Papa's plaster patch! He didn't find it, and Mr. Pochastny was upset."

It seemed an enormous effort for a hunk of adhesive plaster. If the KGB could be that assiduous, so could I. After all, I was—or was I?—the man sent to bring Imre Malar back to the United States. It was about time for me to make my run. "Judy, your father loves to travel. He's all over Europe, speaking to conferences, attending seminars. Why has he never been to the United States?"

She frowned. "I think your State Department doesn't want him."

"I can't believe that. He led the students over the bridge during the revolution. He drew up the fifteen points against the Stalinists."

"Yes, but I think he joined the Kadar government too fast. Your State Department would have liked for him to stay away from them. But of course, then he might have been shot."

That was true enough. But old Malar, old *roué*, looking for some attractive Parisian whore in the Rue St. Denis, quaffing champagne and cognac, swallowing oysters, luxuriating in what was satisfying and sensual, keenly aware of the good stuff of life because he had been so close to the dark pit so often—you wouldn't find him making a last doomed stand for some revolutionary principle. Not any more, at any rate. The thin soup of Marxism wasn't his dish any more. Nothing gives a man an appetite for capitalist corruption like a steady diet of socialist slops.

"Why don't you and Papa come to the United States?"

"I just told you. The State Department turned him down."

"No, not as a guest speaker, as one of those foundation lecturers. Defect. Come for good."

"What?" Judy's green eyes opened wide. "You mean . . . come illegally? Like Svetlana Stalin?"

"Sure. That's the way to go first class. Of course, your dad might have a problem. He isn't a Stalinist, he isn't a real bloody Bolshevik, just a sort of vague Marxist. But still, we can use a few of them, telling us about the red terrors."

She frowned, displeased with my banter. "Don't joke, Benny. That's your trouble. You push a good idea too far and it starts to sound absurd. But—how could Papa come to America the way you suggest?"

I narrowed my eyes and leaned forward. "I can arrange it."

"You are some kind of spy, aren't you?"

I placed a fatherly hand on hers. Across the lobby I could hear Flackman, in a burst of anger, ending his interview. Lights flashed, there was shouting and cursing. The public person was enraged. *Fuck off, fuck off, all of you* . . .

Judy Malar clapped her hands to her ears. "Will I have to listen to *that* every day in America?"

"No, not every day, darling. Think of nice things like Disneyland. Khrushchev never got there, but you and Papa will. And color television. And campus riots. And stores like Korvette's and S. Klein—anything you would ever want at half price."

She shook her head, admonishing me. "Ben, you are making fun. We are a materialistic people, but don't tell us that, or we will be insulted. Besides, Papa is loyal."

"To what? A country that tried to kill him five times?"

"No. To our writers, and our poets, and our history, and our Olympic teams." She lifted her head. "Seventeen medals in the Olympics, from a country of ten million. In case you did not know it, we are a gifted people."

"And so modest." But there was a validity to her innocent bragging. A remarkable people, nurturing their jaw-breaking unspeakable language, ten million of them in an ocean of Slavs, turning out their Szilards and Wigners and Weiskopfs and Reiners and Ormandys and Bartóks and Kodálys. But of course that was Christmas Past; there wasn't much of anything being turned out in Hungary these days. Whatever it was Laszlo Veg had been doing to his white rats, it surely wasn't in a class with Von Karman's work.

"I am not certain," she said. "He might want to go. He might not."

"Judy, let me confide in you." I was about to start lying again and at once I felt bouncy and assured. "I was sent to Paris to bring your father to the United States."

She cocked her head. "I am not sure I believe you."

"It's true. A group of top-level scholars and historians decided that now was the time for Imre Malar to defect. Your papa doesn't tell you everything. You know he's a secretive man—he loves to gossip and exchange jokes with these old socialist pals of his—but he keeps important matters to himself. How else could he survive the way he has? Somewhere along the line he dropped a hint that he was ready to make the jump."

"It never entered his mind to leave in 1956. Why now?"

"In 1956 he had hopes. Now he knows it will be ages, ages before the Russians get their hands off the throats of the eastern Europeans. It's not just their stupid blundering politics, it's the curse of bigness. You get big enough and strong enough and you want to hurt and suppress people. I sometimes think the answer to the world's problems is a limit on the size of nations. Fifteen million at the most and no armies."

She closed her eyes. "I don't know. I don't know what to say. I could talk to Papa. But . . ."

"You're afraid of those Russian wolfhounds, Pochastny and Keramoulian."

"There are many more here. Those two are registered as delegates. But they have a dozen of their men around the conference and at the house."

I waved a hand. "They don't scare me. Once you and Papa decide to make the jump, I take over."

"But . . . who are you? The CIA? The State Department?

I heard the Russians say you were a messenger for the Israelis."

"It doesn't matter, Judy. I give you my guarantee that I can arrange safe conduct for you and your father."

"But why? Why are you so interested in him?"

This was a good question, and one I hadn't thought out. There was a rush to the street. Flackman's bristly head vanished through the door, followed by cameras, lights, a dozen reporters. Warren Cooperage was on the edge of the group, chivvying, keeping his oar in. Seeing him, a response to Judy popped into my head: I recalled Coop's references to Malar's speech.

"It's the speech your Papa is going to make," I said carefully.

"What about it?"

"I understand it is going to expose the Russians once and for all. From the mouth of a dedicated old European Marxist, a man who has been in the forefront of every political battle of the last half-century. If he stands up and blasts Moscow for its brutal stubbornness, for its wanton aggressions against the people of East Europe and the children of Israel, for its meddling and subversion and lying deceits, then he may not be able to go back to Budapest. And, by the same token, he will be warmly welcomed in America."

"Have you seen Papa's speech?"

"No. But I've heard the word being spread. It's the biggest thing that's going to happen at this conference. You see, this damned thing was called to prove that the communists had mellowed, turned liberal, that the Russians wanted to prove their sweetness. But it's a fake. They're big and strong and mean, and they throw their weight around."

"One speech . . . is that important?"

"It will tear the conference apart."

"But the Russians must know he is planning to make it. Just as you do. They can stop him in a minute. They can send him home."

"They wouldn't dare. Not having let him come this far, and

161

not when they are obsessed with the notion of selling themselves to the neutrals and the Third World as swell fellows. You see, Judy, Imre Malar is a big name, an important name, maybe not to Americans or the general public, but to every socialist-Marxist theorist and politician and union leader here."

"You think you are a match for the KGB men?" she asked, with a bitter smile. "Ben, Ben, I know something about them."

Ah, here it was. Bogart. James Bond. A bit of Burton. I leaned back in my chair and took a sip of acrid coffee. Its harsh bite made me wince and did nothing for my efforts at cool disdain. "Stumblebums. I've got some help myself." Lie on top of lie, leading God knows where.

"I shall talk to him. But . . . there is another problem."

"Family in Hungary? Reprisals?"

"No. Mama died two years ago. We have no family to speak of. But, you see, Ben, Papa has a special status. Because he is an intellectual, he is allowed to travel, and speak, and meet other liberals and writers and editors. It is not a bad life."

"It won't be the same, ever again, after he makes this speech. It's one thing to crack jokes about the bad quality of shoes in the Soviet Union, but it's something else to denounce them as enemies of freedom."

"But will he be as happy in New York, with your crimes and riots and dirt—oh, I read about it all the time—as he is sitting in the Vorosmarty Café in Budapest drinking his espresso and chatting with old friends?"

"A good question, kid. I can't answer it. Imre Malar will have to. But at least let's give him the chance."

"I shall talk to him."

"Think of it. He could join some institute or foundation doing research on the economics of Marxism, contribute to *Partisan Review,* and lecture at the New School. You would find yourself a bearded professor of linguistics at Columbia and raise a houseful of small children, across the Hudson River in a Victorian mansion in Piermont, New York."

"And what about you, Benny—our savior?"

"Me? I would slink back to Long Island and think about missed chances." I was feeling like Ralph Bellamy—watching the heroine go off with the young William Holden.

"Oh, you are so funny, so crazy."

She snuggled close to me, her thigh touching mine, her soft hand clutching mine, fingers laced. I had a fleeting vision of her as my naked mistress in a Greenwich Village walk-up, the two of us gasping and tumbling of a rainy October afternoon, full of love and breathy endearments and wistful tears. It was short-lived. I'm no good at this sort of thing. Guilt drowns me. Witness last night: my bold assault on Lila Metrick's fortress. How do some men get so much and all the time, to hear them tell it?

"You must talk to your father at once," I said, as Judy got up to take her post at the Bridge Building table. "Let him make that speech, let him tear those bloody bastards apart, and then let him come with me. I'll make the arrangements. You'll be safe."

Was I pushing this mad charade too far? Was I getting innocent people involved in my lunatic pursuit of status just because I'd been snubbed?

"Ben, don't hurry us. I am afraid. Afraid of Pochastny and the others."

Others? Like someone with a *fleur-de-lis* in his buttonhole? Or an Arab chemist with crazy high sneakers? Or whoever it was who kept lifting letters from my pockets and warning me to stay away from Dr. Veg?

"You have my guarantee. One hour after you leave the Palais de Chaillot you will be on a TWA jet. The next day we all go shopping in Korvette's."

She kissed my forehead. I colored—not with passion, but with confused embarrassment.

163

I'd been warned to STAY AWAY FROM VEG, so I decided not to give him Bloom's letter. Besides, the crafty neurologist probably knew what was in it. He seemed to know everything in advance. It was in Hebrew characters and could have been either Hebrew or Yiddish, neither of which I read. An old Paris hand, I knew there was a Jewish quarter on the Rue des Rosiers, out toward the end of the Rue de Rivoli. I wandered the familiar streets for a while—little tailoring shops, *papeteries, boulangeries*—and on the side streets the same resigned, worn-looking whores who worked the *quartier* ten years ago.

A delicatessen, its window full of unnaturally red tongues and spurious dyed pastrami drew me. I'm no professional *fresser* of kosher meats, I add. A little of it goes a long way; for what it's worth, I'm a Wheaties and Bran Flakes fancier. Inside the small restaurant I ordered a buttered onion roll and a glass of tea and asked the proprietress if anyone in the place read Yiddish.

"*Mais oui,*" she said. "*Mon oncle, le chef.*"

From a kitchen redolent of garlic and chicken fat emerged a bald shriveled little bird in a soiled apron. "*Voilà mon oncle,*" she said proudly, "*M. Gelman.*"

I introduced myself and took out Bloom's letter. As he squinted at the message through gold-rimmed specs, I noted the blue numbers on his right forearm. Slicing salami and washing dishes in his niece's delicatessen . . . was it pleasurable after the years of terror? That old draining sense of guilt emptied me.

"Hebrew or Yiddish?" I asked.

"*Yeedeesh, Yeedeesh,*" he said impatiently. "*Teuer freund, Du bist ein narr,*" he read.

"Dear friend, you're a fool," I said.

The rest was a little harder—my Yiddish is marginal—and we had to use a three-way translating system—Yiddish to French to English—to finish Bloom's short letter. In it, Bloom seemed to be bawling out Veg for not answering his appeals. The whole family—*die ganze familie*—was there (where?) And he was expected. The entire affair, the letter emphasized was a matter of *überleben*. We had some trouble with this, but the niece and I figured out it meant *survival*.

"*Die tseit*," Uncle Gelman read slowly, "*ist kurts und die lager vaxt ernster und ernster.*"

Time is short and the situation was getting graver and graver.

There was something about returning *deinem kleine freund* —apparently a reference to the white rat. Then there was something that appeared to be an appeal to Veg's political sensibilities. *Deiner royte friente zeinen nicht besser als die brauen . . .*

"*Vos amis rouges ne sont pas meilleurs que les marrons*," the proprietress translated. And winked at me. She knew also. Veg's communist pals, the letter warned, were no better than the brown-shirted Nazis.

Feeling guilty, I offered Uncle Gelman ten francs for his help. It was a mistake. He had that quiet innate dignity of small victims. He held his little salami-scented hands up and cocked his head. "*Pour rien, M'sieu.*"

The niece nodded her approval; all that she wanted was that I should recommend my tourist friends to their delicatessen. I promised that I would, and thought mistily of the old Bronx I knew as a boy, the small shops, and street lights, and warmth and closeness of a true neighborhood, and I wondered how we had lost it all.

Riding the metro back to central Paris, I wondered why Bloom had such a case of the hots for that sour pickle, L. Veg. He didn't interest me at all. My quarry was Imre Malar, the bouncy bally of Marxism. I'd pursue him to the ends of the earth, and I would make Cooperage's wild guess a self-fulfilling prophesy. With Malar in mind, I got off at the Ecole Militaire station and walked down the Avenue de la Bourdonnais to the American Library on Rue Camou.

My historian, M. Rignac, had the right dope about the *fleur-*

de-lis. The Catholic Encyclopedia informed me that the Order of the Lily was founded by Pope Paul III in 1564, and was awarded to subjects of the "Roman States" who fought against "the enemies of the Patrimony of Peter." The Pope, I learned, was a Farnese, an "easygoing, worldly-minded Christian." His specialty appeared to be giving jobs to relatives. The logic of papal biographers eludes me. Paul III was described as a "secular prince of the Renaissance" who, through the demands of history, became a "patron of reform." Reform? *Reform*, you say? I read on and learned that Paul III introduced the Inquisition, the Index, censorship, encouraged the Jesuits, and otherwise ran a tight ship. Yes, that man was certainly a reformer. And what a prince! I suppose one man's reform is another man's headache.

There was nothing else on the Order of the Lily. It almost sounded to me like a discontinued model. The Papal States went under in 1870 and maybe some of those honors went with the temporal power. There was some more stuff on Pope Paul III—he commissioned the Last Judgment, built the Scala Regia, and began the Farnese Palace. That's how things get done, I'm afraid. If you want a Last Judgment maybe you have to burn a few Jews and Protestants. Does it follow? I'm not sure.

The Avenue de la Bourdonnais leads to the Pont d'Iena, and this would take me across the Seine to the Palais de Chaillot, where I could catch some of the opening day's festivities. It's a magnificent street—wide, tree-shaded, flanked with massive, handsome buildings, and housing a few first-rate restaurants. I was jealous of the Parisians for having such a city, and for grumbling so much.

As I waited for the green light at the *carrefour* formed by the Avenue Rapp and Rue St. Dominique, I heard a car honking at me.

"Hey, Benny! Wanna lift?" an American voice called.

It was Tom Bragg, the rugged golfer from Darien, and his wife Evie. They seemed full of spirits, undaunted by the way their daughter Vannie had told them to climb a tree (and worse) last night. They were seated in a smart new black Peugeot 504.

"We're off to the conference, and you must be too," Evie Bragg intoned through flaring nostrils. Gad, a husky mare-thighed woman.

I thanked them and got into the rear seat.

"It's a real pleasure bumping into you like this," Bragg said. He'd exchanged his cocoa-colored Panama for an old-fashioned yellow straw katie with an orange and black band. Princeton? You'd never catch him without his O'Connor, not even in August. An orthodox, standard-model WASP, Tom Bragg, and not a bad sort of guy.

"You staying nearby?" Evie asked, turning to smile at me. She looked better under dark lighting. Creases from too much sun and tennis around her eyes; powder a bit spotty. Little Vannie had probably called her a few more names after they left. And Harvey Ungerleider as a future son-in-law! No wonder she looked peaked. Maybe they had been inflicted with more outrages than they deserved. For all I knew they were the kind of decent Republicans who supported the Head Start Program.

"No, I'm at the Bavard. I was in the American Library just now."

"We're at the Hotel Bourdonnais, down the street," Evie said.

"It's expensive as hell," Tom Bragg said, laughing. "Thank God for that good old company expense account."

"You're here on business?"

"More or less. I'm with Academy Fixtures. Don't snicker, Ben. Everyone needs clean sinks and toilets that work. I know that writing guys like you, all you fellows are so full of smarts, think it's funny for a grown man to spend his life selling johns."

"I'd never laugh at you, Tom," I said sincerely. I have come to the conclusion that the threat to American Democracy and

Progress comes not from the Tom and Evie Braggs and their mutual funds, but from the hard-hatted riveter and the overalled welder.

But *Academy Fixtures?* Could a handsome, active, intelligent man spend his life selling toilets? In a sense it served them right. These lords of the earth had seized all the cushy jobs, all the expense accounts, buried their noses in the *Wall Street Journal*, bought up all the big houses in Greenwich and Old Westbury, and look what it had gotten them. A career selling toilets, or sitting at desks initialing meaningless papers and studying sterile figures, for a mere $80,000 a year. And meanwhile, the Jews all became rich novelists and songwriters, and the Negroes halfbacks and vocalists.

The back of Bragg's neck was a scarlet-pink, flecked with golden spicules. His hands were huge, square, the mitts of a tournament golfer, and he wore a monstrous class ring, and a mammoth watch that probably showed phases of the moon. The truth was I found it hard to dislike Tom Bragg. With a hearty handshake and an ivory grin for everyone, he'd barrel around Europe selling bathtubs and sinks, never learning a word of Italian or French or German, but making friends everywhere.

We crossed the Pont d'Iena. I could see, hanging in the morning haze, the twin curving halls of the Palais de Chaillot. It was a good day to motor out of Paris and visit Loire châteaux, to buy picnic lunches—slabs of home-made pâté and crusty bread and fat aromatic peaches.

"Tom and I are always stumbling across people," Evie gushed.

Ah, but how badly had they stumbled?

"How is Vannie?" I asked.

"Okay, we hope," Bragg said cheerfully. "Said she and her pals were going to sleep on the banks of the Seine in sleeping bags. They call it a commune. That kid has lots of smarts."

"I guess she'll be at the conference. I saw her friend Harvey this morning interviewing Arno Flackman."

"Really?" Evie Bragg asked. "He's such an interesting young man. Of course, I don't agree with these student rebels, but he is brilliant, Vannie says. He was on full scholarship at Columbia when he quit."

"What kind of guy is Flackman?" Tom Bragg asked. "Sort of a mad genius, I gather."

"Flackman is an egomaniac who has to convince the world he can beat anyone up if he wants to. He's the only revolutionary who's also a beautiful person, a cross between Ché Guevara and Suzy Parker."

"Gosh, how fabulous," Evie Bragg said. "We sure are looking forward to his debate with my brother Boyle. It should be real fun."

Bragg heedlessly parked his car on the Place de Trocadero in a blue zone. Across from us rose the statue of that grand old screw-up Marshal Foch.

"You'll get a ticket," I said.

He winked at me. "Oh, they go easy on us tourists. I collect parking tickets all over Europe."

As we crossed the street, I glanced back at his 504. It had license plates marked CD—*Corps Diplomatique.*

"Friend at the embassy lent it to me," he said, as we moved around suicidal French cars.

"Pretty nice having friends like that."

"Ben, we're friendly folks," Evie said, squeezing my arm. "We're nice to everyone, and they're nice to us."

It was as if I'd won them in a raffle. Tom and Evie hung to my suede coattails and followed me through the lobby of the Musée de l'Homme into the auditorium. The place was packed, and we had to settle for seats well to the rear. There was no argument about it: Arno Flackman was King of the Conference. Boyle Huffguard, his conservative adversary in the debate, meant nothing, for all his eloquent wit. *Flackman, Flackman,* people kept humming around us. And when he appeared, his black beetling head lowered like El Toro ready to charge, his puissant figure *shlumping* across the stage in that light-heavyweight's pigeon-toed walk, there were murmurs and moans and whispers.

Malar and Veg were not in the audience, nor were the Russian hoods. I did see Tookie Cooperage gabbing with Boyle Huffguard on the stage, as her spouse Warren approached the lectern. Tookie and Huffguard were rival party-throwers and party-goers. Derek Venables was on the stage also, as a conference co-chairman, as well as a Bulgarian physiologist, a Tanzanian editor, and a Norwegian linguist. Lila Metrick, for whom I'd lusted last night—how drown the memory of that impertinence?—sat in a sea of Afro-Asian faces. She always managed something distinctive.

"Gee, Boyle looks dandy, doesn't he, Tom?" Evie Bragg asked her husband.

"Fit and feisty," Bragg said. "Boyle has plenty smarts."

Yes, Huffguard, the articulate and witty voice of the New Conservatism, was a rare bird. Long and pale, like a hothouse asparagus, his skin was curiously pink-toned and he had green teeth which he bared in a death's head grin to underscore all those clever points he made in debate. He had long lank black hair and slanted eyes which he kept shut most of the time, reminiscing about the twelfth century and the Early Christians. He always dressed in funereal black, in mourning, as he put it, "for the death of virtue and honor in the modern gnostic world."

"We welcome the delegates," Cooperage said, in rich tones, "and we are delighted that two such articulate and original American thinkers have consented to open this afternoon's session."

The audience fiddled with their plastic earpieces and began dialing for languages on their small shortwave receivers. You could get Cooperage in French, Spanish, German, Russian, Arabic, and Swahili.

"Mr. Huffguard is a fresh voice on the American political

scene, who, single-handed, has revived conservative argument in America . . ."

"We're proud of Boyle," Evie Bragg said in a loud voice.

"I don't blame you. Is his magazine still in favor of shooting Earl Warren?"

"Oh, Benny," she said, reaching across her hubby's lap to stroke my hand. "Boyle was just needling you silly liberals."

"You guys can't take a joke," Tom Bragg said. "Don't you know when you're being put on?"

"Hey, Tom, there's Vannie," Mrs. Bragg said. She pointed to a distant rear corner of the hall.

Bragg turned in his seat and half-rose. "Yup, that's our gal." As he moved, his jacket hiked up and I saw a small black automatic pistol, an evil insect of a weapon, tucked into a black leather holster in his belt. Evie Bragg saw me staring at the gun and gave me a dopey grin. I said nothing.

"There is no clearer, more trenchant revolutionary voice in America today than that of Arno Flackman, my dear old friend," Cooperage was saying. "Novelist, playwright, poet, critic, a man for all seasons, a man never afraid to put his courage and his strength on the line for his beliefs."

During this honey-dripping accolade, Flackman hunched forward, his huge head almost between his knees. Aloof, secure, he was ill-equipped to hide his contempt for the lesser breeds in front of him.

"You always pack heat?" I asked Bragg casually.

"Beg pardon, Ben?"

"Cut the crap, Tom. I saw John Roscoe in your belt. You walk around Paris with an unregistered piece you can get into beaucoup trouble with the French fuzz. The brass back at Academy Fixtures might have to yank you home *tout de suite*."

"Heat? Oh, the gun."

"You betcha. They catch you carrying that rod, your passport won't be worth doodly."

He crinkled his blunt nose and his eyes were merry. Cold,

but merry. "Like I said, Ben, I have lotsa friends in town."

"Like the ones who lend you a brand-new Peugeot 504 with CD plates?"

A Sudanese lawyer, seated in back of us, shushed me, and I turned to apologize. Dr. Jabali, in white shirt and dark glasses, bowed his head to me.

"Of course I am in favor of hydrogen bombs," Boyle Huffguard was nasalizing. "More and bigger bombs. And perhaps a few might be dropped on the Red Chinese tomorrow, simply to dramatize the firm intention of the Christian West to uphold morality and decency and virtue in a world gone mad. So long as godless communism threatens the world, we must be prepared to kill and destroy its amoral leaders. I daresay Mr. Flackman will disagree with me, but he is, and always has been, an exemplar, a paradigmatic type, an archetype of the left-wing naïf."

When this was translated for the unwashed, there was a good deal of angry murmuring. Say what you will about the assorted intellectuals, scientists, and writers, they didn't like hydrogen bombs.

"Of course I disagree with you, Huffy," Flackman grumbled. "You have murder in your heart. You lack compassion. You lack understanding. I can forgive you your desire to drop hydrogen bombs. That is purely a political matter. But when you depict me as a paradigmatic left-liberal, I bridle. I am no man's political slave. No one owns Flackman . . ."

What was marvelous about these two was their total alienation from ordinary people. *Compassion!* Neither of them had compassion for anything except their own skin. And so they fondled one another in public, simulating great debate and argument, but united in admiration for their flesh.

"Now I'd go into greater detail on this whole matter of the arms race," Flackman said hoarsely, "but I'm in the middle of a major project, a play, unlike any ever done in America, one in which I will restructure the entire shape of drama for a long time, by far the best thing I've ever done, and I'm on a tough

172

schedule, so I don't want to waste too much of my time arguing with my friend Huffy point by point. I respect and admire the man if not his views . . ."

Translation: Huffguard and I are elitist figures, patrician types, and we really shouldn't be obliged to perform in front of you slobs.

"Yes, well said, Arno," Huffguard gasped. "But Red China persists . . ."

There was a good deal of this mutual stroking and licking: Tory and Bolshevik loving one another up to help sales. I was beginning to fall asleep, when I felt Tom Bragg tugging at my sleeve.

"You and I have a few things to tell each other," he said, letting the words slip softly from his mouth.

"Shall we start now?"

"Better if we go somewhere."

Caution, my native cowardice, prevented me from agreeing. "Heck, Tom, you and Evie wouldn't want to run out on Boyle. Even if he and Arno are the dullest act since the Dolly Sisters."

Grinning, he arched his thick neck and scratched imaginary stubble: Mr. Tournament Golfer being coy about that little trick he has for making the green in three off that dog leg on the fourteenth hole.

". . . hope I'm being clear that I wouldn't be on this stage with Boyle Huffguard unless I respected the man, if not his opinions, he and I understand . . ."

More, more, more of this unctuous garbage. And Huffguard responding:

". . . no matter how we differ on politics we regard one another as worthy opponents and we have great respect for each other's talent, each other's gifts . . ."

Respect this, Jack. I've got your *respect* right here in my jockey shorts. A convulsive nausea roiled my guts; reverse peristalsis threatened to explode onion roll all over the Palais de Chaillot. There they sat, rubbing each other down in public—and the public devoured it, absorbed it, was hypnotized by it.

"Tom," I whispered. "You first."

"Leave?"

"Nope. Tell me who you're with. Who supplied the hardware and the CD plates. Then I'll tell you."

"I hide nothing, Benny. Good old Academy Fixtures."

"Bullshit, buddy. Not with that thing you're wearing."

"Evie gets nervous in foreign countries."

"She looks pretty calm. Tom, you were tailing me today. You just didn't find me on the Avenue de la Bourdonnais."

"Coincidence, kid."

An Italian astronomer, one Dottore Mafalda, according to his ID card, shushed us into silence.

"It is my belief," Huffguard drawled, "that the protest marches of our young citizens are, in effect, death marches, symbolizing the West's compulsion to commit suicide, demonstrations by the viscous scum and slime of our society . . ."

This was vintage Huffguard. Flackman had often marched with young protesters and written at length about their goodness and innocence. But there was no protest from him. He and Cooperage merely lolled in their chairs, as Huffguard went on, describing the recent student protests as "the repellent trailings of snails and slugs."

"Yoch, yoch," Flackman chuckled. "My dear friend Huffy goes a little far, but I won't make any major rebuttal because I know he's a sweet kind man, and that his rhetoric outpaces the essential decency in his heart . . ."

"Bourgeois tricksters!"

The voice was the voice of Harvey Ungerleider. He was standing at the side of the auditorium with a dozen of his young battle-jacketed, blue-denim'd band. Vannie Bragg was there, in a khaki poncho.

Heads turned to look at the young people, those ragged anarchists. There was some nervous muttering. Flackman, for the first time, looked uneasy. He had marched with the wild kids, and had written a few complimentary things about them. But the truth was, he detested them.

"Establishment fink!" Vannie screamed. "You won't co-opt us with your cheap lies!"

There were shushing sounds all around. Cooperage whacked his gavel and cautioned Ungerleider's Raiders to be more mannerly; there would be a question-and-answer period later.

"Does it cramp your style," I asked Bragg, "to have a daughter who runs with that wolfpack? Ever file a report on your own kid?"

"Really know how to hurt a guy, don't you, Benny?"

He was one of *ours*. From the flat straw skimmer, the starched pale blue seersucker suit, the crepe-soled cordovans, the huge ring on his thick hand, he was the quintessential country-club jock, a stone-jawed, clear-eyed prototype of middle-class virtue. He was too damn good. No foreign agent would ever believe that such a square, straight Protestant was doing CIA or FBI dirty-work.

"The conservative tide is sweeping America," Boyle Huffguard was braying. "It will soon be worldwide. This turning to freedom, virtue, honor, the old Christian mysteries, the stratified society based on natural law and God-given rules . . ."

As Sam Johnson told us, the loudest yelps for liberty come from the drivers of slaves. Huffguard was heir to a mail-order-house fortune and had once, in his intemperate youth, written that the leaders of the NAACP were "persistently aiding the international communist conspiracy by upsetting the natural order of the republic." Ah yes, a lovable fellow.

"Boyle really told 'em, hey, honey?" Bragg asked his wife.

Evie agreed. "I'm darn proud of the kid brother."

"And the way he handled those two radicals up there."

I stared at Bragg. "They wanted to be handled, Tom. It's their way of life."

Cooperage was concluding the dialogue by praising both

panelists for their "frank and refreshingly literate exploration" of major issues.

"I do hope, as an American writer and editor," Cooperage said, "that our European friends and, even more so, our Third World friends at this conference will appreciate the manner in which Americans who differ widely on important matters can debate these matters in a civil and honest manner . . ."

Anticipating his call for questions, I was on my feet, waving my hands madly. "Mr. Moderator, Mr. Moderator! I have a question for Mr. Huffguard!"

Cooperage's eyes tried to avoid me—he'd barely concluded his browning of the panelists—but he could find no other raised hands.

"Mr. Huffguard, a question for you," I bellowed. "Did I understand you to say that a great conservative tide is sweeping America?"

"Yes. That is evident."

"To what do you attribute this political change, sir?"

"Many things, but foremost the realization of most Americans that they long to be free of tyrannical government edicts and restraints, of bureaucratic strangulation."

"Would you not agree, sir," I barged on, "that apart from all that abstract nonsense, the real reason for this so-called conservative tide, which fills you with such joy, is the utter fear and consuming hatred that many Americans have for black people? And is it not a fact that you and your alleged conservative allies in politics and the press gleefully exploit these fears and hatreds daily, now that the black man is at long last demanding what he deserves? And that what you so airily and happily call *conservatism* is not that at all, but murderous hatred of the Negro? Is not the common denominator, I say, the bedrock *essential*, of every single conservative political candidate in America, all the people you back, a sly, sneaky, and brutal promise to keep *shvartzers* in their place? Is it not a fact that the only, the *only* reason that labor union machinists and AFL housepainters are voting for your kind is that you promise them you will keep Negroes out of their schools and streets? In short, Mr. Huffguard, are you not full of *farfel* when you prate about conservatism—when it isn't that at all, but old-fashioned bigotry that is getting you votes and support?"

The translators had trouble keeping up with my frenzied assault, but I could see I had raised some interesting arguments. A few African delegates were applauding. My pal M. Rignac, the little French historian, was whistling, and behind me, my friend Dr. Jabali called to me:

"Veddy good, Mr. Bloodwart, veddy good."

But I got no rise out of the three high personages on the stage. Cooperage and Flackman agreed with me. They were no dopes and their hearts were in the right place. But the burning terrible truth of what I'd said—yes, folks, what is all this "conservative" crap except a respectable mask for hating blacks?—embarrassed them a little. They'd been loving up Huffguard. And I'd exposed him. They should have been across the barricades from him, not on the same platform.

"I don't think I'll ask Mr. Huffguard to answer that," Coop said firmly. "That question is not a question at all but a polemic. The gentleman was not invited to sit up here and debate, merely to ask a question. Do you agree, Huffy?"

"I really don't mind," Huffguard drawled. "I am inured to slander. Let me advise that person that he has no true comprehension of the breadth and depth of the New Conservatism. It is ridiculous to speak of us as bigots. There is no such thing as a bigoted conservative. But the atrophied liberal mind makes such accusations nevertheless." He yawned.

"I have some questions for Mr. Flackman," I shouted.

"You've had your turn," Cooperage said.

"Let heem speak!" M. Rignac called out.

"*Oui, oui, il doit parler!*"

"*Sprechen, sprechen!*"

And in Swahili, Arabic, and Urdu. By now the gist of my wild assault on Huffguard's "conservatism" had sunk in. More of this and I might end up an official delegate.

"All right, but make it short," Cooperage said. It wasn't

just the rising vote of confidence in me that had changed his attitude. I could see the wariness in Warren's face: I was a spy, a tough cookie, a man in black. Conceivably I was sending coded messages in my attacks on the panel.

"Mr. Flackman," I said, "please identify these historic personages—Wrangel, Kolchak, Denikin."

"Pffft," Arno snorted, lowering his head. "Leaders of the counterrevolutionary White Terror in Russia."

"Correct. Would you bracket your eminent colleague Mr. Huffguard with them politically?"

Huffguard's starved face managed a crooked smile. He crossed his stork's legs and slumped deep in his chair, offering me his I-eat-liberals grimace. Was he registering approval?

"Not the same, not exactly," Flackman muttered.

"But close, would you not agree? Now, Mr. Flackman, identify this name for me—Lev Davidovitch Bronstein."

"Ah, get to the point. Trotsky."

There was a crackling, a gasping in the audience. Mention Trotsky at any of these big left-intellectual gatherings and you arouse something burning and irritating, an endless source of argument.

"Chrissake, Warren, do I have to be baited by that loser?" Flackman called. "Shut him up. End the goddamn thing."

But the crowd was not to be put off. The name Trotsky had put everything in a new light.

"*Noi vogliamo sentire più de Trotsky!*" the Italian behind me yelled.

"*Antwortet an Trotsky!*" a Viennese composer cried.

"Thank you, gentlemen," I said. "I'll direct my question to Mr. Flackman now that I have gotten him to concede that there was such a person as Leon Trotsky. Some simple queries, sir. Do you have direct knowledge, Mr. Flackman, that Trotsky ever sat on a dais with Baron Wrangel, exchanged compliments with him? Did he ever go to parties at the Winter Palace and sip champagne with Denikin and tell him he was a sweet fellow? Did Trotsky ever drop tidbits to

Moscow's columnists, allowing as how though he differed with Admiral Kolchak on many issues, he nevertheless found him to be a generous, good-hearted man, a charming person? Did Trotsky ever do any of these things?"

Flackman got up. "Shut the bastard up, Cooperage, I'm leaving."

"Not yet, Mr. Flackman. I now make my charge. Your self-proclaimed mission as leader of a world revolution of left intellectuals, a man destined by his own brilliance and force of character to turn societies to the left, is a fraud. You not only sit up there with the urbane fellow who advocated shooting Earl Warren and called Martin Luther King a trouble-making captive of the Reds, but you kiss his behind, praise, fondle, and flatter him. Did Trotsky do the same for Kolchak? You bet your grandma's *knishes* he didn't. They'd have skinned him alive if they'd gotten their mitts on him."

The crowd was stirred. What was all this about Trotsky? Who was the skinny American shouting about Trotsky? Even the Braggs were studying me curiously.

"Sir, you have no shame," I cried. "You proclaim revolt, rebellion, cheer the wild children when they burn universities, and you share the same damask and silver tables with Boyle Huffguard, and attend his parties! You cannot, Mr. Flackman, bring down the temple while you cultivate the money-changers! Hors d'oeuvres, sir, are no substitute for bombs!"

"The man is insane," Flackman said. "A lumpen-left provocateur."

Huffguard did not move. He was shrewder than Flackman, and more cynical. He understood that by running with the left he might lose a Bircher here and a Minuteman there, but he picked up guilt-ridden and fearful liberals who wanted the thrill of having him make their flesh creep.

"Ah, Mr. Flackman, a bellyful of smoked salmon and an anecdote in Leonard Lyons' column will not help you on the day Cleveland burns down. Go, go, sir, into Brownsville in your Whitehouse and Hardy shoes and Tripler suit and see if you dare harangue the addicts and pushers and runners and bad mothers the way Leon Trotsky talked to the Fifteenth Petrograd Infantry from the door of a railway coach! But you can't because you are a celebrity!"

Flackman came to the microphone. "This slanderous retching by one of the lower orders of American life needs no response. It will be handled in due time. I won't defend my credentials as a revolutionary. As for my friend Huffy, he can——"

"How does he like the Bill of Rights?" I screamed.

Cooperage slammed the gavel on the lectern. "That's enough, quite enough! Siddown and shaddap, Bloodworth! Next question! Who wants to ask a question?"

"Quite a performance," Bragg muttered. "I've seen covers in my day, but that beats anything."

"My own idea," I said calmly. "The Trotsky ploy. British Intelligence says it's effective in large heterogeneous gatherings."

An East Indian in a white Nehru cap and long coat was on his feet, and he was in a rage. Trotsky had gotten to him. "I demand, I call on the three American representatives of right-revisionism sitting on the platform, three neo-colonialists, to go on record as rejecting any attempt to revive at this conference the teachings of the fascist traitor Trotsky!"

What this meant, I had no idea, nor did anyone. It was incomprehensible Indian dialectic, and the place went wild. A thickset Czech physicist was on his feet shouting that the Indian himself was a revisionist. Rival Italian factions beat each other with rolled-up newspapers. Derek Venables was standing on a seat and shrieking that if Trotsky's name were mentioned again, he would cancel the conference. Delegates began to jostle one another in the aisles and jam the exits.

"Excuse me, Tom. Evie. I have to check in with the Third International." I shoved my way past them.

A furious Jamaican, very black and very angry, was shouting that Trotsky was the father of Frantz Fanon, and that the conference should rise and honor him. "Mon, you told them, mon," he said, pumping my hand.

"Fa Chrissake, Derek," I heard Cooperage wailing. "It's your conference, Derek, shut them up! Quiet them down!"

Somehow the Braggs had shoved their way through the mob and were a step behind me. I waved good-bye and started to cross the Place de Trocadero. I wanted to find Judy and meet with her father. I'd get Malar to America or die in the effort. Just as I was about to cross and shake the Braggs, Dr. Jabali grabbed me.

"Ah, ah, Mr. Bloodwart, what a brilliant speech, sir," he gushed. His shy dark eyes were moist with affection.

"Glad you liked it, Doctor."

"It proves that these silly matters of race and religion and politics mean nothing," he said. "You, a Jew. Trotsky, a Jew. I, a Moslem. All of us in agreement. Oh, I am not a Trotsky-ite, but I believe in brotherhood, nonviolence."

I remembered seeing him lurking around the Lussac when the two Arabs were gunned down. A timed device, the French cop had told me. A scientist—Jabali.

The Braggs were on top of us as we waited for the insane traffic around the Foch statue to ease. "Hey, Ben," Tom Bragg said, "Evie and I are gonna take you to lunch." His mighty right hand seemed to pull Jabali's from my arm. It took over.

"Take Dr. Jabali, the eminent Jordanian agronomist. Dr. Jabali, Mr. and Mrs. Bragg."

"*Shalom*," Jabali said meekly. Like most traveling Arabs, he assumed that wealthy touring Americans were Jewish.

"Later, pal," Bragg said. "We got a reservation at Le Grand Véfour."

"Try Chez Les Anges over on Latour-Maubourg," I said, pulling my tortured arm away. "They make a great entrecôte in cream sauce."

It was no use. They'd made their minds up: I was to be their guest—or something. Evie got a grip on my left arm and the couple stepped off, guiding me through the murderous traffic, leaving Jabali by himself. French motorists played their afternoon game of chicken around us, bent on bloody death. We made it to the opposite side and they walked me toward the Peugeot. I was still in their potent grasp, and my mind was bright with a full-page engraving in my old *Book of Knowledge,* an illustration to a poem called "Eugene Aram" —a man in a three-cornered hat being marched off by soldiers, with the caption, "Eugene Aram with gyves upon his wrists." But who was Eugene Aram?

III

It was distressing how easily they persuaded me, by dint of their strength and their authority, to get into the back seat of the car. Evie drove. Tom sat beside me. Almost as an afterthought, he took the automatic from his belt and pointed it at me.

"Enough of that jazz, Tom," I said. "What is this, a fraternity joke?"

"Just needling you, Benny."

"What would all your pals back in the good old Deke house at Colgate think?"

"Evie and I want to make sure you don't make a run for it. We invited you to lunch, and we intend to treat you real good."

I watched the traffic whizzing around us as we turned into the Rue de Longchamps. Some big lie was called for. "Tom, you saw that Arab I was talking to? Dr. Jabali?"

"Yup."

"He's on my team. He knows you people have dragged me off. I wouldn't be surprised if someone's on your tail right now."

"Yup, we saw him," Bragg said, laughing. "And we saw his sneakers also."

"Sneakers?"

"Al Fatah. He was wearing general issue Al Fatah shoes. They're French Foreign Legion surplus. The dumb bunny is dumb even for a PLO operative. We know all about Jabali. He's one of the prize idiots at this conference. There's a dossier six inches thick on him at the Sûreté, and we've got almost as much. He was in on that bombing at the Café Lussac."

That took care of Dr. Jabali. I'd noticed his sneakers also, and I recalled Moe Bloom saying, in an offhand way, to his wife Sophie, *there's one of them*. And he was my pal, a nice Arab delegate.

"I was faking, Tom," I admitted. "Has it occurred to you that we may be on the same team?"

"We'll sure as heck find out, won't we?" He removed his straw katie and put it over the hand holding the gun.

"This is some way to find out. Pointing a gun at me."

Bragg ignored me. "Hon, turn right on the Boulevard de Lannes."

"You might do better on the Avenue Foch," I suggested.

He was impressed. "Know your way around Paris, hey, Ben?"

"Worked as a newspaperman here."

"We know. Ten years. World News Association, now defunct. Twenty-two, just out of Columbia, where you had a scholarship. You worked the overnight, midnight to eight A.M., in the old WNA offices on Rue de Lafayette. You're married to the former Felicia Amalfitano of the Bronx and you have two children, Edward, aged twelve, and Rosa, seven. You live in Hicksville, Long Island, and make your living as a free-lance writer. Leave anything important out?"

"Yes. I am the son of the late Aaron Bloodworth, a druggist on Southern Boulevard, the Bronx."

"And a founder of the Bronx Socialist Party, Eugene V. Debs chapter."

"And he was six times the man you are, you big shit."

Bragg laughed. "Ben, there isn't a drop of racial prejudice

184

in me. I do this for a living, and for my country."

"You know a hell of a lot about me."

"Our Washington people have lots of smarts."

Evie halted for a red light at the Avenue Victor Hugo. Suddenly we all fell forward with a jolt. We'd been severely nudged from the rear—typical French driving. Bragg and I looked through the rear window. An enormous pale blue Cadillac had rammed us.

"Son-of-a-bitch," Bragg said. The driver of the Cadillac was holding up his hands in a gesture of apology. "Don't get out, hon," my captor said. "Just wave to him that it's okay."

Evie did so. Obviously they wanted no delays, and had no desire to let anyone see me in custody.

"What's it going to be, Tom?" I asked. "Sodium pentothal? Rubber truncheons? The bright lights? I might as well warn you, I am a miserable coward with a low threshold for pain, and I'll say anything you want me to say, if only you stop hurting me."

No reaction from Bragg. He was peering over his shoulder, to make sure the Cadillac's owner had no desire to exchange insurance company addresses. "Hmmm? What say, Ben?"

"Suppose I told you this whole thing is a fake. That I invented it. That I've been telling lies."

"Impossible, kid. You're witting. You're engaged."

"But I'm not. I've been lying. To get some status. You know, with that literary crowd."

"Have to do better than that. Anyway, we'll get the real story in a few minutes. It won't hurt long."

Evie Bragg peered into the rear-view mirror. "Damn that kosher canoe. He's still after us. I think he wants to stop and talk about that bump."

"Ignore, sweetie," Bragg said. "I'll handle him if he stops." There was a steely edge to his voice, and I did not envy the person tooling the Cadillac through the sixteenth arrondissement.

"The damn fool," Evie said petulantly. "Imagine the gall

and the showiness of some people, driving a monster like that around Paris."

"Try turning on the Rue de la Faisander," Bragg ordered his wife. "That should get us to Porte Dauphine."

Porte Dauphine. NATO headquarters. I felt better. After all, they were our shield in western Europe.

"I've always admired NATO and what it stands for," I offered.

"I'm sure you have, kid."

We were stopped again. A moving van was unloading a sofa and easy chairs. French motorists were cursing and honking.

"We've lost him anyway," Evie Bragg said with relief.

"Got me all to yourself now, right?" I asked. "How'd you figure out I was up to something, that I was more than just a hungry American-Jewish writer?"

"You ran errands for Bloom, Benny."

"But that's all they were. Errands. I haven't the faintest idea who Bloom is or what he's up to."

He showed me the snout of the gun again. "Try again, kid. You're a lousy operative."

"Really? Where did I foul up?"

Bragg opened his mouth in a noiseless laugh. "There is no such person as Savino P. DiGiglio."

"Hah?"

"That coded letter you wrote. We ran a quick check of the Little Leagues in Hicksville. The league president is a Mr. Arnold Rainberger. We also learned some interesting things about his wife, the former Shirley Keester. She was Nassau County Chairman for Dietitians for a Vietnam Peace and a few other lefto groups. But you wouldn't know anything about that, would you, Benny?"

"I barely know the Rainbergers. Besides, if that's what's bothering you, I might as well confess. My wife has signed every single peace petition ever circulated. She brought box lunches to the kids who occupied the Sperry-Rand laboratories last year. Eggplant heroes, as I recall."

"Don't get cute. That letter of yours, those figures, the place names—they're a dead giveaway."

"So you're the fink who's been picking my pockets."

"Not me, Ben. A friend. When we cover something, it's covered."

"I guess you're way ahead of me."

Bragg looked in back. "Evie, back up, get up on the sidewalk and go around that goddamn van."

Mrs. Bragg did so. She drove as recklessly and noisily as a Frenchwoman. We careened around the truck, scattering pedestrians.

"We've had the Black Chamber working on that letter all night," Bragg said. "I got to hand it to you, you're giving them fits. Our cryptanalysts are stumped. Maybe you can make their job easier when we sit down and chat. But it really won't be necessary. They'll break it. It isn't a null cipher, or a semagram, or a linguistic concealment. For a while they thought you'd used a plain jargon code. Or an obsolete variant of the Cardano grille. But someone else pointed out no one's tried that since the Crimean War."

I rubbed my sparse beard. "Life is full of mysteries, eh, Tom? You got me on the green in three, but the putt may be harder than you figured."

"In the cup with a par five."

We burst out of the narrow street on two wheels and barrelled onto the Avenue Foch with a rubber-scorching shriek. Evie looked a little distraught.

"Maybe I'll talk," I said. "But before I do, I have to ask a trade."

"No trades, Ben. You're in a weak bargaining position."

"A favor?"

"Maybe. I'm no meanie. This is a job."

"Lay off Imre Malar and his daughter. They have nothing to do with anything I'm involved in."

"Malar? That old commie? He doesn't interest us."

Quickly I asked: "And Veg? Does he interest you?"

"Veg? Veg? Who he?"

His attempt at innocence convinced me he was greatly interested in Laszlo Veg.

"Yes, who he? And who me?" I asked. "Why are you going to all this trouble over me?"

"We don't like loose ends. And yours are just about the loosest in Paris. That's fine, hon. Pull up alongside the ambassador's car, right at the gate."

We double-parked. The NATO building was a huge palace, soaring inside the high walls. There were two uniformed French *flics* at the entrance. Beyond, I could see the bosky dells of the Bois de Boulogne.

"Out you go, Ben," Bragg said. "Don't try to run or make a fuss. This is all routine." He tucked the gun into his belt and waited for me. I walked out stiffly, studying the clouded Paris sky. *Oh they're hangin' Benny Bloodworth in the mornin'* . . .

"One last look at the sun?" I asked. "A sniff of the clear air of freedom?"

"Say, he *is* a writer," Evie Bragg said.

With a savage screech of heavy-gauge polyglass tires, the Columbia-blue Cadillac roared to a shivering halt in back of Bragg's Peugeot. Its blasting horn shattered the afternoon quiet of the elegant street.

"Bastard," Bragg murmured. "You handle him, Evie. I'll take Ben inside." He grabbed my arm and started dragging me to the opened gates. I didn't want to go.

"Hands off, you fascist pig," I protested weakly.

The door of the Cadillac burst open. Out of it flew Moses Bloom, the old gunrunner himself. He was dressed in flamboyant tourist duds—orange turtleneck sweater, two cameras, a checked porkpie hat, outsized sunglasses, a hound's-tooth sport jacket.

"Oi, Benny, Benny, vait a minute, vait for Uncle Moe!" he shouted—in one of the worst vaudeville Jewish accents I had ever heard. Bloom, literate, worldly, erudite, was trying to sound like a boor and not succeeding. Luckily, the pure ears of the Braggs were not attuned to such ethnic nuances.

"Uncle Moe!" I shouted. "So it was you who bumped into us!"

"Dot's right! I been follering you for deh lest ten meenits!"

Bragg looked as if a long pointy icicle had been shoved up his bung. He knew who Moe was and he didn't like the game at all.

"Let's go in, Mr. Bloodworth," he said. "Mr. . . . ah . . . whatever your name is . . . I've arranged a meeting for your nephew. With the NATO cultural committee. We're late as it is."

"Likevise," Moses Bloom said. He grabbed my other arm. A powerful old kibbutznik, a match for Bragg. He yanked at me, and I flew out of Bragg's grasp. "Deh name is Shtarker. Moe Shtarker from Milwaukee, Wisconsin."

"Uncle Moe," I said, "these are two acquaintances of mine, Mr. and Mrs. Bragg. He's a big man with Academy Fixtures."

"Feh. Rotten toilets. I built-it a high rise in Green Bay lest year vit dere toilets and dey broke down. Vot's deh metter mit your company, young men?"

Bragg's eyes had turned to ice-blue points. No, the accent and the costume weren't fooling him, but what could he do? "Funny how you found your nephew like this," he said.

"Vell, I saw you in deh treffick. My vife vent into a drugstore to buy a shower kepp, und ven I vas vaiting, I saw Benny in dis small lousy car. I'm sorry I gave you a smesh in deh beck, but it didn't hoit. Benny, come on, Aunt Sophie is like a vild vomen, she vants to talk mit you."

"We do have an appointment," Bragg said lamely. "Some mighty important people are waiting to meet Mr. Bloodworth."

Bloom looked suspiciously at the NATO building. "Vat is dis NATO? Vat kind of a vaste deh texpayer's money, hah? Besides, you are a toilet salesman, no. Vat is mit NATO?"

"I . . . ah . . . I am on the cultural committee . . ."

"So make a new appointment, misteh." He pulled me toward the Cadillac. The Braggs were glaring at him. A frozen smile bared Tom's terrible teeth.

"*Zeit gezundt*, pipple. Benny, Aunt Sophie is vaiting on pins und needles to see her nephew. All alone she sits in a sveet vun hundred dollars a day by deh Plezeh Etenee. Come, ve'll have a nice lunch, und tonight ve'll all go by deh Crazy Huss."

"The committee will be disappointed," Bragg called after me.

"Denks anyvay," Bloom shouted back. "Alvays a pleasure."

We left them there—two healthy tributes to balanced diets and a belief in the free market. I could see Bragg's lips form an unspoken *son-of-a-bitch*.

We were back on Avenue Foch, riding toward the center of Paris.

"Your accent stinks," I said.

"Good enough for him."

"Who is he?"

"Thomas Ewing Bragg. DIA."

"What's that?"

"Defense Intelligence Agency. Works as a team with his wife. He wasn't lying. He also sells bathtubs. A lot of these fellows moonlight."

"What did he want me for?"

Bloom's burned, creased face seemed to gather in a knot around his parched lips. "You tell lies, you'll get in trouble. I think he wanted you before the CIA got you. People like you they fight over. You're a catch."

"Why? Why am I so special?"

"Inter-agency rivals, boychick. The DIA is new. But it's got muscle. Reports right to the Joint Chiefs."

"You'd think they could afford smarter people than the Braggs."

"Oh, they got them. Those two are small operators." He drove carefully, wheeling the huge Cadillac around sharp turns, threading it through constricted streets.

"What's with the tourist outfit?" I asked.

"I had a feeling you'd be in trouble after the way you were shooting your mouth off. Why do you make trouble for me?"

I sank into the seat. "Sorry, Moe. That literary mob destroyed my fragile ego. Flackman. Metrick. Cooperage. The Fag Kings. I had to assert myself."

"So you told Warren Cooperage you were a spy, that you were sent here to get Malar to defect."

"Well . . . *he* more or less invented that part."

"Did it occur to you it would gum up my dealings with Veg?"

"Frankly, that's what gave me the idea. I claimed another Hungarian."

"The wrong one."

Bloom dropped the Cadillac at a small garage on the Avenue de Versailles. A short Semitic-looking mechanic exchanged a few words with him and we took a cab to a small Basque restaurant on the Avenue de la Motte-Picquet near the Ecole Militaire.

"Listen," I said, "I'm sorry if I've goofed things for you, but you didn't level with me either. You were supposed to be in Budapest. You never left Paris."

Bloom sipped some Badoit and frowned at his *moules marinières*.

"And you were in the Café Lussac when those Arabs bombed it. They were after you. The French police told me. How'd you get in and out so fast?"

"Don't believe what French police tell you."

"And Bragg says that that nice Arab scientist, Dr. Jabali, is a top man with the Al Fatah. He's a Palestine Liberation agent, maybe the head of their whole operation in western Europe. I saw him running away from the café, and he was making believe he was upset."

Moe pushed his steel-rimmed specs on to his lumpy forehead. "Bragg said that? He identified Jabali?"

"That's right. I suppose you knew it all the time."

"Of course. From his brown sneakers."

"And why," I yelled, "does everyone want Laszlo Veg? What's so great about that sourpussed Hungarian?"

"You told him about the seat on the eastern wall?" Bloom asked.

"He wasn't interested. I figured that out myself. The seats on the eastern wall were reserved for the elders of the synagogue, the best-educated, most-esteemed Jews."

"He doesn't deserve it. I've known him a long time, and he's a louse."

"But you're offering him a big job in Israel. What? Head of the Technion?"

"A better job than he's ever had."

"I also had that letter translated from Yiddish. It was all about how the communists were as bad as the Nazis, and that he'd better get out."

Bloom yawned. "Yeh. I saw you go into the delicatessen this morning." He stood up and waved to his wife. She walked toward us.

"Between you and Bragg I'll never walk alone."

Sophie Bloom exchanged a few Hebrew words—I cursed my ignorance—and sat down. She was worried about me. "Is the boy all right, Moe? Maybe you should stop involving other people."

"I'm fine, Mrs. Bloom, honest. I have no idea what Moe is up to, but I'm enjoying it. I think."

"Anything?" Bloom asked his wife. "Any calls?"

The small, pretty auburn-haired woman shook her head. "Not a word."

They were, I gathered, another team. "Why does everybody want Laszlo Veg? He's an animal-trainer, that's all. He conditions rats. Moe, you should see the one he had at the apartment in Gobelins. It beat the hell out of a tomcat."

Sophie Bloom smiled cryptically. "You should see what he's done with monkeys."

Bloom cautioned her with a gnarled hand. "Those two KGB bums—Pochastny and the Armenian. They've got him scared stiff."

"They aren't so tough," I bragged. "I told Keramoulian I knew he was from the Thirteenth Directorate and it shut him up."

Bloom arched his white eyebrows. "Keramoulian has murdered twenty people, sonny. Mr. Bloody Business. Assassinations, terrorism, kidnapping. A guy in Moscow named Rodin runs it, but it's so secret, no one's ever seen him for sure."

I gulped. My appetite for the *moules* was gone. All I could manage was more Badoit. "Holy smoke, Moe, warn me next time."

"You they don't care about," he said. "You're just a pest. They'll figure you out soon enough, and they'll make a deal with Bragg to send you home."

"I'm not going. I'm in this all the way, whatever it is."

"As a matter of fact, Soph, I think Benny can help us, just because of those lies he's told. No one's going to believe he's with anyone. Bragg can't afford to let you run around Paris shooting your mouth off. You're an American. A conference delegate. He'll tell the KGB as soon as he checks you out."

"But . . . but . . . they're enemies . . . the free world and godless communism . . . they aren't supposed to co-operate."

"They can't let an amateur like you, a *patzer*, louse up their business."

"Hah!" I shouted. "That shows how much you know! Bragg is fooled all the way! He tailed me all morning and forced me to go to NATO headquarters! He thinks I'm in black!"

Bloom was rubbing his iron chin; his eyes were shut. The gaudy tourist rig didn't sit with his scarred face. "Wait, wait, this all makes sense," he said. "If you keep up this nonsense about getting Malar out of the country . . ."

"Leave it to Cooperage. The whole conference knows."

"Better. You see, Soph, if we can take some of the heat off us, maybe even get the word out we've given up on Veg, and let Benny keep blabbing about Malar, we might be able to get a second crack at him. I'm not sure, with those Russian thugs around him, but . . ."

"A few questions, Moe," I said.

"Go ahead, sonny boy."

"There was something in that letter about Veg's defection being a matter of survival. Is somebody sick, and needs a top neurologist?"

He frowned. "Yeh, yeh, you might say that. Something like that."

"And why did you pick me out at Orly yesterday to carry the white rat and find Laszlo Veg?"

"You looked reliable."

"Moe knew about you," Sophie said. "You once said some nice things about him in an interview. He never forgets."

No, it didn't matter how old you were, or how long you had fought the literary wars. A kind word was always welcome. It shouldn't have puzzled me in Moe Bloom's case: he was scarred and calloused, but his skin was still tender.

"I'll make you a little speech about American-Jewish writers," Moe said. "There's a whole crowd of them don't know what to do about Israel. It confounds them."

"But I'm no Zionist. I've never been there."

"Doesn't matter," Bloom said. "Don't be insulted, but you aren't important enough, I mean with the literary crowd, to be anti-Israel."

"I'm not offended. Just befuddled."

"I'll explain. First, there are the egomaniacs, the ones who push and promote and show their genitals in public. For them, Israel is an insult. It's tougher and smarter and more original than they are, so they can't stand it. It's also a true *community*, maybe the only one left in the world. And they're only

194

interested in their own skin, so to hell with communities, particularly one founded and run by their coreligionists. I include those fellows who write about beating their meat, beating up other people, all their own personal glorious lunacies. How can they identify with Israel, when the essence of that place is the submergence of the ego to a common goal? Can you see Flackman on a kibbutz?

"Second, there's the ex-communists who never got over it, and the Marxists who still believe. They don't know that as far back as 1903 Lenin was denouncing Zionism as reactionary and regressive. They don't know that the Bolsheviks and the other lefto jerks have opposed us for years, hated us. Well, these people have no use for Israel, and their kids, like that pisspot Ungerleider, go around praising the Al Fatah and hoping that we get destroyed and wiped out again. How full of self-hate can you be?

"And that's the third part, that perverse Jewish self-hatred, which infects both the egomaniacs, the exhibitors as well as the commies. It's convenient to them we got an Israel, so they hate it, or move away from it, or act embarrassed when it's mentioned.

"As for me, the Bolsheviks have had it in for me since I was a kid in Cleveland and distributed Zionist leaflets. You see, I was a traitor. Any smart Jewish boy should have been with them, with all that Marxist crap, which in the long run, turned into another kind of anti-Semitism. They'll even tell you everything is swell in the Soviet Union for our people. Hah! Nothing's been swell there for years. Soph knows better than I do."

The little woman with the sad witty eyes looked at me; she seemed ready to cry. "They killed my parents."

"Who? Who? The Nazis?" I stared at the blue number on her arm.

"The Nazis got most of Soph's family. They were Czechs. Terezin." Bloom took off his glasses and cleaned them with his handkerchief in vigorous, angry motions. The gesture reminded me of my father, who, like Moe, was a short, strong, impatient man, given to quick irritable moves.

"Sophie spent two years in Terezin, near Prague. That's where I met her. Her mother and father were in Moscow during the war. He was Norbert Lebonik. Socialist leader. The Russians told him he could stay in the Soviet Union. Let's face it, Sophie, he was your dear father but he was a *shlemiel*. He should have kept his mouth shut, but he wrote a letter to Stalin suggesting a worldwide alliance of the left, a new Popular Front, all the socialists and communists and all the in-betweens in one big tent."

"Well . . . it was the war," I said. "When someone like Hitler is threatening to kill all of you, you'll take anybody for an ally. Even the devil."

"True," Bloom said. "But don't go kissing the devil's ass unless you have to. Stalin took Lebonik's letter and wrote on the margin two words: '*Shoot him.*' So Beria did. And also Sophie's mother and a few dozen other Jewish intellectuals who were hoping they'd survive Hitler in the USSR. It's a long, dirty story, boychick, but I tell you this just to give you an idea."

"Of what?"

"What we're up against in Eretz. I learned one lesson all these years. It's okay to have friends and allies and treaties. We need them, because we're small. But in the long run nobody is *really* your friend and you have to do it yourself."

Mrs. Bloom was dabbing at her eyes. Moe took her hand. "Sorry, Soph, but it was only to make the kid understand us a little better."

"I do, Moe."

He signaled the waiter. "Let's go to your hotel. I want to see if I can grab Veg by the throat."

Moses and I found Judy Malar in the lobby of the Bavard, handing out brochures at the Bridge Building desk. I introduced Bloom to her; she had not heard of him.

"Is Professor Veg around?" he asked brusquely.

"No. Papa is resting at the apartment, and Uncle Latzi is looking after him. Papa wants to be sure he is well rested for his speech tomorrow."

I told Bloom about the attack on Malar the night before.

"And, Mr. Pochastny, that editor, and his friend Mr. Keramoulian are with them?" Bloom asked.

"Mr. Keramoulian is with them. There is Mr. Pochastny." She pointed across the lobby.

The KGB man, in his rumpled gray suit, was chatting with Dr. Jabali and another Arab in a kaffiyeh.

"Pochastny," Moe muttered. "Real name Antipov. Reports directly to Lubianka. Top echelon, Benny. Speaks perfect English with a New York accent, right?"

"I'm impressed. He knows all about you, also. Says you're with the Shin-Bet."

"I don't underestimate him."

Pochastny started toward us; Judy turned pale. "I . . . I . . . am sorry. But I must not talk to you any longer. I cannot explain." She retreated to her place behind the long table.

"Yeh, yeh, they've put the lid on." Bloom was staring at Pochastny. The Russian grinned back at him. They were sending out signals. "They won't let us get near Veg or Malar. They'll let Malar make his speech tomorrow, escort both of them to an Aeroflot plane, and they'll be out of Paris before we can do a damn thing. Right to Budapest, if they've behaved. Or Moscow, if they've acted up."

"I'm lost, Moe. The word is that Malar is going to deliver a big anti-Soviet blast in front of all these delegates. Why don't they pack him up and ship him home right now?"

Bloom scratched his white bristles. "I got a few theories, but I'm not certain. I'll know when he starts to talk tomorrow."

Warren Cooperage, in a six-buttoned lavender suit, spied us and waltzed across the lobby. "Moses Bloom! Moses

Bloom! Hero of my youth!" He hugged Moe and kissed him. Bloom was impassive.

"Cut the crap, Cooperage." Bloom was not happy with the tribute. "Was it you, or your wife, who called me 'an interesting relic of the thirties, a premature revolutionary possessed of more polemics than personalized art, a professional pitchman for the wildest of the Zionist incendiaries'?"

"I never wrote that about you, Moe."

"Then one of your friends did, one of those masturbators or Stalin-lovers."

Coop smiled his warm smile. "Same old Moe, hey? Still the old paranoid battler for the cause?"

Out of the creaky lift came Tookie Cooperage, on her arm the venerable James Warfield Keen, doddering, lips fluttering. "We have just got the nicest news!" she gurgled. "Jim's book made the Literary Guild!"

There were *oohs* and *ahs* and handshakes, but you never in your life saw three more insanely jealous grown men than Bloom, Cooperage, and myself.

"Wow!" Cooperage barked. "Isn't it great, Jimmy! It's been your *turn* for a long time!"

Your *turn?* Do you see what I mean about these people— the way they pass success around, like a pipeful of opium?

Tookie Cooperage raised her bony arms—gold bracelets made a clanging noise. Her scarlet miniskirt was indecently short; her legs were like a flamingo's.

"Why, why, it's Mr. Bloom," Keen said huskily. "Knew you, knew you back in the old days. Sacco and Vanzetti. Angelo Herndon. Scottsboro. Yes, all the great causes."

"Some were and some weren't," Bloom said. "I liked your exposé of Mrs. Roosevelt in Huffguard's magazine, Keen. And that article proving General MacArthur was a great American who could have saved us from radicals like Harry Truman impressed me also. You certainly have made a big trip, Jim."

"Ah yes . . . yes . . ." Keen's eyes were closed.

"Jim, I remember when we were a lot younger, you once

got beat up organizing the peach pickers in Georgia," Bloom said—not angrily, or wickedly, but with compassion. "My hat was off to you then. You had something."

"Ah, different times, different attitudes."

"And a few weeks ago I read where you wrote that the grape pickers in California are a bunch of troublemaking Mexican traitors and should be glad the growers give them any money at all. How does a man make a trip like that, Jim? How does he end up his life kissing Boyle Huffguard's ass?"

Tookie Cooperage clapped a hand over her mouth. The affront to her was far greater than the insult suffered by Keen. "Ah declare, Mr. Bloom, that sort of talk is uncalled for, and Ah think you . . ."

"No, no, my dear," Keen whispered. "Mr. Bloom perhaps has a point. But I am too tired to argue it right now. Perhaps I had no Palestine to defend, so I lost interest in all my causes . . ."

He shuffled off. The Cooperages helped support him in his creaky passage across the lobby.

Pochastny somehow had moved behind us and had been listening. I had no idea what he made of the confrontation. Or had it been one? In both Keen and Bloom I sensed a mutual respect, a nostalgia for old honorable battles. There was some truth to what Keen had said; he'd lost all his causes.

"Hi, fellah," Pochastny said. "Mr. Bloom, a pleasure. Heard all about you."

"Yeah? From whom? KGB headquarters?"

"Ah come on, fellah. We know who you're with. We know what you want. But you're out of your class, guy. Wise up and tell your friends in Allenby Street they're nuts if they think they can pull it off. I tell you this like a friend. There isn't a drop of anti-Semitic blood in me. Not a drop. This is politics, fellah. Zionism is politics, that's all. Bad politics."

"What's politics to you, Antipov, is life and death to those people," Bloom said softly. "Don't you know you can't frighten a man who's been through Auschwitz?"

"Old stuff, fellah. We beat the Nazis for you people."

"Not for us. For yourself. Good, we were glad. And grateful. I know all about Stalingrad. So we were lucky bystanders. You'd think you would understand what it is to want to live. Or maybe you're just jealous of people who can work together without sticking everybody in jail, or turning secret police loose on them. Ah, the hell with it. I've been having these arguments too long, and I'm tired."

Pochastny rubbed his sweaty nose. "That's the idea, fellah. Why don't you just quit? You're tired." He waddled away from us to talk to Judy Malar. Once she turned to us—as if in appeal—and then, with a grave and fearful face, redirected her attention to Pochastny-Antipov.

Bloom told me to keep an eye on her the rest of the day. She was the only member of our Hungarian party still on the loose. He had some nosing around to do. He walked, in quick steps, to the door, where M. Dunand, the French fuzz, was waiting for him. I couldn't hear what they said, but I could imagine. Bloom, a clay pigeon as far as they were concerned, was being asked to get out of town. I saw Moe shaking his head negatively and Dunand throwing his hands up in annoyance. Then the two of them walked out: Moe was going to be watched whether he liked it or not.

I turned away as they exited. Judy Malar and Pochastny were gone. Evidently they had decided that she, like her father and Uncle Latzi, could not be allowed to roam Paris unchaperoned. It seemed more and more unlikely that I'd have a shot at my Hungarian again, or Moe Bloom at his.

Early that evening, not having heard from Bloom, bereft even of Louise Latour's boozy company, I wandered into the bar of the Bavard and ordered a bottle of Badoit.

"Ah, Bloodworth. May I?"

It was co-chairman Derek Venables. I had the feeling that he'd been lurking around the dim lobby waiting for me. But why? I was small beer in the American delegation, and Venables was a British Cooperage, who knew everyone important and made every conference.

"Please do, Derek." He sat down and ordered a vermouth cassis. Around his neck was the thick golden chain and the golden cross. "Excuse my stupidity, Derek, but I always heard you were a lefty of some kind. Trotsky-ite, what-not. Why the big crucifix?"

"I am a Chwistian. A veddy devout Chwistian."

"Since when?"

"The lahst twenty yeahs or so. Since the death of Stalin. My eyes were opened, as it were."

I chewed on this a few minutes. "You needed his death to tell you he'd been a rat all those years? Man, you're a poet, or a critic or something. Didn't you ever hear of Mandelstamm or Isaac Babel? And the millions of kulaks, the starvings and the murders? He had to die to convince you he was a bad guy?"

"It's quate compwicated. Not atall that simple. Not atall."

There is something about the way the educated Briton pipes out his words that gives him a staggering advantage over boobs like me with their harsh Bronx vowels and dentalized T's. Do people like Venables wake up at three in the morning and sound like that? Your Oxonian or Cantabrigian type can mouth the dullest, most commonplace, most dreary banalities and make them sound like Scripture, golden apothegms, pearly aphorisms.

"And what kind of Chw——Christian are you, Derek?"

"I am an Anglo-Catholic."

"Ah, like G. K. Chesterton. Or Hilaire Belloc."

"Pwehaps."

"Genteel anti-Semites."

"No, no, not atall. If you know anything about me, you know I am fwee of anything wike that."

The Order of the Lily! *The Vatican honor!* Dear Anglo-Catholic Venables! Could he have been the man who jumped his co-chairman in a dirty *passage* off the Rue St. Denis?

"Know anything about Papal honors?"

"I'm afwaid not. My concept of my church is a church of abstwactions, more concerned with the shadows of faith than the substance of medals and bwightly colored sashes and so forth."

"Order of the Lily mean anything? Founded by Pope Paul III as a reward to defenders of the Patrimony of Peter?"

"Haven't the foggiest, old boy."

He couldn't have been lying. Venables was an odd bird, an unpeggable kind of footloose intellectual. What his Anglo-Catholicism consisted of, and why he decided he needed confession and communion after Joe Stalin cashed in his chips, I couldn't figure out. Still, with all my probing, he seemed determined to sit with me, and was not offended.

"I understand Pwofessor Veg has done some wemarkable things with wabowatory animals. Has he spoken to you about his watest work?"

"I'm afraid not."

"With wats? White wats?"

"Well, I've heard a thing or two, nothing specific."

Venables stroked his richly waved locks. His aristocratic nose pointed to the ceiling and I could look deep into his hairy nostrils.

"You bwought him a wat, didn't you?"

"It was killed. Murdered right in my woom. Room."

"Ah, how twagic. Have you seen any of his other wee beasties? I've heard they do incwedible things."

The dainty fellow was working for someone; if not the Vatican, British Intelligence. But he'd get nothing from me. I would not tell him a thing about Tibor, the rat who beat up the concierge's cat.

"You should get him to give a lecture while he's here, Derek," I said. "After all, you're co-chairman. After Malar makes his big speech tomorrow, why not schedule Veg, with a demonstration of his trained rats? It could be the hit of the conference. Of course I'm told that Pavlovian conditioning and reenforcing aren't anything original, and behavioral scientists would know that he's peddling old stuff."

Venables turned his elegant head sideways. "Weally? He's just involved in Pavwovian conditioning?"

"I'm guessing. I don't know."

"Ah . . ." He opened his horsey mouth wide. "Ah . . . I wonder does your fwiend Mr. Bwoom know."

"Ask him."

"Wheah would he be at the moment?"

"At the moment? I guess he's lecturing on the Theory and Practice of the Kibbutz at the Union Israelite. He's sort of single-minded on the subject."

Venables assembled his endless legs and got up. "Shall we get cwacking?"

"Where?"

"Why, the Cooperages' pahty for Keen."

"I wasn't invited."

"Ew."

Careful there, Derek baby. Like his American counterparts, the limey wanted to associate only with equals. I'd seen him cut a few elderly lady translators dead, and I had the feeling he had no special use for me. But the man wanted to pump me about Veg. He'd gotten the word from Cooperage that I knew the Hungarians, and he was willing to overlook my thin credentials. Ah, the Order of the Lily. Or *Opus Dei?* I'd read about them, those hard-working secretive Roman Catholic layman. It was not unlikely that Venables, having made the Grand Tour of the left, was now in bed with the agents of Mother Church, and liking it.

"You see, Der, that crowd doesn't dig me," I said soulfully. "Especially after the way I took after Arno last night."

"Quate. Do come along in any case. Ahfter all, if the confewence co-chairman cahn't invite a fwiend to a pahty, who can?"

Who indeed? Mr. Derek Venables was after something. So long as I maintained the lies of my secret agentry and my inside track with Malar and Veg he'd be after me.

We walked out of the Bavard and into a grim scene on the sidewalk. That young file-crapper and library-burner, Harvey Ungerleider, was baiting Chipper Latour, Louise Latour's nephew, and his dirty, blue-jeaned mob was enjoying it far too much. I knew whose side I was on. Young Chipper had my sympathies; as for Harvey and his Maoists, or what the hell ever they were, they left me with a numb helplessness.

Dear Lord, I know all about their idealism and their political awareness and how they are more noble than we are. But somehow I cannot see how civilization is advanced by burning down Columbia and Berkeley and the Sorbonne; not very far anyway. Let them take their tough talk and dirty words to the hard-hats in the AFL, to the *Force Ouvrière*, and see how far they get. Yes, yes, more participatory democracy, my idealistic children! But you'd better be clear as to who does the participating. Vinnie Calabrese, steamfitter, in a yellow helmet, and Charlie O'Toole, plasterer, in blue denims, will gladly wipe the floor up with you, ideals and all.

"Fuckin' fascist," Ungerleider was sneering. "Goddamn Boy Scouts are run by the Defense Department. What the hell ya' doin' here?"

Chipper Latour's eyes were misty behind his rimless glasses. I didn't see Louise anywhere.

"That's uncalled for," the Eagle Scout said. He was wearing the wide sash with the merit badges. "I didn't insult you because you have a beard."

"Ever go down on someone?" Vannie Bragg hissed at him.

"You needn't be so fresh," Chipper Latour said. "You have no idea what good work the Scouts do in the black ghettos. That was my summer project last year. I helped clean up a whole block in Detroit."

"You stink, you pig," Ungerleider said. "I'd like to tear that lousy uniform off you, badges and all."

"Well, don't you try." Chip looked around helplessly. A small crowd had gathered—a Ghanaian in a yellow robe, a man in a Nehru cap. Young Latour saw me and smiled: a friend.

"Listen, Chipper, go on inside," I said. "That gang of trash may decide to jump you. They're good at beating up professors, researchers, and people with eyeglasses."

"Screw off, Bloodworth," Harvey Ungerleider growled. "Who you workin' for? Hearst? Some other fascist?"

Ah, their innocence, their soiled romanticism. "Ungerleider, your rudeness is equaled only by your stupidity. There are few more liberal organizations in America than the Hearst Corporation. They have done more for hiring blacks than you and your ragbag army of charlatans."

"Hit him, Harve," Vannie said.

"*Au poiteaux!*"

"*Al paradón.*"

"I say," Derek Venables said nervously. "Cahn't we move on? I hate these bwoody stweet confwontations."

Harvey Ungerleider, with the standard bravery of these revolutionary brats—yes, yes, I admire the *others*, the kid rebels who are fair and decent and argue intelligently—was after plains game, meat for the pot.

"That friggin' Boy Scout grosses me out," he said. And he walked up to Chipper and yanked his green-and-gold scarf out of its ring holder. "I think I'll shame you in front of everyone, you racist."

I couldn't bear to watch any more of this. I cannot abide brutality or bullying, or any kind of meanness. Too many big bastards belted me around when I was a kid.

I shoved Harvey Ungerleider. "Get away from him. You are a disgrace to the youth movement. The kid did nothing to you."

"It's all right, Mr. Bloodworth," Chipper Latour piped. He retied his 'kerchief and tucked it into the golden BSA ring.

Ungerleider was studying me carefully. I had a slight advantage over him in height, but he was much chunkier, almost fat, and he was disturbingly broad in the chest, his

205

titties bulging the dirty white T-shirt. "Bloodworth, I may have to settle with you here."

"I'd rather you did with me," the Eagle Scout said. "Why don't you untie my scarf again?"

The crowd edged forward. There must have been twenty people in it. The French could barely wait. They nourish themselves with the misery of others.

"Let's get on," Venables said irritably.

"Untie your scarf?" Harvey asked. "Shitman, you must be out of your tree."

Again he reached for the teen-ager's 'kerchief, and as he did, Chipper Latour belted him in the gut, a dirty, low, unsuspected smash, right in the *kishkas*, one of the hardest, sneakiest blows I have ever seen.

"Yaaach . . . oooch . . . fach . . ."

Harvey Ungerleider went down slowly, doubling over, his face turning red, his hands reaching protectively for his injured gut. Some Eagle Scout—he wasn't finished. He cracked Harvey across the side of the face with the back of a huge flat hand, and the noise drew gasps from the interested audience.

"*Allons, contre le petit con!*" cried one of Harvey's French rebels.

"Kill the motherfucker!" Vannie screamed. "Fascist beast!"

Chipper was ready for all of them. He backed off, his fists up, and I noticed for the first time that his arms were like leather, brown and corded, and he moved with the agility of a trained athlete. In his belt was a long black sheath, and in it, one of those gleaming Boy Scout shivs. He kept circling, his fists up in classic boxer's pose, a menacing figure.

"Attaboy, Chip," I called. "The rest of you bums, scram! Leave the kid alone. And take that sack of guts with you."

They didn't need my warning. None of them had any desire to tangle with Louise Latour's keeper. The kid had developed those muscles, hauling his auntie around.

"Chipper, you go inside now," I said. "And look, kid—if you need help, I'm with you."

206

His fists were up. I wouldn't have wanted to catch that right in my face, or in my belly, the way Harvey had. They pulled Harvey to his feet, but he was having trouble sucking wind into his lungs. When Justice Triumphed, as the *Daily News* would have said.

"Please Mr. Bloodworth," young Latour said to me, as Venables and I started to walk off. "Don't say a word to Aunt Louise. You know how sensitive she is."

I promised.

It was a lovely evening and Venables and I decided to walk to the Ritz, where the Cooperages were staying. Again he tried to draw me out on Veg. Had I had any training in animal conditioning? Was I familiar with the work of a man named Delgado in the United States? How was I on Pavlovian theory? Wasn't there a chap named Watson at Columbia who did amazing things with rats and had I studied with him? And what about an old carnival worker named Getchell back in the forties in America, a man written up in texts, who had a fantastic dog named "Kid," which, according to certified reports by psychologists, understood 4,000 words? Did the initials ESB mean anything to me?

"Der," I said, "I was an English major, and I'm afraid animal behavior is not one of my fields. Also, I can't figure out why a Hungarian neurologist should be so good at it. Seems to me the Americans and the Russians are way ahead in that department."

I wanted to add, *and why should the Vatican care?*

The Cooperages had a three-room suite in the Ritz. With Tookie's money, they always went first class. Warren earned very little, but moved around a lot. Their guest list was far more impressive than the Teagues'. No plastics millionaires and rent-a-car tycoons. But there were a few cold-eyed embassy types, some international jet-setters, a few Beautiful People, including an American actress whose last three films had driven people screaming out of theaters, and some aged literary giants like Vito Anzaletti and Bruno Shockheim.

It helps to have a rich wife. I know a dozen literary types who float around the upper reaches of the writing world just because they have wealthy in-laws. (Wealthy grandparent in-laws are even better, especially if they are old German-Jewish. They will give you anything you want, anything for their darling granddaughter.) These husbands of rich girls can nurture a small talent, behave graciously, go to the right resorts, and know all the editors on a first-name basis, coasting along for years on a short story, an article, a poem. It isn't fair, but if Felicia Amalfitano had been loaded instead of being a fireman's daughter from the Bronx, I'd not have complained. No indeedy, I'd have bought me a red fez and a maroon smoking jacket, a water pipe and an upholstered divan, and reclined, like the Turkish sultan at the Sublime Porte. I'd have written trenchant articles on "The Use of Symbolism in Jacob Wasserman."

Yes, it was a big party, the gold-and-cream rooms crammed with starved models and fat Arabs and Italian exporters and Irish poets and a few broken-down Hollywood directors, floating around Europe in search of backing. There was a flamenco guitarist, a superb one, in tribute to James Warfield Keen's romance with Spain. (The old fellow had fought with the Loyalists, and was thus able to reveal, thirty years later, that he'd been duped by Stalin, and that not only the communists, but anyone, *anyone* who opposed Franco was a dirty Bolshevik and deserved what he got.)

Lila Metrick was there, sulking a bit, but as delectably broad-assed as ever (she avoided my ferret's eye) and the Fag Kings and the Teagues, Bubba and Manuela, looking out of sorts, because they had no use for the conference and did not intend to go to any of the meetings. ("Fuck 'em," Manuela said. "They didn't put Bubba on the list of speakers, so fuck 'em.")

And Flackman. El Supremo lumbered about, head lowered

for the charge, ducking right crosses, affecting that strange Southern accent (he *had* attended the University of Miami) he utilized when onstage, although it tended to come out sounding like my Uncle Hymie, the numbers writer.

After the manner in which Flackman had humiliated me the previous night, I intended to avoid him. But as usual, a mob was gathering around him, waiting for the drama. I must concede he looked marvelous—a knee-length black Nehru coat and a red turtleneck sweater—and he exuded that damned magnetic pull.

Balancing a champagne glass—we were all required to drink to Keen's success, responding to Tookie Cooperage's shriek as to "how nice it is that it's Jim's turn"—I elbowed my way through the mob. To my astonishment I saw Moses Bloom embracing Flackman, hugging him, rubbing his head of frizzy hair. Bloom hadn't told me he had been invited to the Cooperages' party.

"How do you like this kid?" Bloom was saying. "How do you like him? He came to the party just to see me, to see his old friend Bloom."

"Yup, yup, I sure did. Good old Moe, old smuggler."

It was hard for me to believe my ears. Bloom, tough, scarred, cynical, was not fooling. There was something about being touched by Flackman, praised by him, wanted by him, invited by him, that moved even hard cases like Moe Bloom. It was simply that Flackman was magical, mystical. Talented, brilliant, he also knew how to manipulate the public awareness; this rendered him superhuman in the eyes of other writers, including Moe.

"How long has it been, kid?" Bloom asked. "Ten years? Eleven?"

"Too long, too long."

"Soph and I put the kid up for two years in our old place on West End Avenue. Remember, Arno?"

"I sure do, Moe, I sure do."

There was a warm quality in Flackman's normally hostile

voice. I had misjudged the man. He seemed genuinely grateful to Bloom.

"You . . . ah . . . spend . . . ah . . . a great deal of time in Palestine, don't you, Bloom?" James Warfield Keen mumbled.

"They call it Israel now, Jimmy."

"Ah yes. You were always much involved with them."

"Never had to change my mind, either," Bloom said gruffly. "You see, we never had any Stalin to screw up the works. You remember, Jim, when the Writers Union denounced me, back in 1933, when you were its president, because I said the Politburo were a bunch of liars and murderers?"

"Ah . . . so far back . . ."

"It took you thirty more years to discover I was right," Bloom said cheerfully. "But you went all the way around. You woke up and discovered that not only was Stalin a rat, but so was anyone slightly to the left of Herbert Hoover, including FDR, Louis Brandeis, Harry Hopkins, and Leon Blum. You see, Jim, your trouble is you had to be all or nothing. It's a shame I never got you out to a kibbutz."

Bloom was a monomaniac, in his engaging way, but Keen deserved it. Or did he? Poor guy, he was a burnt-out case, an extinguished brand from the burning.

"That isn't quite fair," Warren Cooperage said. Everyone had champagne now. Toasts to Keen were celebrated over and over. "Jim Keen is our guest of honor."

"I'm glad, I'm glad," Bloom said. "Only . . . every time I look at him I think how the communists have been on my ass ever since I decided I was more Jew than Marxist, you understand? I got an idea they still are. What is all that Al Fatah crap? Who are they, those brave people who shoot up children's busses? And when will I hear a word about that from the Red crowd?"

Tookie Cooperage steered James Warfield Keen away. He was a fragile old fellow, for all his boasts about having killed people with his own hands.

"And furthermore, Cooperage," Bloom said, "how come guys with communist records a yard long always get assigned to review my books? Or if not them some fairy friend of yours who wouldn't understand Israel in a million years?"

"That is not so, Moe, that is unfair."

"It's true, Coop," I butted in. "You and your gang decide who reviews what. You always have."

Cooperage spun about. It must have dawned on him that I had not been invited, but he said nothing.

"That her?" I heard Flackman ask Tookie.

"Why, Arno Flackman, how'd you guess?"

Across the crowded room, Miss Katje Westerdoop, the Dutch girl with the pneumatic bazooms entered, her eyes weighted with sorrow and the awful burden of those two volleyballs.

"She's all yoahs, Arno," Tookie murmured.

He had come *just* to see Moe Bloom! A familiar pattern: hostesses often were required to supply raw meat for Flackman, and Tookie had obliged.

I located Moe Bloom, still reviewing the failed gods of the thirties with James Warfield Keen. "Moe," I said, "Flackman didn't come to see you. He came because Tookie fixed him up with that Dutch treat over there."

"Where? Yeah, maybe he did. Well, that's life."

Bloom could forgive. He was larger than life, and as much as he craved good reviews, big sales, better contracts, he had a mission. I envied him for it.

"I wish you'd get over your fixations about me and my friends," Cooperage was saying to Moe. "Honestly, Moe, there is no plot against you."

"That's raht," Tookie cooed. "Y'all do us a disfavor."

Too much champagne—it flowed endlessly at the Cooperages'—loosened my lips. Later the migraine would come. For the moment I was glib, witty, light on my feet.

"But there is a plot on behalf of you and your friends, Warren," I cried. "You review each other's books. You go to each other's parties. It's only outsiders like Moe and myself who get screwed in your magazines. God forbid one of you should get clobbered by a critic you can't control. There's always one of the Cooperages to come to the rescue with a definitive wrap-up in one of your mags."

"Someone shut him up," Tookie wailed.

Across the room, Black Fag King was terrorizing two alabaster blondes with tales of terror and rape. Of all the Negroes in Paris, he was the safest.

"Look at Darrell over there," I shouted. "His last novel was so awful, such a cheap tantrum, such a *tsimmes* of dirty words and tired plotting that every critic who didn't owe you people anything said so. But what happened? Along came Warren Cooperage with an eloquent defense of his pal, a wrap-up that not only praised Darrell's book, but proved that the other reviewers were morons and bigots. So you can't lose. You people never do."

"Would it occur to you," Cooperage asked haughtily, "that I honestly admired his art?"

"It would occur to me," I said, "until I read the book, a cheap gamble for the porno and lip-moving trade. I don't like writers who refer to the cock and the snatch as "the sex" and who use the noun "honey" to describe an orgasm. But you, Coop, made it all right for him, kissed his bubu and made it go away, in your memorable article 'The Art of the Black Avenger.' "

"You'll get your comeuppance," Cooperage said, as a small fascinated crowd gathered around us.

"Dammit, Coop, admit it," I babbled. "You did the same thing for Arno's collection of essays, *My America*. Sophomoric boasts, a display of *putz* in public. Even the English critics hated it." I glanced at Derek Venables as I said this, and I almost felt he was pleased with my venomous assaults on Flackman. "But along came Cooperage, with a ten-page piece in the magazine *In View*, proving that Flackman had extended the frontiers of human experience. It gave his publisher rave quotes."

"And why do we indulge in this sort of thing?" Cooperage asked icily.

"You know each other! You run a closed corporation! You go to each other's parties in Bridgehampton! Jesus, how clear can I make it? You got a good thing going. Why let anyone else in?"

My voice was a womanish shriek, and I barely saw Flackman, in that rolling, head-down gait of his, the menacing walk that warned of bloody violence, coming toward me. And the truth is, I never saw him hit me, but he hit me he did, squarely, mercilessly, one short neat uppercut to my porcelain jaw. So light-headed was I on Cooperage's expensive wine that I hardly felt the blow, but rose vertically, lighter-than-air, as if drawn to the glittering chandelier.

"Hit him again," someone cried.

"Punish the bastard."

"Shut him up for good, the lousy free-loader."

How I got to my feet I don't recall, except that Bubba Teague, who knew a few things about gutter-fighting, was bracing my back and holding my ass with his huge hand. "Kick him in the nuts, Benny," he said. "Ole Arno's got sensitive nuts, kick him one in the House of David."

Flackman jigged in front of me, left out, right cocked on his chest. I heard Tookie Cooperage bawling, and Katje Westerdoop whimpering, and Moe Bloom calling out for someone to stop us, but before anyone could, Bubba Teague shoved me onto Flackman. Bile and gastric juices climbed my esophagus like salmon leaping up a fish ladder. If I couldn't hit him, I might puke all over his Nehru coat. Like lovers entwined, mating fags, we hugged each other, waltzed a few graceful steps, then tumbled over a purple velvet ottoman.

How long was I out? A minute? Five? Ten? You never know after you awaken. It could have been October of the following year, and I was still in the Ritz Hotel. Bloom was squatting over me, pressing ice cubes to my forehead. As the images came into focus, I saw Flackman studying his latest victim, looking not at all unfriendly. He'd proven he could

kick the tar out of me (no great feat) and now he was fulfilled.

"Not a mark on you," Bloom said. "Arno knows how to hit
a guy so it doesn't show."

"No hard feelings, Bloodworth," Flackman said. "But you
have to learn to button your lip."

Had I learned? I wasn't sure. I could hear Lila Metrick
announcing that she refused to stay in the same room with
me, that I was a bloody CIA agent, and she was retiring to the
reception room with a select group to brief them on my filthy
role at the conference.

This pleased me enormously. I was also delighted with the
way Flackman had socked me. It would mark a turning point
in my career. I would be known forever as the writer whom
Flackman decked with one short right. It might get onto my
dust jackets; into my obit.

"No hard feelings, Arn," I said. "I had it coming."

"If you're a pal of Moe Bloom's, you're okay with me," he
said, patting my shoulder. "You're on the team, kid."

Was I dreaming, or was there a microphone in my face?
Harvey Ungerleider, the New Left Youth leader, was squatting beside me, his tape recorder slung over one shoulder,
getting down all these weighty words. "Part of my biography
in sound on Flackman," he muttered. "What a break. I got
the whole thing on tape. How Flackman beat the crap out of
a smartass."

"Wait a minute," I cried. "I may refuse to give you a clear-
ance to use it."

"Tough shit, Bloodworth. It's news."

Ungerleider followed Flackman and his entourage out of
the room. Everything the man did was a public event. Now I
was part of the legend.

"Your head okay?" Bloom was asking. Only he and I were
left in the corner of the living room.

"Yes. I was getting a migraine anyway, and it tends to
neutralize any other pain."

"Okay. Get up. I need some help."

"Another message to Veg? A white rat to deliver?"

Bloom wrestled me to my feet. Surprisingly, I felt strong, alert, ready for an adventure.

"I had a phone call while you were out. We have to grab Veg tonight. I'll explain later. Come on."

No good-byes were said: possibly most of the guests were glad to see us leave. I followed Bloom's stumpy figure into the dark blue night of the Place Vendome, where we got a taxi.

"*Quai de la Mégisserie,*" Moe said. "*Près du marché aux oiseaux.*"

"*Il est fermé maintenant,*" the driver said.

"*Cela ne fait rien. Allons. Vite.*"

"Why are we going to the bird market?" I asked.

"I don't know yet."

"I don't want to buy a canary. Or even listen to one. I've got a flock of sparrows singing in my cranium."

"I need an extra pair of hands."

We stared at the serene muddy Seine on our right, at the looming outlines of the Gare d'Orsay and the Académie Française. On our right was the eternal Louvre. Just beyond the Belle Jardinière department store Moe had the taxi stop. We strolled down the Quai de la Mégisserie, the ancient site of the Parisian tanners. It was now the bird and animal market, but of course it was closed at this hour. The streets and alleys were spotlessly clean, wet from their nightly washing-down.

"Walk casually," Bloom said. "Like a tourist who got lost."

My head was ablaze. The migraine had come on full strength, inevitable punishment for all the champagne I'd guzzled.

"Here," Bloom said. We turned into an alley, a *passage*, too narrow for even a French car, but wide enough for the push-carts from which were sold larks and bulbuls and hamsters and Belgian hares. A rotting fertile odor lay heavy on the air—bird droppings, sawdust, decayed vegetables. The alley, like the quay, was scrubbed clean, but an army of Algerians armed with mops and pails could not erase that laminated stink.

Apparently the crumbling buildings in the alley were used as storerooms by the vendors. In one filthy window, under the dim light of a single bulb, I saw a family of sleeping rabbits. In another, dozens of yellow chicks huddled for warmth.

Above us, someone cracked a whip. *Crack-crack. Nacknack.* Then silence.

"What . . . ? What the hell?" My knees were like jellied madrilene.

Bloom stopped in a doorway and scanned the upper stories. "Listen, kid, if you see a gun in my hand, don't get scared. Just get out of my way."

Feet running? Someone coming down a flight of stairs in a hurry? Bloom cocked an ear, then kept padding down the alley, staying close to the buildings. Near the end of the *passage*, he struck a match and inspected a street door for a number. Then he shoved it open and I followed him into a malodorous vestibule—a zoo stink, menagerie perfume. There were no lights, no concierge. Migraine sharpens my sense of smell. I might have been in the chimpanzee cage at the Bronx Zoo, wallowing in the anthropoidal stench. It also heightens my sense of hearing.

"I hear chattering," I said. "Animals squealing or fighting." I thought of Veg's rats: one murdered, the other a murderer.

"Stay two steps behind me," Bloom whispered. "Don't talk."

The canted steps creaked under the weight of his compact figure. A short man with a heavy tread, like my late father Aaron Bloodworth, Ph.G. It was thirty years ago; I was following the old man's hunched figure to the attic for a crate of Ex-Lax or Ipana. This recollection of my childhood sustained me. I'm not terribly brave. But Bloom's determination, his dogged pursuit of Laszlo Veg, must have mattered a great deal. He'd get him into Israel despite the Tom Braggs and the Pochastnys and the Keramoulians. And like my father, Moe appeared afraid of nothing.

A few steps from the landing he stopped. "Somebody was just here. Those were shots."

"I . . . I still hear something."

"Not people."

There was a chattering, clicking sound, a sort of agitated staccato noise. Animals. But not rats or mice. A bigger beast, with a disgusting human cadence to its prattling. My migraine-honed ears told me: *monkeys*. I'm a veteran of long happy afternoons at the Bronx Zoo amid the kinkajous and binturongs, an old friend of Congo pottos and slow lorises. These were monkey noises and I smelled monkey odors. There's something fearful and occult about them. Remember Mowgli's hatred of the tree people?

At the next landing Bloom walked softly to a decrepit door. A dozen wooden shipping crates were stacked in the corridor. Shredded paper and excelsior festooned the floor. The odor of uncleaned cages, of jungle creatures confined amid their own dung, was overpowering.

Bloom leaned against the door, hand on knob, easing it open, a centimeter at a time. With his other hand he reached into his hip pocket and took out a pen-sized flashlight. With mournful protests the door inched open. As it swung away from us my nose twitched. There was another odor emanating from the apartment, an acrid stench. It cut its way through the animal aromas, sharp as a steak knife. Gunpowder.

"Moe," I said. "The shots were fired in there. I smell them."

"Shhh."

"I'm scared. What if . . . if they're still . . . ?"

"*Shah.*"

"Look, I'm a coward. I have no gun. I'd . . ."

The door was open now. Anyone inside the rooms would surely have heard us. With a kind of blunt courage—tempered I suppose while landing refugees on beaches under

British guns, or bribing pilots to divert airplanes loaded with weapons to secret fields—Bloom entered the room. I followed him. The nervous chattering grew louder.

Moe turned the flashlight on the walls. The room was a wreck. It had once been the reception room of an elegant apartment. At the far end was a closed double door leading to the next room. Plaster peeled in great abstract designs from the old walls. I saw the remnants of regal gold moldings, ormolu curlicues in the corners of the ceiling. There were more empty crates against the walls—larger than the ones in the hallway. On one I could read the return address: *Arpady Utca VI, Budapest, Hongrie.*

"Whoever was here beat it," Bloom said. "I think I know who they were. They wouldn't hang around."

He moved the double doors open and walked across the threshold, my shaking legs a step in back of him.

Suddenly Moe stopped short and I bumped into him. "*Gevald*," he said. He was drawing away from something at his feet. The thin cone of light from the flashlight streamed downward and painted the area around Bloom's feet. There was a furry bundle on the splintery floor.

"What . . . ?" I stammered.

Bloom knelt down. His hands cautiously probed the mass of dark hair. It was an animal, a dead, huge, hairy animal. A dog? A big gray dog? Moe flipped the thing over. The forelegs were too long for a dog. The hind legs were too short. I saw a white flash: long, sharp teeth, bared in a wicked smirk.

"M-monkey?" I asked.

"Baboon."

I squatted alongside Moe. A monstrous, wicked bastard, that baboon. It was a gray-coated Chacma, one of those chesty, angry, intelligent marauders with a long canine snout, a massive chest, thick arms.

Bloom spread the figure out on the floor. "Look at the size of the guy," he said. His hand had turned black. It was covered with blood.

"You sure it's dead?"

"What is this? War paint?" He showed me his soaked hand. Then he pointed to a hole the size of a baseball in the beast's chest. It was maroon-brown and still gushing.

"Who . . . who . . . would want to kill a baboon?" I asked.

"It was a mistake."

In a room beyond us, the dead ape's companions kept up a wild chatter. They knew, they knew. One of their troupe had gotten his; he was bound for that great Kaffir Kraal in the sky, stealing corn and beans from the biggest Voortrekker of them all.

The yellow beam explored the gray corpse. A peculiar harness was strapped around the animal's chest, a few inches above the lethal wound. It was made of two thin leather thongs, and when Bloom flipped the animal over, we saw that they were used to hold a black metal box, about three by four inches, against the ape's back.

"Bastards. Lice." Bloom muttered the imprecations with holy resonance. "They got here before we did." He lifted up the dead baboon and propped it against his chest. Had I not been full of champagne, and more concerned with my migraine headache (they tend to concentrate the mind), I'd have run screaming into the Paris night. Oh mother, the sight of that ape's rheumy red eyes, hideously opened in death, the ivory fangs sprouting from scarlet gums! A dribble of mucus ran down its black snout. It was a match for any hungry leopard and maybe even a man armed with a gun.

"Those shots we heard," I said. "That's what killed it."

"Yeh, yeh. But he was only hit once." Bloom began to probe the baboon's gray coat, peeling back the hairs, as if grooming him, searching for nits and lice and bits of dried epidermis. "They screwed up the job. Look, they didn't get it."

The *it* to which Moe referred was a white plaster patch nesting on the crown of the ape's pointed skull. It was a round patch about an inch and a half in diameter and about a half inch high.

"M . . . M . . . Malar," I stuttered.

"What about him?"

"He's got one also."

"One what?"

"A white patch like that. On his head. When he was roughed up yesterday they tried to steal it. The Russians had people out looking for it."

Bloom let the baboon fall back on the floor. "Yeh, that's to be expected."

The yacketing, the monkey chatter in the next room was louder, more frenzied. Bloom got up and I followed him into the chamber from where the noise came. I wondered idly what it was to be bit, clawed, mauled by one of those vicious Chacmas. Feeling a little like Paul DuChaillu, I trod behind Bloom as he let his light play around the walls. It was another ruin of a room—moldering walls, peeling plaster, the tangled wiring of old fixtures. In the center of the room was an enormous cage, a makeshift affair fashioned of heavy packing crates, set on a long wooden table. It was about eight feet long and five feet high and deep, covered with thick wiring. Inside were three more baboons, but these were not at all dead. Wicked monsters, they showed us their cruel fangs. One of them hurled his gray form against the wire mesh and cursed us in Afrikaans.

Bloom walked slowly around the cage, inspecting the bottom timbers. A hasp at one end had been unlocked, and he secured it swiftly by thrusting a metal bolt through the holes. The baboon flew at him, cursing and spitting.

"They act as if they know you," I said.

"It's the Hungarian in me. They're used to the smell."

"Ah. They belong to Laszlo Veg."

"That's right. His animals."

White rats who beat up cats. Fierce baboons who wore

harnesses and got shot to death. I wondered about Judy's "Uncle Latzi."

"What now, Moe?"

He sat down on a crate. "I don't know."

The bellicose baboon picked up a food pan and started banging it rhythmically against the wooden floor. The other two, somewhat smaller, shrank away, as if fearful of his temper. I noticed that all three of the apes had the same white patches on their skulls. Moreover, they wore the odd leather harnesses around their torsos, the straps securing the same metal box I'd seen on the dead ape.

"You were supposed to find Veg here," I said.

"I think I was suckered. He was supposed to be here and give me an answer." Playing his flashlight against the distant wall, he illuminated a table loaded with what looked like electronic equipment. A shortwave set? There were wires, coils, sets of dials, a kind of jerrybuilt control board. Under the table were some scuffed black cases, the kind used for transporting electrical or medical gear.

"What is this? A radio station?" I asked.

"Something like that." He had been painting the floor with his flash. Now he stopped the beam on a group of dark wet spots the size of quarters.

"The baboon's blood . . ."

"No," Bloom said. "He's in there. Look where those go. Out the back."

Moe got up and gave me the flash. Then he took a gun from his coat pocket. I couldn't be sure, but it looked like a Luger, with the oddly shaped bolt.

"Turn off the light," he whispered. "Come on."

He pushed the rear door open. We were in what must have been a rear bedroom at one time. There was a cot with rumpled blankets. The floor was littered with newspapers.

"Shoot the light on the floor."

Dark round stains, a continuation of the small puddles, left a trail across old copies of *Le Monde* and *Paris Soir*. They seemed to get bigger, more irregular in shape as they marched to the rear of the apartment. There was another door, leading to what was probably a kitchen. We walked in. Stained sink, sagging cupboards, a rusted coffeepot on an ancient table. It was a typical French kitchen. I knew the way the old apartments were built—kitchen at the rear, leading to a flight of service stairs running down to the interior court. A shaft of moonlight fell through the opened service entrance, and in it was a huge pool of blood.

Bloom didn't stop. He walked out to the landing. A bomber's moon flooded the courtyard. "Walk carefully," he said. "Don't step on him."

A tall man in a gray suit was sprawled across the top steps of the stairway. His face was hidden. The blood was spreading in a soaking stain under his right arm.

"Moe, I'm scared."

"So am I. What can you do?" He turned the body over with his foot, gently, deliberately. I didn't need the flashlight to tell me who it was: droopy nose, pendulous cheeks, melting dark eyes. It was Keramoulian, the man from the Thirteenth Directorate.

"Keramoulian," I muttered.

"Yeh. Bloody Business."

Years ago I'd seen a dead man in my father's drugstore. He was a young Italian housepainter and they brought him in from the job still in his stained overalls, gasping in the last stages of a cardiac arrest. I would remember forever the man's offended, astonished eyes, the sucking mouth, as he refused to accept the final insult. There was something of that look in the Armenian's face, as if he were convinced that a serious error had been made.

"Moe, this is awful. Was he really a bad egg? I mean, I always felt Pochastny was the boss."

"Not a bad egg, no. He killed maybe twenty people."

Bloom bent over the railing and peered into the dark court below. The windows around it had remained blackened, sightless. I doubted anyone lived in the old wreck of a building.

"What . . . what happened?" I gasped. "The baboon? You can't tell me Veg trained that big monkey to handle a gun."

But Moe wasn't listening to me. He was staring at Keramoulian. I stared also. A bubble of blood, or saliva, or some body humor formed on his lips.

"Jesus . . . still alive," I whispered.

Moe bent over him, pressing an ear close to the mouth. "*Tovarish*," Bloom said softly. I thought of my father bending over the dying Louie Esposito in his drugstore. The Armenian gurgled, trying to speak. Then he made a terrifying sucking noise. And was silent. Unlike Malar, he had only one life. He was either dead, or close to it. The biter bit.

"He said something," Bloom said. "I think he did, anyway."

"What?"

"*Kolenki*. At least that's what it sounded like."

"And what does it mean?"

"Knees."

"What? Whose?"

"Knees, knees, what you kneel on. *Kolenki*. Unless it's someone's name, and I didn't hear it right." He got up. "Let's get out. Try not to get any blood on your shoes."

"But . . . this guy may still be alive. We can't leave him like this."

Bloom scowled at the Russian. "He's dead." Kneeling, he took Keramoulian's wrist and touched the pulse, then bent his ear to the man's parted mouth. "Dead, dead. Let's go."

The baboons cursed us again as we passed through the large room. We stepped over their companion's bloody corpse, and then proceeded down the stairs to the alley and to the quay.

As soon as we hit the night air, and the ripe aroma of the Seine, my unnerved digestive system backed up. I raced to the embankment; the Dom Perignon I'd swilled at the Cooperages' came up in a golden torrent. Bloom waited patiently until I'd pumped myself clean. It was reassuring how good I felt: courageous, confident, airy.

"Come on, kid, if you're finished," Bloom said. "We'll never get a cab here."

"Place du Tour St. Jacques," I said crisply. "A block from here."

We walked along the quay, and I saw a man come out of the *passage* where we had just been, look at us, then duck back. He was a thin young man in an open-collared white shirt and he was fussing with an elongated valise, the kind used to carry a tennis racket and tennis clothing. He seemed to be putting something in it. Or taking it out.

"There's a guy back there . . ."

Moe pushed me along. "Don't look at him. Walk fast."

"But I think . . ." I swiveled my head and squinted into the shadows. It was Daoud Jabali, the Jordanian soil chemist.

"Moe . . . Moe . . . it's that Arab . . . Jabali."

"Don't look at him. Walk faster."

A long valise. Long enough to carry a carbine, a rifle, a shot-gun, a machine gun.

My emptied stomach rose like an inflated fish bladder, up my gorge, into my throat. Its windy roundness floated me off the ground; any second I anticipated soft-nosed bullets violating my innocent back, my shivering legs.

"He . . . he . . . killed Keramoulian . . . he . . ."

"Shaddap. Turn the corner."

"Him . . . that nice Arab. Keramoulian and the ape. Why? They're allies. I mean Arabs and Russians. He . . ."

Bloom was one of the world's fastest walkers. He barreled, or sort of rolled, on his desert-hardened feet, shoving me along with one tough hand. We got into a cab at the Place du Tour St. Jacques.

"He followed us, Moe," I gasped.

Jabali was standing in front of the Théâtre Sarah Bern-hardt, holding his tennis bag in a strange vertical position.

"Get down," Bloom said.

I needed no encouragement. The two of us ducked our heads below the level of the taxi's windows.

"*Messieurs?*" the cabbie asked. "*Qu'est-ce qu'arrive?*"

With his head down, Bloom responded: "*Gobelins.*"

The driver made a wild U-turn, and we headed toward the Pont au Change. Let it come now, I thought: a fitting end to my brief career as spy. Jabali's Al Fatah bullets would blast us apart—or would he use one of their grenades?—as we sped by the theater.

"Stay down," Bloom growled.

I needed no reminders. My narrow arms, my precious skull were nailed to the floor of the taxi. What the driver thought, I cannot say. He did not notice Jabali—and probably assumed we were two drunken Americans playing some foolish game.

Jabali evidently decided it was not the time and place to dispatch us. When we were out of range, I sneaked a look behind us. He'd vanished in the shadows.

"That murderer," I said. "That bloody Arab killer."

"Shhh," Moe cautioned. "Take it easy."

The cab bounced onto the Boulevard St. Michel and headed south. The neighborhood swarmed with students, street freaks, losers, and weirdos. I felt vastly superior to all of them. Was it Churchill who wrote about how invigorating it was to get shot at in battle? I'd made a run, a mission in black, and although I had no idea what any of it meant, why the baboon and the Armenian were murdered, I felt I was a part of it.

"Jabali, some soil chemist," I said. "That gentle Jordanian in his high brown sneakers. Bragg had the dope on him. A Palestine Liberation agent, maybe their top guy. He set off the bomb at the Lussac that was intended for you. He killed Keramoulian. He just tried to knock us off. And you, you sit there rubbing your chin. Aren't you going to do anything about him?"

"*Avenue du Général Dumont, dix-neuf,*" Bloom told the cabbie. We turned left on Boulevard de Port Royal.

"Look, if you want me to be your extra pair of hands, you have to tell me things," I protested.

He didn't respond. Bloom was upset, his mind elsewhere.

"You got a call while we were at Cooperages'. Veg was going to be rushed out of Paris, and there was a last chance to grab him, right?"

"Something like that."

"And whoever it was called said he might be at that lab where he keeps his baboons, right?"

"Yeh, yeh."

"But instead of Professor Veg, we found a murdered baboon and a murdered Russian. So it was a bum steer. Not to mention that Arab killer standing around. Moe, he was putting something into that long valise, and it might have been a rifle or a shotgun."

"*Ici, ici,*" Bloom mumbled to the driver.

The cab stopped fifty feet from the apartment house where the Hungarians were staying. There were lights burning on the fifth floor, where the Malars and Veg, and presumably, their Soviet guardians, were living. I thought of Judy and I wanted to save her. She had to become an American; I'd spirit her—and her papa—away, and fulfill my mission. Another self-fulfilling prophesy.

"Why are we here?" I asked Moe, as we walked down the deserted street.

"No use kidding around. I'm after Veg."

"You're crazy, Moe. You won't get near him. Why don't you send him a singing telegram? Or a funny valentine? Jesus, a guy got killed tonight."

"You never can tell what might turn up."

A gendarme and my friend M. Dunand came out of the apartment building at No. 19. A step behind them was Pochastny. The three formed a phalanx and approached us.

"Ah, M'sieu Bloom," Dunand said.

"*Bon soir,*" Moe said. "*Eh bon soir,* Antipov."

The French police, I was certain, knew Pochastny's real

name. Still, the Russian didn't appreciate Moe's rudeness.

"Hi, fellah. You guys never give up, do you?"

"I want to see Professor Veg," Bloom said.

"Not a chance," Pochastny said. "He's asleep."

"Someone called me in his behalf an hour ago. I understand he wants to see me."

Dunand shook his head. "I regret, M'sieu Bloom, you are misinformed. I speak with *le professeur* ten minutes ago. He wish to be left alone."

"Make these jokers show their credentials, Maurice," Pochastny said to the detective. "*Ils sont agents, c'est tout. Ils ne sont pas journalistes.*"

"For Chrissake," Bloom said. He took a press card from his wallet, attesting that he was accredited to the *Israel Express*. I showed Dunand my ID card from the conference. The cop turned a flashlight on it, lowered it, and as he did, the beam played on my tan suede Wallabees. The toes were dark, splotched with blood.

The torch lingered over my maroon toes longer than I thought necessary. Dunand and Pochastny both studied my embarrassed feet. But they said nothing. I doubted that they had any idea that Keramoulian had come to a bad end.

"*Vos souliers . . .*" Dunand said. "*Très sales . . .*"

"It's the suede. It gets dirty easily. I stepped in mud."

Dunand shrugged. Pochastny's huge nose widened, as if he were trying to inhale the aroma on my shoes. He knew about blood.

"What right have these Russians to act like a private police force in Paris?" Bloom protested. "And especially to watch over citizens of another state, namely the People's Republic of Hungary? I demand the right to see Professor Veg and hear from him that he doesn't want to talk to me."

Pochastny folded his arms. "Fraternal people's republics, Bloom. The Soviet Union is a friend to all peace-loving nations."

"How about it, M'sieu Dunand?" I asked.

227

"*Non, non. C'est meilleur que vous partiez. C'est rien à faire.*"

Bloom smiled at the KGB man. "I get it. Malar will make his speech tomorrow, and then you'll fly all of them—Malar, Veg, Malar's daughter—out of town, before anyone can talk to them. Pretty neat, Antipov. And you, Dunand, you're going to let the Republic let them get away with this?"

Dunand did not seemed agitated. "*Les Hongroises sont d'accord.*"

"I bet they are. Let's go, Benny."

"Wait a minute," I said. "I have a date with Miss Malar, and I demand that she be let out of that fortress up there."

Bloom actually looked at me with admiration. I was growing up.

"Sorry, fellah," Pochastny said. "Miss Malar left a half hour ago. Had a date at the Plaza-Athénée. And not with you."

I wondered if he were telling the truth. My eyes scanned the windows above, hoping to see Judy waving to me. But the shades were drawn; no one stirred inside the Hungarian quarters.

We found another cab. Bloom was morose. He kept rubbing his big hands together, and he sat on the edge of the seat, as if ready to change his mind and get out of the taxi at a moment's notice. We were heading back to the Cooperage party. If Pochastny were not lying, Judy might actually be there.

"At least they didn't know about what happened to Mr. Bloody Business," I said.

"Oh, they'll know, they'll know. And if you think we have troubles now, wait." He frowned and rested his forehead in his hands. "And those sneaky French. Playing ball with the bums. You like this kind of work, Benny?"

"It beats workshops," I said. And I meant it. I hadn't felt better in years. I was on an exhilarating, heart-thumping trip, taking big doses of the hardest, happiest stuff available.

For a moment I thought Tookie Cooperage wasn't going to let us rejoin her party. She flowed to the door, stared balefully at me, then relented when she saw Bloom's sour face. The old guy was in enough anthologies of "Social and Proletarian Writers of the Thirties" to qualify, even if he were my friend.

"Malar's daughter here?" Bloom asked. "The little red-head?"

"Ah don't rahtly know," Tookie fluttered. "Things have sort of gotten outa hayand." She was mildly soused. Genteel plantation drunkenness, y'all. "Bubba and Arno are at each othah agayan, and Ah do wish they'd stop."

We followed her into the swarm of parasites, free-loaders, self-invented celebrities. The high-priced actress was asking James Warfield Keen about Cinematic Truth and the *Auteur* theory.

"This is the last pahty Warren and Ah will evah, *evah* give at the conference," Tookie moaned. Her lower lip trembled. Tookie, I was told, had low blood pressure.

An inhuman shriek issued from the bedroom. I realized it was the combined howl of several women—shocked, goosed, affronted, raped.

"They all in theah," Tookie said. "Oh, fuss 'n' feathers! Whut are they at now?"

Bloom and I followed her into the huge, be-draped, whor-ish bedroom. Most of the party had gravitated there and were gathered in a drunken, mauling mob around Teague and Flackman. But they did not seem to be fighting; rather a jovial contest of some kind was in progress, with retainers of each giant urging their man on.

"Show him, Bubba!"

"Let him have it, Arn."

"Ah'm mortified," Tookie said. "Ah'm simply humiliated." She shouted over some massed heads. "Warren, do make them stop!"

But no one heard her. Whatever conflict the writers were engaged in had hypnotized the guests.

"No cheating now, Bubba!" I heard White Fag King hiss. "No hard-ons allowed!"

"That goes for Arno also," the lady TV panelist with the slit eyes croaked. "No stroking, no fondling."

Bloom and I pushed our way to the front rank of the audience. Venables was acting as referee. He was glass-eyed drunk and he didn't recognize us. "Lahst time I saw this . . . Cambwidge backs. A wizard show between a don and a Pakistani bwoke who went bonkers . . ."

Oh, the relevance of the artist in contemporary society! Oh, the moral imperatives that guide the writer! Ah, the obligations and responsibilities of the novelist!

Under the Bohemian glass chandelier stood Flackman and Teague, face to face, each with unzipped fly, each holding their members out for measurement. These two men, between them, had earned in excess of two million dollars in royalties, advances, film and TV and stage sales in the last year. And now they were comparing the respective lengths of their cocks.

"Arno's bigger," White Fag King simpered.

"Lak hell he is," Bubba crowed. "Ain't no itty-bitty city boy got a bigger cock than Hennery Pope Teague."

Warren Cooperage chuckled. "It was Arno's idea. They started arguing about who was richer, who was a better writer, who was a better fighter, and everyone got worried there'd be a fight, so Arno decided they could settle it this way. He claimed he had the longest tool of any writer working today."

This somehow rang a bell with me. Dimly, I recalled a much-praised essay of Flackman's in the magazine *Seminal* in which he argued that the novelist's art is akin to the act of pulling your penis out in public to show the world how huge it is. "A succinct, witty, closely argued, and altogether refreshingly honest assessment of the novelist's role," Lila Metrick had said, reviewing the article in *The Discoverist Review*.

"Look, sonny boy," Moses Bloom said. "You see here the state of the arts in America. Behold, they almost cometh."

Both burly men had dropped their pants and underdrawers

and were gentling cradling their tools, side by side. Let me say frankly that neither were bargains. They were ordinary run-of-the-mill pricks, no bigger, no prettier, no more varicolored, no more unique than your average workaday joint.

"Stop that at once, Bubba!" White Fag King shrilled. "You're trying to raise one!"

"Ah ahm not," Teague protested. "Ah kin beat Arno, fair 'n' square, 'thout gittin' me a bone on!"

"Jolly good show," Venables said. "Lahst time . . . Cambwidge backs . . . that bwoody Pakistani had a smasher . . ."

"Now looky hyeah," Bubba Teague said, getting alongside Flackman, waddling as his trousers drooped, "jes' looky hyeah when we side by side! Ah win, Ah win, Ah got me a bigger dong!"

All studied the two *putzes*. Teague was right.

"Looks like you're licked, Arno!" Cooperage shouted.

"You dang said hit, he licked," Bubba crowed. "Y'all know why? He's licked because old Bubba hain't never been snipped. *Woweee! Yahoo!* That's why. Bubba a plain good ole country boy, an' he ain't never been cut short the way Flackman been!"

"Wait a minute," Cooperage said. "Not so fast. I found a slide rule. We're gonna measure."

Warren bent low and carefully applied the edge of a small plastic rule to first Flackman's, then Teague's.

"Hit don't matter," Teague bragged. "Ah got Arno whupped and Arno knows hit."

Cooperage bent low, squinting. "Yup. Yup. Arno, he wins. He's got at least two centimeters on you."

"*Yahoo! Woweeee!*" Teague shouted. "All you rebels join in, and le's heah hit fo' Hennery Pope Teague!"

There were shrieks, applause, thunderous approval of Teague's mighty triumph. Venables stumbled away; so did Lila Metrick. What had they been expecting? A mutual public ejaculation?

"Yoah problem, Arno," Bubba said, as he tucked his shirt

into his pants, "is yo got yo'sef a damn clip-cock. Yeah, you a clip-cock. Cain't no clip-cock git the best of Bubba Teague, who is set up the way Gawd intended him to be set up. *Yahooooo!*"

Flackman also closed shop. Magnanimously he extended his hand to the victor. "You know what they say, Bubba. Long and thin slides right in, but short and thick's the better prick. Yoch, yoch."

Bloom hustled me out of the bedroom. "*Gevald*, there's nothing to learn here."

A mauve face gleaming with pistachio teeth loomed in mine in the vestibule. "Bloodworth, isn't it?" Boyle Huffguard asked. "Asked me those nasty questions today, correct?"

"Yes, Huffy, that was me."

"Join me for a drink. I want to know all about you."

Evie Bragg's brother. Tom Bragg's brother-in-law. "Sorry, Huffy. Where is your brother-in-law tonight? That blond fart who drives around in a car with CD plates and carries a small rod. Tell the bastard I refuse to be kidnapped again."

"How wrong you are," Huffguard said. "They are very fond of you, Bloodworth."

"It's not mutual. Nothing personal, Huffy."

Bloom shoved me toward the door. "Enough, enough of this *narrishkeit*," he growled.

"I say, Bloodworth," Huffguard called. "Tom and Evie would like to see you tonight. Where are you headed?"

"The opposite way from you," I said, with a bow to old Ernest. One of the early short stories, I believe.

Bloom was staying at a small apartment on the Avenue Charles Floquet in the seventh arrondissement, a lovely tree-lined residential street near the Champs de Mars.

Sophie Bloom, in wrapper and curlers, opened the door for us. Bloom was moody, disturbed. With a monomaniac dedication, he wanted Laszlo Veg, and it did not look like he would get him. He slumped into a sofa in the minuscule living room, and Sophie brought us tea with lemon and *petites beurres*.

"Your place?" I asked him.

"Yes and no."

Mrs. Bloom turned on the evening television news. It featured a long film report on the opening of the World Conference of the Arts and Sciences, leading with an update on the bombing of the Café Lussac. A few Arabs had been rounded up. The police now said that the bombers had been killed by police gunfire from an apartment house across the street— telescopic sights, an ambush. It sounded screwy; I don't know why. I saw Bloom scowl as the TV commentator made his report. There was no mention that Moe had been the target of the attack, as Dunand maintained.

By far the biggest section of the report was on Flackman. I could have warned the conference organizers in advance; you didn't stand a chance when Arno showed. The French film crew had followed him around all day (a special ninety-minute report, entitled *"Le Roi"* would be shown at the end of the week) and we saw Arno talking to students, arguing with police, toasting his French hosts, debating with Boyle Huffguard, responding angrily to my wild attacks at the Palais de Chaillot. My voice was dimly heard, the camera and mike never leaving Flackman's rugged phiz.

Moses Bloom yawned through most of this—just as he had found Flackman and Teague's cock-contest a bore—until there appeared onscreen the bushy head of Harvey Unger-leider. The bearded kid and his tape recorder were continually at Flackman's side, shoving a microphone up his nose, catching his pearls, presumably for the New Left magazine to which he was accredited.

"*Et, voici, un jeune journaliste Américain est toujours à côté de M. Flackman, parce que tout qu'Arno dit est valable pour le publique Américain . . .*"

"Who is that fat kid with the tape recorder?" Bloom asked.

"Harvey Ungerleider. New Left Youth leader." I filled Moe in: how Harve had made his rep by defecating in some professor's files, how he had come to disrupt the conference, and at the same time, do a long interpretive article on Flackman for a leftie publication.

"I think the magazine is called *Suck*," I said. "At least that's what his girl friend Vannie Bragg told me."

Bloom's eyes were merry. "*Sucker* would be more like it." He asked Sophie to get him a metal card file from an old-fashioned secretary in the corner of the room. Still staring at the TV—Ungerleider was following Flackman down the Avenue d'Iena—Bloom shuffled through his cards and laughed huskily. "Ungerleider my *tochis*. Take a look."

He gave me a 4 x 5 white card. In the corner was a small photograph of the same Harvey, but without a beard, and with a neat crew cut. He could have been the Student Council treasurer at Manhasset High School. I read the legend at the top:

KANTOR, SHELDON—FBI INFORMANT

Kantor uses a variety of costumes and disguises and often appears at New Left and other youth rallies—hippies, Maoists, rock festivals—to stir up trouble, create disorders, and touch off confrontations with police and other authorities. He has been a reliable FBI informant and courier for the past eight months. Not dangerous, not violent, always unarmed, and in no way connected with espionage or any kind of high-level work.

"Stop, stop," I protested, "you're making it up."

"Like hell I am. That's Kantor. I know his old man. Biggest UJA fund-raiser in Westchester. The kid's been on the FBI payroll for a long time." Bloom chuckled. "So, they sent him here, to liven things up, to check up on the kids."

"He . . . I . . . his dirty mouth . . . Flackman . . ." I was stupefied.

"Listen, the FBI is entitled to make a living. They use

kids like Kantor all the time. Some radical. Normally they don't operate outside the United States, but for this conference, with all the students in Paris this summer, they covered it."

"And his interviews with Flackman? Is that for the FBI also?"

Bloom closed his eyes at my ignorance. "Nah, nah. Anything Arno says is public record. The FBI couldn't care less about him."

"Then why is he with Flackman all the time?"

"He's his *cover*, boychick."

"Who? What?" We were close to some Olympian comic revelation.

"Flackman, the most famous writer here, is Kantor's *cover*," Bloom said patiently. "Look, look, he's signaling."

I stared at the set. Kantor-Ungerleider, holding his microphone under Flackman's face as they crossed the Place du Trocadero in a mob, was touching his eyebrows, then his nose.

"It's a face code, Bloom said happily. "Some of his bosses are watching this show tonight and he's telling them something. Maybe where to pick up a message, or where he'll be later. Simple."

"There's a rude justice in this, Moe. Flackman, of course, has no idea he's being used by the FBI. He's innocent."

"Of course! You get yourself the most unlikely cover in the world. They knew Flackman would be on camera all the time, so if this kid hangs around him, he can always communicate. It's an old trick. I used it myself years ago in London. I made believe I was trying to sell one of my books to a Hollywood producer named Klebanow. I tailed him, went to his parties, dined with him, everything. He had nothing for me, but it was a perfect cover. I was the young novelist hanging around Klebanow's suite in Claridge's."

"You left out, Moe," Sophie said sweetly, "that the suite next door was occupied by Abdul Rahman Azzam Pasha, the secretary-general of the Arab League."

"Of course it was. But what a cover that Klebanow was!" He nodded approvingly at the TV picture: Ungerleider following Arno down the aisle to the stage at the Palais de Chaillot. "Almost as good as what this kid has."

I recalled the manner in which Chipper Latour, the Eagle Scout, had belted Ungerleider earlier that evening. "Some FBI man," I said. "I saw him get knocked down with one punch."

"He isn't an FBI man," Moe explained. "Just picks up a little extra working for them. How do you think these student maniacs keep going? They'd run out of funds and leaders without some help. Listen, fair's fair, and I got no kick against the Bureau. I have other priorities. They never did me any harm." His eyes turned misty. "In fact . . . way back in 1947 . . . I met some pretty nice FBI agents when I was collecting hardware for the Haganah, yeah, some decent boys. . . ."

Sophie refilled our teacups. It was a hot night, but Bloom wrapped his calloused palms around the cup as if needing warmth. Sophie left us. He turned off the TV after the weather report. He looked like a worried drapery-store owner in the Bronx, about to be put out of business by a discount house.

"Moe, what happened tonight at that place? The ape, the Armenian . . ."

"I'm not sure I know."

"Jabali. I know he did it. We saw him there. He had a long rifle or machine gun in that valise."

Bloom shut his eyes and laced his stubby fingers on top of his white bristles. "I'm not sure. I don't know who killed Keramoulian."

"CIA?"

"Maybe."

"Your people?"

"Never. We don't go for that. Unless we have to."

"Who? The Arabs? The French? Was it an accident?"

"Not exactly an accident. I think a couple of groups ran into each other by mistake. One might have been the Social Affairs Department."

"Social Affairs Department? It sounds like a work-study project at Brandeis University."

"Peking. Our friends in Bow String Alley."

"They're boycotting the conference."

Bloom yawned. "They got a big embassy here. And listen, you, you, sonny. You started shooting your mouth off to the Russians what Chairman Mao said. They fed some of that back to the Chinese, and the Chinese decided to look into this."

"Sorry, Moe. It was just to get a reputation."

I had tried to sound contrite, ashamed of my dirty game, but I was engorged with pride, bursting with satisfaction. After all, there are 800 million blue ants in China, all those people doing setting-up exercises and waving little red books, and I'd shaken up their leaders! A few well-placed lies, and I had dragooned them into my charade.

"I'm not blaming you, kid. They had Veg on ice, but we might have had a crack at him. This way, they'll get him out of Paris so fast tomorrow, maybe even tonight, we won't even see his sour puss again." He stared out the opened French windows: they'd turned the lights on in the Tour Eiffel. "They might even get rid of him altogether."

"Kill him?"

"Why not? Pochastny is up to his *pupik* in trouble. One of his agents dead." Bloom looked intense. "I know what happened. Someone tried to steal the baboon. Keramoulian was waiting for him. Shots. The baboon was used as a shield to protect the guy who killed Keramoulian. It took the KGB bullets."

"But where was Veg?"

"Too valuable. Keramoulian found out someone was going to try a heist. So he went to the lab. But the other guy was a better shot."

I looked skeptical. "Moe, how could anyone lift one of those monsters out of the cage? Come on."

"Easy. Tranquilizer darts. I was looking for one in the monkey's hide. Too small to find."

"But . . . the baboons. They're Veg's? And the electronic gear, the radio equipment we saw there?"

"It's all his. He's got refugee pals at the Institute Pasteur. They do favors for him. Ever been out to the zoo at Vincennes?"

"Yes."

"They got an island of baboons there. More baboons than they can handle. Veg's friends bought some of the surplus for him. Then he went to work. The leather straps, the boxes on their backs."

"And the white patches on their skulls?" My eyes widened. "Wait a minute. The rat you gave me, Moe. When they killed it, they scooped out a little piece of his skull, maybe its brain."

"Figures they would."

"Why? Why? What is Veg doing to these beasts?"

"Lots of people want to know."

"And if someone shot Keramoulian dead while he was trying to steal an ape, why didn't the killer take the baboon with him?"

Bloom scratched his head. "Probably heard us coming. Anyway, the dead baboon wasn't worth a fake kopeck any more. It has to be alive to count."

Over my acrid coffee and greasy croissant, I read a special delivery letter from my wife, while across the gloomy breakfast room of the Bavard a Somali editor raised a fuss over not being able to get his morning goat cheese.

Eddie lost his ladder match with that fresh kid Myron Hesseldine. You know the kid—his father is a producer at CBS and his mother is that tall snotty blonde who insulted me one night at the Nuckermans'. She kept coaching her son—he's a year older and four inches taller than poor Eddie—from the sidelines, yelling "Hit it to his backhand, he has no backhand." I wasn't there. Eddie told me about it later. He said if you'd have watched the match he'd have won. As it was, the Hesseldine brat had to go three sets and barely beat Eddie. The score was 6–4, 2–6, 8–6.

There was a mess of fatherly guilt to go with my café-au-lait. I love Felicia, but she knows how to make a man suffer, especially her own husband. *If I'd been there*, Eddie might have won and climbed the tennis ladder. Up, up and away! Yes, that's what we all wanted, to win, to be applauded, to be top, Numero Uno, and earn the envy and fear and admiration and hatred of others. Wilt Chamberlain was right when he said Americans put too much emphasis on winning. But what else is there? How else can a man function? And was I not playing the game at its most daring, its most frenzied? "Winners never quit and quitters never win," Eddie says to me when I'm despondent. And there the kid was—losing at tennis to some tall, lean, blond brat who probably took lessons from a pro three times a week. Eddie taught himself. He uses a two-handed backhand and his serve is soft, but he has courage, he has guile, he never gives up. Would that I were half the man he is at age twelve.

But I had something to show. I was in the middle of some kind of international double-dealing, and an awful lot of important people knew about me. Someday I'd tell my children; they'd think better of the old man. These wild experiences I'd store, like brandy aging in oaken vats, fine tobacco in cedar casks, and they'd accumulate aroma and body with age. My stolid middle-class life—God forgive me I'm a hopeless suburban homeowner, the fellow to whom all those paint and shrubbery and lumber ads in *Newsday* are addressed—would emerge as nothing more than a cover for a life of intrigue.

As I sat in the Bavard's funereal lobby, thumbing through the Paris *Trib* for anything on the murder of Mr. Bloody Business (and found not a word) I thought about my inability, up to this point at any rate, to create an exciting "lifestyle," as the youngsters are fond of saying. I wear Thom McAn shoes and I drive a Rambler, although I often refer to it as a "Nash." A *Nash!* Cultural Lag covers me like fungus.

But all was behind me. Good-bye to All That Crabgrass. Yes, I'd been threatened, punched, witnessed bloody death, passed coded words, delivered messages. It was amazing what this sort of thing did to one's ego. Whittaker Chambers, a low-level courier, was convinced he had changed the world, or would have been able to. Before his death he went looking for bigdome ex-communists like Koestler and Martin Buber's daughter, so that they might reminisce about their glorious careers as workers in the cause. I think it broke poor Chambers' heart that most Americans regarded him as a minor messenger, an informer, and a part-time liar, when he was convinced he was the Lenin of the West. Like James Warfield Keen, who babbled about killing men with his hands, like Black Fag King's threats of murder and rape. Fantasts and jerk-offs—these seem to be the ultimate metamorphoses of writing fellows.

But was I happy? I think so. Maybe I would make it a life work. I'd gather up my courage, desert Felicia and the children, and float around Europe with a succession of bony models on my arm, lolling on obscure beaches in Turkey and Greece, in mountain cabins in the Tyrol and crumbling apartments in Trastevere.

"Good morning, sir. I'm having trouble making myself understood to the concierge. Could you help me out?"

Chipper Latour, in full Scout rig, was standing shyly to one side. A decent kid. He reminded me of home, green lawns, barbecues. He had on his green shorts, knee-length socks with the sassy green tabbed garters, a pale green scarf, and a wide-brimmed campaign hat. His shirt gleamed with countless insignia, an antipasto of embroidery.

"Sure, kid. Glad to."

It was a simple matter of buying stamps. I concluded the deal for Chipper, who busied himself with a stack of postcards.

"How's Aunt Louise?" I asked.

"She's asleep, sir. I think we may leave early. You know this was her publisher's idea."

"Chipper, I admired the way you belted that snotty Ungerleider last night," I said. "He sure asked for it." An interior chuckle warmed me: Ungerleider, real name Sheldon Kantor, an FBI plant, an operative sent to report on New Left Youth activities. Some agent! He'd played his role too well and gotten the crap beaten out of him by an Eagle Scout. I found myself studying Chipper's bare forearms: they were thicker than I recalled and rather hairy.

"I didn't want to hurt him, Mr. Bloodworth. I only wanted to teach him good manners."

"You're a convincing teacher."

"I was head of Senior Patrol last year," Chip said, licking stamps, "and that involved a lot of instruction. First Aid, self-defense, and so on."

He dropped his cards into a letter slot, turned and his eyes were looking at my Wallabees. "Golly, look at those stains on your shoes."

"Spaghetti sauce," I said. "We had dinner last night in a little Italian place on the Left Bank. The waitress tripped."

"I've got some carbon tet in my room. Would you like to come up? I can clean them in a jiffy for you."

"Good deed so early in the day?"

Chipper smiled. The light flooding in from the Bavard's open doors obliterated his eyes, and two rimless ovals stared at me. Bereft of his eyes, I saw that there were hard lines around his mouth. He hadn't shaved too closely that morning.

"Aunt Louise and I think a lot of you, sir. Any favor we can do. An important writer like you shouldn't have to wear bloodstained shoes."

"Spaghetti sauce. Marinara."

"What made me say that? I guess I got mixed up with your name. Bloodworth."

"I guess so."

"Aunt Louise would love to see you today. You cheer her up."

"You said she's sleeping."

He grabbed my right hand. "Say, why don't we surprise her? We'll have breakfast sent to the room and go up and join her for coffee. It'll make her day start off nice."

Chipper was crushing my hand, drawing me close to his khaki chest. It was insane. There was a touch of menace in him, and I remembered the way he had decked Ungerleider with one swift blow to the gut. Insolence, firmness, a kind of *do-it-my-way* arrogance one encounters in certain young Jaycees or radio announcers. He wasn't seventeen; he'd seen his seventeenth birthday years ago.

"Some other time, Chipper. I have a busy morning."

"Really, Mr. Bloodworth?"

I was on top of him, immobile, helpless, his powerful hand holding me close, but I still couldn't see his eyes. The brilliant patches and badges on his broad khaki chest dazzled me. A bouillabaisse of emblems, awards, memorabilia. My goggling eyes came to rest on the BSA insignia: the eagle with the shield on its breast and the motto BE PREPARED, bird nesting in a huge golden *fleur-de-lis*.

"Ah . . . ah . . . the *fleur-de-lis* . . ."

"What about it, sir?"

"N . . . nothing. I'm admiring the way yours is embroidered. And this one. INTERNATIONAL JAMBOREE 1967."

"Yes, that was a dandy event. Our troop staged a reenactment of the Mountain Meadows Massacre. We won second prize for dramatic spectacles."

"Ever stage any spectacles in the Rue St. Denis, Chipper?" I asked shakily. "Two nights ago?"

"I don't get you, sir."

"Zapping old Hungarian radicals?"

"I think you want to come up to Aunt Louise's room, but you're shy. We can talk everything over up there."

He turned slightly, almost as if signaling someone with his head—the lunacy, him in his ANZAC hat!—and I saw, reflected in his specs, the seersuckered figure of Tom Bragg.

The DIA man, that traveling salesman for Academy Fixtures, had entered the hotel, paused at the concierge's desk, and was watching us.

"Too bad you didn't know enough to grab Malar's plaster patch, Chip," I babbled on. "The KGB was after it also. They sent their men to the alley where you jumped the old man and I think they found it. You get no merit badge for ambushing, kid. How'd they ever let you into the Order of the Arrow?"

Bragg was walking toward us. Latour had signaled him. But he wasn't saying anything. I'd be damned if I'd call for help. Clearly, they knew each other, and they wanted me. Having failed yesterday, thanks to Bloom, they were after me again. As Moe had said, they didn't appreciate *shlemiels* like me spreading lies. No loose ends, Bragg had said. And yet they were my countrymen, and I wasn't sore at them. I just wanted to be let alone, to play out my own part.

"I say, Bloodworth! Bloodworth!"

Derek Venables had come out of the elevator and was gliding toward me, much agitated. Chipper Latour saw him and released me. I rubbed my mauled hand. The little bastard had an iron fist. He'd deformed three fingers. Bragg, the big lox, began studying a copy of *Newsweek* on the concierge's desk and turned his back on us.

"Morning, Der. You know Chipper Latour? Mrs. Latour's nephew."

He ignored the Scout. Lord Baden-Powell would never

have approved. "I say, old man, we are in a bit of a stew at the workshop on Journalism as History. Our Wussian fwiends dwopped out at the lahst minute. Mr. Pochastny was going to chair the bwoody thing, but he just called to say he's indisposed."

"Really? That nice Mr. Pochastny?"

"Yace. Says he has a pain in his chest. Bit of indigestion."

A severe case, I was certain. But not nearly as severe as the pain in the chest suffered last night by his gunman, Hrant Keramoulian. There were no remedies left for that sucker, no analgesics or sedatives. He had suffered a bad attack of angina, cardiac arrest, coronary occlusion, myocardial infarction.

"How can I help, Der?"

"Won't you sit in? I mean, I cahn't let you chair the meeting, that would be infra dig. But you can take Pochastny's pwace. Come along."

"Oh, it's right now?"

"Yace. Heah in the hotel."

Chipper wouldn't quit. He hooked his arm in mine. I didn't like the look of the gleaming Boy Scout shiv in its black sheath. "Gosh, Mr. Venables, Mr. Bloodworth was going to visit my aunt. She isn't feeling well, and he promised to cheer her up. It'll only take a minute."

Bragg had replaced *Newsweek* and was facing us. Ah, the vagaries of fortune. To be saved by a queen!

"New, new, new, that won't do atall," Venables protested. "The workshop is alweady underway, and it's short of confewenciers. Come along, Ben. Young man, do let go of him. That's a good chap."

"I'll visit Auntie later, Chip," I said. "Say, isn't that good old Tom Bragg over there? The well-known toilet salesman from Darien? Hi there, Tom. What's new with the greens committee this year?"

Bragg grinned. "Hi, kid."

"You do seem to know everyone, Bloodworth," Venables said. "Now, come along. I'll intwoduce you. Remember, it's called 'Journalism as History.' Anything you want to say will be fine."

We floated across the lobby to the workshop. Bragg turned to leave. Nothing passed between him and Chipper Latour.

As it developed, all I rated in the workshop was a chair against the wall. The regulars at the conference—M. Rignac, Katje Westerdoop with her balloons, the usual Nigerians and Thais—sat around a long table laden with Perrier and peanuts. The rest of us were "observers." While Venables was out rescuing me from my fellow Americans, they'd filled the open spot at the big table. Venables shoved me in and left; he was everywhere at once, co-chairing like crazy. Somehow Cooperage had become chairman of this workshop. Boyle Huffguard was slumped in a chair. Party regulars.

"I'm of the opinion," Cooperage was saying, "that journalism is every bit as valid as history. It *is* history. History in the making. All of us in this room are accomplished journalists of one kind or another, and we can claim to be in the vanguard of this new synthesis . . ."

"The speaking drum is the purest form of communication," the Nigerian said.

"I'm sure it is, Majaka, and we'd love to hear more from you on that subject in a moment, as soon as I finish my introductory remarks. I foresee the day when journalism departments at our universities will be part of the history department, or perhaps vice versa."

"Yes, I think you have a point, Warren," Huffguard muttered. "The kind of reportage in which I deal, in-depth, interpretive reporting, is more akin to the academic disciplines than to mere day-to-day gathering of facts."

I couldn't take any more of this. "Mr. Huffguard, would that include your brilliant piece on the assassination of Martin Luther King? You know, the one in which you argued that the man had caused a great deal of trouble, that he had rocked the boat, disturbed the public order and aroused unwarranted desires on the part of happy black people, but that all things considered, he didn't deserve to be killed, as you phrased it?"

"Hmmm . . . yes . . . I believe I wrote that . . ."

You had to hand it to Huffguard. He stood by his garbage. "Well sir, if he didn't *deserve* murder, what did he deserve? Chains? Pillories? A job as a bootblack? Or perhaps he could have been turned to stone, painted gaudy colors, and put on your front lawn in Muttontown, as a warning to uppity colored people?"

"Mr. Bloodworth, can't you wait your turn?" Cooperage asked. "There'll be an open discussion in a moment. Can't we set up ground rules?"

But he was cautious, respectful. You didn't *futz* with a top spy. Cooperage knew who mattered. I had never felt more confident, more buoyant. Half the people around the conference table must have gotten the word. You watched your step with Bloodworth.

"I don't want to address myself directly to the gentleman's comments," Huffguard nasalized, "but let me say, in general, that history as it is written at our universities tends to be false and misleading because most of it is in the hands of secular, humanistic, liberal, gnostic clerks, descendants of the French Revolution. Recognizing this, we must start anew, with new modalities, new ideals, new concepts . . ."

"Like what, Huffy?" I called out. "How about a blast at Galileo? We could rewrite the story to prove the Pope was right all along and that Galileo was a soft-on-communism liberal. Or maybe he was a little wrong, and they had some justice on their side. Or maybe they were misunderstood."

Huffguard bared his pea-green teeth at me in his best Sparafucile grimace; he enjoyed the banter.

"Please, Mr. Bloodworth," Cooperage said politely. Katje Westerdoop was looking at me with soulful admiration. By heavens, I'd breach that Dutch dike. To hell with Flackman;

246

she may have been his partner last night, but I'd take seconds. A man living on the edge of danger deserved the best.

The debate meandered along—more on the speaking drum from the Nigerian, more self-congratulations by Huffguard. Finally, I'd had enough.

"Mr. Chairman," I said, "we lose sight of one thing. Journalism is immediate, swift and offhand. It has no time for contemplation, analysis. Hence it is often misleading and wrong. Even the weekly columnists and monthly magazine intellects are often hampered by a lack of correct information. History has time on its side. Let me give you a simple example which you can multiply a hundredfold. In World War II, it was reported that Captain Colin Kelly bombed and sunk the Japanese battleship *Haruna*. But at the end of the war, we found the *Haruna* still afloat. Why? Well, we needed an early war hero, and Kelly was fine for the newspapers. But everyone read about the feat in the papers, and we all believed it. That's journalism. Years later, a historian could write that the *Haruna* was in action, firing its guns, right to war's end. That's history. Is everything clear?"

"No, that's not fair," Cooperage protested.

"What do you mean, not fair?" I cried. "I've just given you the basic difference. I suggest that this workshop is irrelevant and without legitimacy, and I intend to file a separate report with the co-chairmen to that effect."

They looked at me as if I'd gone barmy. That's my trouble. I am too far ahead of my time. I see things too clearly. Was a PhD in Mass Communications necessary to realize that journalism and history were *not the same thing*?

"Ah, yes, hence the speaking drum," Dr. Akokawa said. "Please go on, sir."

"Thanks. Let's take a hypothetical case." I scanned all the faces around the long table. Now I was ready. I'd marry my two careers—writer and spy. "Let us suppose that an important delegate to this conference were murdered."

"Ah, who has been murdered?" the Nigerian asked.

"Hypothesis," a Greek editor said. "Hypothesis only."

"Right, Mr. Diodakis. Let's further assume he was a top member of a communist delegation. And let us assume he came to Paris to engage in matters that went beyond his attendance at a conference on the arts and sciences. Let us assume he was shot to death in an old building in an obscure quarter of Paris . . ."

They were fascinated. As I talked, I noticed that Venables had loped back into the room and was lounging in the doorway.

"Now let us suppose the press reported this murder of an important delegate," I went on. "What might it say? Well, it might say that this Russ—this dignitary was found dead of gunshot wounds in an old apartment house near the Louvre. What would it mean to us? What would it mean to the professional journalists covering the case? Not much. Robbery. A mistake. A political murder."

I stopped and looked around the table.

"The speaking drum would not equivocate," Dr. Akokawa said.

"Perhaps not," I said.

"Go on, go on, deah boy," Venables called. "What is your point?"

"My point, Der, is that the truth, the reason why this Russian was assassinated, or murdered, or accidentally shot to death, might remain a secret for years. Suppose . . . suppose he were a spy. Or a trained killer. Or engaged in some sort of underhand skulduggery. But whatever theory was advanced in the daily newspapers, by ordinary reporters, might be completely wrong. The truth might remain buried in Lubianka for years to come. History might someday present us with a correct version. Delegate X came here to perform mission Y and was killed by Z because of A. But we would never learn about it from any journalist covering the story as the murder of a delegate in an old building."

"Fascinating," the Nigerian said. "When did this take place? Who was it who was killed?"

"Hypothesis," the Greek muttered.

"Brilliant, brilliant," M. Rignac said, tapping his cane. Well, my little French *historien* was on my side. He'd been no help on the *fleur-de-lis*, but that hadn't been his fault.

"Ah, but Ben, deah boy," Venables piped. "Suppose you were a mere journalist, as you put it. And you were confwonted with this murder. How would you go about finding the twuth? Why should we have to wait yeahs and yeahs for it to come to wight?"

"Good point, Der. If this Russian were murdered, and he were a delegate, and I were a co-chairman, I'd get hold of my other co-chairman, and I'd start by interrogating every Russian at the conference about their dead colleague."

"Ah . . . yes . . . yes . . ."

Did he know about Keramoulian? Maybe he knew a lot more than I did. Did he know more than Daoud Jabali, stuffing that long rifle into a valise last night?

I saw Judy Malar's red curls pop into view behind Venables' draped form. She poked her pretty head in and waved to me.

Leaving, Venables looked long and longingly into my eyes. Was it love, or was it interrogation?

Bloom was sitting stolidly in a corner of the lobby. He had taken a seat that afforded him a view of the rest of the hotel, and the street. He was in no mood to provide an easy target for Daoud Jabali, or Pochastny's friends, or anyone else. On the coffee table in front of him was a bulging zippered briefcase. He wore his standard, a tieless short-sleeved shirt, Ben-Gurion style.

As we walked through and around delegates, I heard Louise Latour *tak-tak-taking* for a fresh drink. "Hey, Bloodhound," she gargled. "C'mon, talk Louise."

"Sorry, Louise, no time." And where was Chipper? Practicing karate chops? Honing that baloney slicer in his belt? If the fat lady ever sobered up, I intended to give her a piece of my mind about her phony nephew.

I said nothing to Moe about Chipper Latour in Judy's presence. I was learning all the time. Shooting your mouth off was a useful part of faking, but when you become operational, silence was the rule. It was too bad that espionage didn't pay better; I was enjoying it so heartily, I could have made it a life's work.

"They let you out?" Moe asked Judy.

"Yes. In fact Mr. Pochastny said he wanted me to be friendly to you and to Ben."

Bloom shut his eyes. "And Keramoulian?"

"He was not at the apartment this morning."

"That's understandable," I said.

Judy looked puzzled. "Why? There were six more men hanging around—some Russian, some French, one looked like an Algerian. Mr. Keramoulian was usually in charge of them when they came."

"He's busy, he's busy," Bloom said. "I think he's going to take part in a seminar on External Trade." He leaned forward. "After your papa makes his speech this afternoon . . . what are you going to do?"

"I am going to stay through the conference. And so will Papa. They have assured us of that."

I darted a look at Moe. He thought differently and he was usually right. With Keramoulian dead in a gunfight over one of Veg's baboons, they would take no more chances. The Hungarians would be spirited out of France. Russians are good at this sort of thing. I recalled the way they'd deceived poor Imre Nagy—one of Malar's colleagues after the revolution—by coaxing him out of his sanctuary in the Yugoslav Embassy, and then shot him dead, dead, dead.

"Listen, young lady," Moe said wearily, "the KGB is not going to let any of you stay in Paris after your father makes his speech."

"It depends on what kind of speech he makes, doesn't it?" I asked.

Bloom shook his head. "No. No. It doesn't matter any more."

Did I imagine it, or had Louise Latour, highball glass in hand, moved closer to us? A fat female Buddha, in nirvana with her morning booze, she was trying to eavesdrop. I recalled the day I'd met her at the elevator, her monstrous barf, the way I'd helped her nephew Chipper—we had accounts to settle—ease her into the lift. Then I realized what they'd done. She, or Chipper, had stolen Bloom's letter to Veg. And last night they'd lifted my fake letter with Eddie's batting averages. Tom Bragg had seen that letter. Tom Bragg had shown up magically an hour ago when Latour had tried to wrestle me to his hotel room. Bragg–Latour. They were working together. That they were on our side cheered me only marginally.

"Listen, little girl," Bloom said, "I am telling you this for your own good, your own safety. You and your papa should make a run for it after his speech."

"Oh . . . Mr. Bloom . . . there are dangers . . . all those men Mr. Pochastny has around my father."

"It can work. Benny will be in charge of you. I'll work details out in a little while. What's important is that you go with him—it'll be broad daylight, they won't try any funny stuff in the open in Paris—you go with him to the American Embassy, you and your father. You'll be safe there."

Ah, the fox, the old *rebbe!* I knew what he was up to. He didn't give a damn about Malar or Malar's daughter. He lusted only for that rat-trainer, that baboon-conditioner—Veg.

"I plan to make a fuss, not much of a fuss, but a loud one when your papa finishes his speech. The hall will be jammed. Photographers, reporters, newsreels. When I get through, they'll all want to talk to your papa. You and Benny run to the stage and start guiding him out the back door. It'll get crowded in the corridors and Pochastny's thugs won't be able to get any closer to you than the reporters will let him."

"How about when we get outside?" I asked.

Judy had turned pale; her little fists were clenched.

"You know how to skate-board?" Moe asked.

"Me?"

"You, Benny Bloodworth. You ever been on a skate-board?"

"Sure. My son is the skate-board champ of Hicksville. He taught me."

"Okay. I can't plot this any further, but when you start down that ramp in back of the Palais—you know where? there's a big statue of Hercules there, another of a goat or a bull?—you'll see some kids using skate-boards. Children from the diplomatic corps. They come there every afternoon. A kid in a white yarmulka will look for you. Actually, he's seventeen, but he's small. Embassy kid. His name is Ayal. Do what he says."

"That's your plan? We're in the hands of seventeen-year-old Israeli kids who skate-board?" I looked at Judy. "Judy, you don't have to go through with this if you don't want to."

Before she could respond, Bloom held up a hand. "She'll go, she'll go . . ."

"If you think it is safe . . . I cannot bear the thought of Papa being sent to Moscow . . . or to prison again in Budapest . . ."

"Then take your chances with me."

"Moe, what will you be doing all this time, while Judy and I are escorting her father out? I mean, apart from this diversionary tactic?"

"Guess."

"I know already. Can I mention it in front of Judy?"

He shrugged.

"You'll be sneaking Laszlo Veg out of the auditorium. He's all you give a damn about, isn't he? Diversion, hell. We're the diversionary force in this battle plan. Of course. You'll stir up a big *tsimmes*, you'll send the press flying to Malar, and while everyone, including those Russian guns will be after us, you'll do something to Veg, stick a gun in his ribs, and walk him out the front door."

"That's the idea. You'll get Malar. I'll get Veg."

Naturally he was giving me the wrong Hungarian. But I didn't care. Malar was my man. Hadn't Cooperage and I settled that? Wasn't that the reason someone had sent me to Paris?

"What happens after I meet this Israeli skate-boarder?" I persisted.

"Follow him. Listen to him. Arrangements have been made." He unclipped a large orange fountain pen from the breast pocket of his drip-dry shirt. "You might need this but I doubt it. It's better than Mace. If any of those Russians get too close or too nasty, give him a short squirt. It works from the top, one little push."

"I feel as if I'm being bar-mitzvahed. Today I get a fountain pen."

Judy's mouth was trembling. "It will be dangerous, Mr. Bloom. I know it. You make it sound as if it will be easy, but I am afraid. You are sending Benny, and my father, and me on this crazy adventure, so you can capture Uncle Latzi. It is not fair."

Bloom scowled at her. "Girlie, I can't force you to do anything. The signal for you to start moving to the stage will be when I throw a bunch of papers up in the air. As soon as you see the papers flying, start for the stage. Also get to the hall early and get seats up front, so you'll have less distance to travel."

Confidently I clipped the orange fountain pen (did the Ladies Auxiliary of B'nai Jeshurun give me the same kind of pen when I made my covenant?) into my shirt pocket. For a timid man, one who ran from fights and violence, I was supremely at ease. I almost hoped one of Pochastny's hoods would get rough with us. I couldn't wait to give him a faceful of Bloom's Little Miracle Spot Remover.

Tak-tak-tak. Louise Latour was dry again. I glanced at her, and I sensed a sullen frustration in her sodden face. She hadn't gotten close enough to catch more than a word.

Bloom had a phone call to make and he excused himself.

"Are you willing to try this?" I asked Judy. "Is it worth it?"

She was upset. I took her hand. "Look, Judy, your papa is a big name, an important man. This is Paris, daylight as Moe says. The Russians don't get rough out in the open. They hate to look bad. They have guilty consciences. I think it'll work."

"Ben, I hope so."

I stared at Bloom's bulging briefcase. The leaflets he spoke of, the papers he would toss about, were probably inside. Along with my new sense of identity, my pride in my calling, I had developed a conviction that I could stick my nose anywhere I wanted to. Novelists, of course, feel that way all the time when they write. Now I was merely extending this compulsive curiosity into my life. So I zipped open Bloom's briefcase.

The leaflets—three pages of mimeographed material stapled together—were there, but so was something else.

"Someone's old shoes," Judy said.

Indeed, someone's old shoes. Crushed, pliable tops folded over the hard brown rubber bottoms—Daoud Jabali's desert sneakers. I lifted one of them out.

"They are strange shoes," Judy said. "For sports?"

"You might say that."

They were dusty and scuffed, and I inspected the hard thick rubber toe, and the doubly thick sole with its cunning ridges and indentations, to afford footing in sandy wastes or rocky heights. I'd seen them for sale at Abercrombie & Fitch. Made in France. French Foreign Legion surplus. Like an old bounty-hunter, Bloom had relieved his victim of ears, a tail, a paw. I had not the slightest doubt that he, or one of his people, had gotten fed up with Jabali and his bombs, his long-range rifles, his sneaky game. And the irony of it! I guessed— as I saw Bloom finish his call and start toward us—that somebody had tricked Jabali into a confrontation with Keramoulian in Veg's private zoo. Maybe the timing had gone wrong; they were supposed to be allies, Big Red Brother and Little Moslem Brother. But it hadn't worked out. Mr. Bloody Business was dead, and looking at those pale brown, high-top sneakers, I was convinced that the polite little Arab agronomist had eaten his last plate of *hummus*.

Bloom saw me zipping up his briefcase. "*Nu?* What are you poking around for?"

"Sorry, Moe. I was curious about those papers you were going to toss around this afternoon."

"That was Dunand on the phone." He glared at me. "Jabali's disappeared. Gone."

"I imagine he left in a hurry," I said. "Someone scared him right out of his shoes."

Bloom snorted. "Ah, he never bothered me."

"He damn near blew you up. And last night he——"

"*Shah, shah.*" Moe looked at Judy. "Anyway, it's a help. When we try our run this afternoon, you and Miss Malar with her papa, and me with the professor, it'll help if there are fewer French cops there, if they have Jabali on their mind. He's a suspect now. Let them run after him."

"What are the chances of his running after *us*? He may decide he wants his sneakers back."

"Listen, boychick, they were *kockers* in 1948, they were *kockers* in 1956, and they were *kockers* in 1967, and they're still a bunch of *kockers*. Of course, there are big, powerful *kockers* helping them out now, but a *kocker* is a *kocker*."

"I don't understand your friend Mr. Bloom," Judy said. "Can we trust ourselves to him? I do not mean to be rude, but I sometimes am not certain what he wants, or what he is doing, or who he is doing it for."

Bloom got up. "Girlie, you have to trust somebody here, and it might as well be me. Remember, Benny. The kid with the skate-board."

"Thanks a lot. Now I'm Leader of the Skate-Board group."

"Don't be insulted. Emerson called Thoreau captain of a Huckleberry Party. *Shalom*, kids. I'll be somewhere in the middle of the auditorium."

He walked out of the hotel in that impatient brisk stride, a solid immovable man.

"Ben, I am frightened of this," Judy said. "I am afraid of Mr. Bloom."

"Moe? Come on, Judy, he's an old Zionist activist. He needs Veg for some kind of experiment, some process he's invented with animals. Probably has to do with increasing the butterfat content of cows on the kibbutzim."

"No. He is a dangerous man. The way you looked at those old sneakers. You were frightened also. I have the feeling they belong to someone he has killed."

I was thinking the same thing, but I said nothing. "No, not Bloom. He's a humanist, a liberal. They don't kill people." I told her a little about Moe: the gunrunner who once spirited an entire bomb factory, in parts, across Europe, in trucks labeled UNRRA. "We're in safe hands. Who else ever planned a getaway from the KGB on skate-boards?"

"You are joking to cheer me up."

She began to sniffle, small discreet noises into her handkerchief and then she unloosed a few genuine sobs, and I felt like a rat, a deceiver, a self-serving phony. I was hot stuff all right, blabbing (but didn't Cooperage invent the part for me?) how I'd come to escort Imre Malar to the West. It was true that I hadn't asked him. But wouldn't any freedom-loving American assume that an old Marxist radical, under the boot of revived Stalinism, wouldn't he have to assume that such a fellow craved America, and Korvette's and Nassau County and a reliable publisher? I saw the dust jackets dancing in front of me: *I Chose Scribners. Twenty Letters to a Friend at Macmillan. Out of the Night and into John Day. Conversations with Stalin, Simon and Schuster*. Malar would be inundated in lecture-circuit bookings at top dollar. He'd show up at Hadassah luncheons, Rotary meetings, high school graduations. A vibrant rewarding new life beckoned.

There was a small hitch. He might get killed in reaching for this new life I offered him, and he was, after all, a belly Hungarian, a goulash communist. And he did have a deal of sorts with his bosses. They let him out frequently to show the genial face of the survivor, the house intellectual. See, see? they could ask. Malar is a free spirit, a nine-lived cat, a friend to the West, and we let him roam around Europe making small jokes and small criticisms of Stalin! *Aren't we liberal!* It was even possible that Malar liked his job. Lecture bookings on Ohio campuses might not appeal to him that much.

But then there was Judy. I owed her a better break. That ivory-skinned auburn-haired kid with the wide green eyes—an ethnic beauty. Amalgam of Tatar, Slav, Teuton, and who knows what else, that makes Hungarian women such prizes. I thought of her in her drafty gloomy apartment in Budapest, working over dresses on a rattling Singer, laboring at her job with the state publishing house—it paid her thirteen dollars a week—and I wanted painfully to give her something better. All those kids in Prague and Warsaw and Budapest, the ones who march across the bridges, face the tanks, cry for a breath of air, for ideas, for stimulation, for liberation, for a new dress and a decent pair of shoes and a small car! You have to love them; and I loved her.

And still she wept.

"Come on, Juditka, *nicht weinen*," I said. "We are in good hands. Tomorrow we will all be in New York—you, me, your father."

Damn Bloom! He was leaving the Malars to me while he ran off with Veg. There were too many loose ends, too many Irish pennants flapping from the mizzenmast. Where to? The U.S. Embassy? And who do we ask for? And how do we get out?

As I pondered these problems—I took it as a sign of emotional maturing that I wasn't terribly worried about any of them—I saw Chipper Latour walk up to his drunken aunt and whisper in her ear. The two of them stared at me. Louise's pouchy face was impassive, dispassionate. The Boy Scout's was cold and contemptuous.

When I caught his eye, I formed the words carefully with my lips, exaggerating the movements, so he'd get the hint.

"Up yours, too, Jack."

IV

Harvey Ungerleider and his mob were demonstrating outside the Palais de Chaillot when we arrived. The bearded boy seemed to have recovered from the clout in the *kishkas* Chipper Latour had fetched him. That bit of business I hadn't yet figured out. Harvey was—according to Bloom—an FBI plant, an agitator and informer among the youthful leftos. Latour was some kind of CIA agent. Why compete? I had two theories—one, that neither had any idea of the other's fakery; the other, that they did, and staged the fight to head off suspicious characters like Moe and myself. It was comforting to me, that I, a total charlatan, was wise to both of them.

"No more diversionary conferences!" Harvey yelled. "Death to bourgeois revisionists who try to co-opt the Third World Revolution!"

Vannie Bragg was waving a huge placard on a stick reading:

AGAINST THE WALL
FUCK EVERYBODY HERE

At least it was impartial; the kids had no use for any of us. They were a hairy, scraggly, sorrowful crew, and I pitied them. They had no real power, neither in Europe nor the United States, and they were born suckers. The FBI and the French cops, and lots of other smarter, tougher people, sneaked spies

and informers in their midst—Harvey, you lying bastard!—
and they were left naked and exposed. Someday they'd learn
that the right things get done only for the wrong reasons, and
the civilization progresses, however haltingly, through deceits,
lies, frauds, and back-door entrances—not via dirty words
shouted in the faces of those who control the switchboards
and the arsenals.

"What are they protesting?" Judy asked, as we walked up
the steps into the left wing of the Palais de Chaillot. (The
building, I should explain, consists of two identical wings. On
the right is the Musée de l'Homme and the Naval Museum.
The one on the left houses an exhibit of models of French
monuments, plus theaters and assembly rooms.)

"Anything," I said. "They hate all of us."

"Up Against the Wall, motherfucker!" Harvey shouted at
me.

Judy put her hands over her ears. "Such words! In Budapest
we would not dare."

"In Budapest kids demonstrate for air to breathe, more
books, better homes, and a Volkswagen. These children want
to burn and get burned."

I stared at Harvey. "Whaddya say, Harve, baby."

"Screw off, Bloodworth. We're getting a line on you."

"Likewise, Harvey. Heard from J. Edgar lately?"

He dissembled badly. His mouth twitched, but he recovered, looking hastily about to see if Vannie or the dozen or
so French kids in field jackets, milling around him, had heard
me. They hadn't, but now he knew a little more about me. I
couldn't be too sore at Ungerleider (Kantor) because of the
ingenious way in which he was using Flackman as his cover.

"*Ché, Ché! Viva Ché!*"

"*Arriba la revolución!*"

"*Mort aux fascistes!*"

"Off the pigs!"

"Drop dead, you Nazi bastard," Vannie screamed at me.
"You murderer of peasants!"

Ah, Lord, Lord. Do they not know about the gradations of evil—and good? Is it possible that while our State Department is not such a hotsy-totsy outfit, and we do nasty things —like all big nations—that we aren't quite the SS, or Hitler, or even Stalin?

"Smart fucker, aren't you, Bloodworth?" Ungerleider sneered.

"Anybody in your group named Sheldon Kantor?" I asked casually.

No response. I hustled Judy into the auditorium.

We'd arrived early. So early, in fact, that we bumped into Pochastny and a half dozen of his galoots, clogging the lobby. The "editor" looked as if he'd had too much sour cream with his morning blini. The bluff cheeriness was gone. And who could blame him? It must have been a nerve-wracking night— identifying Keramoulian, phoning Moscow, awaiting orders.

He spoke to Judy in what sounded like German. She nodded her head. "Papa is with Mr. Venables."

"Oh?"

"Mr. Venables is arranging for an escort for Papa—the most famous people at the conference, to pay tribute to Papa for his efforts in behalf of freedom."

"Say, that's real sporting of you to let Mr. Malar go," I blurted out. "I mean, the way he's been under wraps."

"Can it, fellah," Pochastny said coldly. "It's your own people have been making trouble here. Dirty hooligans."

"Don't look at me, Mr. Pochastny. I'm a novelist, a delegate."

"I bet. Lemme give you some advice, guy. Don't try any fancy stuff with that gangster Bloom. You don't stand a chance. You Zionist hoodlums think you can get away with anything you want. But I got news for you. Nobody has any use for you. Nobody'll lift a finger to help you. Not the French, or the Americans, or anyone else."

"A domineering, elite people, hey, Antipov? Like old de Gaulle called us?"

"Yeah. This is a law-abiding country. You Jews break the rules all the time, but you won't get away with anything here."

"You misread me, Antipov. As Chairman Mao said, 'When rules inhibit the proletarian revolution, leaders must create a new set of rules.' "

He didn't appear to be fooled by this. I'd run with Bloom for so long, they probably had me carded, indexed, and filed as a Shin-Bet agent. It didn't matter any more. We were in the last inning, and we either got the runs or we were beaten.

As I walked in with Judy I saw Pochastny dispatching his troops: some to one side of the hall, some to the other. I didn't like their looks. A few looked like the Russians I'd seen outside the apartment in Gobelins—lumpy, potato-faced *bul-vons*. Two others appeared to be dark, furtive French types—Corsicans, southerners—the professional gorillas, guns-for-hire, so common at public events in *La Belle France*. Another had the grim, furrowed air of an Algerian. All of them looked as if they wouldn't hesitate to pump bullets into anyone who got in their way. And Bloom had us escaping from these monsters on skate-boards, yet.

The hall was half filled when we walked in. With a verve born of my new life, I led Judy to the cordoned press section, flashed my ten-year-old WNA press card, and we took seats. We were well up front and just a few yards from the side door that led through a corridor to the ramp and esplanade in back of the Palais.

We waited. The room began to fill, and I saw Pochastny's guards take up standing positions in either aisle. The "editor," so recently bereaved by the death of his KGB sidekick, took a seat in the second row, in front of the lectern. Two more hoods materialized and sat down in back of Judy and myself.

"*Bon jour, et bienvenue*," I said to them.

No response. No smile. They had one-inch brows, coarse hair, and one gave off a faint odor of Pernod.

"I am frightened, Ben," Judy whispered.

I took her hand: a reward of faking it. As I have been frank to point out, I am not a notably brave fellow. But now I was clearheaded, absolutely unafraid. Since I was a fraud, it occurred to me that the gun-bearing brutes in back of us, and guarding the aisles, were similar charlatans. We were all actors.

"Ben, I am wondering if we should go through with this," she whispered. She squeezed my hand. "Poor Papa. He doesn't even know you are going to try to rescue him."

There was truth to what she said. Old Malar hadn't the vaguest notion I was about to save him from communism and bring him to freedom. How could he object?

"It will be all right, dearest," I said softly. There was no quaver in my voice, no hesitancy. I believed. I was deceived by my own masquerade.

The hall was filling. Moe Bloom trudged in, unnoticed, a thickset white-haired geezer in a white shirt, carrying a briefcase. Did he still have Jabali's sneaks in it? I thought of my Arab gentleman friend. *Zeit gezundt*, Daoud. Moe had had him taken care of, dumped somewhere, silenced. Or had done it himself? For reassurance I fingered the bar-mitzvah pen he'd given me. Would it stop the thugs on Pochastny's payroll?

Bloom sat down at the center aisle, folded his arms, and seemed to fall asleep. Almost instinctively, his eyes flicked open when Laszlo Veg entered the auditorium from a rear door, and, like a wading bird, walked in stiff strides to a front-row seat. Veg, I gathered, had been backstage with Malar and his honor guard, cheering up his friend.

It was getting close to speech time. The hall was overflowing—standees in both aisles. Malar was a draw, a hero to these people. I'd kidded him about his narrow escapes, his brushes with hangmen and firing squads, his agility and his resilience. But after all the jokes had been made, the old Marxist meant something, a great deal, to these Pakistani physicists and Norwegian editors, Brazilian biologists and Ivory Coast poets,

Cambodian astronomers and Canadian playwrights. He was a survivor, a witness, a man not given to murder and brutality and violence, a sort of interested bystander, a beggarly humanist, a pensioner of an older gentler politics.

"Ah, Mr. Malar is to give the lie to communist mythology, am I not correct?" a kerchiefed Burmese behind me asked a toothy Englishwoman in tweeds.

"Sew Ay am tewld."

"Good, veddy good. His is a voice we can all respect."

"Yace."

"Imre Malar has never compromised, never surrendered, am I correct?"

"Yace. Sew they say."

There is a good deal to be said for decent survivors. Was I doing the right thing yanking Malar out of this hall and across the Atlantic? Was it possible his role as the Robinson Crusoe of Marxism was better suited to the mushier, easier ways of Europe?

A scattering of applause: Venables wafted into view from behind a maroon curtain. He appeared to have had his blond locks washed and set. Alone on the stage, he was an authoritative presence—flapping gray Daks and a dark green jacket, nibbling at the sidepiece of his horn-rimmed specs, abashing everyone with his Oxonian sinusitis, breathing culture and erudition and snobbery.

"Yew all know of course why we are heah," Derek began. "There will be but one speakah, and he is of course my esteemed co-chairman, a bewoved and honored figgah, a wegendawy figgah in the intewectual wife of Euwope. No man has worked harder at building bwidges between our many worlds—East and West, Science and the Humanities, bwack and white, devewoped and underdevewoped nations, Jew and Gentile, in short all of the dispawate and sometimes antagonistic dichotomies of our twoubled times. He has witnessed massive changes in governments, societies, national twends, upheavals, and he has expewienced wifetimes of

264

twavail, stwuggle, honowable toil in the vineyards of politics and social undertakings, not to mention the gweat cultural upheavals of our century. He is a man who knew Freud, counted Bartók and Kodály as fwiends, suffered in pwisons with the gweat weaders and minds of middle Europe, defied tywants and fought the good fight.

"He is thus superbwy quawified to addwess this confwence of world intewects, to make its keynote speech, to inspire these scientific and cuwtural weaders . . ."

Venables went on too long. The audience wanted Malar. As I picked up the buzzing around me, I understood they wanted to hear one thing from him: a denunciation of communism, once and for all. He'd played footsie with them an unbearably long time; the accounting was long overdue from someone as scarred, beaten, and calloused as Malar.

"And so, as an earnest of the deep wespect this confwence has for Imre Malar, we have ahsked that an escort of notables bwing him to the stage for his addwess! Gentlemen!"

Whoever Venables was working for—*Opus Dei? The Mattachine Society?*—they had hired a shrewdie. The escort of honorary brains would get Malar away from the Russians for a few minutes before his speech. He'd have time to sneak a note to someone, deliver a message, make some arrangement.

Rising, applauding, the conference was paying tribute to Malar. Judy cried a little. The notables came down the center aisle. Malar, shuffling along like my Uncle Moishe, was in the middle, looking embarrassed, waving in awkward gestures to the cheering crowd.

"*Viva Malar!*" a Uruguayan shouted.

"*Nous ne pouvons jamais oublier cinquante-six!*"

A lot of them would never forget 1956 and the brave Hungarians. I stretched my neck to look at Pochastny. He stopped applauding on cue when the date was mentioned, and he turned even sourer when the chant was taken up.

"*Vive la révolution de cinquante-six!*"

"*Cinquante-six! Cinquante-six!*"

Ah, the tender sensitivities, the thin skins of bullies and hoodlums! Mention 1956 to a Russian and he sweats and stammers. It is the same today. Soviets don't even want to argue about their bloody business in Israel. After a few mumbled lies about Zionist imperialism, they shut up and sulk, their feelings outraged. How dare anyone suggest that they are a gang of strong-arm bastards?

"Cinquante-six! Cinquante-six!"

The chant became a roaring surf, a breaking wave of sound, gushing into the Russians' offended ears.

"They remember him," I said to Judy, putting my arm around her. "They remember the man who led the students across the Erszebet Bridge."

"Yes, yes, Benny, I know they do. I hear them."

A group of Czechs in one corner had climbed on chairs and were shouting: *"Prague, Prague, Prague!"*

By now the honor guard was at the edge of the stage, and Malar, alone, was shuffling to the steps to ascend it. They'd given him quite an escort—Flackman and Keen from the United States, a Nobel Prize-winning chemist from West Germany, Anzaletti, Shockheim, a Japanese film director, an Indian poetess. But for all the glamour of these worthies, it was the spontaneous tribute from the mass of delegates that was most impressive. He was a shred of decency in an indecent world. The poor old left! It had been sold out, betrayed, devoured by its own monsters, eaten by its own children, subverted, co-opted, de-balled, de-fanged. There had been a few giants, but they were all dead. And Imre Malar, if not a giant, was a larger-than-life legend, an Old Pretender to a Kingdom long vanished.

"You know, your papa doesn't look too bad," I said. "He still has the patch on his head, but there's color in his face."

"The applause is helping," she said, smiling. "Papa loves an audience, especially a friendly one."

Malar was at the lectern now, waving to the delegates. The honor guard took seats on the stage. Don't ask me how or why, but somehow Cooperage and Lila Metrick were up there also, not quite members of the escorting party, but above the groundlings.

Malar took a rumpled sheaf of papers from his inner coat pocket and opened them on the lectern. Once he patted the patch on his gray head, then put his rimless glasses on and studied his speech a moment. He was a despairingly unheroic man, a shabby, scuffed, unraveling, aging trimmer and dodger, a walking tribute to man's bounciness, an outlaster, a Marxist chicken whose neck had been wrung a half-dozen times, but never long enough to force a final croak from his throat. No wonder they admired him.

"Mr. Chairman," Malar said to Venables, "distinguished fellow delegates to this conference, friends, members of the press! I greet you as a survivor!"

The waves of affection formed deep in the back of the hall, rolled across the chamber, crested and broke in a warm and wild shout. Again and again they called his name, chanted their slogans.

"*Vive Budapest!*"

"*Prague! Prague!*"

"*Dachau! Buchenwald! Auschwitz! Vorkuta! Lubianka!*"

Judy shook her head. "Papa can do this to people. I hope the excitement does not exhaust him."

"He's thriving on it."

Malar was a performer. The affection of the international audience buoyed him. I had the feeling that we'd hear his speech the way he wanted us to hear it. Inured to beatings and bright lights and long interrogations, he'd always bounced back. For whatever reasons they had, the Soviets were willing to let him mount this public forum and blast them. I could only conclude that either the speech would not be too abrasive, too defiant, or the Russians simply didn't give a damn what burnt-out Marxists had to say at conferences.

Wiping away a tear of gratitude, Malar was trying to stop the chanting, the burst of feverish applause. "My dear friends," he said, "I am not worthy . . ."

"Yes! Yes! *Da! Oui!*"

"Malar *Sì*, Stalin *No!*"

"Malar *Sì*, Brezhnev *No!*"

This last was a bit close to the nerve and I saw Pochastny muttering to one of his hired guns. It could get sticky before Malar was finished on the stage, maybe not from what he said, but from the audience response.

"Dear friends, I am not worthy of such an accolade," Imre Malar said shakily. "Others have given much more, including their lives, to the endless struggle for intellectual freedom. I am merely an elderly Hungarian, a used-up humanist, a tattered liberal, a ragged believer in the free spirit, trying to make some sense out of our terrible times."

"*Liberté pour l'esprit de l'homme!*" my small historian, Rignac, cried.

"*Liberté pour tous les gens créatifs!*" shouted a lady translator.

"Sinyavsky! Daniel! Ginsburg! Grigorenko!"

These last came from a group of eastern European writers-in-exile—Czechs, Poles, Hungarians.

"And freedom for the Jews of the Soviet Union!" a hoarse, hard voice cracked out. It was Bloom, of course, standing on his seat. "Freedom for the enslaved Jews of the Soviet Union!"

This was more than Pochastny could bear. He was on his feet, hurrying to his squad of gunsels at the side aisle, hurrying back to his seat, looking around the vast room.

There was a sudden silence, and the voice of Vito Anzaletti, Nobel laureate, was heard, clearly, firmly: "*Ricordi Budapest, caro Imre!*"

"Remember Budapest, dear Anzaletti?" Malar asked. "How can we ever forget Budapest of 1956? Or Prague in 1968. Or Hiroshima. Or My Lai. Or Lidice. Or Ouradour. Or Dresden. Or Auschwitz, Sobibor, Dachau, Buchenwald, Mathausen, Treblinka, and Terezin? We are cursed, our generation, with the gift of remembrance, and if we do not remember and swear to learn from these remembrances, what are we here for?"

268

More applause. Malar was speaking English with his pleasurable unspecific *mittel-europäische* accent: misty memories of student meetings in dingy cafés on spring evenings, cheap red wine from Hungarian farms on the shores of the Balaton, sad Gypsy music, shabbily dressed young men, their pockets crammed with leaflets, all talking feverishly about social injustices, cruel governments, a brighter future.

"We move on, fellow delegates," Malar said, "and the topic of my address is 'Europe Moves Ahead.' The topic is not of my choosing, but I respect the wishes of the Program Committee, who selected it for me." A sly smile: Uncle Moishe telling my father how he put a fast one over on the shop steward. "Of course, as many of you know, words have often been selected for me."

A great roar of knowing laughter went up. Even Pochastny grinned.

"He seems fine," I said to Judy.

She was biting her lip. "I hope so. Ben, I hope so."

"All of us want Europe to move ahead, our beloved Europe, this goodly, rich, creative, fertile place, peopled with the descendants of Japhet, the progeny of the white bull. The only question is, my dear friends, in what direction will it move?"

I glanced at Laszlo Veg. The neurologist had stuck a cigarette in his mouth, probably one of his redolent Kossuths, and lit it with his PX lighter. It was like some kind of amulet or fetish to the skinny scientist. Slouching, legs crossed, he didn't seem remotely interested in Malar. No doubt he was mourning his baboon.

"In what direction, I ask?" Malar continued. "Unfortunately, and I speak as a realist, we unarmed and disorganized intellectuals possess limited powers in determining that direction. For it should be apparent to most of us at this late stage in the twentieth century that intellectual freedom exists in many parts of the world only insofar as it does not, does *not*, I say, threaten the existing political power. Indeed, I am grieved to add, there are parts of Europe where this precious freedom of thought, of creativity, is crushed and annihilated even when it poses no threat at all to the centers of power!"

"Bravo, Malar!" Anzaletti cried out.

"Hurrah for Malar!" one of the Czech exiles, a sad, tormented-looking man shouted. "We know what countries you are speaking of! Tell us about the writers in jails in the Soviet Union! Tell us who silences the intellectuals in Russia!"

"Name them! Name the oppressors!"

"A *bas les tyrants de gauche et droit!*" M. Rignac called out.

"Patience, friends," Malar said. "My speech is short and I think it will be responsive to the questions you raise. You know my life and my work. You know that Imre Malar has never compromised . . ."

Old rubber ball! I turned to look at Moe Bloom, and on the word *compromised*, he had clapped a hand to his forehead, as if to say: *Gevald*.

". . . so I speak today of that priceless freedom of the artist, the intellectual, the scientist, to work unfettered, in the open air, to have his say, to proceed freely and without threats, to pursue the truth. Three thousand years ago, the philosophers of ancient Greece, from whom we trace our descent with pride and gratitude, understood this necessity. Why, I ask this conference, has it taken so long . . . so . . . so . . . long . . . for . . . certain polit . . . political . . . to . . ."

Judy gasped and grabbed my hand. Malar had stopped talking. His hands were gripping the edges of the lectern, as if he were fearful of falling. His mouth was ajar and he was opening and closing his eyes, as if momentarily disoriented.

"Papa . . . Papa . . ." Judy moaned. "Ben . . . they have hurt him . . . I must go to him."

"Steady, kid. Maybe he's just tired."

Venables had gone to him and was holding his elbow, speaking gently. Malar's eyes opened wide, he grinned, and then he yawned. It was a crazy grimace. Again, and a third time, he yawned prodigiously. Then he nodded to Venables, as if signifying that he was all right. The audience began to buzz.

"He has been hurt," Judy said. "I know it."

Malar released the lectern, and instead of resuming his speech, he walked away from it, to his right, paced off a small circle, as if strolling about his study, shook his head, and came back to the microphones. He drained a tumbler of water.

"They beat him up," I heard one of the eastern Europeans mutter.

"Antipov, the policeman, is in charge, what does one expect?" another said.

As stunned as Malar, I turned in my seat and looked questioningly at Bloom. Moe ignored me. He was hunched forward, staring at Malar.

"Excuse me, ladies and gentlemen," Malar said. "A temporary seizure of petit-mal." He patted the patch on his head.

"He's fine," I said to Judy. "The excitement, the big crowd got to him."

"He is used to big crowds."

"I was speaking . . . speaking . . . of the Greek philosophers. What a sublime example they set for us in that misty, distant past! Dear friends, were they living and working among us today, those noble souls, Zeno and Themistocles and Plato, they would applaud and appreciate the progressive labors of the Soviet Union in advancing the cause of freedom among the fraternal, peace-loving peoples of the world. Those ancient Greeks would understand the unselfish work of the international socialist movement guided by the Soviet Union, to preserve peace and promote goodwill among all peoples."

Malar had rattled this lunacy off so effortlessly that it took some seconds before it sank in.

M. Rignac was one of the first to realize what he'd said. "*Trahison! Trahison!*" the historian cried.

"Untrue! Untrue!" a refugee Pole shouted.

"Malar, you betray us!"

"Malar, what do you say?"

"Good friends, we must be truthful to ourselves," Malar said. He sipped water. Then he lowered his head, took a deep breath, braced himself at the lectern. His contorted gray face had the look of someone trying to break invisible bonds, to spring free from a restraining grip.

"After more than fifty years," Malar said slowly, "it would appear that the men who rule in Moscow would realize that all men desire freedom, to speak freely, to exchange ideas, to experiment, to act in accordance with . . . with . . . the . . ."

"Ben, he is ill, my poor father is ill," Judy sobbed.

He'd stopped talking. Again, his lower jaw dropped, his mouth opened and he unloosed one of those ghastly yawns. And again. And again. Venables and Cooperage ran to him, but he did not see them, or made no sign that he did. Once more he stepped away from the speaker's stand, and went into that madman's gavotte, a short walk to his right, a small circling stroll, his jaw moving, his head trembling.

"Perhaps you wish to postpone this, Imre?" Venables asked him.

"Derek, I am fine. A bit of indigestion."

"Malar!" a booming Slavic-accented voice called out. "Please tell us what the men in the Kremlin do not realize!"

"Yes, yes, go on!"

"I shall, my good friend. They have failed to realize the treachery of their enemies. The men in Moscow are tolerant and friendly men, who look with fraternal feelings on all intellectuals, who encourage these international meetings, and have generously sent observers here. Is this not evidence of their goodwill?"

A slender blond man was leading the shouting and the angry questions. "Malar! Malar!" he shouted. "You are destroying our hopes!"

Venables raced to the front of the stage. "You are out of

order, Dr. Milic! There will be an opportunity for questions when Mr. Malar has finished."

"Truth is never out of order!" Milic shouted. "Where is the free press in the Soviet Union, or in those nations where its puppets are in control? Where the right to strike? Freedom of assembly? Of religion? The right to protest? Where, tell me, are free elections held?"

Several dozen people were on their feet, shouting at poor Malar.

"Friends, friends, *mes amis, amici, amigos,*" Malar responded multilingually. "I will make all this clear to you. I have always been the partisan of truth and of liberty, and I would not change my views before so august a gathering."

Malar lowered his head—I saw the white patch glistening under the fluorescent lights. Coughing, he then raised his ravaged face and spoke with effort. "I know what has happened in eastern Europe. It is not a story I enjoy relating. But let us be courageous and tell that story again." Malar raised his right fist—not in the communist salute, but in defiance of them.

"After more than half a century, the rulers of the Soviet Union continue to live in fear of even the slightest allusion to freedom of thought," Malar said tensely. "Censorship, suppression, the crushing of artistic and intellectual freedom continue. Dialogue is nonexistent. Debate is anathema. The air is sterile and stationary. And worst of all, the citizens of these oppressed nations seem to have grown weary of the struggle. Those who dissent are punished. And sometimes dissent is not even required to invite brutal repression. The Jews of Poland and Russia see again the terrors of the Czar inflicted on . . . on . . . them . . . these innocent . . . inn . . ."

It was horrible. This time Malar behaved as if he were strangling on his own words. God knows what they'd done to him: drugs, beatings, electric shocks. Like a man possessed by an evil spirit, a dybbuk, a familiar, he writhed and wriggled, straightening his back, convulsing to a crouch, trying to shake off a demon forcing him to behave against his will.

"Enough! Enough!" Judy screamed. "Let him alone!"

"Speak, Malar! Speak!" Dr. Milic shouted. "You are a brave man, and you are telling the truth!"

Then it came again: that hideous yawn, contorting his face, as if he sought to unhinge his jaw. And then the mad promenade away from the lectern, in a circular path. He returned clear-eyed, relaxed, ready to resume his speech after a sip of water. Venables was conferring with Cooperage and others on the stage.

"Forgive me, friends," Malar said lightly, "but I suffer attacks of vertigo occasionally. I am fine now. Yes, more water." He downed half a glass and rested an arm on the stand.

"History is a demanding teacher," he said airily. "We must pay close attention to her. And history tells us that what artists and intellectuals, in their special way, conceive to be freedom is often not freedom at all, but irresponsibility, license, disorder, and other manifestations of the counterrevolution."

"Traitor!" someone yelled. "Stalinist!"

"Apologist! You dare not apologize for October 1956!"

"Ben," Judy wept. "They have destroyed him."

The room was bursting with noise, shouts. They'd come to hear the last brave voice of independent liberal Marxism. Instead they were watching a bemused old man, yawning, acting in an incoherent and disturbed manner, alternating between courageous attacks on the Kremlin and cowardly apologetics in their behalf.

"Friends, do not be upset," Malar said. He was grinning! "I am in good health. I am happy. I am a man fulfilled, to be here with so many old comrades of battles past. I can state with assurance that Imre Malar has no enemies, hates no man, and bears no grudges."

"Even against Rakosi, who tortured you?" someone cried.

"Let me say that in my old age, I understand him better."

By now his performance was so incredible, so unbalanced, that the delegates were beyond protest. They were stupefied. A soft, numbing cloud appeared to have settled over Malar; he almost appeared to be laughing, his eyes crinkly with grim humor.

"We must learn to trust our friends in the Soviet Union," he went on. "Why speak of a thaw? The waters of fellowship were never frozen. It was frozen only for those who wished to remain out in the cold. Communism has always been a warm and comforting bath, a mineral spa, to revive and refresh us, like the invigorating sulfur baths of my native Budapest."

The hisses and boos started again. Building in intensity, they arose from all over the chamber. I looked about the vast room. Bloom was zipping open his briefcase. Venables, Cooperage, Flackman, and the other wheels on the stage looked stunned. The most relaxed man in the chamber, other than Malar, seemed to be that heartless bird, Laszlo Veg. His legs insolently crossed, he was lighting another Kossuth, releasing the noxious smoke in a camouflaging cloud.

"Nothing is gained from perpetual hostility," Malar said. His voice was liquid, as persuasive as an insurance salesman's. "I have learned to shrug at so-called restrictions on my so-called freedoms. The greatest freedom in the world is to be agreeable and pliable and to get along with the other man——"

"When he points a gun at your head?" Milic cried.

"—because he has got his problems also, and I would rather try to understand them than go around looking for fights, with my teeth clenched and my face in a snarl, like a gunman in an American cowboy movie."

"This is the worst, the most idiotic, the most awful speech Papa has ever made." Judy was so angry she had stopped crying. "It is not his style. It is not the way he writes."

"He seems to be making it up as he goes along."

"I—I cannot believe it, all this garbage he is saying."

275

Her old man blathered on, expressing his admiration for just about everyone he'd ever known—Mao, everyone in the Kremlin, Richard Nixon, and even his jailers of years past: Horthy, Szalasi, Rakosi, Khrushchev, Kadar, the whole roster of nice customers who'd ruined his digestion. This toadying *bonhomie* so astounded the delegates that they had almost stopped interrupting him.

"In all his life," Judy said, fury lighting fires in her green eyes, "Papa has never read words written for him by someone else. He has always been his own man."

I sucked in my breath. "Judy, he's someone else's man today. And I intend to find out whose."

"—and I hold no grudge of any kind against the people of the United States of America. I like them. I like their government. What is essential is the shedding of all these hostile tendencies. That is essential to the writer, the artist, the scientist. We must reach upward for an elevated state of transcendent perceptions, of spiritual enlightenment, in which we lose these destructive predilections for anger and violence. It has perhaps been an error of my political life that I have too often been bellicose and contentious. But I am not too old to mend my ways.

"Yes, I have traveled a long, hard, and winding road, but today I feel only gratitude toward my Soviet associates, and I applaud their efforts to bring peace and socialism to the Third World! Any friend of Chairman Kosygin's is a friend of mine. I have never met a communist I didn't like. And let us not bury poor Stalin's memory too soon. He was, after all, a good and farsighted man——"

"Stop him! Stop him!" shouted Dr. Milic, who, I learned later, had spent sixteen years in one of Stalin's prisons. "He is betraying us! May God forgive you, Malar, for these vile statements! You, who led the revolt against the Soviet monster! You, who spent time in their jails and was tortured by their police! Malar—go tell these fairy tales to the dead freedom fighters in Kerepesi cemetery, to the martyrs of Prague, to the

276

writers starving in Russian prisons! Tell them to Sinyavsky and Daniel!"

"Tell them, Malar! Tell them!"

"Tell us of Budapest, Malar! The Russian tanks!"

"Where is there a free press in Russia?"

"*Traditore!*"

"*Trahison!*"

"Stalinist murderer!"

"Tell us of your affection for Rakosi," Milic cried. "He who pulled out your fingernails and fed you stale bread for six months!"

"I have no sense of enmity toward that misguided man," Malar said. "I am a friend to all, enemy to none."

Staggering slightly, he turned away, and seemed to wink at Venables. He patted another grotesque yawn into oblivion and addressed his co-chairman. "Derek, some questions perhaps . . ."

As if they hadn't been throwing questions at him all afternoon!

"But only friendly questions," Malar said idiotically.

Venables came to his side. Behind them, Flackman, Cooperage, and Metrick were huddling, discussing the outrageous performance, the way he had changed course in midspeech at least three times, the manner in which he had betrayed every prediction about the brave attack on communism he was supposed to deliver. Flackman, of course, was annoyed for another reason: he wasn't the star.

"Well," Venables said cheerily, "let's see who had their hands up first . . ."

A plantation of waving arms confronted them. There were irate Bulgarians, furious Brazilians, seething Ceylonese, enraged Guineans. They'd come to hear Malar, one of the last of the undefeated, and they had been deceived, gulled, by a man not in possession of his senses, a blathering, nattering old nut.

"Get ready, Judy," I whispered. "Bloom may not get a

chance to pull his stunt. We may have to grab Papa fast."

My heart battered against my sternum. Action, action. I craved it, after the torrent of nonsense Malar had unloosed. I was not afraid; *I'd get him out.*

"There go the Bad Guys," I said. Pochastny had nudged a galoot seated next to him and signaled to two others in the aisle. They began to move toward the stage. Two other gunsels walked to the rear of the assembly hall. Shouts, cries, threats rose from the audience, and Venables had trouble recognizing anyone.

"What have they done to you, comrade?"

"Who tortured you? Show us who!"

"Malar, speak, speak! They forced you to do this!"

Judy and I got up and walked to the apron. Venables seemed petrified by the savage, chaotic reaction of the delegates.

"Imre!" cried a man I knew to be a Hungarian refugee leader in Paris. "What about your friends? The murdered freedom fighters? What of Rajk and Nagy and all the others?"

To this cry from the heart, this anguished shout, Malar responded:

"Those were all misunderstandings, my friends. Old history. Of no account."

"You betray your own revolution!"

Malar smiled stupidly. "It was not a revolution. It was a counterrevolution. The regrettable events of 1956."

Judy was staring at her father in disbelief. "He is drugged," she said to me. "I did not believe they would dare, but they did. They have filled him with drugs and forced him to do this."

I heard Moe Bloom's bellow echoing across the tumult. "Mr. Chairman, Mr. Venables, if you are chairman, please keep order here," the Zionist shouted. Ever the parliamentarian, Moe. He might have been attending a wild session of the Knesset.

"Ah . . . the gentleman . . ." Venables looked around

the field of waving arms, shaking fists, raging faces.

"I ask to be heard!" Bloom boomed. Yes, he had the power to command. You earned it, I supposed, smuggling concentration camp orphans past British sentries, or manning a rickety machine gun against Arab raiders.

Moe had a sense of the dramatic too. He waited until the shouts had subsided, a tough, paternal, broken-nosed figure, as adamant as the Golan Heights. An Italian reporter from a right-wing newspaper standing next to Judy turned to a countryman from the communist *l'Unità* and asked: *"Chi è?"*

"Si chiama Bloom," the Red answered. *"Ebreo-Americano, vecchio scrittore, vecchio condottiere."*

Among the international brotherhood of communists, Moe always claimed, he had never been forgiven. They still hadn't —a Red reporter remembered him and thought he was a bandit. Bloom would have been complimented.

"Mr. Chairman," Moe thundered, as he climbed his chair and waved a handful of the mimeographed sheets about, "Mr. Chairman, I have here in my hand copies of the speech Imre Malar was going to make to this meeting! And I challenge him to state whether or not this is, in fact, the speech he intended to make before someone forced him to change his mind!"

The audience was hushed. Malar appeared to be almost grateful. Pochastny also listened politely.

Bloom squinted through his eyeglasses and began to read.

"Fellow delegates, I am here as a witness, a survivor. I am here to tell you some unpleasant truths about the Soviet Union and the men who control it today. They mean well, they claim they are trying to be decent, and that they are not cruel men. But they are afraid. They fear freedom. They fear free speech and a free press. They tremble at the thought of dissent. They are haunted, for all their power, by the specters of discussion, protest, dialogue, experiment, intellectual liberty. For all their promises of an emerging humane Marxist philosophy, of a system softened through free inquiry and unfettered minds, we must be frank with ourselves and admit that these promises are false, specious, misleading. Our hopes have been dashed. Our good wishes were wasted.

"Fellow intellectuals, artists, writers, scientists, men of goodwill, let us confront these terrible truths with courage and without blinking, and say to the rulers in Moscow, and their puppet rulers around the world, you must change, you must let thinking men think, creative men create, honest men debate issues, and let society develop, and grow, and mature along humane, liberal, progressive ways—without the heavy tread of the policeman in the night, the eternal threat of the cold prison cell, the scaffold, the firing squad."

They'd never let Bloom finish; they went wild. There were cheers and shouts and applause and a surge toward the stage. For a moment I thought they would storm it, and carry the old man off on their shoulders. Pochastny was moving up the stairs, but he couldn't get through the biggies, who were giving Malar—or Bloom's reading of his original speech—a standing ovation.

"That is Papa!" Judy cried. "Those are his words!"

Malar himself smiled secretively; he wasn't saying yes, he wasn't saying no.

"Mr. Chairman, there is no need for me to read the entire address," Bloom shouted. "I shall hand out copies so that the delegates and the representatives of the world press can see for themselves what Imre Malar intended to say to this conference, before agents of a foreign power forced him——"

"The Soviets! The Russians!"

"Point them out!"

"—to change his mind, almost in mid-sentence. Further, I promise all of you that in time the diabolical means used to bend Malar's will, and the people responsible, will stand exposed and revealed for their unspeakable crimes against freedom!"

With that, Bloom hurled his papers high in the air, and they fluttered and hung and wafted about, like confetti at a political convention. Delegates scrambled for them; reporters ringed Bloom, while others, including platoons of cameramen, rushed to the stage.

As quickly as he had started his *confronta*, Bloom seemed to vanish. I saw him scurrying down front—to Laszlo Veg. Then I lost sight of both of them, as Judy and I allowed ourselves to be swept forward in a churning, thrashing mass of reporters, still cameramen, and newsreel types. I maneuvered Judy in front of a TV newsfilm team—a huge Frenchman lugging an Eclair camera, and a surly litle fellow with a Nagra recorder slung over one shoulder—knowing that they'd get close to Malar and run interference for us.

The audience was still shouting, now that they had a chance to read the Hungarian's original speech. Aroused at first, they were now furious; many screamed threats to the Russians, others wept.

"*Vergogna! Vergogna!*" an Italian socialist cried.

"Mr. Chairman," the English lady in tweeds shrilled, "I demahnd that the Russian observers be ahsked to leave this conference at once, or make cleah what they have done to Mr. Malar!"

Pochastny's goons were moving in. But with the crowd in its inflamed state, with the Russians exposed as brutes and torturers, they were hardly ready to seize Malar and rush him out of the hall. Besides the strategy was working. The reporters wanted him and had formed a ring around him, some on the stage, a mob of them below, some waiting at the side steps.

"Go get Papa," I told Judy.

She ran up the steps, rushed past Venables and Cooperage, who were supporting the wavering Malar, and they exchanged Magyar endearments. Judy took her father's arm and led him to the steps, as cameras clicked, lights flashed, and questions were hurled at the co-chairman.

"What did they do to you, sir?"

"Have you been drugged, Mr. Malar?"

"Est-ce que ce papier est votre discours original?"

"Vas fur Tortur, Herr Malar?

Malar didn't respond, but permitted himself to be led down the stairs and toward the rear door that led to the esplanade of the Palais. I noticed, with some amusement, that Flackman and Metrick had detached themselves from the drama. They almost seemed to be sulking. It wasn't their show; they had no starring roles; and so they sat back and observed it with a lofty *apartheid*.

As Malar and Judy neared the door, I turned to the agglutinized mob of journalists and shouted: *"M. Malar a quelque chose très importante à dire—mais, dehors! Allons!"*

That was all they needed. With the enormous Frenchman leading the charge, they practically lifted Malar and his daughter off their feet and propelled them through the exit. Pochastny's thugs lingered at the edge of the crowd—the dough-faced Russians, the dark Corsicans, the sinister Algerian. They would not attempt a snatch in front of the press. When all is said and done, these animals are sensitive, tender people, who want to be loved.

"Were you beaten, sir? Threatened in any way?" a *New York Times* man shouted, as a woman from *Agence France Presse* dug him in the kidneys, and she, in turn, took an unintentional but firm goose from the representative of *Osservatore Romano*.

"Perchè ha cambiato i suoi paroli?"

"Malar! Herr Malar! Wo gehen Sie jetzt?"

"Pochastny, est-il KGB, M'sieu?"

Rolling, floating, born on an inexorable wave of sweaty bodies and determined wills, our feet barely touching the ground, we progressed, cushioned and insulated, through the hallway as lights flashed, curses were unloosed, questions were hurled in five languages. Malar said not a word. Judy and I were on either side of him now, and we kept assuring the journalists that he would have something to say as soon as he caught his breath.

Afternoon sunlight blinded us as we burst out of the doors onto the *terrasse* of the Jardins de Trocadero. Immediately, as we found ourselves freed of the binding confines of the corridor, the pursuing group spread out, and I began to worry. I had reason to. One of the Russians and the Algerian were working their way toward us. But the cameras kept whirring, and the questions kept coming. We hurried Malar down a short flight of wide steps that led to the long ramp, on which, according to Bloom, the children from the foreign embassies went skate-boarding every afternoon.

"*Un mot d'explication, M. Malar!*" the woman from AFP howled. "*Seulement un mot!*"

The man with the Eclair was joined by three other newsfilm crews, who stayed close to us, forming a protective ring of heavy gear around the Hungarian. Right behind them were the KGB's hired hands. The Russian was grinning at me, pointing to Malar, trying to explain that he, good old Ivan, or Gyorgi, or Pavel, would now take over.

"*Shalom.* I am Ayal."

A whey-faced squirt in short pants handed me a skateboard. He was wearing a white yarmulka.

"*Shalom.* What do I do now?"

"You vait mit me. Mr. Malar and daughter go in deh texi."

A pale green Peugeot 404 cab was parked, motor running, at the head of the ramp. One door was open.

Judy looked at me with terrified eyes. Was this lunacy necessary? Was my dream of getting Imre Malar to defect a doomed enterprise, meaningless, of value only to my hungry ego?

"Get in, Judy. I'll catch up with you."

She hesitated. The reporters again formed a clot around them. Malar seemed to bend and sway; his hand went to the white patch on his skull. He looked awful—putty skin, filmed eyes, his lips working noiselessly.

"Go on, darling," I said. "You're safe. Bloom arranged it."

She helped her father into the cab and got in with him,

then shut the door. It started down the ramp, slowly, to avoid the kids on their skate-boards.

"Plizz, I am friend of fommily!" the Russian shouted. He began to dogtrot after the taxi and grabbed the handle. I must say he moved swiftly for an overweight man, a glutton full of borscht and blini. The Algerian started after him, and the two of them pursued the taxi as it rolled in low gear down the roadway, and toward the Avenue de New York.

"Now get on your budd," Ayal ordered me. "Following like me."

I mounted the skate-board. The Israeli kid got on his. "What do we do now?" Some journalists were a few steps behind. Most of them, however, had stopped at the crest of the hill, assuming that Malar was through for the day.

"Right into dem," Ayal said. "Fest. Hit dem fest."

We began to roll. I balanced artfully—my son Eddie taught me how—and the boards picked up speed on the steep ramp.

With his hard little head lowered, Ayal smashed into the Russian's lower spine, knocking him off his feet. I followed, crashing into the Algerian's liver. But I hadn't hit him hard enough. As the Russian tried to extricate himself from the thick hedges along the ramp, the Algerian, a scrambler, light on his feet, regained his balance and grabbed the rear bumper of the slowly moving cab. This time Ayal and I, after getting off to new starts, picking up speed, and taking aim, smashed into him from the same side. He went ass over tea-kettle off the road, and the Israeli kid went with him, shouting Haganah war cries as they rolled into the bushes.

"*Gardez! Gardez!*" a reporter cried.

"*Circonstance critique! Police!*" I shouted.

The green Peugeot made it to the Place de Varsovie at the bottom of the Trocadero Gardens. I mounted my skate-board once more, and, unimpeded, rolled down the hill. A backward glance told me we were home free. The cameramen were taking photos of the Algerian and Ayal, and a mob of reporters had surrounded the Russian goon.

I reached the taxi the instant that the traffic light on the corner went to green. I had no time to get inside the cab with the Malars. So I did the next best thing. Still balancing on my skate-board, I grabbed the Peugeot's bumper as it turned onto the Avenue de New York.

"Stop!" I screamed. "Lemme in!"

But the driver had other ideas. There was little time to be lost if we were to make it to the American Embassy before Pochastny's mobile reserve caught up with us. There we went, on six wheels—the taxi's four, my two—across the sixteenth arrondissement, barreling toward the Place d'Alma. Horns honked at me; tourists guffawed; a *flic* blew his whistle at me, demanding that I stop.

"*Jesus, lemme in!*" I wailed.

The skate-board was wobbling dangerously. Under the best of conditions, a man can get killed by a car in Paris by merely stepping out of his house at three A.M. on a Tuesday in August. Now I was a moving target, a clay pigeon, a poor work in progress. The bloody appetites of Parisian motorists would make an end of me and my dumb charade, and I would be laughed at and mocked by the Flackmans and the Cooperages, forever and ever.

On the Avenue Montaigne, we blasted past the ateliers of the couturiers, and an elegant woman in her sixties, parading a brace of apricot poodles, shouted at me: "*Quel fou!*"

By now, I was adjusted to the motions of the car—a Peugeot is a smooth-riding vehicle—and my clever feet had grafted themselves to the smooth pine. The oiled wheels were an extension of my ego, an affirmation of my dazzling talent.

I had the feeling, as I clutched the bumper and glided and balanced skillfully, that it "was the way it should have been all my life." It was like Hemingway shooting those ducks in the Venetian marshes early in the morning, those "white-eyed pochards."

"*Arrêtez! Arrêtez!*" a gendarme shouted to me from his tower in the Rond-Point.

But there was no stopping the car; no stopping me. I rolled

along the streets of Paris, agile, graceful, airy, oiled, sinuous, as free a soul as ever skate-boarded on the Champs Elysées. Never had my mind been clearer, my *esprit* higher. Never again would I feel inferior, snubbed, ignored, in the presence of demigods like Flackman and Metrick and Keen. As for Cooperage, I would someday thank him for supplying me with a role. My lungs burst with electric ozone, my skin prickled. Gently, as the airline offices and banks and elegant restaurants of the Champs whizzed by me, I shifted one foot, then another, maneuvering the weight of my body to stay erect, rolling, rolling, rolling forever . . .

Near the Clemenceau metro stop, the cab halted for a light. I was exhausted, enervated, drenched in honest sweat. I trembled—an inch in each direction—so violently that I knew I could not continue my rash balancing act. So I stepped off the skate-board, and as two *flics* studied me with bemused ruddy faces, I climbed into the front seat of the taxi, next to the driver.

"To the American Embassy, I guess," I gasped.

"That's right," the woman driver said. It took me a moment to recognize her. Her curls had been tucked into a peaked cap: it was Moe's wife Sophie.

"Mrs. Bloom?"

"Don't be surprised. I drove the armored busses between Tel Aviv and Jerusalem for a whole year. The Latrun run on the monastery road. This is nothing for me. At least we are not getting shot at by Jordanians."

I looked in back of us. "But maybe by Russians." How pleased I was with the evenness, the calm of my voice. "Sophie, have you met Mr. Malar and his daughter, Judy?"

She nodded. "Mr. Malar I met many, many years ago. His daughter I have not. How do you do, young lady."

"I am pleased to meet you," Judy said. Then she screamed: "Watch out! Watch out! Wa——"

Sophie Bloom, with a lightning reflex action—I suppose you learned that guiding armored busses in 1947—wheeled

286

the Peugeot onto the sidewalk of the Avenue Gabriel, scattering surly French and frightened tourists.

"The bastard tried to ram us," I said.

From out of a side street one of Pochastny's black Citroëns had come at us—its sharklike snout aiming at the Peugeot's soft flanks. They'd missed us by inches, coming to a shrieking, rubbery halt as we swerved away. The doors of the Citroën flung open and two of the KGB's paid guns came running out—the lowbrow Algerian and the Russian I'd knocked galley-west on the ramp. Sophie stopped in front of a café table, deftly backed up, and bounced into the street again. We were off, home free—almost—to the American Embassy.

The taxi stopped at the corner of the Avenue Gabriel and Rue Boissy d'Anglas. "I'll wait here for you. Moe says you should come out and report every ten minutes."

I kissed Sophie and opened the cab door for Malar and Judy. Then, keeping an eye alert for the black Citroën—it had started again, moving toward us, but Mrs. Bloom did not seem concerned—I escorted my wards, my precious defectors, into the elegant court of the embassy and then into the foyer. I wanted to kiss the flag, to hug the shave-headed Marine sergeant behind the high desk. I had done it. I had pulled it off. I'd be in the newspapers. From now on my books would not be reviewed, but *I* would be, and these notices would have to be favorable.

As I walked up to the reception desk, I had an unnerving quaver of doubt, like the first troubling stab of diarrhea in the lower bowel after a Mexican dinner. After all, I'd told nothing of my daredevil escapade to anyone at the embassy. I had no appointment. I knew no one in the place. I had no credentials. I could hardly say to this handsome, pink-faced Marine, aged twenty-two, that I had two defecting Hungarians on my hands, and that there was a carload of Russian gangsters outside ready to grab them—and me—unless they were flown to America at once.

"May I see the first secretary?" I asked coolly.

287

"Do you have an appointment, sir?" He was staring at my skate-board. For some odd reason, perhaps because it represented security, safety, flight, I'd lugged it out of the taxi, and was holding it by the wheels.

"No, no appointment, Sergeant."

"I'm afraid he's gone for the day. And so has the second secretary, and the commercial attaché. The press secretary is at the conference at the Palais de Chaillot." From the skate-board, his innocent green eyes had wandered to my sparse beard, my beads, my denim bell-bottoms. Clearly, I was suspect. And the stooped foreign-looking man in back of me, the pale, shivering girl—they were no help either.

"Judy," I said, "you and Papa sit down. I'll try to work something out." They took seats at the side of the lobby. "Judy," I called after her, "if the Russians come running in, the sergeant will protect you. He can handle a whole division."

"Russians?" the boy asked.

"Sergeant, I can't kid around any more. Who is in charge of defectors here?"

"De——?"

"Citizens of communist states who want to leave illegally. That man over there is a Hungarian, a leading intellectual, and he wants to come to America. The young lady is his daughter. She wants to come also."

"Hungarians are a problem, sir. We've been warned about them. That priest in Budapest—he's still in the embassy. Once they get in . . ."

"Mindszenty, young man. No, this is nothing like that. They don't want to set up housekeeping here, they just want to go to America. Preferably tonight."

"Sir, I can't——"

"Look. Here's my passport. My ID card from the conference. Listen, Sergeant, there is a black Citroën full of KGB assassins outside, and unless you let me talk to someone, you'll be an accessory."

He was frowning at my passport. "Hmmm. Bloodworth. That your name?"

I moaned and clapped my hands to my ears. "Jesus."

"Sure it's his name," Tom Bragg said.

I spun around. Bragg had emerged from a side door and was standing right behind me. His teeth blinded me; the afternoon sunlight glinted on his shaved head. It had seemed unlikely that I would ever welcome Tom Bragg's robust, ruddy Darien Country Club face, but I loved the man at that moment. "Tom! Tom! Am I glad to see you! Look—look——" I pointed to my charges. "That's Imre Malar, Tom, eastern Europe's leading Marxist voice, its conscience. He wants to defect."

"Sure he does, kid. But later."

Bragg's golf-hardened fingers dug into my right forearm and he began guiding me to a rear door. Yesterday Moe Bloom had rescued me from him; that morning, Venables had interrupted as he and Chipper Latour had tried to pin me down. But now I went with him willingly. He was my—our—savior.

"But can we leave Malar there . . . and Judy . . ." I mumbled.

"Safe as in their home," he chuckled.

"That isn't very reassuring, Tom. Can't we bring 'em in with us, and I'll explain?"

"In a minute, kid."

As he whisked me through the door, I shouted: "Sergeant! I'm holding you responsible! Judy! I'll be right back!"

The door slammed behind us. Bragg did not release me. I was getting annoyed with the big lox. "Tom, leggo, willya?" I yelled. "Listen, that's pretty stupid leaving Malar out there. The guy wants to go to the States. I have connections at State. You're just a small-time DIA operative, Tom, I know all about you. You don't land a big name like Malar every day of the week."

Ignoring my harangue, he began punching out a combination on a set of push buttons set into a recess in a wall, near a metal door. There was a faint click after Bragg had punched out the message, and the door moved aside, into the wall. We passed into a bleak corridor, and I had the feeling that we were moving into a different building. Then he ushered me into a small windowless room: gray walls, gray carpeting, a desk, a phone, two chairs.

"Be my guest, Ben."

"Tom, for God's sake, listen to me. Malar is a big fish. We've got him. I pulled it off. This will make every newspaper in America, the biggest defection since Stalin's daughter. I know your field is weaponry and body counts, but it wouldn't hurt you to diversify."

Bragg sat down behind the desk and waited until I slumped into the chair. Then he stared at the ceiling and ran his hand over his blond fuzz twice.

"How's your uncle, Benny?"

"My uncle?"

"Yes, the old gentleman with the funny accent and the big Cadillac."

"Oh, Uncle Moe. He's fine and dandy. Touring the Loire châteaux today with his wife. Now look, can't we cut this crap and get to Imre Malar and his daughter? If you keep *futzing*, there's going to be one hell of a shoot-up in the lobby of the embassy. There are a bunch of guys from the Thirteenth Directorate, paid killers, waiting around the block for him."

Bragg's eyes opened wide and he fiddled with the collar of his button-down shirt. "Really picked up all the lingo, didn't we, Ben?" He jerked forward, leaning over the desk; they must have taught him that in a Dale Carnegie total immersion course. Forceful. Direct. Sincere. "Benny, you don't have any Uncle Moe. That dialect comedian was Moses Bloom, an American citizen, and a shifty troublemaker who runs errands for the Shin-Bet. We've got our eye on him, and anyone who does favors for him."

"Better not touch him, Tom. He's clean. He's more anti-communist than you are, and he has been for fifty years. Besides this is an election year."

"Bloom is no concern of ours," he said. "Listen, kid, you read the papers. We've got lots of sympathy for those people out there. They have lots of smarts, and who can love Arabs anyway? So long as Bloom operates within the law, we don't care. We even help those people out from time to time. Bloom and company aren't on our priority list."

"And I am?"

"It's a possibility."

"Well, if I'm so damned important, how about listening to me? There's this fellow Malar, see——"

With that naïve rudeness that grows out of total confidence in one's estate, race, religion, job, and capacity for martinis, Bragg yawned in my face. Wide, wide, opened his Standard Goy of New Jersey mouth and I saw his mighty choppers again. It was a mouth nourished on a thousand Gristede shells of beef scorching on a thousand charcoal briquet fires. As he stretched I noticed that his left hand was bandaged, a thick white wrapping, covering palm and the lower parts of his fingers. It had not been bandaged yesterday when he had shoved the automatic into my short ribs. In keeping with my new life, I realized that his wound might have some significance. One of the advantages of being a faker was that you could try anything, anything at all. And sometimes you hit the right combination, just the way Tom Bragg had opened the sliding door with the correct sequence of push buttons.

"Getting your rabies shots, Tom?" I asked.

"Hmmm?" He tried to be offhand, but I detected an iciness in his eyes.

"A baboon can give you a wicked bite. You go around grabbing baboons they'll sink those big white fangs in you."

"Ah . . ." He turned his head sideways. "Ah. Uncle Moe tell you all this?"

The sheer joy of being so full of crap you can say anything you want to! In this new realm of lying and deceit, I was truly at home, casual, adjusted, as content as a suburban house-holder mowing his small lawn, spreading fertilizer, dusting his roses. Utterly confident, I barged on, jabbing a finger at Bragg now and then to underscore my points.

"Forget about Bloom," I said airily. "I got to Veg's secret zoo just after you left in something of a hurry. You tried to steal one of Veg's apes, didn't you, Tom? You shot it full of tranquilizers—I located the dart in the ape's hide—and then you tried to haul it out of the apartment. The monster bit you. Then a nasty Russian named Hrant Keramoulian, a professional assassin who reports to Rodin, caught you in the act. You exchanged shots with Keramoulian and you killed him. But in the gunfight, you used the baboon as a shield, and it was killed. I had a few words with the Armenian before he went off to that great collective farm in the sky. When you heard me and my friends coming up the stairs, you beat it out the back way. A badly botched job, Tom. One dead Russian. One dead baboon."

Bragg applauded noiselessly. "You sure are a pistol, Benny. And a lot tougher, a lot smarter than I thought." He held his wounded mitt out and studied the bandage. "Damn. That baboon was a lot stronger than I figured. Filled the bugger full of knockout juice, and he still kicked and screamed."

"And he died too soon, didn't he, Tom? He's of no use to you dead, is he? Whatever it is Veg is doing to those animals you'll never know from a dead ape, will you? I have the notion that neither you nor Keramoulian knew about that lab until late yesterday. He went there to get Veg, you went there to steal a baboon, and you met. You were meant for each other. Anyway, as an American, I'm glad it was you who got him. Bloom says he killed twenty people, so he isn't much of a loss to anyone, except maybe the Thirteenth Directorate. I wonder if they'll give him a state funeral."

"Bloom, hey? You did this all by yourself, but you keep coming back to Bloom."

"Moe and I help each other out."

"He took you to Veg's place, didn't he? On a phoned tip?"

"No," I lied. "I took him."

The phone rang: a low, discreet buzz. Bragg picked it up, listened to someone briefly and nodded. "Fine, fine," he said. "No, that's okay. Thank you." He hung up.

I leaned forward. "Is that the Marine? Is that about Malar?"

"Relax, Ben. We have lots to talk about." He shook his head. "Boy, you are a rare bird. I never know when you're putting me on. I mean, you may be a fake, and you may not, but you've got lots of smarts."

"You ought to get that rabies shot. I think it's a course of twelve. Right in the la-bonze, and they hurt. Of course, what's important is to determine if the animal is rabid. They'll have to get that dead baboon, cut some brain tissue, and run tests on it. But that may be a little difficult. Veg has probably done away with the body. Or Pochastny. Incidentally, Pochastny's real name is Antipov, political section, First Department."

Glibness is my strong suit; I could always rattle on, put words and sentences together. Thus far, I felt, it had given me an advantage over the DIA man. But I knew that over the long haul, his dull, dogged manner would win. I couldn't keep up the mad baiting forever. And he could sit behind that desk all afternoon, study me, prod me, and unmask me. Moreover, I had to keep in mind—it wasn't easy—that my primary mission was not to con this bathtub salesman, but to get the Malars into the United States.

"This letter signed by Mr. DiGiglio," Bragg said casually, taking it from his inner jacket pocket. "It's a doozy, Ben. The cryptanalysts have been up all night with it." He spread it on the desk alongside another sheet of paper.

"It doesn't mean a darn thing, Tom. It's my son's Little League batting averages."

"Sure it is, sure it is."

Damn! I couldn't even tell the truth any longer! I tried, and no one believed me. All credibility was gone forever.

Mendacity, brazenness, fraud, masquerades: these were my weapons.

"Screw that letter, Tom. It's a false trail. I wrote it because I knew someone would lift it, just the way they lifted Veg's letter. I'm interested in only one thing. Getting Imre Malar and Judy Malar on a plane as soon as possible and into the United States. Forget who I'm working for, or what my job really is here. You'll find out soon enough."

He was shaking his head slowly from side to side; I was infuriated.

"And while you're at it," I shouted, "get that phony Boy Scout off my back."

He stopped moving his head. "Scout? What Scout?"

"Tom, you never made it to that Actor's Studio they run at Defense, did you? You know who I mean. That hood Chipper Latour. Louise Latour's alleged nephew and keeper. Some Eagle Scout! He, and someone else, maybe you, jumped Malar off the Rue St. Denis the other night and tried to get the patch off his skull. I have a feeling Latour was with you last night when you tried to heist Veg's ape, got bit, and knocked off the Armenian. Incidentally, he muttered something about 'knees' before he died, and I figured out what he meant."

"That a fact?"

"Yup. Bare knees. Chipper was in his scouting shorts. It was the kind of detail that a KGB killer, breathing his last, might remember."

"You're just loaded with smarts, aren't you, Ben?" He wasn't happy with me any longer. Fun time had ended.

"I made Dean's List at Columbia regularly. But I missed Phi Bete because I couldn't pass physics."

Bragg tapped the desk. "I never had the advantages of an Ivy League education. Did my undergrad work at good old North Dakota State."

"I had a scholarship, I worked my way through, and I lived in the Bronx with my parents," I said. "And I don't have to apologize to a big smoked salmon like you. Now come on, Tom, let's cut this nonsense and do something about the Malars. Get on the phone and call someone. Get one of those wafer-assed State Department flunkies off the golf course and get him here——"

"Yes, you are a pistol," Bragg said, staring at the papers in front of him.

"I try hard."

"Maybe too hard, kid."

"Hah?"

His eyes were on mine—pupil-to-pupil, a laser beam gleaming between our orbital sockets. "Bupo," he said softly.

"Bupo? Up your Bupo, buddy."

"You're Bupo."

"What does that mean?"

"Ben, we've cracked this cipher. All the clowning and lying and fakery and false clues in the world won't help you, any more than this ridiculous cover about some Hungarian hack and his daughter. You see, kid, we know who is paying you and who sent you here, but we'd like to know why. We'd also like to zero in on your tie-in with the Shin-Bet, even though they aren't your principals. But we'll get it all on paper before long."

"Start writing, Jack. That letter was a fake, I repeat. My son Eddie's batting averages. Chipper Latour picked my pocket, the way he did opening day. Light-fingered little fart. After he took Bloom's letter to Veg and then returned it with a warning, I figured I'd give him something else to steal. He did. That's a cute trick he has, using that drunken lady as a cover, asking *shlemiels* like me to cart her around, and rifling my pockets when I'm laboring under her heft and avoiding her foul breath."

"Bupo, Benny, Bupo."

"Jesus, cut that baby talk. Is Bupo like Maypo?"

"You know darn well what I mean. Tell us about the *Bundespolizei*."

"West German? East?"

"Try again."

"Austrian? I give up."

"Say, we do play a dumb game, don't we? *Bundespolizei* is the Swiss counterespionage organization."

"So?"

"You're working for them."

"You're out of your tree, Tom."

"Don't deny it. It's all here in this letter to the nonexistent DiGiglio. The cipher clerks broke it last night. I was going to pick you up at the hotel before, but that queer Englishman got in the way. So it worked out fine, you coming here with those two Romanians——"

"Hungarians, Hungarians."

"—whatever they are. A shrewd move, Ben, and the old Bragg hat is tipped to you. You probably were so sure we wouldn't crack the code, you figured you could keep going forever."

"This is fascinating. Tell me what I said."

"Well, to begin with there are those names—Cavatelli, Kupperman, and Deegan. These are codes for three important border crossings between Switzerland and her neighbors. Cavatelli is Simplon, Kupperman is Schaffhausen, and Deegan is either Alstatten or Buchs. The figures you list, when properly transposed and extrapolated, are the net weights of certain products. We're not sure what they are. If they turn out to be narcotics, I feel sorry for you. Interpol doesn't take a kindly view of this sort of trade. Anyway, what you seem to be doing is gathering and transmitting information on illegal shipments that enter Switzerland at different border points. It's curious, and relevant, that the three crossings encoded are adjacent to different countries—Italy, West Germany, and Austria."

"And I thought I had you fooled."

"It was rough. The cryptanalysts tell me that it was pretty ingenious the way you modified the Baudot alphabet."

"That's standard Bupo procedure. Surprised they weren't aware of it."

"Swiss pay you well?"

"Enough to send me to international conferences. Say, there's something crazy here. If I'm working for them, how come I could also be involved in narcotics smuggling?"

"Benny, we've reached the point where we can believe anything about you. You're a free-lance. We have the feeling you'll do anything for a buck."

"Almost anything."

"We had some uneasy moments with this cipher," Bragg said. "You darn near fooled the black chamber with the Little League gambit, until I discovered that DiGiglio was a phony, and that Arnold Rainberger was the actual head of the league. A beautiful feint, kid. Especially since Mrs. Rainberger had a record a mile long as a peacenik and lefto. I'm glad to report she's in the clear on this business."

"Don't be too sure," I lied.

Bragg chuckled, got up, and put on his cocoa-brown straw hat, which had been on an old-fashioned clothes tree. He sat on the edge of the desk, the short-brimmed O'Connor pushed back, reporter-style. "Give it to us straight, Benny. Working as a spy, any kind of agent for a foreign power, even a neutral like Switzerland, is bad business. It doesn't matter whether you're in white, just gathering data, or in black, on a run, you can get into *beaucoup* trouble. You can be put away for a long time." He waved the letter. "And it's all here, in your own words."

"That goddamn letter is a fake. Cavatelli is a body repair shop. Kupperman is a supermarket. Deegan's fuel oil. They sponsor teams."

His voice had a hard edge. "What are you doing running errands for Bloom? Why are you so interested in Veg? Why are you busting into his lab at night?"

"You should talk. Who tried to steal his baboon? Not me. And those baboons are hard to get. He has to buy them, surplus apes, from the Vincennes Zoo."

He stretched. I saw his gun again. "I want you to tell us about the tie-in between Bupo and the Shin-Bet. You and Bloom are up to something. It involves Veg and his animals."

"I don't know. I ran errands for Bloom as a favor."

"Why?"

I felt like an idiot; what I had to say would be lost on Bragg forever. "I admired his books. He was a hero of mine when I was a kid."

Bragg laughed. "Oh boy, do better than that. Look, kid, we have no kick against the Israelis. We admire them. I'm military myself, and I respect any country that runs an army the way they do, and the way they beat the crap out of those flea-bitten Arabs. You know yourself about the Phantom jets, and the economic aid. In effect, we're in the same ball park. Any country that has compulsory military training for women can't be all bad. It would do my daughter Vannie some good, much as I love the girl, to put in some time drilling and shooting."

"Sorry, Tom. This appeal to my latent Zionism won't help. I'm leveling with you. Now let's do something about the Malars."

"Not until you tell me about this Swiss-Israeli arrangement."

"Okay. You've got me. It's a barter deal. Don't you want to make notes? It's quite detailed."

Bragg tapped the desk. "We're recording everything."

"Oh, of course. Ready? It's Swiss cheese for Jaffa oranges. That's what those figures represent. You have to extrapolate, as you put it, the left column, and you get gross tonnage on oranges, while the left, using a different increment, gives you the same on Emmenthaler and Gruyère. Incidentally, it's all predicated on base seven."

He got up and paced behind the small desk. "I'm not sure I buy that. I'm not sure you're playing fair with me. We're American citizens. I have your record. You're not a bad sort of a guy. Never were a commie, or an SDS sympathizer, just a hard-working *shnook* in Hicksville, Long Island, with a mort-gaged house and a car and two kids. By the way, we were impressed with your wife, the former Felicia Amalfitano——"

"You dirty son-of-a-bitch! You interrogated my wife?"

"No, no. Settle down, Ben. It's all on cards, at our data center. Seems your father-in-law is a past president of the Firemen's Post of the American Legion in the Bronx. That's all in your favor."

"Good. Now let's get the Malars someplace safe."

"Hold it, kid, hold it. We don't beat up Americans, nor can we force you to talk, but this crazy business of running after Veg, doing favors for an old hustler like Bloom—you can get hurt. You saw what happened to Keramoulian."

"Yeah. Was it you or Chipper knocked him off?"

"I'll ignore that. I'm authorized to give you a terrific oppor-tunity to serve your country."

"Are you sure you can trust me?"

"We take chances all the time. Ben, I am empowered to double you."

"Double me?"

"That's right. Walk around it a little."

I had not the remotest idea what he was talking about. So I told the truth, and naturally, he assumed this was further evidence of my cunning. "I have to admit, Tom, I don't know what that means. You mean you'll get a guy who looks just like me, and send him out? A *doppelganger?* Fellow wrote a book once claiming there were *two* Lee Harvey Oswalds——"

"Benny, the dumb act doesn't go any more. You know what doubling is. We make you a double agent. We send you out, free and clear, but you're working for *us* this time. You go back to *Bundespolizei* headquarters, play along with them, but you report to us regularly. Don't fake me any more, buddy. You know what a double agent is."

"No deal."

"Why? You want to help the Malars, don't you?"

"Yes, but this thing has gone far enough. I made believe I was a spy to get status with that literary crowd. I don't think you'd understand, but I was sick of being snubbed by people like Cooperage and Flackman and Metrick. So I invented my part. It is true Bloom gave me a letter and a white rat for Veg and had me try to reach him later. But I have no idea what Bloom wants. You know more than I do about that. You've seen those baboons. That's the truth. I'm faking it."

"This whole act is for—what did you call it?—*status?* With a bunch of half-assed writers?"

"That's the truth."

"And I'm to believe *that?*"

"Until I can think of something better. No, I take that back. It's the truth. Cooperage invented the mission for me, getting Malar to defect. I was just going to spread a few lies, write some fake letters, insult a few people. Then Cooperage decided I'd been sent here to snatch Imre Malar and get him to the States. Well I just did it. I'm proud of myself. He's in the lobby with his daughter, and they're ready. It's up to you now to fill out the papers and get them on a plane."

"That's the whole story?"

"That's right. You'll have to put the screws to Moe Bloom to learn anything about Laszlo Veg. I couldn't care less."

He didn't budge; he was frowning. Maybe at long last, I was getting through to him. "What makes you think we want Malar?" he asked, sitting behind the desk again.

I blinked. "Want? *Want?* Tom, he wants us. He wants freedom. This man is the most respected, the most listened-to voice of left-wing anti-communism in eastern Europe. He's the man who practically started the Hungarian Revolution. What a coup for us! The State Department could send him on lecture tours. He could write books exposing Moscow, and Stalinism, and the new terror . . ."

"Malar is a communist."

"No, no. He may have been one a long time ago, but not for years. And he was his own special kind, a liberal communist."

"We know all about him and we have absolutely no interest in him. Try the Ford Foundation. Or the Institute for Behavioral Sciences. Of course, they'll have to go through regular immigration channels, and I have a hunch that our people won't touch him with a ten-foot pole." He winked. "Or a ten-foot Hungarian."

"You're out of your mind! And your jokes stink. This guy has been risking his neck standing up to the Stalinists for years! Long before you got your first gun!"

"The way he did in that speech to the conference today?"

Sharper than I'd figured him, Thomas Ewing Bragg. Yes, that speech, that sniveling, crawling, pusillanimous speech, that stupid apologia for the Soviets.

"They forced him to do it," I protested. "If you weren't there, you must have gotten a report. He started to make a speech attacking the bastards. But they'd done something to him—drugs, hypnoses, threats of some kind. That's standard for them, except I was amazed they'd do it so blatantly. Bloom had the original text of the speech and distributed it. Read it, Tom. You'll see what kind of a guy Malar is. They worked him over."

Bragg shook his head. "A slippery article, Malar. No, I don't think we want him. We don't want him as a defector, as a visitor, or a spy. What does he do for a living anyway?"

"Do?"

"Yeah. I can't get a fix on the guy. What is he, exactly?"

"He's an intellectual. He's a critic. An editor. An essayist. For Chrissake, he's a writer."

Bragg sneered. "See what I mean? Who needs writers?"

"*What?* What are you saying?" Rage empurpled my face; my throat constricted and my mouth turned arid. Anger furred my lips and swelled my tongue. "Why you dumb shit!" I exploded. "You big handicap golfing turd! You goddamn thick upper-middle-class barbecue asshole! *Who needs writers!*"

"Settle down, Benny."

"Like hell I will! It was the writers who started the Hungarian Revolution! You cops and spies and strong-arm men never do a goddamn thing except take orders and worry about body counts! Malar's got more guts than a roomful of hoodlums like you and Keramoulian and the rest! Writers and poets and intellectuals and editors are going to jail every day, are being tortured, for their beliefs, for freedom! No cops are jugged in Russia, but writers are! It was Hitler who knew where the power was—he murdered every writer, every thinker, every professor who disagreed with him. He didn't worry about soldiers and cops or even union leaders—those bastards could be bought off, or won over to violence. But not writers, you big prick! How dare you sit there and put Malar down because he's a writer! You goddamn toilet salesman!"

He wasn't insulted. Sticks and stones might break his mammoth bones, but names would never hurt that smooth, strong exterior. "Don't get your bowels in an uproar. It's just that we consider writers low priority."

"Oh, you do, hey? Well what about neurologists? Behavioral psychologists who train baboons and rats?"

"Getting close to pay dirt, friend. Got any leverage with Veg? Has Bloom? We could work a deal. Those Israelis need lots of stuff. Hardware. Know-how. They got lots of smarts, but they could use some of our specialized merchandise."

"Ah, trading time. My Swiss employers might not care for this. Still, if you'd agree to stick Malar and his daughter on a plane for New York tonight——"

Yawning, Bragg stretched; an obscene, rude grimace. The summerweight voile shirt went taut across his huge chest. "Forget it. You had your chance. I think you're unreliable. We'll get around to Professor Veg on our time, without you or Bloom, or Bupo, or any of your pals."

I stared stupidly at him for a moment. "Sure you don't want Malar?" I asked, sounding pitiful, plaintive. I'm a lousy salesman.

"Positive."

"Tom, let's be practical. What do I tell Cooperage and

those other *machers?* I deserve some consideration. I risked my neck bringing him here. We had to run a gauntlet of KGB hoods. And his daughter, the poor kid. She's quite a looker, Tom."

"Let your friend Bloom take care of them."

"Tom, Moe is only one guy, and he's running a small operation. He can't take on Pochastny's army. Besides, he isn't interested in Malar either."

Bragg clapped his hands together: triumph. "See? See? What did I tell you? Nobody wants an old leftie writer. They're a drug on the market. You're so proud of your buddy Bloom, and look at him. He doesn't want that moldy Hungarian either."

He pounded the desk with that huge blond fist, then bounced up. "Well, we've gone as far as we can. You don't want to be doubled, and you won't tell me about Bloom and Veg, so we're finished. And give my regards to Stoefli in Geneva. He's a good man, and I'm surprised at him for giving you such a responsibility."

Forcefully, his hand guided me to the door and into the long corridor. As we approached the metal sliding door with the coded push-button control, he asked casually: "And what has Mr. Bloom done with Dr. Jabali?"

"I don't know."

"Pair of bloody sneakers turned up at Palestine Liberation headquarters an hour ago. You wouldn't know about them, would you?"

My voice suffocated. Bloom, whom I admired and worshipped . . . The nice agronomist from Jordan probably deserved it.

Thoughts of the murdered Jabali and my failure to secure sanctuary for the Malars had me shaking when we passed into the large sunlit lobby. A premonition of doom shivered me: the Malars were gone.

"Those people . . . the man and the young lady . . ." I was blubbering at the Marine sergeant.

"Sir, they just upped and walked out by themselves."

"No one came in and talked to them? Threatened them? Was there anyone outside, gesturing to them?"

"No, sir. I've been here all the time. About ten minutes ago they got tired of waiting and they just chatted a bit and strolled out without a word to me."

Bitterly, I turned on Bragg. "Thanks loads, Tom. You deliberately kept me up there, threatening me, leading me on, pumping me, for no damn reason. You lied to me——"

"Look who's talking."

"—and while you did, the KGB grabbed the Malars."

"I doubt it, Ben. The Russians don't care that much about old Hunky writers either. Guys like you and Bloom and Malar—you don't count. You got no muscle, no clout. You can play games, but that's all they are."

"I hope those rabies shots knock you on your ass. Maybe you'll get a bad anaphylactic reaction and strangle. It couldn't happen to a bigger fink."

"Change your mind about doubling, let us know."

I fled from his healthy, ruddy, overweight body into the sun-flooded courtyard. There was no sign of Imre Malar, or Judy Malar, or the green Peugeot taxi which Sophie Bloom had been driving. Nor did I see the black Citroën with its party of killers.

I'd almost climbed Everest, but I'd faltered and collapsed short of the summit. Malar was in my hands; free; willing; and I'd lost him. Now Cooperage would find out and tell it on the mountain, over the hills and everywhere, as Mahalia Jackson used to sing. I'd be exposed, deballed, exhibited before a mocking world as a bumbler, fraud, poseur, and incompetent. And did I deserve any other kind of treatment?

Where to? What next? I wasn't going to quit. I'd stay on Malar's trail, and I'd help Moe Bloom. *Quitters never win and winners never quit,* my son Eddie says. Traffic roared and screeched around the Place de la Concorde. Dizzy, I watched it, vertigo muddling my efforts to think clearly. Where had

Malar gone? Why had he run out on me? And Bloom! That single-minded, hard-nosed smuggler! Had he succeeded in getting his greedy hands on Laszlo Veg? And what had he done with Jabali? I shuddered; I suspected. Good Christ, what had I let myself in for?

A quick tour of the streets around the U.S. Embassy told me nothing. I walked down the Rue Boissy d'Anglas to the Rue du Faubourg St. Denis, then in front of the Hotel Crillon and the Ministerie de la Marine. By God, I wasn't dead yet. I'd come close with Malar. That in itself was a feat, considering the way the Russians had tried to grab him. Bloom's planning had helped—the fuss in the auditorium, the leaflets, the press, the kid with the skate-board, the Peugeot. Everything had worked superbly until Tom Bragg had turned me down. Who did he think he was? Admissions officer at Amherst, passing on applicants?

At the corner of Rue Royale I bought a late edition of the Paris *Trib* and collapsed into the big sidewalk café at the Place de la Madeleine. I ordered a Perrier, and at once experienced Bloodworth's Law—no matter how dreadful a man feels, something in any newspaper can make him feel worse. I'd skipped Flackman's immortal coverage of the conference that morning, but in my vinegary mood, I felt the need for Numero Uno's prose. There was a two-column photograph of El Lider, glowering at Ungerleider (*hah! wait till Arno learned who the kid worked for!*) and a two-column headline above the article.

Flackman approached this assignment with reluctance. Long hours of his valuable time wasted at previous gatherings of the frustrated and the fussy and the failed should have warned him off. At the time his publishers and his agent approached him with the assignment—an extremely lucrative one, even by Flackman's demanding standards—he was at work on a play, by far the best thing he had ever done. Then Flackman seized the challenge; he picked up the gauntlet; and he knew he would be crowned again. What he did, making notes on back of an old bit of stationery from the Claridge Hotel, was to create the basis for an *entirely new art form*. The great cultural détente of the century, the in-gathering of brains and egos, could only be done justice in a new and hitherto untried literary form, and Flackman was obviously the only writer in the world capable of creating it.

A belch worked its way up my esophagus and exploded like a bangalore torpedo across the café. Outraged patrons glared at me, and I belched again. Flackman's ego has that effect on me, and what he was perpetrating here was manure of such loamy texture, such agglutinative consistency, that I was certain I would be afflicted with a duodenal ulcer before I was through.

This new form is not journalism. It is not fiction. It is not history. It is all of these, and yet it is not. And it is superior to all of them. Flackman decided to call it "personalized testimony." What is "personalized testimony"? It is hard to say, except that only Flackman (Flackman understood at once) had the wit, the intellect, the erudition, the energy, and the powers of observation to carry it off. It would make enormous demands on the writer. But it would make even greater demands on the reader and the critic.

My impulse was to put the newspaper on the floor and urinate on it.

The bell was tolling for the opening sessions, and to Flackman, it was the toll of doom. To Flackman's tastes, the conference was not sufficiently revolutionary, and he felt there was something to be said for the dirty, mindless, aggressive young agitators—Maoists, Third Worlders, Weathermen—who baited the delegates. Flackman laughed at them; they could be handled. Not by some soft-palmed, wispy-voiced, lisping poet, or some gray broad-beamed lady translator, but in language they understood: the left jab and the right cross and the left hook. They would learn about these refinements of forensic procedure in due time, Flackman assured them, and from Flackman himself.

There were references in this "personalized testimony" to Flackman's prodigious drinking powers, his endless capacity for satisfying women, his innate superiority to everyone in Paris. There were some gossip-column revelations—Venables wore a truss, Anzaletti had once praised Mussolini, Bruno Shockheim looked like an old queen—but it was a standard Flackman blivit, three pounds of shit in a two-pound sack. I read no more.

The paper had no mention of Dr. Jabali—with or without his bloody sneakers. I stopped for a moment. *Bloody* sneakers? So Bragg had said. But when I had stolen a peek in Moe's briefcase, I had seen no blood on them. They were crushed and dusty, but not stained.

The conference itself was largely ignored; apart from Flackman's thunderous piece, trumpeting his "entirely new literary form," there was only a small article on the opening ceremonies, the addresses of welcome, the Flackman-Huffguard dialogue.

On the rear page, I began to read the classified advertisements. They permitted me to indulge in airy reminiscences about my newspapering days in Paris, when Eddie was an infant, and Felicia and I had been married a little over a year. We had made do in a drafty, sloping room in the Rue Soufflot, and it had been fun. At least we made believe it was fun.

Under the personal notices, I read:

Latzi. Come quickly. All arranged.—Kitti.

Judy Malar had referred to Veg as Uncle Latzi. There couldn't be that many Latzis in Paris. Besides, everyone seemed to hunger for Veg; why not someone named Kitti? I memorized the message—what had been *all arranged?*—and wondered if Bloom had succeeded where I had failed. Had he glommed onto the neurologist? Or had Pochastny's goons swept Veg out of the Palais? If Moe had failed, there were no more options available to us. Malar had made his speech—not a smash hit from the Russian standpoint—and now they would surely spirit the Hungarians out of Paris. Veg, and whatever crazy process he was using to make terrors out of rats, to electrify baboons, would be gone, probably forever.

For the moment I was planless, adrift. Then I remembered the cozy apartment at Avenue Charles Floquet where the Blooms were staying. Sophie had been supposed to wait for us outside the embassy, but she'd vanished. There was a possibility she had taken the Malars to the flat, and I hailed a taxi, my feet tingling with the sensation that I hadn't failed at all, that I'd still deliver my Hungarians.

Two Oriental kids were kicking a soccer ball in front of 34 Avenue Charles Floquet. A lot of diplomatic people lived on the street. I rested under a chestnut tree, got bombed by one of those vile Parisian pigeons, then rang the outside bell. The concierge was friendlier than the one at Gobelins, and even smiled at my good French. Yes, the Blooms were at home and they had visitors.

Outside the high doors on the sixth floor I jabbed at the buzzer a few times. Someone opened the door, retreating with it, so that I could not see who it was.

"Cut out the kid stuff, Moe," I said. "It's Benny."

I stepped in, turned, and started to shake a little. Dr. Daoud Jabali was pointing a short, ugly machine gun at my midriff, holding it lightly with one hand, the other pressing a telephone to his ear. He motioned for me to sit down.

"You . . . you . . . you're dead . . ." I mumbled. "You . . . Bloom got rid of you . . ."

He held a finger to his lips. Apparently he was talking to someone named Kenneth, because he kept repeating his name —*Ken, Ken.* Semitic languages are not my dish of tea, but I assumed he was speaking Arabic, contacting one of his PLO killers.

What had he done with Bloom? And with Sophie? The pattern began to form in my marbled mind: Jabali was working with Pochastny, a marriage of convenience. The Malars had been grabbed or tricked outside the U.S. Embassy, delivered to the KGB. Jabali, meanwhile, believed to be dead, had been turned loose on Bloom. He'd tried to kill Moe at least once, at the Café Lussac, and he'd tailed us to Veg's zoo on the Quai de la Mégisserie, and now he'd shown his hand again. I didn't like the short, stubby weapon in his hand, and I didn't like a disturbing change in his manner. Jabali had been so sweet, so apologetic, a gentle Jordanian. Now I detected a brusque coldness in the man. And he'd abandoned those nutty high sneakers for a pair of brown loafers. If I had not been utterly certain—it was Jabali, the long beak, the soft eyes, the creamy skin—I might have thought him to be a different man.

"Ken . . . ken," he was saying.

My clotted brain responded. He was talking *Hebrew. Ken* means *yes.* Vague memories of *cheder* on Olmstead Avenue wafted back to me: the gnarled ancient language had assailed the fortress of my baseball-cluttered head with small effect. But I remembered *ken.* And now I heard *atah* (you), *ani* (I), and something that sounded like *zahal* (army).

He ended his conversation and looked at me with a bland, contemptuous stare.

"You . . . you got rid of the Blooms," I said. "But you won't get away with it."

Again, he held a finger to his lips. "Do not leave that chair," he said. He crossed the reception room, stopping at the opened double doors, still covering me with the machine gun.

"You were speaking Hebrew," I said. "I gather Al Fatah is training a higher type murderer. Look, Jabali, you'd better smarten up. It's not just Bloom and the Shin-Bet you're messing with, it's the United States of America. I've given them a full report on this business, and they're on your tail."

"*Moishe,*" Jabali was calling in the other room—and then some words in what was surely Hebrew.

Bloom entered. "Oh. It's Benny. He's all right, he's all right. Put the Uzzi away, Shlomo."

"I demand an explanation," I shouted. "Who is this guy? Where's Malar and Judy? I don't like having Uzzi machine guns pointed at me. Besides, he's Jabali, and you murdered Jabali. Bragg told me. They found his bloody boots."

"*Shah, shah,* boychick. There's another call for you inside, Shlomo."

Jabali—or Shlomo—nodded and left us. He even walked differently now. As Jabali he had sort of shuffled, or sidled, apologizing with his feet. Now he seemed more erect, tougher, a thoroughly unbending and untouchable young man.

Bloom took me out on the small balcony and closed the louvered doors. Below us stretched the eternal beauty of the city—on our left the Tour Eiffel, on the right the Ecole Militaire, distantly the Sacré Coeur.

"Who is he?" I demanded.

"Colonel Tal," Bloom said. "That's enough for you."

"Your boss."

"Colonel Tal. Keep your mouth shut about him. He's getting out of Paris tonight."

"Ah. No more cover? Wait, wait. You had to set up a fake murder of Jabali, so he could get out. If Jabali's dead, then there's no Tal. And the sneakers. When you had them in the briefcase, they were clean."

"So?" Bloom arched his brows.

"You stained them with blood, somebody's, an animal's maybe, and left them for the French cops. A broad hint."

"Ah, routine, routine."

"Yes," I said. "And Jabali—Tal—shot those two Arab bombers at the Lussac. It wasn't the gendarmes who were holed up in the apartment across the street when the bomb went off. It was that cold-eyed colonel. He knocked them off with a telescopic sight after they tried to blow you up. I think you were staked out there like bait—the tethered goat to draw the tiger so the hunter could get a clear shot. But why all that fuss over a couple of PLO *Kockers?*"

Bloom raised a hand to quiet me. *"Shah, shah.* We had to clean up before we made a pass at Veg. We had to get those *Kockers* out of the way."

"What was Shlomo Tal doing outside of Veg's lab the night we found Keramoulian?" I asked. I remembered seeing "Jabali" stuffing a weapon—it was probably the same sharp-shooter's rifle he'd used on the bombers—into a long valise.

"Covering us, what do you think?" Bloom said. "You know too much already, and he's a little sore at me for bringing you in. That's why he shoved the Uzzi in your face."

"I'm glad the guy is leaving. I don't like that look in his eye."

"Shlomo? He's a gentle boy, one of our best."

What a long, long way we had come from the Tal-mudical scholars, the born victims, the white-faced, soft-limbed sacrificial lambs of the *shtetl!* What a joy to be known for your soldiers rather than your philosophers! I envied Colonel Shlomo Tal as much as I feared him.

"And Veg?" I asked.

"Lost him." Moe said, scowling. "You did a good job, kid. Sophie told me. Professional."

"Will you get another crack at him?"

"I doubt it. I'm trying to figure out some way to keep him in Paris a little longer. They had too much manpower at the Palais. Plucked him out of my hands."

I told Bloom about the notice I'd seen in the Paris *Trib.* Someone named Kitti was asking Latzi to come quickly.

"In today's paper?" he asked. "That gives us some hope, if the jerk reads the *Trib.*"

"What does it mean? Who is Kitti?"

"I'll tell you some other time."

"Where are the Malars?" I asked.

"They're safe."

"I almost did it, Moe. I think he and Judy got scared and ran out on me. It was murder in there with that crud Bragg. He accused me of working for the Swiss police, tried to bleed me on your activities, and worst of all, he didn't want Malar. Figure that."

"I could have told you that. They wouldn't take Malar on a silver plate. You see, if he were a real Bolshie, a real bastard, they might be able to use him. But he's been everything. He's backed everyone. They can't get much mileage out of him."

"You're kidding."

"No. They—Bragg, the CIA—they have tabs on everyone here. They're a good group, very professional. Besides, they have to know about everyone at the conference, they're picking up the tab for it."

I almost fainted. The chestnut trees below me revolved, and I grabbed the balustrade to keep from pitching over. "The CIA? They're paying for the conference? This meeting of the minds and talents of East, West, and the Third World?"

"Why not? Somebody's got to pay for it."

"But . . . but . . . the Russians?"

"Cheap bastards. They wouldn't pay, but they went along with the gag. They know the CIA is signing the checks. You see, Benny, both outfits have nothing but contempt for these people—writers, intellectuals, even the scientists. So they got them all in one place where they could look them over, and maybe steal a few notions, or screw them up. Of course, the only one here with any new ideas, with anything worth stealing——"

"Is Laszlo Veg."

"You might say that."

Sophie Bloom's face appeared between the opened French doors. "Moe—hello, Ben—it has been arranged. Mr. Malar just spoke to them."

We entered the apartment. Malar and Judy were standing

in the living room, looking at me guiltily. Colonel Tal was gone. I had the feeling I would never see him again, in Al Fatah sneakers or in brown loafers.

"I am sorry, Benny," Malar said. "I could not go through with it. It is a game to you, and sometimes even to Mr. Bloom, but not to me. It is my life."

"You'd have had a new and better life in America," I said.

"I cannot be sure. I gather that they were not too interested in an old socialist."

"That was just one dumb agent," I said. "If you want to reconsider . . ."

"No, no. The matter of my defecting is over. I shall not defect. I never intended to, and I want you to so advise Mr. Pochastny."

I was shattered. I had just pulled off the coup of the conference, and it had turned to dust in my hands. A defector who wasn't wanted by the host country—and who didn't want to defect! How could I face Cooperage again? What kind of sarcastic laughs would Lila Metrick and Arno Flackman have on me now?

Judy looked at me sorrowfully. "Papa could not go. He has important work in Budapest. He has friends. And . . ."

"And I am still part of the revolution."

Old social democrats never die, I thought, they just write for Hearst. But not so in Malar's case. He'd been betrayed, cuckolded, shamed, beaten and mocked by his amour propre, but he still lusted for those creamy thighs and melon breasts, or at least the youthful memory of them. Lady Marx was a haggard crone now, a harridan, but when Malar looked at her, he saw the clean-limbed, bright-eyed temptress of his revolutionary youth. And I suppose he saw her clearer in Budapest than anywhere else.

"So . . . what now?" I asked.

Bloom took over. "You, Benny, will return these people to Pochastny."

"What? That killer? That hoodlum?"

313

Judy touched my arm. "It's all right, Ben. We just spoke to him. He understands it was an error. You will tell him that you forced us to go to the embassy against our wills. He is prepared to accept this explanation. In fact, he spoke to someone there, who verified this."

Someone? Thomas Ewing Bragg, of course. Now I saw the design clearly: Bragg and Pochastny, enemies, but professionals, united against the amateur! Like two high-priced hookers, they resented the competition of the round-heeled girl who did it for kicks. They had finally realized—in spite of Bragg's crap about my connections with Bupo—that I was at best an erratic part-timer, and at worst, a total fraud. They'd joined forces to keep the game honest.

"Go on, it'll be all right," Bloom said wearily. "He's waiting in a black Citroën on the corner of Avenue de Suffren and Rue de Saix."

I escorted the Malars to the door. "What next?" I asked Moe. "What else can I do?"

"Go back to the hotel. I'll call you in an hour or so."

We were silent in the elevator. Malar looked dazed, exhausted. I felt like apologizing, but I didn't know for what. I'd offered him freedom, royalties, lecture tours, and a new life—and he'd spurned me.

Judy squeezed my hand. "It's all right, Ben. We will be all right." She was sniffling. I kissed her cheek. The old man had chickened out, but she had wanted to make the trip.

We approached the corner of Suffren and de Saix and I saw the Citroën with the venetian blinds. I couldn't tell how many people were inside, but Pochastny got out, beaming in triumph. He hugged Malar, pinched Judy's cheek, and then snickered at me.

"Tough luck, fellah," he said. "You lose a lot."

"Mr. Malar and his daughter were unwilling to go along with my attempt to bring them to America," I said frigidly. "I deceived them. I told them we were showing a Shirley MacLaine movie at the embassy, and they said they'd missed it in

Budapest. They never had any intention of leaving France or defecting."

"I'm with you, fellah."

"While we were at the embassy, I decided it might be a good time to try to arrange a travel grant for him, but I didn't succeed. So he's all yours."

"Right, guy." He edged closer to me. I didn't appreciate the glow of his sweaty nose, or his halitosis. "Stay away from him, you dig? And also from the professor. We're wise to you. You're a fake. We know all about you. We know all about Bloom. We know he killed the Jordanian, and we'll hang him for it. The French will be happy to get rid of a Zionist murderer."

I was tempted to blab, to shoot my mouth off. However Bloom had set up Jabali's murder, he had important people believing it; which meant Colonel Tal was safe for a while.

"Golly, that's awful," I said. "I never dreamed Bloom was that kind of a guy."

"You dirty revisionists," Pochastny said. "You lousy cosmopolitans, internationalists."

He almost sounded like Bragg. "You left out intellectuals."

"Yeah, all that jazz. You guys'll get paid off before this is over. We don't tolerate your kind of interference."

Braving his bad breath, I bent my head low. "Antipov, if I may use your square monicker, did you know Semichastny?"

"Don't kid me. Of course I knew him. Former head of the KGB."

"He once told the Central Committee that if they let him arrest one thousand of the most active members of the Russian intelligentsia, he would guarantee absolute tranquillity in the USSR."

"So? He was right."

"It can't be done, Antipov. We'll always be around. Arrest a thousand, there'll be another thousand. You may have the guns and the knives, but we've got our brains, and we'll lick you yet."

"Don't count on it, fellah."

He got into the car. I stuck my head in the window.

"Antipov, I'm warning you. No reprisals against these people. I was the one who sneaked them away. They had no intention of leaving."

He started to roll the window up and I would have been guillotined if I'd kept my head there. As I withdrew, I saw Judy putting her arm around Malar's shoulder. Papa looked dazed, drugged, at the end of his terrible trial. Judy wept; I felt guilty.

A few of Harvey Ungerleider's wild children were handing out mimeographed sheets outside the Bavard. I glanced at the heading: LIBERATION NEWSLETTER. But who are you liberating, darlings? Who wants your advocacy? Someday, thanks to their obscene lunatic assaults, we will all end up in concentration camps on Staten Island.

I checked my mailbox—nothing—and sank into a lobby chair, ordering a Perrier. The handout read as follows:

CONFERENCE EXPOSED AS CIA PLOT

The bourgeois American press, usually toady and lickspittle to the American Establishment, today revealed the true nature of the World Conference on the Arts and Sciences now meeting in Paris. An Associated Press dispatch from Paris, by-lined by two Establishment servants named Winton Talley and Samuel I. Fels, reveals that the American Central Intelligence Agency financed this alleged "meeting of East, West, and Third World." Money was made available through the revisionist English publication *The Discoverist Review*. Apparently the Soviet secret police knew about the arrangement and agreed to go along with the plot. Is it any wonder that the conference thus far has been a mishmash of false trails, lies, and bourgeois deceits?

Serious questions are raised about the credibility of the conference co-chairman, Imre Malar, the purported "father of the

Hungarian Revolution" and Derek Venables "the poet of rebellion."

My eyes then popped and my heart did the hop-step-jump in record time, as I saw my own name.

Their roles remain ambiguous. There is no doubt, however, that the chief CIA operative in Paris is the American novelist Benjamin Bloodworth, 34, a minor literary figure, sent here to file reports, spread lies and confusion, and insinuate himself into important positions, thus enabling him to feed information to Washington and disseminate "disinformation" to the delegates. Bloodworth is engaged in some special mission involving the Hungarian delegates.

Bloodworth is believed to have been a member of the assassination team that killed Che, and later invaded Communist Party headquarters in Hermosillo, Mexico. His real name is Hyman Schlabfeder and he is a graduate of CCNY, where he majored in urban sociology.

It was hopeless. I'd created my own monster—*me*. I'd faked so well, told so many lies, that I couldn't stop the thing. It grew of its own accord, waxing fat on its own nutritive juices. Bragg had me working for the Swiss; these kids had me in the CIA; the French had me in the Shin-Bet; only Pochastny thought I was a fake, and I think he still had lingering doubts.

For a few minutes I sat there, feeling a corona, a mystical gold haze forming around me. Yes, I was something special, a man of mystery, Joyce's "Man in the Mackintosh," the Shadow, Zorro, the Lone Ranger, Mycroft Holmes, the most brilliant man in London.

That the conference had been partially paid for by the CIA, I really didn't care. Dammit, I was an American; the CIA wasn't *all* bad. We had to have them, even if they fouled up now and then. The Russians had theirs. We needed someone to counteract the Pochastnys and the Keramoulians. And why not spend their money on a fairly decent conference, bringing all these Burmese physicists and Finnish critics together for a few days in the loveliest city in the world? It couldn't do any harm.

I slouched off to the elevator, and heard Warren Cooperage's voice attack me. "Bloodworth! Bloodworth! You rat, you fink!"

Cored and flayed, I turned toward him. He'd gotten up from a table in the bar: Flackman and Metrick were there, and James Warfield Keen, dozing, gray head resting against the faded draperies.

"You leaked this," Cooperage said. "Couldn't keep your damned mouth shut, could you?"

"Leaked what, Coop?"

He had a wrinkled copy of the New Left flyer in his hand. "This. This garbage about the CIA financing *our* conference. Even if there's a little truth in it, how do you think we feel? All my friends are humiliated because of you."

"I don't believe any of *that* nonsense," Lila Metrick sniffed. "The CIA put out the story to discredit us. As for that boor, that fool over there—Bloodworth, or Schlabfeder, or whatever his name is—he's part of it, and I am going to urge more strict screening committees next time."

"If you have a minute, I can explain the whole thing," I said.

"I doubt we're interested," Cooperage said, as I trudged toward the table of *k'nockers*. "And I made the mistake of befriending you, of letting you in on things."

"Coop, I gave you my seat on the bus, didn't I?"

And then I became aware of a marvelously heartening, invigorating truth. They were all—except Keen, who slept on—staring at me with *envy*. No question about it, they were jealous. I knew things they didn't. I'd taken risks they hadn't. If the embassy didn't invite me to the big party, they did so for good reason: *I was undercover*. Some apogee, some zenith of my career had been reached, but not without arduous travail, nifty footwork, acts of legerdemain, and an intellect humming along on all sixteen cylinders. But I was top. And they knew it.

"We don't want to hear anything from you," Lila Metrick said. There was a cavernous echo in her Boston voice, as if she were spelunking.

As they all studied me—envious, wondering, frustrated— M. Rignac, my little historian friend, and Katje Westerdoop, the Dutch girl with the balloons, came by and stared at my bearded, chalky face.

"*C'est lui*," M. Rignac said proudly. "*C'est l'espion Bloodwart, l'agent Américain. Gardez, quel élan. Et, il est, naturellement, mon ami.*"

I nodded at them coolly. This was the summit. My name, my identity, was being utilized by *a man trying to get laid.* I was a status symbol. Just knowing me might help a fellow get a well-earned piece, and I realized at that moment that it would be difficult to go any higher. Silently I wished M. Rignac good hunting.

Entering the elevator, Cooperage called after me: "Where's Malar, Bloodworth? And what have you done with Venables? You bastard, I'll never forgive you."

"Fuck him, fuck him," I heard Flackman mutter. Poor guy, he was forever two people—revolutionary and celebrity, and he could never reconcile his two selves. It was as if every time Trotsky had tried to organize the Petrograd garrison, Boris Thomashefsky would show up and start reciting *Richard III* in Yiddish.

My hotel room door was open. It didn't surprise me. I expected to find the French fuzz in residence, or maybe a messenger from Bloom. He'd hinted that he wasn't through with Veg, that a last run after the gloomy neurologist was imminent, and I might be involved.

Evie Bragg was in my room. I smelled her Detchema before I saw her, and my viscera started to prance and pirouette.

"Hi," she said—and my blood jellied. It was that drawn-out nasal quality that got me; Greenwich Country Club and obscure dainty women's colleges in Boston for big, blonde dumb *shiksas* with huge hams, rearing rumps, and low SAT's.

"Hi yourself, Evie."

Late afternoon sunlight gilded the sheen of her sheer stockings. I lusted for those pale tanned hairless legs, a bit thick in the calf and flank, but capable of lecherous moves and turns, hardened and made supple by years in the saddle, years of strenuous doubles on clay courts. Yum, yum. She was there for *me*. Pure Protestant Republican middle-aged lady, for me, dirty left-wing Jewish intellectual.

"Surprised?" she asked.

I sat down on the narrow dormitory cot, a few feet from her perfumed, iron-bound figure. "Yes, as a matter of fact. And delighted. I've had a bad day, and that includes a séance with your hubby."

"Tom? Have you seen him?"

Was she lying? Who cared? I had no immediate assignments as a spy. A man driven as I was needed surcease from his toil, a bit of slap and tickle to revive himself. As I studied her long, well-favored body—she was wearing a turquoise suit of some light nubby stuff, and a strand of pearls, all very matronly and proper—I started to feel Master John Thursday rise, unbidden, in my jockey shorts. I'd never be any good as a seducer; I want it all, right away, in a frenzy—slobbering, grabbing, tearing, thrusting, no subtleties.

"I paid Tom a visit a few hours ago," I said. "At the embassy."

She bit her lower lip, shamefaced. "Oh dear, you know about us then. But I hope you won't hold it against us. We're all working for the flag, aren't we?"

"Yes dear." Passion was making my hands tremble. I'm no good at this. My desire explodes too blatantly, like an overloud radio commercial. Instead of enticing, it offends. But Evie appeared friendly. She didn't recoil.

320

"Like a drinkie?" I asked. "I'm out of booze, but I'll call room service."

"No, thanks. I just wanted to chat." She smiled: long, white teeth like her husband's. A short, square nose, a square chin, nicely spaced green eyes. Late thirties? I studied the discreet wrinkles where her neck met her clavicle. They aroused me unmercifully. I'd kiss them away. My knees were like watery oatmeal and there was a Fourth of July sparkler sputtering under my belt buckle. Her roguish tweedy odor overwhelmed me.

"No drink?"

"I don't think so." She leaned forward and touched my hand. We're touring the homes of famous people in Fairfield County, ladies. This is Mr. Bloodworth, the Jew Novelist. Works at home, you know. He's available most afternoons for a quick *shtup.*

"I thought I saw your daughter Vannie outside," I said, "handing out these. Or maybe just some of her friends."

"Vannie? I don't think so. She's getting a checkup at the American Hospital. Tom insisted on it."

"Ah. All that sleeping out-of-doors. Say, have you read this scandal sheet?"

She touched her lips. "Yes. It's atrocious! What lies! Claiming that the CIA is sponsoring the conference. And those terrible things it said about *you.*"

Careful there, Bloodworth. According to Bloom, she worked as a team with hubby. Behind that smiling facade, that dull stupidity, that false front of selling toilets and mangling foreign languages, they worked for the Defense Intelligence Agency.

"I have a broad back, Evie," I bragged, squeezing her hand. "I can take it. These lefties don't scare me."

"My brother Boyle claims the conference is stacked against him because of the left-wingers. He's leaving tomorrow."

"I bet Mr. Flackman leaves with him. They can hold a joint press conference at Kennedy. Boyle can denounce the conference as a left-wing scheme, and Arno can denounce it as a CIA plot."

"You're so perceptive. I love to hear you analyze political matters."

I got up, bent double, and raised her by the arms, out of the chair, over to the bed. She came along willingly, a large-bodied, perfumed, desirable woman, a strong, firm-assed daughter of good breeding and marginal education; I wanted her for all her mindless superiority, for all the status and power and sure-footedness she'd won simply by being born.

We sat thigh to thigh on the side of the bed. "A fellow might have the right to ask why you came to see me."

She shook her burnished hair. "Bored. Unhappy. You're the most fascinating person I've met here."

"Naughty. You tried to kidnap me yesterday."

"Ben, can't we forget that?" She stroked my hot hand. "You know all about Tom and me. We do a little white espionage. Just information-gathering. Nothing terrible. Maybe I came here to prove to you that I'm not, well, all bad."

Ye gods, she wanted me. I could sense it. I got the vibrations through the protective layers of silk, nylon, elastic, rubber, all those maddening articles of clothing I'd have to peel off before the conquest. And I would give myself to her. I bent her backward, and as her skirt moved upward I saw the bottom of her hard, cruel panty girdle, its garter-teeth sunk into her stocking tops. Like insane white doves, my hands fluttered over her armored thighs.

"You, ah, didn't see Mr. Bloom anywhere?" I gasped. "I wouldn't want him busting in here while we are *in flagrante delicto*."

Her lips parted. "No. He wasn't anywhere in sight." I kissed her, probed her mouth, and felt as if I'd eaten *trayf* for the first time: a *yeshiva scholar* corrupted by a cherrystone clam.

"I must tell you, Evie," I said, as I dragged her skirt up,

with one hand, and fondled her ear with another, "that I have never wanted any woman as much as I want you now."

"But . . . I'm so old . . . a middle-aged lady with a teen-aged daughter? Are you sure, sweetheart?"

"Oh, yes, yes. I've arrived. It's some kind of fulfillment."

"Then take me, dearest, take me."

I nibbled her ear. "You came here . . . you wanted me . . . you understood how much I wanted you. Something passed between us, Evie, some signal, some magic, some electricity. Unspoken, unseen, but deeply felt. It was an epiphany, a moment of mystery, as Joyce termed it."

"Joyce who?"

My flying right hand slithered up and down that damnable metallic corset she wore. As much as I hated its apparent impregnability, it intrigued me. Yes, yes, I admit it, I'm a hopeless, abandoned fetishist, and the sight of a garter, a zipper, can send me up the wall and onto the ceiling. You'd be surprised how many men are. Some are queer for the rear straps of brassieres and others are hung up on petti-pants. Oh, they won't admit it, but it's the truth. So here was that contraption Evie was wearing, a panty girdle of medium length (a prudent woman, she didn't go for short skirts and those one-piece leotard-type garments), sheathing her firm full form, from midriff to a few inches above her sturdy knees. An elastic-nylon carapace, a scented, stretchy shell, driving me mad. And within its cunning prison, pressed, crushed, molded, was her captive aromatic flesh! My duty called: that cursed suit of armor would have to come off, peeled, unzipped, unstrapped, ungartered, to reveal her steaming rose flanks and her silken peach belly. I would bury my face in her unsullied flesh, kiss, caress, lick, and embrace those restricted areas. On her vast, spreading flamingo pink *tochis* I would scrawl, with her own carmine lipstick: Dietary Laws Observed.

By now I had her skirt almost under her chin, and I was clawing at the lower edges of her girdle. My hands shook so that I could not get a purchase on the resistent elastic stuff.

"Relax, dearest, relax," Evie said. Her voice was flat, dispassionate.

"That was James Joyce, sweetheart, who called these moments epiphanies."

"You're so well-read," Evie said appreciatively. "But look how you're sweating."

"Can't help it, ma'am. I don't get much."

"Naughty."

"Leastwise of such a high calibre. You're what I've wanted all my life." My hands began to probe the fierce elastic waist of that damnable apparatus she wore, and I now realized that in my enervated and tremulous condition, it would be no easy matter to yank it off. Neurotic anticipation had fragmented me. I was a lot of little Benny Bloodworths, all of them suffering malnutrition.

It then dawned on me that I was being resisted. Somehow, with artful moves of her behind and thighs, she was eluding my sneaky attempts to peel off the impediment to my lust. "I get it," I croaked, "you want to be forced into this. Animal strength is what you respect."

She was a strong one, age-for-weight, every bit as powerful as Lila Metrick, that other tall, thick, hard-bodied, blonde goddess I'd tried to pierce. Evie Bragg, mother, housewife, and spy, would be no piece of cake, no can of corn. And as she artfully resisted me, passion flamed and raged in my starved gut.

"Oh, I'll be gentle, Evie," I gasped. Determined I'd win this one, make the big score, show that rat Tom Bragg who had the real *cojones*, I paused to rest and study the problem. I understood the basic design and principle of her protective pants because I am an incurable reader of the advertisements in the Sunday *New York Times Magazine*. Many a morbid rainy Sunday afternoon has been brightened by those art photo ads, in glorious living color, of the world's most beautiful girls, tantalizingly modeling bras, girdles, panties, and stockings. As I've said, Evie's was a gleaming white affair, with a huge satin diamond spread across her flat abdomen. I jabbed at it a few times: tungsten steel. It hugged, secreted, formed, tortured, and imprisoned her, and it defied my fluttery hands.

"Ah, do you, ah, have a detachable crotch?" I asked.

"Silly. Do you?"

She was mocking me, the minx. Now I was steady on course, certain in my mind that I would have her. This conquest, was, after all, merely another aspect of the role I'd been playing so brilliantly. I'd force her into whimpering surrender, give her a taste of that wild Bohemian Jewish literary life she craved. Cunningly I worked my febrile paws up her rear, toward the top of that adamantine garment, until they found the pliant flesh of her midsection, the soft demilitarized zone between brassiere and girdle.

"Port of entry," I gargled. Great pearls of sweat rolled down my forehead, my nose, into my gaping mouth. It was more than I could manage. Feeling faint, yet triumphant, I rammed both hands down the rear of the girdle as far as I could, my burning fingers scorching the moons of her behind.

"Ai, ai," I moaned. "All systems are go. We have lift-off."

She was more or less under me, but propped on one elbow. What I desperately needed was a little more leverage, one swift yank, to peel those cursed football pants down, over belly, thigh, knee, over the slender calf, divesting her, in one surgical operation, of girdle, stockings, and pale green Papagallos. First I tried to shove my hands farther down. There was nowhere to go. Then I tried to raise my hands, the better to secure their grip on her nether cheeks. They would not move upward either. In effect, I was trapped by the implastic trousers.

"This is a bit embarrassing, dearest," I said. "I'm afraid I can't move my hands. Could you move a little, just to your right, so I can navigate better?"

"Are you really trapped, hon?"

"Yes, lover." I tried to raise all of her with a sharp jerk of

my arms, but she was heavier and stronger than I had anticipated. In certain Indian villages, I had read, the natives trap
monkeys by enticing them with coconuts into which a hole
has been bored. The stupid apes can jam their greedy fingers
into the hole, but withdrawal is impossible, so the monkey is
caught, weighted down by the nut. That was precisely my
situation. As Virgil remarked about the descent into hell: it's
not hard to get in, but leaving may present a few problems.

"Give me a hand, darling," I whispered. "Goodness knows
I need one."

Evie sat upward suddenly, hauling me up with her. Hand-
cuffed, my two mitts locked into her undergarment, I smiled
at her in relief. "Yes, that's better. I believe I can manage." I
started working my fingers upward, stealing pinches as I did.

"Downsy for you," she said. And with a brutal shove, her
hands slamming into my narrow chest, she reversed our positions. She crushed me beneath her heft, and Detchema
hovered over me in a misty cloud. Was this the way she got
her kicks? Asserting herself over supplicant Semites? Good
enough. I'd play her game. Indeed, the feel of her potent
torso and heavy limbs on top of me gave me a new depraved
thrill. Once again I tried to get my jailed hands out of her
girdle, wiggling them upward, but I simply had no strength
left.

"What now, love?" I asked. "Shall we soar to the heights?
Roll our passions up into one sweet ball?"

"Gee, you're well-educated." For some reason she began
searching my breast pocket.

"Stop, stop, Evie. I'm ticklish."

Moe Bloom's orange bar-mitzvah pen stared at me. She'd
extricated it, and was pointing it at me.

"Eve, my angel, I don't want your autograph, I want your
ass."

Drawing back as far as possible, she kept the butt end of
the pen perhaps a foot from my nose. Then she let me have it.
A sweet synthetic odor enveloped me, as a misty spray ex-

326

ploded from Moe's weapon. My eyes teared and my nose flamed. I tried to talk and the words clotted in my throat. "Evie . . . oh, you didn't have to . . . oh, shit . . ."

The room was getting smaller, darker. Walls caved in. The ceiling descended slowly. Soon all I could see was her prim matronly face. A lacy handkerchief was pressed to her nose.

I was sitting in the back seat of a car. Evie Bragg, having slipped me my own Mickey Finn, and having extracted my hot hands from the inside of her girdle, was seated next to me. Apparently she realized that I was a gone goose, because even when my eyes opened from time to time, she did not appear perturbed. My limbs were paralyzed, nor could I speak. There was an efficient masterful air about Mrs. Bragg; she was like the chief nurse in a wardful of senile alcoholic males, full of thick sex, contempt, and reproachful glances.

Beyond her blonde head I saw the preternaturally green fields of rural France. We must have been in the outskirts of Paris. I seemed to see, distantly, surrounded by dark cypresses, the gray mansard roof of a small château or manor house. Some fifty feet from the car was a sort of small corral, post-and-rail fencing, with chicken wire rolled around the exterior. Two men in dark suits were standing outside the fence. One was Laszlo Veg. He held a lean leggy dog on a short leash—a greyhound. The other man was slender and had a gray straw hat on his small head. I couldn't see his face, but his figure seemed familiar: someone I'd met the past few days.

As I watched the proceedings, I decided that it was a dream. The parklike fields, the distant mansion, the desirable matronly blonde next to me—all these had the look and the shape of a nightmare. Then I heard Laszlo Veg's thin, sarcastic voice:

"Are you ready, sir? I shall release him if you are."

"Goddammit, let him go. We haven't got all day."

Veg brought the greyhound—it was a lithe handsome

beast, pale fawn in color, with a great whip of a tail curving over its lean back.

"Greyhounds hunt by sight, not smell," Veg said. "A peculiarity of the breed."

"You don't have to teach me about greyhounds," the man said irritably. "I've seen coursing fifty times since I was a kid."

Veg brought the dog to a space between the rails and let him slip the leash. With a graceful leap, the greyhound bounded into the enclosure. Coursing involved the chase of some stupid hare; it ended with a kill.

"And there is your hare," Veg said.

"Big bastard," the man said. "But not big enough to handle a greyhound."

I lolled against the back of the plastic-covered seat, my eyes fixed on the bright green field, the corral, the watching men. An animal ballet, a terrifying dance of death was taking place inside. The greyhound saw the hare, sped toward him, and the quarry soared vertically, landing on its side.

"That's called a *trip*," the stranger said. "My old man used to score coursing meets. Jesus, look at that turn."

The hare had regained its feet, and raced for the perimeter of the fenced-in arena, and the dog turned sharply, bumped it with its nose once, and pursued it across the field.

"And they call that a go-by."

He knew a great deal about the horrid sport. The greyhound had pulled ahead of the hare, but the frightened prey, hugging the earth, clinging to its bunny life with guile and speed, managed to avoid the snapping jaws.

Twice around the arena they flew, a third time, and on the fourth go-round, the hare flew vertically again, at least three feet high, like an ascending helicopter, hit the grass in a furry bundle, rolled away from the dog's teeth, and was off again.

"Smart rabbit," the man said.

"And courageous," Laszlo Veg said. "Are you quite ready?"

"Yeah, yeah."

The hare was sitting up on its haunches, a brown-gray, long-eared fool of a mammal, exhausted, breathing hard, waiting for the next rush by the killer. Across the enclosure the greyhound pawed the green carpet, lowered its long skull and bounded off to its dinner.

Veg was lighting one of his stinky cigarettes. I almost thought I smelled the vile smoke of the Kossuth and I saw the huge lighter flame in his hand. And then I saw the greyhound stop dead in its tracks and crouch low, its head dipping between its forepaws, its curving tail wilted.

"Son-of-a-bitch," the strange man said.

Had I been able to speak I would have expressed similar sentiments. The hare had sprung from its corner and, with a flash of white teeth and a squeaking noise, began to chase the greyhound across the grassy stadium.

They must have shot me full of something when they realized I'd been staring. I barely recall the two men walking toward the automobile, and Evie Bragg rolling up my sleeve. I felt no needle prick, but I went out cold again.

When I awakened I was on a narrow cot. There was a sheet under me, and a sheet and thin blanket on top of me. I tried to wiggle my feet and could not. My hands were numb, unresponsive. But my mind was alert, and oddly enough, I had that euphoric glow one gets after coming out of a deep Demerol sleep. The mists lifted slowly; my head was stationary but my eyes perceived light. Beyond my lifeless feet was a vertical rectangle of light—the space between opened double doors. I focused on the illuminated space, feeling relaxed, confident, unafraid on my narrow bed. Was it a hospital?

I tried to review the wild events I'd just raced through—the attempt to convoy Malar and Judy to the United States and my rejection by Bragg, the disappearance of my two prize Hungarians, the revelation that Daoud Jabali, my Arab terrorist, was a high-ranking Israeli officer named Shlomo Tal, my shamefaced delivery of the Malars to Pochastny's hands. And then had come my *confronta* with Flackman and Cooperage and Metrick, all of them convinced, thanks to the New Left brats, that I was a CIA biggie, and my conviction that they *envied* me. Finally, I'd been trapped in Evie Bragg's iron pants, my hands locked on her *culo*, from which vulnerable state she'd stewed me in my own juice and delivered me to someone who watched Laszlo Veg make a rabbit scare a greyhound. And now I was—where?

None of these adventures bothered me terribly, or maybe it was the happy drugs they'd shot into my innocent arm. What did disturb me was the way Moe Bloom had failed to keep me informed. He'd failed on Veg, clearly. Veg was out demonstrating "coursing" to some unknown American in a dark suit. And I was . . . my nose twitched. I smelled animals, dirty animals, an odor I'd recently encountered. Monkey stink. Baboons, to be exact.

I knew where I was. It was the rear room in Veg's decrepit apartment off the Quai de la Mégisserie. As my eyes grew accustomed to the darkness I saw the curlicues in the corners of the ceiling, the dirty newspapers spread on the floor. Veg. Now I seemed to recall him, not outside the green corral, but bending me over, wearing a white coat, holding an enormous hypodermic needle over my bared right arm. That bastard, that evil, scheming old manipulator of animal psyches! I'd seen his rats that terrified cats, his hare that frightened a greyhound, and his vicious baboons, and I feared him. I began to understand why so many people in Paris wanted him.

My ears sharpened. I heard again that high-pitched angry chattering, that quarrelsome chorus of monkey voices. The stink hit me full force, clogging my nostrils—urine, dung, rotting fruit, a stew of stale stenches.

". . . an iwwegular pwocedure, I should think . . ."

How's that? Come again?

". . . my pwincipal is not awtogether convinced . . ."

Venables. Derek Venables, that ruddy, tweedy snob! What

was the co-chairman of the conference doing here?

"I am sorry, Mr. Venables," I heard Veg say. "But this gentleman insisted on the demonstration immediately, and with other interested parties present."

What time of day was it? Late afternoon? The middle of the night?

"Get the show on the road, Veg," a harsh American voice said. It was the voice of the man I had seen at the exhibition of coursing. "I'm in a hurry."

"Of course," Veg said. "You understand the rules?"

"You'll drive me up the wall, Veg," the American rasped. "I said we'd abide by any ground rules you want."

"You are an impatient young man. I know that you are an important member of the Central Intelligence Agency, and I know you have a right to demand I move ahead. On the other hand, Mr. Venables', shall we say, *employers* . . ."

"I know who they are," the American said. "And so do you. We've had him tabbed from round one."

"Good," Veg said. "It is best for us to know one another. In any case, Mr. Venables wishes a full briefing." There was a pause. The floor creaked. It sounded as if the Hungarian were pacing, like a teacher starting a lecture. "Neither of you has any training in neurology? I thought not. What about electronics?"

"I know some," the American said.

"Hmmm. A bit."

My limbs were feeling stronger. The legs were still weak, but the arms were regaining strength, and I was now able to prop myself up on the elbows. With a sigh of gratitude, I discovered that my neck was not paralyzed. The doors leading to Veg's zoo had been opened wider, possibly to allow some air into the fetid dump, and I could see the long cage on the table.

"Before we proceed to more sophisticated matters, let us begin with a simple demonstration with my Chacma baboons," Veg said. I saw him walk by the cage. One of the three baboons bared his scarlet gums and ivory teeth and began to jabber.

"Okay, but not all night," the American said. "I came here to make a bid."

"And so you shall," Veg said. "As shall Mr. Venables. But it is only fair to him to have the techniques explained to him. You, sir, are less in need of explanations. You and your associates have been making determined attempts to steal my secrets for the past few days, beginning with the killing of the white rat in that stupid novelist's hotel room. I could have told you in advance, it was of no value to you, or Mr. Bloom, or anyone but myself."

"Wait a goddamn minute," the American said. "I don't have to sit here and be insulted."

There was a noise of chairs moving, bodies changing positions. Veg moved into my field of vision. He had on his white lab coat, and he seemed to be feeding something to one of the baboons. "Then you may leave, sir," he informed the American.

"You know damn well I won't."

The American came into view—a thin man in a dark gray suit, a pale-faced bespectacled man wearing horn-rimmed glasses and a thick black moustache. It was Chipper Latour, Louise Latour's Eagle Scout. Had I been more alert I would have made the connection when I had seen him watching the greyhound and the hare. He was a Nebraska boy—I believed that he really was Louise's kin—and Nebraska was the coursing capital of America. He kept telling Veg that he knew all about greyhound coursing. I had no doubt that he did; and he probably knew about killing rats and KGB agents also.

"Splendid, sir," Veg said. "But if you or your agents have any lingering notions that you can steal my procedures from a white rat, or from the plaster patch on a man's head, you must be more realistic. Only I can impart the knowledge you seek, and you shall—one of you shall—pay for it."

The Hungarian, tickling the baboon under the throat, and

the American agent were almost directly in front of me. "Something is fishy here," Latour said. "How come Pochastny is letting you get away with this?"

"They are more concerned with Mr. Malar's security, ever since that fool tried to kidnap him."

So. Bloom's crazy plot had not been a complete failure. The Russians were still worried about Malar.

"I don't buy that," Chipper said. "Who the hell wants Malar?"

"Believe what you will. Would it surprise you to know that Mr. Pochastny is not even aware of this laboratory?"

"Balls. Keramoulian knew."

"Indeed he did. He caught you here while you tried to steal an animal. You and some colleagues. You killed him here, did you not?"

Venables gasped. "I say . . ."

"I wouldn't tell you even if I had. Listen, Veg, if he knew about this setup, the others did. Who's to say they haven't got this bugged? Or that you aren't working for them right now?"

"Mr. Keramoulian's body was removed by certain refugee friends of mine. It was discovered in an abandoned Citroën outside the Franco-Soviet Cultural Society in the ninth arrondissement."

"Can we get on?" Venables piped.

"You are right, Mr. Venables. I merely felt it my obligation to assure you that this work is clandestine and you are both privileged. Now please. Both of you stand near the center of the cage while I go to the control board."

Derek Venables moved into my field of vision. Veg departed. The Englishman—buddy to buddy—leaned toward Chipper. "This chap Bwoom, is he involved at the moment?"

"Bloom's been taken care of," Latour said grimly. "He won't show."

Had I been able, in my semiparalyzed state, to shudder, I would have. Yes, they were the big time. They'd rendered me comatose, trapped in Evie Bragg's girdle, and they'd put Moe Bloom on ice.

"As you know, gentlemen," Veg said, "I specialize in radio-controlled stimulation of the brain. That is not a new field by any means. I have simply refined and advanced the techniques."

Venables and Latour were turned toward his droning, didactic voice. The baboons seemed relaxed, intent on their lice-infested pelts.

"We have long known," Veg went on, "that electrical stimulation of the brain, ESB, can affect motor responses. Blinking, salivation, and so on. In the past few years, we have also proven that social behavior in which an animal has a choice can be altered, heightened, diminished, or eliminated by electrical proddings."

"Fasc'natin'," Venables said.

Latour was silent; I had the feeling he knew the basics already.

"Let us explore a trait like aggression, the tendency to attack and fight and dominate, and its opposite—fear, withdrawal, cowardice. What can ESB do to these traits?"

He moved into view again, and he was holding a white rat in his hand. "Tibor, an ordinary white rat. Look at the small white plaster cap on his skull. Beneath it, I have implanted four hair-thin intercerebral electrodes. When these are stimulated by radio impulses, Tibor becomes a demon. There is not a cat in the world that can face up to him."

I knew, I knew. I'd seen Tibor in action. I'd also seen the white plaster patch on Imre Malar's skull; I was way ahead of Veg. With sickening clarity, I understood what the bastard was doing.

"As I have already said," Veg went on, "the rat stolen by Bloom's Budapest agents was a control animal, and you, Mr. Latour, wasted your time trying to steal it, or pry secrets from its innocent brain."

But what about the secrets in Malar's innocent brain? I

wondered. I'd grown cold—cold, weak, terrified of the neurologist.

"So, to our Chacma baboons," Veg said. "By nature these animals are aggressive competitive beasts. I regret that Zoltan, who was boss of the group, is dead, murdered by you and your people. No matter. Ah, here is Kitti, dear Kitti. *Kommen Sie hier, Kitti.*"

Kitti. The note in the personal column in the *Herald Tribune.*

"Kitti is the only female in the group. She is rather gentle. She lets strangers tickle her back, and she will even kiss me."

Kitti paraded in front of them, a dark gray, red-rumped monster, studying them with baboonish contempt.

"There is a plaster cap on her skull, presumably to cover the electrodes. On her back is a box containing a small radio receiver. But she has not been implanted, she has no electrodes in her brain, and her radio receiver is dead. In short, I cannot stimulate her with radio impulses."

"She's the control animal," Chipper said quickly.

"Excellent, sir. You are better trained than I imagined. The other two baboons are males. The big fellow is Erno, who, since Zoltan's death, is boss of the cage. He gets the best food, and makes love to Kitti when he desires. Do not get too close to him. He can remove several fingers with one bite. *Erno! Erno, kommen Sie hier! Erno! Setzen Sie!*"

There was a crash; a thud. A mouse-gray monster bounded across the cage and smashed into the wire with such force that the entire table shook. Then he backed off, spitting and cursing, rolling his red eyes. Venables retreated; the American held his ground.

"Big bastard, isn't he?" Latour asked.

"Yes, and vicious and intolerant. He has been implanted. There are six hair-thin electrodes leading from the plaster cap on his head through a burr hole in the skull into the rostral area of the caudate nucleus of his brain."

"Repeat that, slower," Latour said.

"No, that will not do," Veg said. "You are seeking some free information in the event you lose the bidding to Mr. Venables. But gleanings will not help you. What you shall witness in this baboon family is a mere refinement of experiments already tried in your own country. It is my specialized work that is of value, and you will need more than a good memory and a notebook to steal that from me. In any case, I shall repeat. The electrodes reach into the rostral area of the caudate nucleus. They are directly connected to the radio receiver strapped to his back.

"The third baboon is Gabor, that smaller fellow. He is a coward. He is barely tolerated, and even Kitti will sometimes steal his food. *Gabor! Hier, Gabor!*"

An undernourished, droopy ape skittered across the cage, stared at the men, then rolled over on its side in craven supplication, like a whipped dog.

"He is implanted, like Erno, but in his case, the electrodes reach into an entirely different area of the brain—the rostral part of the red nucleus, near the zona incerta."

"Zona . . . ?" It was Chipper again, making notes.

"Ah, Mr. Latour, you should take my word that this sort of knowledge is known to your own physiologists."

"Then why the devil are we heah?" Venables protested.

"You will see soon enough," Veg said.

"Let's get the show on the road, dammit," Latour said. He was getting jumpier. The pressure on him must have been enormous. Me, in my relaxed, semidoped state, I felt no pressure. As a faker, a fraud, a charlatan, I had no worries.

"Stay where you are, gentlemen," Veg commanded—he was out of sight, across the room, "while I activate the panel. At first, I shall not stimulate the animals but let them behave normally."

There was a humming noise as the radio controls were turned on.

"Now keep in mind," Veg said, "that Erno is the boss, Gabor the coward, and Kitti the woman. She cannot be stimulated. They can. Mr. Latour, there is a bunch of bananas on the packing crate near you. Shove them under the wire near where Gabor, our coward, is resting."

I was fully awake now, up on my elbows, seeing everything clearly. Chipper Latour grabbed the bananas and put them inside the cage. Gabor looked grateful. Poor guy, he probably never got enough food. But as soon as his hand touched the fruit, Erno, with a shriek, leaped across the cage, cuffed him around the ears, nipped at his ass, and yanked the bananas away. Gabor skittered away, wailing. Erno squatted in the middle of the cage, peeled a banana, and began to eat it with finesse and dainty movements of his savage teeth. He munched sedately, secure in his supreme strength. He was the Flackman of the cage, Numero Uno, all balls, all ego.

Kitti now sidled up to Erno and reached for a banana. He cracked her on the cheek, but she took it anyway and scampered off to a corner. Erno scrambled after her a few steps, chattering and showing white fangs, but he let her eat it.

Emboldened, Gabor the yellow-belly slunk up to the boss, circling him, his knuckles scraping the floor, his tail perched high above his red rump, like a hairy erection, pleading, begging for a banana. Erno had no pity for him. Barking, he leaped at the loser, sending him into whimpering retreat. Boss, cocksman, dispenser of goodies, arbiter, master of the revels, Erno was unshakable in his primacy.

"That, gentlemen, is the *natural* order in this colony," Veg said. "An aggressive male boss, a male coward, a neutral female. So, we shall begin to stimulate them with radio. The apparatus is now functioning. Let us begin with our boss-baboon, Erno. I shall stimulate his brain with exponentially falling waves of one minisecond pulse duration, up to twenty-two volts, directly into the caudate nucleus of his brain. Note that the animal experiences no pain. So, with Erno. Observe him."

There was a clicking sound across the room, the humming became louder. Erno shook his huge head a few times, as if

337

getting rid of tsetse flies. His eyes opened wide. With his jaws poised over the half-eaten banana, he decided he wasn't hungry and tossed the fruit to the floor. And then he yawned —a great, jaw-breaking yawn exposing all of his alabaster teeth and his blood-colored mouth. *Malar. Malar yawning during that awful speech.*

"Extwadinary," Venables said softly.

"I am still stimulating him," Veg said. "Typically, he has lost interest in food. Also, the ipsilateral movements of his head and the yawning are part of the behavioral pattern. There is a general inhibition of activities, a lassitude."

Erno rose from his haunches and began to shuffle around the bananas, making a small circular journey, then dropping to a sitting position again. His brutal hairy arms dangled in front of his chunky body. His eyes blinked a few times, and then he shut them. As he appeared to doze, Gabor, the hungry one, came sneaking back to the bananas.

"Gabor has not been stimulated," Veg said. "But he is a bright subject and has been through this several times. He understands what has happened to his tormentor."

Gabor snaked a long arm out, grabbed a banana, and raced away. Erno, who had beaten him unmercifully a few minutes ago, yawned. He had no interest in bananas, combat, or status. Kitti now scampered by, snatching a second banana as she did. *Erno had been nullified by Veg's electrical jolts.*

"I shall now stimulate Gabor," Veg said. "I shall use the same exponentially falling waves, with intensities of one to two milliamps. Gabor's stimulation will start at once, but I shall continue with Erno's—a prod of five seconds, every minute, a routine ESB procedure."

Again I heard the clicking and the intensified humming.

"It begins already," Veg said. "Gentlemen, notice how Gabor's hair is rising. Pilo-erection, a certain sign of imminent aggressive behavior."

A dull-eyed baboon, Erno remained in a gray lump, center-cage. But Gabor, gingered by Veg's magic juice, was not sitting down for anyone. His brain humming with messages, he was walking *erect*—grabbing at the side of the cage for support like a deformed man, asserting himself. Once he circled Erno, in that short tour—the way Malar had walked about the lectern!—and once he climbed the wire. Then, in a stand-up pose like a boxer, he confronted the bully.

"Watch carefully," Veg said. "He is at the peak of stimulation. He actually believes he is courageous."

A low rumbling noise issued from Gabor's throat, an unnatural sound, unlike any I'd heard from Veg's apes. *Choo-coo-roo, choo-coo-roo,* Gabor informed Erno. He got down on all fours in front of the drowsy boss. The hair on his back was a bristly ridge. His ears flattened. Then he bared his teeth and cursed Erno, showing teeth, spitting, letting him have it in Afrikaans and Swahili.

"Good heavens," Venables gasped.

"I'll be goddamned," Latour added. "That lousy punk became a terror."

Tail up, jaws open, Gabor threw himself at Erno, biting, clawing, scratching. The bully didn't fight back. He rolled, stumbled, scrambled through the underbrush of shredded newspapers, to the safety of a distant corner. He was a whipped baboon, an ape with no more interest in combat or his primate primacy.

Something was going *buzz, buzz, buzz* in a part of Gabor's brain, assuring him he was a battler, a terror. And something was going *buzz, buzz, buzz* in a different part of Erno's brain, convincing him he could not fight. And what had gone on in poor Imre Malar's brain?

"I'll be goddamned," Chipper said again.

"The potentialities of electrical stimulation of the brain, or ESB, are very great, gentlemen," Veg said. "You have seen a simple demonstration with laboratory animals." The Hungarian walked into my field of vision and tapped at the wire. Gabor, transformed into a raging monster, hurled himself at the scientist, trying to eat his fingers. "See how he is convinced of his bravery. The effect will last about forty minutes. When it wears off, he will be his normal cringing self, and Erno will reassert his dominance over the colony."

"I understand all of this," Latour said. "Now let's get to those refinements you were telling us about. My people wouldn't have sent me here if they didn't know you had something better to peddle."

' "Ah, how commercial you make it sound, Mr. Latour. Typically American."

"You should talk, Veg. You're the one who wants the big money." Latour's fake moustache drooped, and he pressed it against his lip.

"So I do. Look, look at Gabor, how his stimulated brain tells him he can do whatever he wants."

Gabor was king of the hill. Having bolted a banana, he was now on top of Kitti, humping away. The sight of Chacma baboons making love is not one of the more inspirational visions in the world, especially in the middle of the night—morning—when one is full of deadening drugs and isn't even sure why he is watching. Why had I been dragged to Veg's secret zoo where I could overhear the double-dealing? They knew I worked with Bloom; they knew I'd blab to Bloom.

"What about Malar?" Chipper asked brusquely. Gabor was pumping away on Kitti, a sex maniac unloosed, caressing her neck with tender bites.

"Yes, Mr. Malar," Veg said. "His behavior was something on the order of what you saw here, but more refined."

Now we were getting down to cases. My ears grew pointed, supersensitized.

"You had no control panel," Latour persisted. "Those radio waves have a limited range. Also, he only had a patch on his head. I didn't see any wire leads going into a receiver."

"You are an impatient young man," the neurologist said. "All will be made clear. But first, you must believe that I, Laszlo Veg, have absolute confidence in the originality of my work. I am unique in the field. I have moved the whole question of behavioral control via ESB into a new dimension."

"Then I still don't know why the Russians are letting you do this," Chipper said.

"I have told you. They are unaware that I wish to leave Hungary. Moreover, they *are* aware of a great deal of my work, but not the specifications of the techniques we are here to discuss."

What a con man! What a Hungarian! I thought of the old recipe for Hungarian chicken. First, steal a chicken . . .

"I repeat the conditions," Veg said. "First, price. Second, sanctuary and safe conduct. Either to the United States, or in Mr. Venables' case, to a neutral country acceptable to me and his employer. I shall surrender all my animals, my papers, my research, and my own talents."

"In perpetuity?" Latour asked.

"Yes sir, insofar as anyone can give such a guarantee."

Definition of a Hungarian: a man who follows you into a revolving door and comes out ahead of you.

I felt much stronger. With an effort, I might have been able to talk. My breathing was regular, but I doubted that I would gain anything by shouting. It was better to rest, to watch, to remember everything I saw and heard.

"Poor old Malar," Venables said. "He had ewectwodes in his bwain."

"And still has," Veg said.

"Just wike these apes," the Englishman said. "Dweadful."

"Did you have his permission to fix him up like that?" Latour asked.

"I am afraid not. A fortuitous accident occurred in his bathroom last week. A scalp wound, some bleeding. When he came to my hospital, the Lenin Institute, I put him under anesthesia and under pretext of cleaning the wound, introduced multilead electrodes into the caudate nucleus of the brain, and some smaller electrodes into the thalamus and central gray areas."

"How was this done?" the American asked.

341

"The same as on my animals. Through small burr holes in the skull."

"Any pain?" Latour asked.

"None. Nor has he any now. Nor is he aware that he is implanted."

"And the idea," Latour said, "was to reduce or eliminate his hostile feelings and make him friendly, controllable, good-natured?"

"Precisely."

There was a hiatus in their palaver. I suspected that both Venables and Latour, like me, were repelled by Veg. The man was a fiend, a cynical brute. Malar, his old friend, had been transformed from a rational, thinking, creative man—a slippery one, no doubt—into a robot who responded to radio stimulation. It was hard to accept the appalling truth. But I had seen the white rat terrify the cat. I had seen the rabbit chase the greyhound. And I had seen the way Veg's electrical jabs had transformed the baboons.

"Yace, yace," Venables said. "That would be the Soviets' idea of a good show. They wanted Malar to speak at the confwence, to spwead the word that he would attack them—and then force the bugger to stahnd up and make that awful speech pwaising them."

"You are free to speculate on that," the Hungarian said. "I am not required to respond. You are customers. I am seller."

Chipper Latour was laughing—a cynical chuckle. "Jesus, what a scene. You kept shooting radio waves into that guy's brain. Every time he tried to make his original speech attacking the Russkies, you derailed him. He got the message—say nice things about the big boys in the Kremlin. What a gas."

"And now you want to sell it," Venables said. "How perfectwy Hungawian."

"You bastard, Veg!" I shouted from the cot, rising to a sitting position. "You lousy son-of-a-bitch! You didn't fool anyone! Moe Bloom showed you up! He had the real speech! The Russians never looked worse! Everyone knows they did something to Ma . . . Ma . . . Mal . . ." My voice suffocated in my parched throat.

"Ah, he is awake," Veg said casually. "I should have given him another injection."

The neurologist opened the doors wide. I saw the laboratory unfold—the control gear, the long cage, the chattering, obscene apes. Three faces studied me—Venables', bland and indifferent (no wonder the fink had been trying to pump me about Veg), Latour's contemptuous, and the sour professor himself, advancing on me with a hypodermic syringe.

"Shove that needle up your ass, Veg," I said. "I'm an American citizen and I have some clout. Latour, you're with the government, protect me from this maniac. You heartless scheming prick, Veg, you Frankenstein, you jammed electrodes into Imre Malar's brain and made him a machine. You ruined one of the finest minds in Europe, the last of the liberal intellectual Marxists. You crud, you turd, you fartleberry, I could strangle you with my own hands, if I had any strength."

"Mr. Bloodwart, do not agitate yourself," Veg said. "This is only a mild sedative."

I tried to move away from him, but succeeded only in collapsing on the bed when he gave me a gentle shove. "Chipper! Latour, you phony Eagle Scout! That moustache doesn't fool me! *Ouch! Ouch*, you bastard!"

He'd gotten me right in the soft part of my upper right arm.

"Chipper, I befriended you and your Aunt Louise! You picked my pockets and killed the white rat! Don't let this madman do me in!" I was wailing, screaming. "Venables! Who the hell ever you are! You'll get screwed! Stop this guy! Malar was your co-chairman! Oh, oh . . . Jesus . . . I'm going . . ."

Afloat in analgesics, I barely felt the prick of the needle. But I was outraged, consumed by a fiery anger that could not be appeased, but would scorch and sear my ego for life. It was like the time a gang of Italian kids had jumped me on Arthur Avenue, pulled down my pants, and rubbed horse-shit on my genitals. They had laughed, pummeled me, yanked and kneaded my privates with manure, and then run off, leaving me weeping and cursing in the gutter. That day I swore I would kill them one by one, dropping them with a long rifle, shooting the bastards between the eyes.

Sedate tears rolled down my face. They traveled in warm rills down my starved cheeks, onto the soiled pillow. "Ah, Veg, Laszlo Veg," I bawled, "you have no heart. You stinking animal trainer, you brain-implanter." I did not cry long; the intravenous injection stilled my ravaged nerves and I began to doze again.

"Okay, how about the controls?" Latour was asking. "How did you control Malar?"

In fuzzed outlines I saw Veg hold up his huge cigarette lighter. He clicked it a few times; it flamed. "With this," the Hungarian said. "These are my radio controls. It is like the remote switcher they sell with American television sets, but infinitely more delicate. The entire system is inside the body."

"But . . . but . . . wheah was the weceiver on Malar?" Venables stammered. "He had no box on his back, wike the baboons."

"It was contained within the plaster patch on his head," Veg explained. "A small transistorized apparatus, connected directly to the implanted electrodes, and fixed beneath the plaster."

"You kidding us, Veg?" Chipper asked. "You need a whole panel, a console almost, to handle the baboons. How can you get enough juice out of that lighter? Lemme see it."

I saw Veg pull his arm back. "Not yet, sir. Part of the agreement is my right to withhold information until the price is agreed on. You will observe that part of the agreement. You may not examine the transmitter or the receiver. Some of my cards must remain face down."

Perhaps I was getting inured to the drugs; but now I

couldn't fall asleep. I remained in that semidazed state, the way I was when I saw the greyhound and the rabbit. I couldn't talk but I could see and hear. I heard the cigarette lighter going *click-click*, and I recalled the first day I'd met Malar and the way he acted strangely, yawning, his eyes glazing, when Veg was nearby lighting his Kossuths. And the cigarette lighter again—when I saw Tibor the rat beat the tar out of the concierge's cat. And again at the conference. And outside the coursing arena. And now.

"The question of behavioral control of large populations through electrical stimulation of the cerebral cortex is a complex one," Veg said. "Your American scientists say that it is unfeasible. They argue that the anatomic and physiologic variability of human beings makes such a mass control program unlikely."

"Yace," Venables added, "not to mention the difficulty of impwanting miwwions of people."

"In the mass, yeah," Latour agreed. "But individuals? Selected people? Hundreds? Thousands? What about ESB for them?"

"Oh, that is another matter," the neurologist said. "As you surely know, the technique has already been used on epileptics, people suffering depression manias, sexual aberrations. Many have been implanted and have shown good responses. My work, of course, is more advanced, because I can change specific attitudes, modes of thinking."

"Yeah, yeah, we know," Latour grumbled. "Get to the point, Veg."

Sleep, finally, devoured me. I floated under a warm gentle sea. Effortlessly, I glided around day-glo reefs, varicolored tropical fish. Friendly groupers nuzzled me, and I saluted a passing jew-fish. A benign octopus tickled my face and a porpoise kissed me. Drenched, de-boned, fileted, I felt no pain in my warm watery home, sensed no danger, and was satisfied with my subaqueous life. All my life, from now on, would be million-dollar royalties and tax exemptions.

The clicking of Veg's cigarette lighter roused me from this oceanic reverie. I awakened smiling, a child in front of a penny candy counter, clutching a dollar bill. But I was no longer on the hard cot. My boneless body had been stuffed into a nubby maroon easy chair. Fetuslike, I nestled in its woolly embrace, warm and secure. It was the same room where I'd been on the cot, but a large floor lamp had been lit, and I could see the soiled and cracked walls. Across from me Venables and Latour sat on a sagging sofa, studying me. Nearer to me sat Veg, in his white coat, stiff in a wooden kitchen chair. The cigarette lighter was in his right hand.

"Hi there, sports fans," I said, "this is Stan Lomax with the day's doings in the world of sports. First, a look at baseball." My voice was strained and distant, my arms and legs were weighted.

"You sure he's right for this?" Latour asked. "He's a goddamn clown, and I don't like clowns."

"You chose him, sir," Veg said, and crossed his long legs.

"Well, we all agreed on him," Chipper said. "You and Venables were in on it also."

"And Mr. Bloom," Veg said, smiling at me.

Chosen? For what? And why by four people, all involved in some kind of underhanded business?

"Yace," Venables sniffed. "We did agwee that he was a good subject. All that posing, the bwagging and boasting."

"Okay, okay," Latour said. "So we all chose him."

"For what, Chipper?" I asked hollowly. "For what? You . . . Oh, Chip . . . you dirty bugger . . . what did Bloom . . ."

"Besides," Latour groused, "he's so full of drugs, how can we be sure of anything he says or does?"

Laszlo Veg scowled and stared at the ceiling. "The drugs

are only temporary. Besides, they cannot withstand the force of the radio waves. He is not in pain, and as you will see, he is lucid."

The warm sea in which I swam turned to Arctic waters. Chunks of ice formed in my hands and feet, and my throat was filmed with frost. I knew why I was sitting in the maroon chair.

"You bastards," I moaned, "you fiends. You monsters."

With every smidgin of strength left in my right arm, I raised it slowly and patted the top of my head. On the crown, in the midst of my innocent pate, a small area had been shaved and there was a smooth white bump of some kind of plastic material. *I'd been patched.* Like the white rat, like the baboons, like Imre Malar.

"Veg, you assassin, you killer, you destroyer," I wept softly. "You drilled a hole in my skull. You bored into my brain."

"It is only a small hole, Ben."

"Don't call me by my first name, you Hungarian murderer. You villain, you savage, you Nazi. You jabbed electrodes into my brain. They're there under that plaster. You are going to try to control me, the way you did your buddy Malar."

"Ben, they are tiny little things. Less than fifty millimeters of needle are in your brain substance. It is an absolutely safe and antiseptic procedure. There is no pain involved. I did this to you with nothing more than a local anesthetic. There is no danger of infection, and when we are finished, the electrodes can be easily removed."

"But . . . but . . . why me? Why'd you guys pick on me?"

"You were more or less elected by a committee. These gentlemen here and some others decided you were an ideal subject for a demonstration."

"What's that about Bloom?" I bawled. "What did he have to do with this?"

"Mr. Bloom betrayed you," Veg said.

"I—I don't believe it! Moe would never do that!"

347

"You shall have a chance to discuss it with him," Veg said. "When we are finished with you, of course."

Was it possible? Evie Bragg conveniently finding me alone in my hotel room? Moe tipping the Braggs off about me? No, it was impossible. They were telling me this to destroy my confidence in Moe.

Tears began to stream down my face. Again, I touched the plaster mound on my head. Within, the sinister electrodes penetrated my secret brain. Never again would I be my own man. My tears gushed forth; huge hot sobs.

"Stop your wailing," Chipper Latour snapped at me. "You're a disgrace to your country. Loudmouth. Liar. Running around making up stories about what a hotshot spy you are. You dumb meddler. Here's your chance, Bloodworth. Let's see who you're really working for."

He infuriated me; anger evaporated my fears. "Full of snotty remarks, aren't you, Chip?" I crooned. "Smartass Boy Scout. You dirty little pickpocket. I'll file a report on you when I'm home."

"Watcha gonna do, Ben?" he smirked. "Report me to the National Council?"

"Yeah, you and your fat aunt. Who is she? Mata Hari?"

"I say," Venables piped, turning toward Veg. "He doesn't appeah conditioned atall. He's evewy bit as wicked and as foulmouthed as he was two days ago."

"You too, you Sassenach faggot. Good old Der! You and Flackman and Cooperage and Metrick and all those fancy gropers, coming here on CIA money! Who's your conduit, Venables? Who pays your way?"

Ignoring my abuse, Venables walked toward me and touched the plaster on my head. I felt nothing. I was so full of pain-killer, I could stand anything. "Hands off me, you lanky fart," I snarled.

"He is well implanted, gentlemen," Veg said.

"Yeah, but we got to take your word," Latour said. "You

kept us locked out when you operated on him."

"One of my cards with its face down," Veg said. "You agreed."

"Yeah, yeah."

"I trust you will not entertain notions of running off with the subject and treating me in the rude manner in which you treated Keramoulian."

"He shot first," Latour said.

"And killed the baboon," I offered. "And the baboon bit your associate Bragg. It should have bitten your balls off, Chipper. I have more respect for those poor apes than I have for you."

The two bidders stood in back of Veg. Could I make a break for it? I knew the layout of the apartment, the back stairs leading to the courtyard. I tried to move my feet: they were hobbled. But even free, I doubted that I could run.

"He is almost ready," Veg said. "I want the drugs to wear off, so that he exhibits his normal hostile, jealous traits." The neurologist smiled at me; I saw a gold incisor. "I think you will prove an excellent subject. Almost as good as my poor Zoltan. He was a wonderfully bad-tempered baboon."

"Getting the picture, Bloodworth?" Latour mocked. "See why you were selected?"

"Thanks a million, Chip."

"You met the requirements. A snot, a loudmouth, a braggart, a liar. When you popped off at Huffguard and Flackman at the debate, we decided you'd be perfect."

"Good old Tom and Evie Bragg," I said. "They dug me, hey, Chipper?"

"That's the idea."

"You sneak. You're a disgrace to the uniform. I'll sue all of you. You just don't drill holes in a man's skull and jam electrodes into his brain without having to answer to someone. By God, you'll answer, Latour."

"When the interrogation begins," Veg said, ignoring my exchange with the CIA man, "feel free to join me in asking questions. We want to arouse as fully as possible his capacity for belligerence, outrage, jealousy, and so forth."

"I say," Venables said, "this should be a jolly good show. Bit of pwodding with wadio waves, and he'll go fwom hate to wove. That is the idea, isn't it?"

"Precisely," the Hungarian said. In the next room the baboons jabbered and scolded. The normal pecking order had been resumed—Erno sat center-cage, cuffing Gabor when he came too close, grabbing at Kitti's naked scarlet behind.

"Veg, you are a traitor to science," I said. "These other guys, and I shudder that one is my countryman, they are paid agents, hirelings. But you are in the tradition of great men like Salk and Sabin and Szilard and Bohr and Wigner and Weiskopf and Semmelweis. What would they think of you, tampering with the minds of innocent victims?"

"Shut up, Bloodworth," Latour snapped. "Don't try sucking up to the professor."

Laszlo Veg sat in the chair opposite me, fondling his cigarette lighter, the diabolical gadget that would soon be shooting electricity into my violated brain.

"You're Nazis, all of you, killers," I went on. "And curse all of you, you won't make a laboratory monkey out of me."

Veg jerked up in his chair. "Gentlemen, we can begin. Now, as in the case with Malar, there will be a powerful conflict between what the subject *wills*, and what the electrical stimulations force him to do and say. I suspect this subject may not be as resistant as Malar, but we shall soon find out."

"Yeah, you'll find out, you goddamn fascist," I cried. "Shove that PX Zippo up your Hungarian bung and burn your hemorrhoids."

Veg was not even looking at me. "I shall begin with a five-second stimulation, using unidirectional pulses of point-five miniseconds duration, at a frequency of one hundred cps. Stimulations will range from five to ten volts. Mr. Latour, you may stop taking notes."

"You madman," I said softly, "you mind-murderer. You're

no better than those Nazi doctors. You're a disgrace to your country, your profession, your religion, and even to those poor lab animals who trust you and whose brains you destroy. And you should hang your head in shame for selling your genius to whores like Latour and Venables. You are beneath my contempt, Veg, and I put on you the curse of my grandmother, may you grow like an onion with your head in the ground."

"He appears to be ready," the neurologist said.

Latour and Venables were staring at me. Chipper moved the floor lamp, the better to illuminate my ravaged face. Veg held the cigarette lighter forward and pressed it twice. The flame leaped. It made a wickedly loud clicking noise.

Did I hear a faint humming? I listened carefully. Yes, a distant noise, barely audible. A painful dryness afflicted my mouth, and my throat was constricting. My mouth began to open, my jaw drooped, my lips stretched and my features, willy-nilly, contorted themselves into a grotesque yawn. I seemed to yawn for minutes, the way Malar had. It was not an unpleasant sensation, rather like a good stretch. I yawned again. So this was ESB.

"I'd like to take a walk," I said. "Just a little stroll around the room."

"I know you would, Ben," Veg said amiably. "That is a normal reaction. But in your disturbed state, we have had to restrain you. Imagine you are walking. It is almost as good."

"Yes, a little walk. The way Malar did on the stage."

"Jesus, I can't believe it," Latour whispered.

"Involuntary reflexes," Veg explained. "These motor responses—yawning, strolling—are typical, and not of great importance. But the imminent changes in his emotional behavior, in specific responses to names, ideas, concepts, is what you shall find original. It is my intention, gentlemen, to metamorphose this person from the obnoxious, envious, hate-filled boor that he is, to a loving, understanding, tolerant fellow."

"Try it, buster," I sneered. "You'll fall on your ass."

351

Like a man switching from channel two to channel four, Veg clicked the lighter again. And again my throat went taut, my mouth and my tongue arid. I yawned hugely and wanted to take a walk. My feet tugged at the leather belt binding them.

"Please do not strain," the Hungarian said. "You cannot move."

"Go on, work on him," Latour snapped. "So far you haven't proved a thing except you can make him yawn."

"Proof will be forthcoming," Veg said. "I am ready to begin." The fiend smiled at me: I was no better than his rats or his baboons, a laboratory creature, to be handled gently before being transformed.

"Screw you, Veg. You don't scare me."

"I am sure I do not. Why should I, Ben? I am not going to hurt you. Now. Some questions. How do you like your family?"

"My family?"

"Yes. Wife, children."

"I like them fine, you *shmuck*. I love them."

"And your home community. Hicksville, I believe."

"Say, Chipper has really briefed you, hasn't he? I like it, yeah."

"And your publisher?"

"No better, no worse than other publishers."

Latour got up and began to pace the side of the dingy room. "For Chrissake, Veg, those questions don't mean a thing. Get on with it."

"If you please, sir," the Hungarian said, "a subject must be eased into interrogation with neutral, nonpolarizing questions."

"That's right, Chip," I added, feeling a kinship with Veg. "If you'd earned a merit badge in lab techniques, instead of *futzing* around with bee-keeping and vegetable gardening, you'd know that. And to think, my taxes pay the salaries of half-wits like you."

"What is your opinion of the World Conference on the Arts and Sciences?" asked Veg.

"It's a fraud."

"Why?"

"The CIA, with the KGB's consent, is paying the freight. It's filled with egomaniacs like Flackman and ass-kissers like Cooperage. The poor innocent Malaysians and Danes and Lebanese who came here are being taken. And that includes you, Venables, you schemer, letting Malar be humiliated, playing your dirty double game. This conference is a lot of crap, proof that the cops run the world . . ."

I almost leaped out of the chair. He must have given me the full ten volts. His hand clicked the lighter more than a few times. My jaws tried to unhinge, and I wanted to take a long, long walk, not just in a semicircle, but for miles and miles.

"Again, your opinion of this conference."

Latour and Venables were standing in back of Veg staring at my contorted face.

"This conference," I said, as the words oozed from my lips like ribbons of toothpaste, "is a fake . . . fraud . . . run by police . . . it . . . I . . ." Dammit, I'd show them. My superior brain would never bow to Veg's radio waves.

"You don't mean that, do you?" Veg asked.

"This conference," I hissed, "is a . . . a . . . lousy . . . rotten . . . is . . . a . . . is truly a gathering of the great minds and eminent talents of the age. It is a platform for intellects from far and near, a meeting ground for East and West, a convocation of men of goodwill, no matter what their politics. I mean it. It's a peachy conference. It's dandy. I like everyone here, including Mr. Venables."

When I stopped babbling, I was breathing hard, covered with sweat. I had not believed a word of what I'd said, but the pandering, soft-soaping, words had gushed forth from my mouth, as involuntary as my yawning.

"Wizard," Venables whispered.

"Damn," Latour said. "Damn, I don't believe it."

"Well done, Ben," Veg said. He turned to his customers. "He is an excellent subject because of his reflexive desire to be insulting and hostile. But, as you have witnessed, simple stimulation of the caudate nucleus of the brain, with a few electrical prods, forced him to forego his aggressive responses and speak in friendly, compliant tones. He is actually a better subject than Malar, who has made a career of being elusive. With Ben here, we have no such problem. By nature an outraged, offended fellow, his immediate reaction to almost anything is a hateful one. I tell you, gentlemen, that it is a challenge even to my techniques to change him from a crank into a benign comrade."

"Try again," I said. "I'm wise to it now."

"Yes," the neurologist said. "We shall see remissions to his normal state. That will last only until the shocks exercise a pronounced spread effect."

"Spread this, you Nazi."

"Your opinion of Warren Cooperage, Ben."

"Hah! A self-promoting, celebrity-sucking snob. His nose is permanently brown. When he shakes hands with me at a party, he's already looking over my shoulder to see if he's missing any *k'nockers*. He's the House Critic, the mobile reserve who does the wrap-up rave review if any of his pals gets hit hard by the other critics. He and his rich wife run a tight little preserve . . . you're in or you're out. I can't stand either of them, if you must know——"

Click. Click. Click. Click.

My head began to swivel, my eyes bugged. My jaw flew open and I had an almost uncontrollable urge to urinate. "Veg," I wailed. "I got to take a leak."

"A normal reaction to a longer stimulation. Be patient, Ben. First tell us again what you think of Warren Cooperage."

"I say," Venables gasped. "The buggah is stwuggwing with himself. I cahn't bewieve it. He's two men."

"Coop . . . Coop . . . Cooperage is a rotten . . . is a

. . . a . . . truly original and germinal mind, a first-rate intellect, one of the gems of mid-twentieth-century letters. Head and shoulders he stands above the run of American critics, one of the last of the great belletrists, a man of facile style and pungent wit, a catalyst bringing the most dazzling talents together, a master of the revels of the haut monde of the American Writer, a man of grace, charm, and candor, a kind and generous person, supplying a much-needed role. We are all the richer for his elegant, incisive, and insightful comments on the American Novel and the Art of the Essay."

"And his wife? Mrs. Cooperage?"

With each new subject, I was learning, I was able to summon up my true feelings before being buzzed. So I fought back.

"Tookie . . . Tookie Cooperage . . . is a Southern-fried *kotchka* with nothing to recommend her except her money. She is flat-assed and flat-chested and full of hominy grits . . . she can buy and sell editors and critics and publishers with her goddamn parties . . . but she doesn't fool me a minute . . ."

"I am disappointed in you," Veg scolded. I braced for the electrical jolt, but this time Veg spared the electricity, and merely pointed the Zippo at me, like a Melanesian medicine man pointing the bone at a rival. The juice didn't come, but I did.

"Tookie Cooperage is . . . a . . . a . . . charming and sparkling woman, a credit to the Old South and the plantation way of life, a gracious hostess and a generous befriender of artists. With her witty husband Warren, they comprise the most with-it, switched-on, trendy couple in Gotham's literary circles, and their kicky, kinky parties are where it's at. If you haven't attended one, you simply aren't into the mad, Mod New York scene."

"You sure you didn't give him that crap to memorize, Veg?" Latour asked. "The jerk sounds as if he learned it by rote."

"A common phenomenon with verbal persons," Veg said.

"He makes his living with words. They come easily to him. Under ESB, this facility is heightened."

I couldn't shut up. "Oh, such marvy people. Warren and Tookie can make life worth living. Believe me, folks, if they tap you for fame and wealth, you deserve to be tapped. They're as sweet as they're gay and as witty as they're talented."

"Doesn't he seem rawther to be overdoing it?" the English poet asked. He was fingering his gold crucifix.

"The spread effect has begun," Veg said. "I can now reduce his stimulations to one every three minutes, and his genial, approving, friendly manner will not diminish."

"Gosh, I like all you fellows," I burbled. "Even you, Chipper. How's Aunt Louise? Gee, she's a warm human being."

"Another peculiarity of my work," the Hungarian said. "Feelings of goodwill are transferred to persons nearby, relatives and friends of such persons."

Latour was scribbling in his small book. Veg did not reprimand him; he merely scowled as if to say—*write, write, I shall keep the secrets to myself until I am paid.*

"More questions, Laszlo, more questions," I pleaded.

"Of course, Ben. Your opinion of Mr. James Warfield Keen."

God, I wasn't out yet. No sooner did I hear the name of the prize-winning ancient than I curled my upper lip and showed them my incisors.

"Keen," I sneered. "Old-time socialist, later a commie. Marched with the copper mine strikers and led the Wobblies. Organized the tool-and-die workers and collected funds for Sacco and Vanzetti. Party member in the thirties. But woke up one morning to discover that his hero, J. Stalin, had been a bloody murderer. So Keen, feeling betrayed, threw out the humanist baby with the communist water. As a result, the old cinder has ended up writing poison for Boyle Huffguard's rag, proving that McKinley and Coolidge were much-loved, misunderstood heroes, and that Martin Luther King was a secret

Bolshie. He hates the memory of Mrs. Roosevelt and will confide to you that FDR betrayed him personally. A sad case of ex-communist blues, hardly worth my contempt . . ."

I guess Veg decided that the spread effect wasn't spreading fast enough. My recuperative powers must have astounded him, because I'd put the blocks to Keen. Naturally, he clicked me again, hitting the lighter at least four times. To my astonishment, he forced me to switch attitudes in *midsentence*.

". . . were it not for the fact that this noble and much-loved figure in American letters has emerged in his twilight years as a fresh and honest conservative voice, a truth-seeker and plain-speaker, ever ready to point out to us the deceits and lies of that arch-hypocrite Franklin Delano Roosevelt, who sold this country out to bolshevism by cultivating the mass-murderer Stalin, and whose cozened and favored appointees in the State Department betrayed Chiang Kai-shek to the bloody killers of Mao. We rejoice that intellectual patriots like James Warfield Keen have exposed for all time the perfidies and plottings of Eleanor Roosevelt, Harold Ickes, Herbert H. Lehman, Fiorello LaGuardia, and the whole pack of running dogs of international communism."

"Mr. Huffguard?"

Rage gripped my tonsils again. "A lisping, black-hearted reactionary knave, who hides his hatred of rationalists and reformers with a veneer of elegance, a wicked rearranger of facts . . ."

"You must be nice, Ben," Veg commanded. And clicked away.

". . . but nonetheless an urbane, witty, and wise man whose closely argued and well-structured essays remind us of the rebirth of an erudite and humane conservatism at a time when it is most needed. Let me say, sir, that I applaud the public appearances of Mr. Huffguard, especially his enlightening, entertaining debates with Mr. Arno Flackman."

"Miss Lila Metrick?"

"I'd like to *shtup* her. What a nerve she has wasting that big round *tochis*! A fake, that's what she is, full of phony demands for more and better orgasms, but afraid to make the keister available. Hah! Metrick and her Brave New World of come and cock, she's full of dried straw, not blood, and her notions of art will ensure fascism in America . . ."

"Ben, I don't like your attitude."

I got no message from the Zippo, but I obeyed anyway.

". . . but not before she restructures every lingering traditional concept of art, literature, film, and theater. A gifted and engaging critic and commentator, plastic and poignant, whose views on the current crisis in writing are a watershed in American letters, a landmark, a breakthrough, a free-fire zone for all who care, an exegesis long overdue of the with-it, trendy, thinky, kinky ambience in which we now live. Yes, Lila Metrick deserves our praise and our love, despite her stinginess with her big ass."

"For Chrissake, Veg, turn him off," Latour snapped. "I can't stand the dumb bastard any more."

"Please note," Veg said sourly, "that I no longer need stimulate him. The mere sight of the control instrument, or a word from me will arouse his feelings of goodwill, of friendliness, of approbation. He now sees the world around him in a warm, satisfying glow."

"Veg, that warm satisfying glow will be in my pants in a minute. I have to wee-wee in the worst way. A nice guy like you should let his buddy go to the john."

It wasn't only my bladder. My entire complement of vital organs seemed to have been tickled, titillated by the bombings of my caudate nucleus. My lower bowel demanded release, my heart bounced, my kidneys danced, and I was getting a lazy erection.

"Of course, Ben," Veg said, soothingly. "A final question first. What is your opinion of Mr. Arno Flackman?"

No. No amount of voltage, no electrical jabs into my brain by this Hungarian monster could ever temper my insane jealousy, my envious contempt for Numero Uno. So convinced was I that I would get the better of Veg's electrodes, poking into my private brain, that I even stalled a little, the better to savor my triumph. "Sure, Latzi," I said. "But first let me pee."

"It will pass," he said. "It is a mere motor reaction. I think you will soon experience a pleasurable sexual urge."

"Goody. Then this isn't a total loss."

"Come now, Ben, now that you are in a good mood. Tell us about Arno Flackman."

A white rage burned his electrodes out of my brain, the way a lit cigarette will force a leech to let go. To hell with Veg and his implants. There is nothing in the world, I could have told him, more potent, more virulent than a writer's envy. My consummate hatred of Flackman and his toadies, his world, his money, his fame, crisped the thin wires in my gray matter, and I was ready.

"Arno Flackman," I said, in a low, calm voice, "is undoubtedly a man of talent and intelligence. But he has forfeited his right to be heard, because he is a full-time professional celebrity who runs after Beautiful People, and snubs and ridicules those beneath him. He is arrogant and vainglorious and greedy when it comes to the literary world. But he has so ingeniously bullshitted the Establishment, notably the influential critics who are his neighbors and want to attend his parties, and crave a good word from him, that he has become impervious, unassailable, eternal. Flackman's nonfiction, for all its insightful brilliance and flashes of style, is indigestible manure, because it is chock-full of embarrassing and puerile personal references and ego-trips, which in lesser minds would be condemned as borderline psychoses. Flackman spends one night in a jail in Ithaca, New York, and he contrives to report it as if he had just done four years in Auschwitz. More disgusting are his reports on his relationships with various girl friends and assorted *nafkas*, all new versions of Heloise and Abelard. An adoring public now swoons over accounts of how he shines his shoes and buttons his overcoat. Oh, Veg, I've got you by the short and curlies now. No jolt in the world can get me to say anything nice about Arno Flackman!"

Venables looked mortified; Latour was mopping his forehead, and his false moustache had slipped to a forty-five-degree angle. The whole devilish contraption was going up in smoke. Veg hadn't reckoned with my hatred of Flackman; he'd pushed his luck. Now there'd be no big money, no sanctuary, no flight from communism. His ESB was a fake.

Then he began to work the lighter. He must have clicked off a dozen: *click, click, click,* doing their work in my brain. My eyes opened wide; I yawned forever; and my skull felt as if it had been plugged into a transformer at Consolidated Edison.

"More on Flackman, please," Veg ordered me.

"Gaaah . . . gaaaah . . . Earl Browder in evening clothes . . . Bela Kun doing the boogaloo . . ."

Click. Click. Click. Click.

"The man is a genius, nothing less," I proclaimed. "He is our only genius, a genius who will withstand the test of time. He deserves the Nobel Prize immediately. Flackman is responsible for extending the realm of sexual experience in literature to new and throbbing areas, and his plangent prose is a stunning breakthrough, a seminal, germinal, and an unarguably original mode for the new novel, the old essay, and the middle-aged short story. On so many different levels, Flackman is *sui generis,* at once sinuous and sinewy. By making the general specific and the specific general, by transposing the existential equations with which so many novelists try to solve problems but only muddle them, by courageously flaunting his multifaceted talent for character, plot, theme, and erotic fondling, in the face of the doubting Academy, he proves again that the artist speaks for all time and all men, not only of this time, of this place.

"When the cultural history of our troubled era is at long last writ large and eternally on tablets of adamantine, the name of Arno Flackman, born in Cleveland, Ohio, to humble Jewish parents, educated at the University of Miami, the world his oyster, will loom large, despite the shite-poke critics, the sniveling dissenters, the rodent-minded pedagogues and mincing aesthetes who so pathetically misinterpret the man's princely and universal mission. I regard Arno Flackman as the most wonderful person, the most unforgettable character, I've ever met."

"Ah, turn him off," Latour said. "I believe you, Veg."

Veg got up from his chair and patted my plaster bump. "You are a good boy, Ben, a good boy."

Exhausted, I lowered my head. My chin fell on my chest; my eyes closed. What I had just uttered about Flackman, even though forced from my lips by a madman's insidious tricks, was clearly the nadir of my life. Those words were a retreat from sense and honor so appalling that even as I mouthed the gassy clichés and the standard critic's fertilizer, I despised myself and what I had become.

"Laszlo Veg," I said, raising my tear-stained face, "you have just done the worst thing anyone has ever done to me."

"What is that, my boy?"

"You made me talk like a literary critic. You monster, you beast. You filled my mouth with existential equations and seminals and germinals. Veg, that was a vile and contemptible thing to do, and you shall not go unpunished."

"Oh, cheer up, dear boy. As soon as the stimulation wears off, you will be your angry self again. You can save all your hatred and envy of Flackman for those delicious moments."

Veg was finished with me. I'd served his purpose. I was like the white rats, the baboons, the hare. "Gentlemen," he said to the two agents, "that is all, I repeat, all I will show you. Per our agreement."

Latour was on his feet, fiddling with his moustache. He walked into the room with the baboons, studied them a moment, then came back.

"Listen," the American said. "I want to see the receiving

apparatus. I don't care whose—in the rat, one of the baboons, or in this jerk's head. I want to look at it."

"Yace. That would be a good idea." Venables was up also.

"No. That is final." Veg put the lighter into the pocket of his white smock. "We so agreed, and that is all you will see."

"Lemme think a minute," Chipper said. I liked him better in his Scout shorts.

"If you are ready to submit bids," the Hungarian said, "I shall release Mr. Bloodworth."

"Keep that clown tied up," the CIA man snapped. "He stays out of circulation until this deal is over. He'll run to Bloom and shoot his mouth off."

"But I got to pee."

The three of them had wandered back into the room with the apes. Veg tossed some bananas to the baboons. Latour was still complaining about not seeing the receivers. I tried to rise; it was impossible.

"*Kitti, schoene, Kitti,*" Veg said. He tickled the female baboon between the ears. "*Erno ist böse. Aber Kitti ist schoen.*"

The personal notice in the *Tribune* bugged me again. *Latzi and Kitti.* The three came out of the big room, Latour and Venables still arguing, Veg barely hearing them. As the Hungarian came near me, I grabbed the tail of his long white coat and pulled him close.

"Professor . . ."

"Yes, Ben. You must urinate. In a moment."

I dragged him closer. "*Latzi,*" I whispered, "*come quickly, all arranged, Kitti.*"

"Yes?" he asked. But he darted a look at the two buyers, who were arguing whether they had the right to demand an explanation of the radio receiver. Latour now wanted to examine the lighter also, with its tiny transmitter.

"Personal column," I whispered. "Today's Paris *Trib.* I know all about it. Let me go, Latzi, and I'll follow up. Bloom can help."

These haphazard lies had their effect. Veg was studying me, eager to press me. Latour's irritable voice interrupted us. "Got a phone I can use, Veg?"

"Yes. In the reception room."

He walked out. Venables wasn't going to let him get too far. I could hear Chipper ask for a number, and then his angry, prissy voice, bawling the daylights out of Tom Bragg.

"What the hell do you mean you let Bloom get away? He's a murderer. He killed Jabali, didn't he? You have any trouble, get ahold of Dunand. You goddamn fool."

He talked another thirty seconds, then came back in, Venables trailing. "Here it is, Veg. A quarter of a million dollars and safe conduct to the United States. We guarantee your security."

It didn't take Venables more than three seconds to react. A lisping nance he may have been, with limited knowledge about biology and electronics, but someone had given him his marching orders. He hadn't been required to phone anyone for last-minute instructions.

"My people will match that offer," Venables said smoothly. "And we guawantee youah pwotection in any neutwal city of your choice—Geneva, Stockholm, Vienna, Colombo, whatever."

Chipper Latour rubbed his nose. He seemed a little upset; perhaps he hadn't expected Venables to match him. Feigning disinterest, he wandered toward me, glancing at the plaster patch on my noodle.

"You rat," I said. "You let them do this to me. Fellow American."

"Since the offers are equal," Veg said, "you must give me a moment to weigh them."

This bit of hesitancy on the Hungarian's part told me something: I had a chance. Was it my imagination? Was my play-acting creating self-fulfilling prophesies? "Professor Veg," I wailed. "You promised you'd let me go to the john. I'll flood my pants if you don't."

"Ah, of course, Ben."

There was a conciliatory tone to his normally cold voice. He helped me rise but did not untie the leather belt hobbling my feet.

"Keep an eye on him," Chipper said. "All we need is for that jerk to start blabbing before you settle the deal."

"He is quite harmless," Veg said. "He is hobbled and he is so full of sedatives he can barely walk."

Veg lied. My limbs were strong and I was neither dizzy nor as weak as I had anticipated. He guided me to the next room, actually a dismal water closet off the kitchen. Outside the can, he knelt and undid the belt. As soon as it was loose he looked up at me, and in a firm stage whisper, said: "Kick me gently in the chest. Then pull the fuse box from the wall just above you. I shall shout, but you run down the rear stairs and keep running. Do not stop. Count three and proceed."

I held my breath. Inside I could hear Chipper Latour, in his loud voice, asking Venables to join him in a final demand to see the receiver in my skull, as well as the transmitter in the cigarette lighter.

"Thanks a lot, Latzi," I whispered—and kicked him easily. He sprawled backward convincingly, waiting until I got to the fuse box before shouting. Knowing French apartments and their electrical systems as I did, I knew what would happen. The ancient wires shredded; there was a dart of blue fire and a harsh yellow crackling. The lights in the room where I'd been exhibited went out. I raced to the kitchen door and flew down the winding stairs to the court, hearing Latour's curses and Venables' womanly cries. Veg was moaning in Hungarian; he wasn't a bad actor.

Latour must have had second thoughts about shooting at an American. After all, I'd helped him drag his sodden Aunt Louise around the conference. I thought I caught a glimpse of his gun poking over the railing. But he didn't shoot.

"Bloodworth! Bloodworth, you dope!" he called after me. "You're in trouble! You can't run around with those goddamn needles in your brain! Come back here!"

I didn't answer him, and I knew he'd never chase me. Not with Veg almost on the hook. The first morning light illumined the ugly grays and dirty browns of the courtyard. I fled through a door into the lobby of the old building, then into the Quai de la Mégisserie. Surprised and delighted by the strength in my limbs, I raced along the Seine toward the palatial walls and heavenly roof of the Louvre. I thought of all the blissful hours I had spent in its cool halls, and these reminders of eternal excellence and beauty almost neutralized the freezing fear I had of Veg's evil electrodes stabbing at my innocent brain.

V

It was six in the morning when I stumbled into my room. There was no room service available. No mail had arrived. They were out of morning papers. I couldn't sleep. Occasionally I studied my violated head in the mirror. The area shaved could not have been more than two inches in diameter. The plaster patch—it was some kind of gummy material, like the stuff dentists use to make molds—was pure white and shiny, and rose about a half inch above my pate. Oh, that Veg! Within that tiny mound he had secreted a whole damned radio receiver, to transmit wicked signals to the needles plunging into my caudate nucleus!

I shivered. What would he be able to do to me? And who, who in the world except Veg could remove the damned thing? About the only encouraging part of the horrid affair was that I felt no pain, not even a dull ache or an occasional twinge. Now and then I would poke at the plaster, or try to lift it, expecting it to fly from my head with bits of brain and bone. It was firmly anchored, no question, but there was no pain.

At about 7:30 A.M. I called the Israeli Embassy and asked for Moses Bloom. A sleepy duty officer said they had no record of anyone by that name. For a moment I wondered whether I should ask for Colonel Shlomo Tal, Bloom's boss, but then I thought better of it. I did not have Bloom's phone number at 34 Avenue Charles Floquet, and the operator had no listing either. So all I could do was wait. But for what? Who was I? Who was I working for? Then it dawned on me that I no longer controlled the game I'd started. From activist, provocateur, double agent, man in black, I'd suddenly been revealed as a victim, a patsy, a miserable lab animal, no better than one of Veg's rats.

Worse, my mission, or missions, were hopelessly botched. I'd performed a small miracle getting Malar and his daughter to the American Embassy—only to discover that they (at least Tom Bragg) didn't want him, and that he really didn't want to defect. That pitiful man! Cored, decorticated, reamed, implanted by his dear friend Veg! Malar was still the adaptable man, the free-style Hungarian intellectual, but he was something more, and something less.

And Veg. Bloom needed him urgently in Israel. I'd never been any hot-shot Zionist, but as a marginal coward, I had nurtured a sense of affection and admiration for those hard-bitten Jews on the littoral. Anything to help them survive. "A *matter of survival*," Bloom said to Veg in his letter in Yiddish. And was it un-American of me to want them, rather than my own country, to have Veg's technique? The Americans, with their billion-dollar labs and huge budgets and platoons of scientists would learn Veg's secrets sooner or later. Why not let the Israelis get first crack at it?

I thought of Venables. A nice game he'd played, with his mincing and his crucifix and his hoo-hoo conferences. Now I understood his kindness toward me, sucking up, putting me on one of his hoo-hoo workshops where I could talk about journalism as history to Nigerians. As spy or literary operator, they worked the same way: you do something for me, I'll do something for you. I had told him nothing, but he—and Latour—had found out anyway. And worse, they'd used me as their damned subject. By what seemed a rising vote in espionage circles, I'd been elected. They had even claimed that Bloom was in on it!

As for my performance, I was a little disgusted with myself.

My hatred of Flackman, Cooperage, and their world should have been potent enough to have resisted Veg's electrical jolts. Oh, I'd battled him, right down the line—the way Imre Malar had when he'd made his address—but when the crisis came, I'd folded, and I'd said those slobbering, ass-kissing things. I only hoped they hadn't tape-recorded me for posterity.

At 8:00 A.M. I went down to the Bavard's lobby and ordered a café filtre to burn away the fungoid fuzz covering my mouth and throat. I sat despondently in a corner of the empty, dreary room, so that no one could see the shameful patch on my skull. The *Trib* had finally arrived, and the coffee roiled my bowels as I started to read Flackman's by-lined report on the conference.

> The delegates, Flackman sensed immediately, fell into two categories. There were makers and fakers. Flackman naturally gravitated toward the makers, the important and creative people like his old friend and fellow combatant, Warren Cooperage and his charming wife, and gentle and sagacious adversaries like Boyle Huffguard. With these, Flackman felt at ease, understood, appreciated.

> On the other hand, there were the fakers and frauds—the boors, freaks, and climbers, minor talents sucking after their betters.

This was meant for me, of course, but Arno was too shrewd to mention me by name. As King Space-Grabber, the Prince of Puffery, the Original Advertised Man, he knew better than to waste newsprint on worms. There were a few more comments about the lowly hacks with whom he was forced to associate at the conference, and then he disposed of the CIA matter, in this ingenious fashion:

> Flackman was not surprised to learn that the Central Intelligence Agency had helped finance the conference. Why not? They financed everything else. Nor did the revelation that the CIA

had helped pay a few bills at *The Discoverist Review* disturb him. Many members of the magazine's staff were close friends of Flackman, sharp-witted, acute commentators, and they would take the money and run from the bungling gumshoes who gave it to them. Flackman was less concerned over these matters than the Stalinoid children, miserable, failed wretches who contaminated the streets around the conference hall, and tried to bait him. Small excrescences, spoiled embryos, they impressed him as gropers and masturbators, filthy little nits, afraid of a decent shouting orgasm.

Translation: I've got to stick up for the conference because a lot of my friends, some influential critics and editors, are involved. So I'll kiss off the whole CIA business.

There was this on Malar:

As the most politically astute person at the conference, Flackman understood at once that the KGB's medicine men had worked some rough magic on Malar. From a purely literary standpoint, Flackman had never had much use for Malar's constipated and derivative style, but he had found the creaky Marxist an engaging boozing companion at previous conferences. But all judgments on Malar apart, Flackman was horrified to observe the manner in which the Russians, somehow, had controlled him. This outrage against Malar's person—to be honest about it— was equaled, Flackman understood shrewdly, by the outrage committed against the leading figures of the conference. The people on the stage honoring Malar, Anzaletti, Keen, Cooperage, Shockheim, Metrick, Venables, and not least of all, Flackman himself, were the cream of the international literary world. The insult to Malar's mind was no less dreadful than the affront to his hosts; Flackman was furious. He was not accustomed to serving as a stage-setting for a grand fraud.

Translation: I am angry at the Russians for what they did to Malar, but I am even angrier because they stole the show from me.

Ten minutes later the concierge awakened me with an airmail special delivery letter. It was from my son Eddie. He'd lost to Myron Hesseldine again in a ladder match at Salisbury Park. Eddie had had the tall blond kid 5–3, but Mrs. Hesseldine, his tall, blonde mother, kept shouting "Hit to his backhand, son" and Eddie lost, 10–8, 6–4. "If you come to the next match when I play him, Dad, I think I can beat him," the kid wrote.

Yes, the Hesseldines of the world had to be beaten. All those tall, lean winners, the father a CBS executive, the kid raised on tennis lessons. Eddie, my Eddie! I suddenly hated myself for running out on them, for deserting Felicia, to make my big play for fame at the World Conference on the Arts and Sciences. And what did I have to show for it? A reputation as a CIA bungler—or a Shin-Bet man, or a Bupo spy, or something else—and the eternal ill-will of the Cooperages and Flackmans and Metricks, the makers and breakers. Bad reviews and closed doors for the next twenty years!

"*Bonjour, M'sieu*," M. Rignac said politely.

"*Ah. M. Rignac. Mon historien. Bonjour.*"

"May I join you for coffee?"

"Please."

I'd liked the little fellow ever since we'd chatted about the Order of the Lily. (I didn't let on that it was a wrong turning: the *fleur-de-lis* Malar saw was Chip Latour's BSA emblem.) And I also had admired the way Rignac had hopped on the communists during Malar's speech.

"You are up early," he said. Rignac seemed a bit wary. He looked around us twice and waited until the waiter had left.

"I didn't go to sleep."

"Of course. In your line of work . . ."

"Work?"

"M'sieu, I have read the brochure put out by the Maoist students. Whether it is true or not, I will not say. But I do congratulate you on your modus operandi. I have my sources.

I am told your handling of Malar and his daughter was a masterpiece of planning and timing."

"Standard operation, Maurice."

His eyes rose over the pince-nez and he fussed with some obscure lapel decoration. "I am not so sure. It was more than standard. It was brilliant, and it is too bad that the obstinacy of your countrymen prevented you from fulfilling the mission."

He was fishing. "You're a historian, Maurice. Why are you so interested in my line of work?"

Rignac leaned back and sipped his café filtre. "I am a naturalized citizen of France," he said enigmatically. "I was born in Lausanne, and still lecture at the university there. Does that suggest anything to you?"

"No. Except maybe why I liked you the first time we spoke. I find the Swiss eminently civilized."

"You are *très gentil.* My wife is a Swiss citizen, as are my sons and my grandchildren. Only I changed my allegiance. Are you somewhat more aware of what I am trying to say?"

"Not really."

"When a gentleman at the American Embassy interrogated you yesterday he accused you of working for an organization called Bupo, short for the *Bundespolizei,* the Swiss counter-espionage organization. Is that correct?"

"How . . . how did you know?"

"No matter. Somehow his intelligence was faulty. There is a Bupo agent in Paris attending the conference. Can you guess who it is?"

"Maurice Rignac, historian."

"*Mais certainement.* In some obscure way, the reports filed to that gentleman, a Mr. Bragg who sells toilets and bidets, were garbled. So you were accused because of me."

I rubbed my eyes. The patch was itching slightly but I didn't want him to see it, so I arched my neck and kept the back of my head high and stiff. "Now . . . now why do you tell me this? Why do you surrender your cover so easily?"

Rignac coughed politely and looked around before respond-ing. "Because, M'sieu, I am authorized by my superiors in Geneva——"

"Stoefli," I said glibly—recalling the name used by Bragg.

Rignac's eyes goggled. "Ah, my instincts were correct. You are a brilliant operative, an original. Yes, I am authorized by my superiors at the *Bundespolizei* to offer you immediate em-ployment in our international branch. I have reported to them that I have never witnessed a more daring, ingenious, and confusing cover than the one you have here employed—that of a jealous writer. Every one of your moves has been a master stroke. I congratulate you again, sir, and ask you to think about us. We would be willing to double you and let you continue working for your employer, whose identity, I confess, is still unknown to us, or start anew as a man in black for Bupo International."

All the vapors I'd experienced after reading Eddie's letter vanished. I was top again. "Maurice, I have never been paid a higher compliment. And rest assured everything you have told me will be kept in utter confidence."

"I fear you are going to reject my offer."

"Afraid so, Maurice. You see, this has been too much of a strain on my nervous system. I like the work, and I think I delivered a dollar's worth of work for every dollar paid me. But after the conference ends, I'm giving it up."

"Yes, yes, I understand. But remember, *cher ami*, the offer stands. There is a man named Rudi Zimmerman, a waiter at the Pavillion de Genève restaurant in New York. Should you change your mind, please call on him and say that Maurice sent you."

We shook hands—two old pros, two old cons—and I was heartened and sustained by Rignac's high estimate of me. I turned to go to the lift and he saw the white patch on my head.

"*Sacrebleu,*" he gasped. "*Vous aussi. Comme Malar. Ils sont monstres.*"

"Monsters can be defeated," I said casually. "They are, after all, only myths." I had no idea what this meant, but Rignac was nodding his approval as I entered the lift. "Thank your superiors in Geneva, *mon ami*," I called to him.

Resting on my bed of pain, I decided to leave the conference as soon as I could get on a flight. I'd not wait for tomorrow's closing session. No, I'd creep back to Hicksville, still the man of mystery, and help Eddie climb the tennis ladder. Then I thought of the electrodes probing my brain, the cursed filaments under the plaster. How? What? Who would take them out? Would Veg be able to control me forever? Would he put his cigarette lighter on a transoceanic frequency, bounce signals off satellites, and have me in his power forever? And why had he let me escape? Was it possible he suspected I knew something about the cryptic "Kitti," whose name had roused him?

There was a knock on my door; I feared no one any longer. "Come in," I said drowsily.

It was Judy Malar, smiling, a shaft of morning light giving her red curls an edge of gold.

"You okay?" I asked. "They are still letting you out?"

"Everyone is okay."

She sat on my penitentiary chair and crossed her legs. Beauty is the most potent of weapons. It endows the bearer with natural dignity, grace under pressure.

"But . . . Pochastny . . . isn't he angry?"

"Papa has made his peace with them. They are accepting his version—ours. You forced us to go to the American Embassy. You are on the KGB's list of enemies, but I don't think they will bother with you."

"I'm not afraid of them," I said—truthfully. The old Ben Bloodworth would have had a case of the runs; the new BB shrugged and ignored them. My cool was the cool of a man who had nothing to lose. "I only hope you and Papa don't live to regret the opportunity you missed. You could have made a

373

run for it, when the Blooms had you in their place."

"No, no, no," she said—not too convincingly. "Papa will live out his life in Budapest."

"Writing just what they let him write. Making speeches that they want him to make. Yes, he'll have his freedom. The kind of freedom the cat gives the mouse."

"Do not make me feel worse than I do now, Ben," she said. Her lip trembled. "You are thinking of that awful speech. They forced him to do it. They frightened him. But how? What terrible thing did they do to him?"

I wondered whether I should tell her. Then I thought of that cynical cruel bastard Veg, and the way he controlled the brains of animals and humans. I turned my head and showed her the patch.

"Oh . . . oh, Ben . . ."

"See that, Judy? Your Uncle Latzi, your papa's buddy, Laszlo Veg."

"What . . . what does it mean?" She got up and touched my shaved pate tenderly. "Oh, poor Benny. Does it hurt? Why . . . why . . . the same bandage as Papa has?"

I pulled her down and sat her alongside me; the cot creaked its Gallic protest. "Laszlo Veg is a fiend, Judy, a genius, but a fiend. He has invented a way of controlling human behavior by digging tiny wire electrodes into the brain. He controls them with his cigarette lighter which is a radio transmitter. The brain gets these electrical signals and is no longer its own master. Veg can make people hostile, aggressive, combative, sleepy, happy, cheerful, friendly, stop sexual urges, arouse them, and goodness knows what else. In your father's case, he implanted him with these wicked wires so as to render him amiable, friendly, kindly disposed to everyone, especially the tyrants who tried to kill him and who have infringed on his freedom of intellect. He did it to your papa as a favor to the Russians, to make sure that the voice of Imre Malar would be a whining, weak, conciliatory voice, not the clarion sound of freedom. Your papa fought valiantly against the radio waves, but they were too much for him."

374

"Oh, dear God, dear God," she cried. "They have destroyed him. And you, you, Ben? Why to you?"

I laughed grimly: Jake Barnes telling Brett about his condition as *castrato*. "Veg did it to me last night. A demonstration of his techniques to two potential buyers. He wants something from them—money, safety, sanctuary, but something else—and he came to Paris to sell it. I think part of the deal with the Russians was to implant your father while he was in Veg's hospital in Budapest, and thus control him here. Bloom ruined that little act for them, and now they aren't sure what to do with Veg. He's kept a lot of his stuff—his laboratory, his methods—from them."

She began to weep. "Those awful needles! Stuck into Papa's head! Ben, Latzi is a Nazi, a wicked, insane man, to do that to an old friend, his best friend! How will Papa recover?"

I put a strong arm around her shivering shoulders—how frail she was! "Steady, kid. He can't be controlled unless Veg is around with his Zippo. And Veg has probably left the country by now, or is being hidden somewhere before he's escorted onto a jet. Besides, he told me that they won't cause any pain or infection, and I have an idea a good brain surgeon could probably take them out. You see, they're right under this little mound, through a hole in the skull . . ."

She wailed. I'd been prattling on too long, stupidly proud of my plaster patch, wallowing in my stoic acceptance of fate. "Papa! Papa! How can we help him?"

"I'll think of something," I lied.

She leaned against me. I stroked her back—the back of a thin twelve-year-old, supple, lean, fileted. Smooth, young, edible. I could have had her, I was certain. Unlike matronly Evie Bragg, poured into her bronze carapace, Judy was almost nude—a pair of dime-store panties and a wisp of a bra, I imagined, under a minidress. Off I went on one of my fetishistic flights. Veg, you bastard, try to control me now. I kissed her quivering bud of a mouth, her wet eyes, her tiny Magyar nose. My tongue vibrated over her face. She responded; she hugged me; she whispered my name.

Why not? Why not, indeed? I'd adopted her and chaperoned her since coming to Paris; I had almost gotten her to the States. Something ere the end, some work of noble note may yet be done . . .

Why prolong it? As I caressed her smooth young limbs and fiddled, hot-handed, arthritic, with the snap on her bra, there was a sharp rapping at the door.

"Get lost!" I shouted. "*Allez vous en!*"

The intruder rapped again, then began to kick.

"Story of my life, Judy," I said. "Let me get rid of this pest and we'll resume." I straightened my clothes. She retreated to a prim position on the chair.

I opened the door. It was Ayal, the skate-board champ of the Palais who had helped me yesterday. He had shifty eyes, and he wore his yarmulka pushed forward on his forehead in a cocky manner.

"*Shalom,*" he said rudely. "Meestah Bloom vants you."

"Tell Mr. Bloom to run his own errands."

He refused to budge; a stocky, pale squirt. "You godda come. He's donstezz."

"I'm not going."

"Und I dunt live ontil you come."

The accent was out of a Bronx chicken market, but the arms and legs were muscled and hairy. I looked at his pale hard face, and I understood those border *kibbutzim* under Syrian guns that refused to move.

"What are you waiting for?" I said. "Now beat it. I'm through with Bloom after what he did to me. Tell him I'll see him back in New York."

Ayal's eyebrows arched; he shoved the yarmulka back on his head. "He vants you should help him find de professeh."

"Veg?"

"I dunt know."

Damn Moses Bloom! He knew I wouldn't refuse. Not with a chance to get hunk with that scheming neurologist who'd raped my brain. I'd pursue Laszlo Veg to the ends of the earth, even if it meant giving up a morning's dalliance with Judy Malar.

"Judy," I said, "I'd better go. Where can I find you later?"

"At the Palais. Papa will be in the chair, but he will not make any speech."

I kissed her and followed Ayal out.

One of those odd boxlike Citroën vans was double-parked in front of the hotel. At the wheel was Bloom, wearing a peaked navy-blue cap and a navy-blue field jacket. The words *Air France* were embroidered over the breast pocket. "Get in," he said hoarsely, after giving Ayal some Hebrew marching orders.

We headed toward the Etoile. Bloom looked drained, disgusted. That air of confidence he usually exuded, a kind of sunburned, squinting, desert assurance that someday the Negev would flourish, was gone.

"Some friend," I said. "Some friend you are. Turning me over to those bastards."

"Who told you that?"

"All of them. Veg. Venables. That Boy Scout. You were in on it."

"Not exactly. Don't be sore at the old man."

I glared at him. "Anything for *Eretz*, hey, Moe? Including giving up your buddy, the one young writer who remembered you with affection, to a crazy Hungarian who stuck needles in his brain and can control him now with a Zippo lighter."

"Nah. Nah. It wasn't that way. Bragg got hold of me when I tried to grab Veg. I almost had that Bohunk convinced, when Bragg and his wife came along—they had help—and pulled me off. We sat in their hotel room over on the Avenue de la Bourdonnais, and we made a deal. We *hondled*. You can always *hondle* with a fellow American, which is why I told Bragg I wouldn't get him fired."

"From the DIA?"

"No. Academy Fixtures. His boss is a big UJA contributor."

"And part of this deal was to surrender me to Veg?"

"More or less. Latour had decided you were perfect for the experiment. He got Veg and Venables to agree. Not only do you hate almost everybody here, but nobody will go to bat for you, the way you've been tabbed as four different kinds of spy, and all the lies you've told."

"I get it. The only one they were worried about was you, or the Shin-Bet. So they got your approval."

"Ah, it was a hard thing for me to do," Bloom said, as he turned the clumsy truck onto the Avenue de Friedland. "All I said was I wouldn't make a fuss if they took you. I made them pay for it."

"I'm glad. I'm really glad you got something for me. A nice price, I hope."

"A concession. If Latour and Venables turn Veg down, if they won't meet his price, I get a crack at him."

"And what about my head? My brain? Jesus, you're inhuman."

"Oh, that. Your brain. Well, yeh." He stared at my shaved and patched pate. "*Gevald*. They let you have it. Well, I have some doctor friends in town. We'll see them after we finish work."

"Naturally. The electronic destruction of Bloodworth can wait. As long as Israel marches on."

Bloom scowled at me. "That's the general idea. You'd rather be at the Suez Canal, boychick? Waiting for the SAM missiles? Or in a bunker on the Golani?"

"But who elected me such a hot Zionist? Moe, I'm no hero."

"Start here," Bloom said. He shoved an airline schedule at me. "I didn't have a chance to check the flights. It's Pakistani International Airways. Look up tonight's schedule. See what they have going to Peking."

I thumbed through the leaflet. "PIA 214, originating in London," I said. "Stops in Paris, Warsaw, Moscow, Teheran, Lahore, and Peking. Leaves Paris at 8:05 P.M. There isn't another one until late Saturday."

"They'll get him on tonight's."

"Veg sold it to the Chinese. Then Venables . . ."

"That's it. On orders from the Social Affairs Department, Bow String Alley."

"And I thought I'd gotten Veg off balance with that business of the ad in the *Trib*."

He frowned at me. "What ad?"

I reminded him about the message to Latzi from Kitti.

"Yeh, that should have helped," he said wearily. "I think maybe he's gone nuts, bananas. No good to anyone—I hope."

"But who is Kitti?"

Bloom yawned. "Kitti Balint. Hungarian beauty. Professional actress and amateur whore. Left the country in 1956 and Veg hasn't been the same since. She's supposed to be the greatest piece since Madame Pompadour. Forty, looks twenty-five. Screwed her way into the communist *apparatchik*, then screwed her way to the United States. If you saw Veg's wife—she weighs two hundred and has three hairs growing out of her nose—you'd know why he wants Kitti so badly."

"But . . . Latour matched Venables' offer. If he wanted her, why didn't he take the CIA up?"

Moe shrugged. "I don't know. I don't know much any more." We stopped, Bloom cursing at a cabbie as we tried to make a left turn into the Rue Mogador. "Kid, reach in back of you. There's another jacket and cap like this—Air France Express. Put 'em on."

I did so. "What now?"

"Last chance on Veg. And don't make a fuss if you see Latour or Bragg. They haven't quit either."

"But . . . but . . . why to Peking, the jerk?"

"Maybe the Russians decided to make him go there. He could get his quarter of a million and then meet Kitti in Switzerland, or Sweden. Maybe the Russians figure the Chinese won't be able to do a thing with his electrodes."

Bloom slammed the van into the loading area in the rear of the big department store, the Galeries Lafayette.

"What's up?" I asked. "I don't need any tourist-discounted perfume."

"*Foire de Chine*," he said. "Chinese trade fair. Come on, pick up the clipboard and act as if we're waiting to be loaded."

Several trucks were backed up to the platform. Crates moved from the rear of the department store, manhandled, or on small dollies.

"Veg had to promise to ship his baboons and his rats and any other animals he had here, to seal the deal with Venables," Moe whispered. "What they didn't figure on was that it isn't that easy to ship live animals out of France. They won't fit in a diplomatic pouch. All kinds of medical tests, papers, forms. Some of our people work here at the Galeries. We had a call."

"The baboons might go out in some of the Chinese merchandise?"

"Yeh. They're big on lacquered chests, coffers."

A battered black van was backing into the platform. Moe dug me in the ribs. "They're here. Come on." Two surly galoots sat in the front seat.

We walked into the rear of the store, up a flight of stairs. The second floor looked like downtown Hong Kong. The floor was full of those curly-mouthed, toothy, pop-eyed lions and dogs, huge vases, furniture with bronze handles and bright decorations. It was apparently the last day of the *Foire de Chine*. Much of the merchandise was being crated, tagged, hustled out to the rear for shipment.

Bloom's eyes scanned the floor. "They're supposed to go out in a real antique. It was just on loan."

Migraine nibbled at my skull. I wondered what Veg's evil wires would do to my propensity for headaches. As I rubbed my left temple and eye, Bloom looked at me quizzically. "Headache?"

"One of the worst."

"Start sniffing." I'd told Moe about the way migraine

heightened my senses of smell and hearing. "Smell any baboons?"

"No. Just French sweat, wine, and garlic."

Three Chinese in blue smocks were pushing a dolly. On it was an enormous antique chest, over six feet in height, perhaps a yard deep. It was half-crated—held firmly in place by a cage of two-by-fours. We followed it; the Chinese wheeled it into an elevator. Bloom and I raced downstairs and got to the loading area first.

The doors of the black van were open. One of the *barbouzes* was waiting at the rear. He seemed impatient, anxious.

"If they're in that," I asked Bloom, "how come they're so quiet?"

"Tranquilizers."

The dolly bearing the enormous chest—a chiffonier? a chifferobe?—lumbered onto the platform. Bloom walked between it, and the rear of the opened van. He waved a sheaf of fake papers. "*Attention, messieurs! Le coffre est le mein! Je suis avec Air France! A mon camion, s'il vous plaît, là-bas.*"

The Chinese ignored him, and the thug shoved Moe rudely away, into my arms. "*Va-t'en, sale con,*" he advised Bloom. He slammed and bolted the door of the truck. As he raced to the front seat—the motor was running—Moe recovered, dragged me with him, and we flew to our own van. Too late, we started the engine and swung out, trying to intercept the huge black truck. With a clang and a crunch, the truck bearing Veg's apes sheared off our right fender, and with gears grinding and rubber scorching, it roared onto the Rue Mogador.

We weren't hurt, but the fender of our van had been crushed against the front right wheel. We couldn't move.

"Taxi," Moe shouted at me. "Come on, run."

I raced after the old man toward the corner of Boulevard Haussmann. "Moe, Moe," I gasped. "They must have disinfected the apes, I didn't smell anything."

Like two thieves, we kept running. "Yeah, yeah?"

"But I smelled something else. I know I did. Those stinky Hungarian butts Veg smokes."

We leaped into a waiting cab. "He's in there, boychick."

We roared over the Pont d'Iena, made a two-wheeled turn in front of the Eiffel Tower, sending plastics millionaires and expense account warriors scurrying for cover, and then spun crazily under the elevated tracks on the Boulevard de Grenelle. Moe had shoved a one-hundred-franc note at the driver and informed him that we were in a *"circonstance critique."* The route was pure guesswork on Bloom's part.

I knew the Boulevard de Grenelle well. The side streets leading off it and into the fifteenth arrondissement house some of the best food shops in Paris, and some of the most reasonable. Felicia and I used to shop there years ago, and I had warm memories of ripe *Reblochons*, fat *poulets de Bresse*, crusty *pain campagne*.

"We lost him," Bloom said. "The whole shebang. Truck, Veg, baboons."

At the corner of Rue de Lourmel, a street I remembered well, because it contained a *crémerie* that sold the whitest, tangiest *chèvre* in the world, a gendarme halted us. Up ahead, I could see that traffic was jamming up, cars turning off, making illegal U-turns under the elevated tracks.

"On ne peut pas continuer?" Bloom asked the cop.

"Non. Accident de voiture. Tournez."

"Un grand camion noir?"

"Oui, mais allez, allez."

Bloom flew out of the cab, and, in that impatient, bow-legged half-run, took off. I dogtrotted alongside him.

"Bragg," he puffed. "Got there first. May be good for us."

The *Nation-Etoile* express rumbled over us, shaking and shivering my ravaged head, my violated skull. The awful noise seemed to pour right into the burr hole, coursing through the electrodes and into my caudate nucleus.

The accident had occurred at the point where Avenue de la

Motte-Picquet crosses the Boulevard de Grenelle and becomes Rue du Commerce. Traditionally, there was an open-air market under the El tracks on Thursdays, and part of it was a small, gaudy children's fair—a ferris wheel, a whip, a carrousel.

The black van had rammed into the carrousel, lifting it on its side, mangling a pink horse and an orange bear. A respectful, interested crowd of French had gathered in front of the corner kiosk and the café, where I used to sit sipping a café-au-lait after shopping.

A dozen cops had gathered around the van, which was resting on its side, two embarrassed, gently spinning wheels uselessly suspended in midair. There was a good deal of yelling from the *flics*. I saw our friend Dunand, in his blue raincoat and dyspeptic face, talking to a high-ranking uniformed man, and then I saw Tom Bragg approach them, nod a few times, and go to the rear of the van with a crowbar.

"I was right," Bloom said.

"How come Bragg has so much clout?" I asked. "Why are the French letting him . . . ?"

Bragg, my captor, the man I wanted to cuckold, Academy Fixtures' hot-shot salesman, was prying at the door with the heavy bar.

"Cashed in a few IOU's. The French hate everybody equally, so they do a few favors for the Russians, the Chinese, the Americans. Oh, they got something in exchange all right."

"But . . ."

"It's like getting a good review for a new book. What have you done for me lately?"

With a ripping, snapping noise, the rear of the van opened. We heard a high-pitched chattering, and from the dark interior of the van, Erno leaped forward, flashing his wicked teeth, baring his bloody gums. Bragg moved away, but the big clod was smiling. He had Veg's apes. Gabor and Kitti appeared at the opened doors. They looked frightened, hesitant.

"*Oh, c'est un cirque!*" the French cried.

"Gardez le grand singe!"
"Oh là là, quel singe!"

Erno studied the audience of police and pedestrians with baboonish contempt. His spunky tail arched high over his swollen red behind, and he paraded about on his knuckles, cursing everyone in sight.

A half dozen of the gendarmes were unrolling a large net, walking stealthily toward Veg's king ape. Erno looked at them with grand superiority, then bounced away and clambered up the small ferris wheel. At the summit, he settled into the top gondola and began to rock back and forth. The children applauded; the crowd laughed.

Dunand ran to the concessionaire and told him to start the wheel moving. The man obliged, but Erno was way ahead of them. As the wheel began to move, he nimbly climbed out of the gondola, clung to the frame of the wheel, and settled into the next one, and so on, chattering and screaming, spitting out his Chacma contempt for his anthropoidal relatives.

"There he is," Bloom said.

Into the late afternoon light emerged the starved figure of Veg. He was holding hands with the docile Kitti and the craven Gabor, walking stiffly, like a man forced to sit in a cramped position too long, a baboon clinging to each side of him. Tom Bragg walked up to him and they began to chat easily.

"Latzi!" shouted Moe Bloom. "You'll be sorry! You can have your own laboratory in Rehovoth! The people need you!"

Veg wasn't buying. He made a sorrowful gesture with his shoulders, and for the first time since I'd seen the sneaky neurologist, there seemed to be an air of contrition, of humanity about him.

A gray panel truck had now pulled up to the curb, and two men in white coats and peaked hats walked out. They carried portable cages and those long poles with loops on the end for entrapping animals. But they weren't needed for Gabor and

Kitti. Veg coaxed the two drugged, frightened apes toward the cages, and they were promptly secured. Then Tom Bragg ushered the Hungarian into a black Peugeot with CD plates —the one they'd tried to kidnap me in—and got in with Veg. Apparently feeling he owed us something, he stuck his head out the window and called.

"Sorry about everything, Moe," he said good-humoredly. He almost sounded sincere. "And Benny. No hard feelings about last night. You still have plenty smarts."

"Okay, Bragg," Moe said. Professional-to-professional. "Better you than *them*, but better us than *you*. Look out for that Hungarian. Read the fine print in the contract."

Veg did not show his face. He had pushed himself against the corner of the Peugeot. Was the monster unhappy? Was he sorry for what he had done to Malar, to me?

"My best to General Amit and the rest of those guys at Allenby Street," Bragg said jovially. "Talk about smarts, they've got it."

The Peugeot blasted away. I looked helplessly at it. There went Veg—Bloom's prize, my enemy. "I hope he shoves those wires up Bragg's nostrils and short-circuits his brain. They deserve each other. What the hell is the Pentagon going to do with that stuff? Implant Senator Proxmire?"

"Right to Orly," Moe said huskily. "He'll be in Washington tonight. Ah, sometimes the world is a pile of *dreck*."

Gabor and Kitti were caged and in the gray truck—it belonged to the Jardin Zoologique according to a sign on the door. The two men in white coats stood in front of the wrecked ferris wheel and studied Erno, still scrambling around the upper reaches of the ride.

"Come on," Bloom said. "We'll do something about those needles in your head."

We crossed the Boulevard de Grenelle, both of us darting a farewell look at the baboon Erno, shrieking fearfully as the two zoo attendants began to climb toward him.

The driver of the small zoo van had come out and was

385

watching the attendants. He was a thin dark fellow in dark glasses and a dark short beard that covered his cheeks and chin.

"That guy," I said to Bloom. "The skinny guy with the beard . . ."

"Don't look at him. You never saw him before."

I had, of course. And so had Bloom. It was Colonel Shlomo Tal.

At the American Hospital in Neuilly, I shivered in the waiting room while Moe sought out a certain Dr. Halevy. He refused to talk to anyone else, and after a fifteen-minute wait, during which I tried to stifle the tremors in my gut, I was ushered into a small examining room.

"Will it hurt?" I asked Dr. Halevy. He was a thickset, ruddy man with an unidentifiable accent, surely not French.

"I don't know till I look," he said.

He sat me in an examining chair and began to touch the patch on my head. Nausea, panic, a sense of doom permeated my enervated bones. I was finished, washed up. Courier, spy, tough-guy, man in black. And finally a guinea pig, with wire filaments stuck into my brain.

"Any pain?" he asked.

"Not yet." I bit the bullet. I'd show them.

"It's some kind of synthetic gel," he said matter-of-factly. "Like what the dentists use. You say there should be a burr hole under it?"

Bloom nodded. "Yeah. I've never seen one, but I read the literature. Maybe an eighth to a quarter of an inch in diameter. There's a metal plate on top, and then a thin rod with the electrodes."

Damn Bloom. He was devoid of pity, rattling off my condition as indifferently as if I were one of Veg's rats. An odor of medical alcohol flooded my nostrils. Dr. Halevy was swabbing the bald area on my head.

"But the plaster isn't attached to the metal plate?" the physician asked.

386

"As far as I know, no. It's just a protective cover." Bloom was standing next to the doctor, the two of them staring at my head.

"All right, let's peel it back," the physician said.

I felt nothing; nothing at all.

"What do you see?" Moe asked.

"*Garnicht*," the doctor said. "Nothing. *Rien*."

"Look again," Bloom said.

"Look yourself, Mr. Bloom. Look, look. There's nothing under it. A plaster patch, all right. But no hole. No metal plate. No electrodes. Mr. Bloom, what are you doing, playing games with me? I'm a busy man here, and while I have obligations to you and your people for old favors, I can't waste time on this kind of nonsense."

"It has to be there," Moe insisted.

"Listen, I know about brain implantation, just a little. And this man's head is intact. They gave him a little shave and patched it, but there was no boring into his skull." His artful fingers kept parting the hair on my pate, like Erno grooming Kitti for bits of dried skin and cooties.

"It must be there," I said plaintively. "They wired me for controlled behavior. I was Veg's slave. I did what he wanted . . ."

"*Shah, shah*," Bloom said. He was pacing the room, his brawny arms folded on his chest, his creased features gathered in a knot around his taut mouth.

"May I go?" Dr. Halevy asked. "May I please return to my patients? This is ridiculous. Pay on the way out. They'll want cash."

"No!" I cried. "Look again! They did it——"

Dr. Halevy's white coat vanished. A nurse chased us out.

"Hypnosis," Moe said, as we sipped hot tea in the apartment on Avenue Charles Floquet. "But that was only part of it. Are you suggestible?"

"Hell, yes. At the men's club at the temple one night this hypnotist had me flapping my arms like a chicken in three minutes. An hour later when he was working on Arnie Rain-berger, up on the stage, I fell asleep all over—without a direct cue from the hypnotist."

"That was it," Bloom said. "They kept talking about radio-controlled behavior in front of you. The baboons, the grey-hound. Veg hypnotized you while you were under sedation. When he finally got around to you, with the lighter, all you had to do was hear it clicking and you responded. Without anything in your brain."

"But why?" I asked.

"Who knows? He might have been unwilling to take a chance on actually implanting you. Venables or Latour might have double-crossed him—run off with you, stolen a look at the electrodes, watched him when he was supposed to be operating on you. Veg is a goddamn genius, I told you. He figured you were an easy mark, that he could get you to obey the signals without an implantation."

"And he was right, the dirty fascist. God, Moe, what a disgrace. The things he got me to say. I still can't believe it. He had me sitting there babbling compliments, saying nice things about all the people I detest—Cooperage, Keen, Flack-man, Metrick. He made me do the worst thing I've ever had to do in my life—talk like a critic. I was spouting seminals, germinals, and jejunes all over the place."

"I admit it, that's pretty good for autosuggestion."

"What a come-down. Thank God it was secret. I end up an Establishment suck. Moe, that bastard Veg had me mut-tering about 'existential equations' and prose that was 'sinewy and sinuous.' "

Bloom smiled crookedly. "When you were a kid, did you ever walk pigeon-toed so people would think you were an athlete?"

"How'd you guess?"

"It figures. A perfect syndrome. You're a frustrated actor, Benny. No wonder Veg wanted you for the experiment. The *momser* owes me one for letting you go."

"You're a cold-blooded old man, Moe."

Bloom made a do-me-something gesture. "Also, Veg figured after you watched Malar perform, you'd imitate him. I had the boys at the Weizmann Institute send me some stuff. Everything he did was in accordance with the literature, with previous experiments. Those head movements, the yawning, the crazy little walks he kept taking, the uncertainty. You saw Malar reacting, and you figured if Veg could do this to a tough bird like Malar, it could be done to——"

"A *shlemiel* like me?"

"No, no. It's only that you haven't been in Gestapo prisons or had your nails pulled out by KGB police."

I drank my tea and got up, walked out to the balcony to clear my bursting head with a view of eternal, magnificent Paris, and came back in. "There are a lot of screwy things about this, Moe," I said. "First, Veg took a chance not implanting me. I understand that he was afraid Latour might grab me. But they needed Veg also. I gather he carries a lot of his technique in his head. But why did Veg let me run away?"

They had to let you go sooner or later. Maybe he was afraid Latour was going to examine your head. You said he was still insisting on it."

"But there was nothing in my head."

"That's right. Veg is a slippery bastard. He covered himself both ways."

"But then he decides to go with the Chinese. Why?"

Bloom laughed. "Ah, but he didn't end up with them. Maybe he changed his mind."

I fell onto the green velvet couch. "And what's the application of this damned ESB?" I asked. "Is it worth all the effort? What's the CIA going to do when it gets it perfected? Sneak into the Kremlin and shove electrodes into Kosygin's skull? Or Brezhnev's? Or Mao's?"

"Don't knock it, boychick. Look what they did to Malar."

The phone rang. Bloom conversed in Hebrew a few minutes.

"Tal?" I asked.

He didn't answer me directly. "Veg's gone. They ran that car into the mouth of one of those open-end Bristol transports at Le Bourget. They're going to land at a military airfield in England and then bring him to Washington on an Air Force jet. He'll be there tonight."

"A quarter of a million dollars richer, and with his actress whore waiting for him."

"Yeh, yeh. Well, it could have been worse."

"For him?"

"For us."

Bloom had not given up. And therefore neither had I. The relief that came with the knowledge that I had not been implanted and forced to obey Veg's will, but had rather been the victim of intense hypnosis and suggestion, buoyed me and filled me with a renewed sense of destiny. I was back in the swim, ready to run errands for Bloom, lie, fake, and adorn my image as spy, double agent, courier.

For the last time, I pinned on my delegate's ID card, and Bloom and I walked toward the Palais de Chaillot for the final session of the conference. Never had I felt more relaxed, confident, valid. Like Churchill under fire in the Boer War, I'd come out of my ordeal a better man.

In front of the Palais, Harvey Ungerleider's youngsters, all those idealistic children, determined to insure the success of fascism in America, were holding a mass meeting.

"Look at them," I said to Moe. "You'd think they'd know by now. There's more people in Levittown who go bowling and drink beer and like Gomer Pyle than there are of *them*. Lots more. Ninety percent of Americans thought that not enough kids were shot dead at Kent State."

"Yeh, yeh." I had the feeling that anything not directly connected with Israel interested Bloom only marginally.

"The trick is not to insult and abuse and ridicule Americans, but to infiltrate them and con them, the way Roosevelt did."

"Maybe you got a point, kid."

"And do they know who Ungerleider is?" I asked. "Sheldon Kantor, FBI stooge. Look at him. With the microphone under Flackman's nose."

King Arno, reluctant to let the long-haired children dominate the scene, had climbed on the roof of a Renault. He had a bullhorn in his hand, and he shook his curly black hair and taurine face a great deal. Ungerleider was standing on the hood of the small car, the tape recorder on his shoulder, the mike a foot from Flackman. The FBI would get a full report on everyone. Actually they cared little about Arno Flackman; to them, he was a harmless party-goer, a face on the cover of *Newsweek*, and as such, could not be taken seriously as a revolutionary. He was of the non-torturable class.

"Let me say to you that I'm with you in spirit, if not in action," Flackman growled. "The only reason I can't march with you to the American Embassy today is that I'm on assignment here. I'm working on a book for which I have a deadline, by far the best thing I've ever done——"

"Screw you, you motherfucker, and up your royalties."

"You don't speak for us, you speak for Suzy Parker."

"Up Against the Wall, bourgeois prick."

"Join us, join us, Flackman!"

"*Avec nous, avec nous.*"

"Yes, thanks, I'd love to," Numero Uno said, "but I really have to finish this piece I'm doing, a really original piece of writing, a new literary form unlike anything that's ever been done in America before——"

"Stick it up your ass, Flackman."

"Tell it to Lennie Lyons, Arno."

"Go, go in before I puke," Moe Bloom said.

"Wait, I have some unfinished business." I elbowed my way through—there wasn't much of a crowd, no more than fifty kids—and braced myself against the Renault.

"Listen," I shouted. "This is Bloodworth speaking."

"That's the CIA fink," Vannie Bragg said to a French girl in a jump suit next to her. "Don't tell him a thing."

"Listen, folks," I shouted. "Harvey Ungerleider here, the man with the tape recorder, is really Sheldon Kantor, of Larchmont, New York. He is a paid informer and agitator for the FBI. He is recording everything you kids say and do, and he is using Flackman as his cover. If I were you I'd get his tapes and burn them."

Someone threw a vanilla ice cream cone at me. It hit me in the left eye. The kids became violent, pushing and shouting—some going for me, some for Harvey, who began to shout that I was a liar, a pig, a fascist, an M.F., and a murderer, and a few clawing at Flackman, who dropped the bullhorn and made for the Palais. Bloom locked his iron arm around me and dragged me away.

"That's it," I called to the milling children. "Get his tapes and burn them. And the photographs he took."

They obliged. I could see Harvey Ungerleider's recordings unreeling, great twisted ribbons of quarter-inch magnetic, flying through the air like streamers at a boat departure.

Bloom and I took seats in the rear of the conference hall. It was only partially filled. Some of the delegates had left early: Malar's performance had disheartened and disgusted many of them.

"The old Hungarian is back," I said to Moe.

Malar was on the platform, nodding, waving, exchanging chitchat with Derek Venables. Well, you couldn't keep good men down. There was something about the literary life that endowed a fellow with limitless resiliency.

"And look who's going to make the wind-up speech, the big summary," I whispered to Moe.

It was Warren Cooperage, of course, in a maroon blazer, tossing his wheat-blond hair, shaking a hand here, kissing another there, acting as if nothing, nothing at all, had happened on that stage the day before."

"This has been a difficult time for intellectuals," Coop began, "a time of testing, from which we emerge better men.

We have talked, argued, exchanged views, learned something of each other's hopes."

A Ugandan ethnomusicologist, a purple-black man in a green robe, leaned toward me and asked, "Who is the gentleman speaking and why is he so important?"

"Hard to say, Dr. Zadako," I said, reading his ID card, "but you better be on his side."

". . . and we reject out of hand the reckless charges that certain government agencies paid for this conference. That some have *contributed* toward its expenses, we do not deny. Well say I, and all of my friends here, good. What better cause? I don't approve of everything the CIA does, or the KGB, for that matter, but if they want to pick up some bills, why not?"

I glanced at Pochastny, rubbing his potato nose, his eyes shut, wondering how he'd let Veg slip away, how he'd blown Malar's performance. He'd have a bit of explaining to do back in Lubianka; the man named Rodin would have some interesting questions. And why, Comrade Antipov, did you permit Comrade Keramoulian to track the professor to his secret laboratory, without anyone covering him, or protecting him? And why, Comrade, did you let this bourgeois adventurer, this madman Bloodworth, who, as nearly as we can establish, was a double agent for the Swiss, pretending to be a Shin-Bet man, with connections to the CIA, why did you let him get so close to Malar, when you knew that the meddler Bloom was in Paris?

"Why did Pochastny give Veg so much free rope?" I whispered to Moe. "Why did he let him run to Latour and Venables?"

"I'm not sure. Maybe Veg didn't have anything to show them. They're way ahead on ESB at the Pavlov Institute."

". . . we must be more selective in the future. Those of us most concerned with the success of the next conference, my friends and I, shall appoint a screening committee to filter out the poseurs, agents, crypto-writers, and pseudo-scientists.

These frauds and troublemakers and two-faced operators must not be allowed to muddy the waters of pure intellectual give-and-take. They will no longer be able to make mischief, spread lies, confuse issues . . ."

Bloom held a hand to his mouth and whispered to me, tough-guy style: "He is referring to you, boychick."

". . . a wide-ranging proposal for more cultural exchanges, for the opening of windows and doors, for a united, but pluralistic, community of scholars and creative people . . ."

"Any bets on Malar speaking?" I asked Bloom.

"Hmmmm. I think he will. The old bastard's got guts."

"I shall refer only briefly to yesterday's demonstration," Cooperage said airily. "I make no apology for Imre Malar's speech. He is his own man, his own voice, and while we may wonder at, and some of us disapprove of, the odd duality here witnessed—the words he spoke on this platform, and the words in the alleged original—I will not be the man to point a finger at Imre Malar, or anyone else. Someday, when he is ready and when the occasion is right, I am sure that this beloved figure will tell the whole story, and we will admire him all the more for it."

"Don't hold your hand on your *tochis* till it happens, Warren," Moe said softly.

"However, since I know he wishes to make some final statement to the delegates, whatever its nature, I now invite Co-chairman Imre Malar to say a few words." Cooperage beckoned to him.

There was applause, a few angry shouts. Most of the exiled Czechs and Hungarians and Poles had left. Malar's performance yesterday had sickened them. And Imre himself was having none of it. He was making those short, lateral eastern European gestures with his right hand, patting his injured skull with the left, grinning stupidly. Then Cooperage walked to him, almost lifted him to his feet, and he and Venables waltzed Malar to the lectern.

"Look, look," Bloom said, grabbing my sleeve and turning me toward Pochastny-Antipov.

394

The KGB boss was on his feet, staring at Malar and waving an admonitory finger at Malar, as if to say, *nyet, nyet.*

"No more chances," Moe said. "They'll kill him if he opens up."

"That's right," I responded. "No more Laszlo Veg to shoot radio waves into his brain."

Malar opened his mouth. "I . . . I . . ."

"Five will get you ten he doesn't speak."

"No bet," Bloom said.

Malar was trudging back to his seat. We were both right.

We cornered him in the lobby. An Ecuadorean professor of romance linguistics and the Ceylonese lady in white were trying to grab his attention, and Judy was trying to rescue him.

"Free for lunch, Malar?" Bloom asked. "We want to tell you about your friend Veg."

Malar bowed to the Ceylonese lady, promised the Ecuadorean he would correspond with him, and looked at Bloom intently. "Oh, my dear Mr. Bloom, my dear Zionist agitator. I know all about Professor Veg. The CIA has kidnapped him against his will. They were aided by your own Shin-Bet agents, and possibly the French. He is being held in Washington and will be tortured until he reveals his secrets."

"*Merde,* Malar," Moe said. "You can stop that nonsense right now. There aren't any radio waves shooting into your brain. Veg's not here with his lighter."

Only Judy remained at Malar's side. The old radical looked about craftily—no Pochastny, no Venables—and winked at us. The crudest, fattest, most cynical wink I'd ever seen.

"Yes, a national disgrace, which the participants may never live down," Malar went on, in a husky, parched voice. "Imagine, a citizen of the People's Republic of Hungary, an eminent scientist, kidnapped in broad daylight off the streets of Paris by the CIA and the Israeli secret police . . ."

What was he blathering about? I recalled Colonel Tal, that

dark, lean hawk, the former Dr. Jabali, standing next to the gray truck.

"Worse than the Mehdi Ben Barka case," Malar said. "Much worse. Protests will be made on the highest level to the French Foreign Ministry, the American State Department, and the Knesset. A telegram is being sent to the United Nations."

Bloom was on his tippy-toes staring at Malar's white patch. "How's the head feel, Imre? Better?"

"Oh, yes. I shall be able to remove the plaster in a day or two."

"How about lunch? Bygones be bygones. You remember Carl Sandburg. He said the past was a bucket of ashes. Come on, you and your daughter. Benny and I will spring for a good lunch. Joseph's."

Someone was going to have to yank those electrodes out of Malar's skull. Moe intended to be around when that happened. Dr. Halevy out at the American Hospital would have another chance later in the day.

As Malar mulled the invitation, Tookie Cooperage floated up to him in her fluted Grecian robes. "Oh, Imre, y'all invahted to the fayerwell lunch Warren and Ah are givin' at Le Grand Manoir. Evahbody's goin' to be theah—Derek and Jimmy Keen and André and Vito. Y'all come, hyeah?"

Bloom and I, naturally, were not invited.

But we went to Le Grand Manoir anyway, a restaurant that embodies everything I find meretricious, greedy, and over-rated about Paris. It was a fine place to conclude the conference.

The Cooperages, as always, went first class. They had a long outdoor table, set for two dozen people, agleam with silver service, four sparkling glasses per setting, and an Alençon tablecloth. Ten waiters and two wine stewards fluttered around the guests. Bloom and I sat a few yards away, at a small table near an outdoor men's room—a small stone building, perhaps once part of the estate which preceded Le Grand Manoir.

"They'll be disappointed in the food," I said to Moe, as we watched the guests assemble. Malar had the place of honor, on Cooperage's right. "The kitchen here stinks."

Bloom didn't hear me. He was squinting at Malar. He would track him down before the day was over.

A one-eyed waiter hovered over us.

"Asparagus, thirty-five francs?" I asked no one in particular. "Seven dollars *pour les asperges fraiches?*"

"Order some Perrier and a cheese sandwich," Bloom said.

He shaded his eyes and stared up at the leafy branches of the splendid shade trees. Nature was in tune; the air was invigorating, but it was hard to enjoy anything in a place that charged seven dollars for asparagus when most French workers' children were raised on hard bread and had rickets.

I ordered two *omelettes aux fines herbes*, and took small solace in the fact that Malraux had snubbed Cooperage's love feast.

"To the health of our dear friend and co-chairman, Malar!" Warren Cooperage shouted.

Glasses tinkled, laughter drifted across the verdant parklike setting. The hazed summer air resounded with the joyous noises of the anointed. Yet I did not feel hurt, or snubbed, or left out. After what I'd been through, after what Moe Bloom had made me part of, I would never again envy those people. In the checkered shade, Bloom and I watched and waited. The scowling waiter brought us our Perrier in a silver ice bucket.

"Got any idea what this will cost Tookie?" I asked. "A plate of fried spuds, twenty-five francs. Wait till they get to the *Boeuf Wellington* and the *Quenelles de Brochet.*"

"Money helps," Bloom said.

"Can your expense account stand this?" I asked. "And what are we here for, besides making goo-goo eyes at Malar?"

"He's got weak kidneys from being beat up so much. Pretty

397

soon, when that champagne starts down, he'll have to run for the john. That's why I wanted the table here. We'll grab him there."

"Grab . . . ?"

"I want to take a good look at his *kopf*."

"Whatever you say." I'd given up trying to keep up with Bloom. "They say they have a new Siamese chef here, and his native dishes tend to induce constipation."

Bloom didn't hear me.

"A Siamese cook. He's the Thai who binds."

The omelettes were dry, undersized. I told the waiter so and he curled a lip at me. Don't try that in a French restaurant, especially if your French is good. I shoved it away and sipped the cold Perrier. Lunchtime; seven dollars for a plate of asparagus; and the place was jammed.

"There he goes, Benny," Bloom said quietly.

Malar, shuffling, nodding apologies to no one in particular, was walking toward the outdoor lavatory.

"Go, go, in the stall next to him," Bloom ordered me.

Casually, I got up and strolled behind some protective trees to the stone house. Moe was a step behind me. Malar was standing at the urinal, sighing, blinking. What heels we were to accost the old guy like this! He couldn't even relieve himself without Bloom and me coming after him.

"Ah, Ben. Dear boy. Charming restaurant, no? It reminds me of Gundel's in Budapest, in the summer under the trees."

"An old radical like you, Imre," I said, "you should be ashamed of being seen in this ostentatious dump. Those prices. And the French worker can't afford meat twice a week."

Malar was shaking himself dry. "No, no, Benny. Such feelings of guilt, of pity for the oppressed proletariat must never interfere with our own earthly joys. If we are denied the thirty-five-franc asparagus, will Jean and Claude and Huguette have more pork on the table?"

"It's possible."

398

"But only possible. Meanwhile, in transitional periods, such as the one in which we now live, why should I not have my caviar and vodka, if he cannot? After all, I am his friend, his advocate. You see, dear boy, socialism must adapt——"

Bloom had sneaked up on him just as he zipped up. Malar let out a whoop as Moe embraced him rudely and hauled him away from the white vitreous enamel *pissoir.*

"Please, gentlemen, some respect for your co-chairman," Malar pleaded. He didn't seem afraid. The old organizer had been manhandled by rougher customers than Moe and me.

"Take it easy with the patch," Moe said to me. "I'll hold him, you peel it off, but easy. I don't want the electrodes to come off."

"Ai, ai, gentlemen, that stupid thing," crooned Malar.

It slid off easily—a smooth, white mound. Bloom and I stared at his shaved skull: nothing. No hole. No plate. No wires. No electrodes.

"Get him in the light by the window," Moe ordered. We hustled him across the slippery floor of the john. The afternoon sunlight spilled over his haggard face. Obligingly, the last voice of humane Marxism in eastern Europe bent his head. We stared at the pale pink piece of scalp surrounded by moist gray hair.

"Nothing," Bloom said. "What I suspected. Another fake."

"Naturally, dear Bloom," Malar said. Moe released him. Malar fussed with his tie, straightened his soup-stained jacket.

"What the hell is this, Imre?" Bloom demanded.

"You and Veg are two phonies," I said. "He didn't control you. He couldn't. He hypnotized me, and he fooled Latour and Venables."

A phlegmy laugh, a noise originating in a stuffed cabbage deep in Malar's throat, emanated from his mouth. "Yes, my dear Zionist agents, a big fake."

"Why?" Bloom demanded. He had Malar cornered, and I felt he'd kill him unless the Hungarian spoke the truth.

"You have probably guessed by now, Moses. You are a

clever old *condottiere*. You know the tricks. Why? So Latzi could get to America, with a small, as you say, stake."

"To be with Kitti Balint," I said.

"Oh, indeed, yes indeed. Thighs like bowls of sour cream. A woman in a million. Breasts like summer melons. The softest belly, the silkiest hair. Latzi could not live without her. He was being driven insane with the memories of their love."

"Why didn't he just defect?" I asked.

"Kitti needed the money to finance a *nouveau vague cinéma vérité* motion picture. Those were her conditions. It was an impossible situation, because Latzi was under constant surveillance. He was under no circumstances to be allowed to leave Hungary. Not even Budapest. His wife is a member of the Central Committee. She spied on him, kept him under guard."

"Ah, but you, *you*, Malar," I said. "The tame communist, the nice Hungarian. You were permitted to go anywhere you could to make a speech to an international gathering. They knew you would always come back and that you would be critical enough to make the outside world think about more freedom, yet never critical enough to anger the Central Committee."

"Oh, if once you saw Frau Veg, friends, you would know why Latzi wanted his Kitti so desperately, and why I, as his oldest and best friend, and a romantic in my heart, was obliged to help him. Frau Veg—the hairs growing from her nose, the cotton stockings, a body like an abandoned tractor."

"Kitti Balint," Bloom snarled, "is a superannuated whore. She will take that quarter of a million Veg gets for his phony technique, buy jewelry, and go to bed with the next guy who offers her more."

"Please, please, Bloom, your Spartan Zionist idealism blinds you to certain corrupt pleasures. She is a goddess between the sheets. And I wish them both happiness." He kissed his cropped fingernails and blew the kiss across the fetid air of the lavatory. "Once, only once, I was privileged to enjoy her favors, and the memory of those thrashing white thighs and that glorious belly sustained me through years of cold jails and stale bread."

"A goddamn fake from start to finish," Moe said. "You faked the fall in your bathroom. You went into the Lenin Institute. Veg pretended to have drilled a hole in you and to have implanted you. Maybe the two of you even staged a little show for the Russian ambassador in Budapest?"

"Yes, more or less. As you know, Latzi had already done much interesting work with implantation of animals. But to be truthful, nothing in advance of what the Americans at Harvard and the Russians at the Pavlov Institute have already done."

"The KGB got word that Veg could control human behavior in a refined, specific way," I said. "And then you leaked the word that you were going to attack Moscow in your speech in Paris. They began to worry. Some genius in Lubianka, Rodin, or maybe Antipov himself, decided here was a chance to cross up the whole conference. To force you to make a pro-Russian speech."

"Yes, yes," Malar said, enthusiastically, his amber eyes gleaming. "As you Americans say, they walked into the trap. It was intended only to get Latzi out of Hungary, in a position to go to America, with a great deal of money for his lost love."

"Beautiful," Bloom said. "The Russians figured they couldn't lose. The word would go out how you, Malar, the most respected voice of the old left, would denounce them— but thanks to Veg's implants and his cigarette lighter, you'd end up praising them."

"What's in the lighter?" I asked.

"Lighter fluid," Malar said, chuckling.

"No wonder he refused to let Latour or Venables look at it, or at my head," I said to Moe. "They weren't even allowed in the room when he was supposed to be shoving the wires into my skull."

Interrogation concluded, the three of us strolled into the afternoon sunlight. "At some time during the conference," Bloom said reflectively, "the Russians must have realized that you two Hungarians were phonies. You were playing some sneaky game, but they weren't sure what. When Benny showed up with his crazy mission—to get you and your daughter to defect—they were really upset. Veg was a fraud, okay. But they had to let you go through with the act, because shutting you up would be worse. Also Keramoulian got his, another botch. But since Veg was a liar, and had nothing to sell, they decided to let the Americans and the Chinese pay for it. That's why Veg was allowed to run loose and stage the demonstration on Benny."

"That is rather what happened," Malar said. "They were quite disturbed over Mr. Keramoulian's demise. He was the sort who killed others joyfully, but did not get killed. They are cautious people. So they gave Latzi and me low priorities and decided to let nature take its course."

"Especially since they liked the idea of the Chinese or, more likely, the Americans, coughing up a quarter of a million dollars for nothing."

"Oh, not for nothing," Malar said slyly. "After all, Latzi and Kitti will be reunited. That is not nothing, Benny, that is something of great moment."

Malar waved at the Cooperages, who had left the High Table and were looking for him. "It is all right, friends," the old free-loader called. "I am in small conference with colleagues."

He agreed to join us for Perrier. The Cooperages retired; conference ended, they had no use for Bloom or me.

"Why did Veg choose Peking's offer?" Bloom asked.

"Greed, Bloom, greed. He would get his quarter of a million from the Chinese, go to his neutral city, and then get perhaps another one hundred and fifty thousand from the Americans for the second rights."

"I see," I said. "Like options on a novel. It could go on forever."

"Of course. If he went to America, he would not get paid twice. No foreign power would give him ten cents for something the Americans already had. Your generous CIA, on the other hand—look how generous they have been to our conference—would not hesitate to pay a large sum for a slightly used, somewhat outdated technique. You are aware of what is paid out daily for obsolete bombers and nonworking missiles."

"Clever bastard," Bloom grumbled. "Of course, if he got to Peking, and they had time to find out he was a fake, they'd have killed him. No money. No life. No Kitti."

"I have not been able to talk to my friend Latzi," Malar said sadly, "but he may have had second thoughts and gotten word to your Mr. Bragg. Hence the interception today."

"You know what?" Bloom asked him. "It would serve that scheming Bohunk right if the CIA refused to pay him also."

"They will pay, they will pay," Malar said cheerfully. "Process, no process, implants, no implants, they will pay so that their reports to their superiors will look proper."

"What would we do without the CIA?" I asked. "They sort of keep everyone in business."

"And a nice business it is," Malar beamed. "If one can stay alive."

Bloom was smiling. "So. I saved a little money. Not to mention not getting stuck with a fake. Some scheme. You and Veg. Just to make sure Latzi got his *tsatske* again."

"*Tsatskes*, Bloom, can be as important as revolutions," Malar said.

"But . . . to screw up a whole conference, to keep all these people running around, spending money, making speeches, so a friend can get into the sack?" I was scandalized.

"Sack?" Malar asked.

"Bed. Love-nest. A place to perform the sexual act."

"Ah, sack. But what is more important?"

"To a Hungarian," Bloom snorted.

"To anyone," Malar said emphatically.

Cooperage was braying at him to come back. They wanted Malar. I didn't begrudge him his champagne and oysters in

403

Paris. He shook hands with us and trudged back to the table of wheels, a hunched, shuffling figure, the old belly Hungarian. Fire and plague, bullets and ropes; he'd been through it all, and he was still around. He watched with outraged tearful eyes as they shot his bosses and hanged his comrades; but he still could scheme and plot to get a friend into the right bed. I saw him glance up at the green leafy wonder of the Paris sycamores, and I appreciated his grasp of life, his joy at being allowed to experience the magic city another sunny day.

"I don't think he was the wrong Hungarian, Moe," I said. "He was the right one."

"In some ways," Bloom said.

"Malar will ruin their business someday."

"Whose?"

"The KGB. And the CIA. And maybe even yours. Is there anything beyond the Pleasure Principle?"

"There is, boychick, but not everybody understands it. Me, I can take Malar or leave him."

I raised my Perrier in toast. "To thighs like bowls of sour cream."

Later I sneaked out of the place with Bloom, waving ruefully to Judy Malar. She got up as if she wanted to come after me for a final word, but Bloom and I—I wanted it that way—cut hurriedly across the park, like two excited college boys on their first day in Paris.

VI

I'm back in Hicksville, Nassau County, Long Island. It could be worse. Felicia gets out of the house every morning to shop, or go to her classes at C.W. Post College. I'm the only man at home during the week, and you'd think I'd make out like crazy, but the local wives—jazzy types in curlers, wrappers, and wedgie shoes—know better. They know I'm a total loss. I write mornings and play tennis, usually with my son Eddie, in the afternoon.

Something that happened to me in Paris helped Eddie beat the Hesseldine kid at tennis, and climb over him on the ladder. I'm not sure what. But when Eddie went out to challenge young Hesseldine again, there was Mrs. H., lank blond hair, gold clip, long tan legs. She had me muttering apologies at first, but the first time she yelled at her brat: "Hit it to his backhand, Myron," I shouted at Eddie, "Lob it deep and run to net, Eddie, he can't handle the lob."

Eddie did, and he beat Myron Hesseldine, 6–4, 8–6. Afterward, Mrs. Hesseldine looked down her short nose at me and sniffed: "Oh. You're the writer. The fellow that was mentioned in the write-up of that conference."

What could I expect of the wife of a CBS producer? People who never worried about insurance premiums or good colleges for their kids. "Do you know my husband Arch?" she asked. "He hires a lot of writers."

"This writer is not for hire, lady," I said. "Leastwise not by television. Besides, CBS couldn't afford me."

Of course, these were all lies. I'm for hire, like anyone. It's just that I've learned the need for being on one's toes all the time.

Her kid was bawling as they left. "You never know the kind of element you come up against on public courts," I heard her say, as she left with her All-American son.

Element this, lady. I've got your element, right here in my jeans. Eddie and I laughed all the way home. We had a pizza to celebrate. Oh, the joys of winning!

Felicia, for a while at any rate, kept bugging me about all the affairs I had in Paris. I denied everything, and why not? My record had hardly been one to be envied. I can't even talk about my failures, they were so ludicrous. Round one: Lila Metrick, tumbling me, humbling me, so that I misfired. Round two: trapped in Evie Bragg's iron girdle. Round three: alone with Judy Malar, and interrupted by that Israeli skateboarder, Bloom's aide-de-camp. Was there anything to discuss?

The World Conference on the Arts and Sciences was behind me when two events occurred to revive memories of those rich, bursting days in Paris, my tour as self-appointed spy.

First, the Sunday *New York Times Magazine* ran a lead article on the meeting, with by-lined contributions from Flackman, Cooperage, Bruno Shockheim, Vito Anzaletti, and a couple of eastern Europeans—but, curiously, not Malar.

My eyes raced through the piece looking for my name. After all, I'd made a stir. I'd posed as a spy. I'd interrupted meetings, baited protean figures like Flackman and Huffguard, and I had almost gotten Imre Malar to defect. And I was one of the few people who knew the full story of the Hungarians. But there was no mention of me. Not a word. (In the earlier news reports on the conference, the *Times*, the only paper to cover it, had even ignored the New Left kids' charge that I was a CIA operative. Probably they were afraid of a libel suit.) I was mildly insulted. But, reading on, I decided that it was just as well that I was ignored. It was deadly dull palaver, except—I give the man credit—for Flackman's account of the meeting, which dispensed at once with any politico-social content, any informed judgments of the great East-West confrontation of intellectuals, and restricted itself to vain, contentious, insulting gossip. Flackman was good at this, very good indeed.

Flackman [he was on that third-person kick again] stared at Venables' pale green eyes, the eyes of a laboratory frog, or a mounted salmon. The limey stared back. Glassy, cold, unblinking. There was a see-all, know-all, hate-all superiority in those Cambridge eyes, those apple-green orbs, that set Flackman off. Neither smiled, for each man, at the summit in his chosen field —Venables in poetry, Flackman in prose—understood that this would be a battle to the finish. They knew an enemy when they saw one. Venables would be a tough man to overcome on the podium. Those constricted sneers and upper-crust vowels, those frigid put-downs and patronizing little snickers would mean trouble for the old Cleveland street brawler. So Flackman summoned up all his slum-bred cunning, his dirty tricks of in-fighting and clinching. He'd need them to claim victory over the gracile Englishman.

Translation: I'm just a tough Jewish boy from Ohio, and it will be hard to top this elegant bastard in the open field, so I'll insult him a little. Besides, he may be a better poet than I am a novelist.

There was this on Malar:

Here was the legendary Imre Malar. There was something elusive, unnamable, unlocatable in his seamed doughy face. The cheesy features, the ragged moustache, the darting eyes. Flackman knew Malar's history—the prisons, the beatings, the torture, the narrow escapes. Yet it was hard for him to summon up pity for this Hungarian fox. Yet . . . what was his attitude?

Curiously, as Flackman studied this ravaged Marxist, Flackman kept thinking about a desirable woman he had made love to only a week ago, the lustful beautiful wife of a New York publisher, much besieged but never breached by ardent writers, including some friends of Flackman. . . . The connection was an odd one, but it seemed to Flackman that Malar's dusty, crummy, soup-stained world was not worth a damn, while Flackman's, for all its cop-outs and compromises, was.

Translation: Imre Malar, whatever his faults, is a real revolutionary, jailed, beaten, tormented, a witness to the upheavals of the age, a sufferer and survivor. He is something I will never be. Hence I must cut him down by bragging about all the rich perfumed twat I get in New York.

But I gave Flackman credit; he forced me to read his article to the end, whereas Metrick's peanut-butter prose lost me after three paragraphs, and Keen's neo-conservative ramblings were grotesque parodies.

The second reverberation of my career as a spy came in October when Moses Bloom phoned me one night. "How's your head, boychick?" he asked.

"It's beautiful. How could it be bad? He never put anything in it. By the way, did your people ever figure out how he got the white rat to beat up the cat, or the rabbit to chase the greyhound?"

We'd discussed this before I left Paris. Veg could not have been a total fraud.

"Delayed reactions. Probably drugs. The animals may have been implanted, but obviously he didn't have any radio control over them. Not such a big deal."

"Where's Veg now?"

"Hollywood. He took Kitti out there. She's using the money he got to start a television film company. Enough with those Hungarians. Come see me in New York tomorrow. I'm covering the United Nations."

"For the Shin-Bet?"

"Don't be a *shlemiel*. For the *Israel Express*."

The next day I met Moe in the lobby of the General Assembly building. He had a press pass for me. Wearing a dark blue suit and a tie, he looked older, more sedate.

"Big day, kid. Egyptian foreign minister. Katib."

"Oh, yes. I read that he's here for the opening debate."

We found seats in the press gallery. "There he comes," Bloom said.

There was a standing ovation for the Arab leader, deafening applause. Katib, a stunningly beautiful man, his face gleaming, stood at the microphone.

"Mr. President, Mr. Secretary-General, members of the General Assembly," he began. "We face today another grave crisis in the Middle East, a crisis provoked by one aggressor nation, one alien and hostile presence in our midst . . ."

He stopped abruptly and reached for a glass of water. As he bent his dark head I saw the white patch on his skull. He drank deeply, set the glass down, and yawned. Then he yawned again, and shook his head, as if clearing his ears.

"But . . . but . . . this . . . presence . . . this state," he said hesitantly, "this . . . Israel . . . must be our friend and we must be Israel's friend. We seek no more wars. We offer our brotherly hands to our fellow Semites, to the people of the book, and we stand ready to discuss all issues with them, with the Israelis, our neighbors, our allies, the people with whom we share a common destiny. We have fought too long and too hard to seek solutions with armed might . . ."

The entire assembly was on its feet—cheering, applauding. Delegates, press, the public galleries exploded in what I was later told was the most emotional outburst in UN history. And the applause would not stop. The Egyptian studied his speech, patted the plaster on his head again, and resumed:

"Peace, peace, we cry! And we stand ready to make peace with our Israeli neighbors. Let us be true friends, let us unite to guard the holy places, we whose past is so closely interwoven, whose cultures are so closely related . . ."

He yawned again, sipped water, walked away from the lectern, came back. Reporters flew out of the gallery to file the sensational news.

Bloom nudged me. "See if you can find him," he said.

"Who?"

"The controller."

My eyes searched the Israeli delegation. A slender dark man in a stone-colored suit was toying with a large silver cigarette lighter.

"That's him," I said. "Who is he?"

Bloom smiled grimly. In a few seconds the man turned his head, and I saw the lean features, sunken cheeks, and long nose of Colonel Shlomo Tal.

"Ah. Part-time neurologist?"

"When necessary."

". . . peace, peace we say unto Israel, and I assure my fellow heads of state that we mean it sincerely . . ."

"He's laying it on thick, isn't he?"

"He gets buzzed, he talks nice."

The gallery was in upheaval. Messengers kept flying in and out. Men were racing to telephones. Typewriters were clacking frantically.

"But Veg's technique was a fake, Moe. He couldn't control behavior. Not any more than the Americans could. He had no baby transmitter and receiver."

"So we advanced it a little. We got the big baboon on the ferris wheel. Took him back to *Eretz*. A change here, a modification there."

"You used Veg's ape as a starter, and refined it?"

"The hardest part was planting the doctor in the Cairo hospital."

". . . extensive cultural exchanges between our peoples, a Nile River Valley project, joint operation of the Suez Canal and a mutual defense treaty, a Middle East Olympics . . ."

"Come on," Bloom said, "it's going to get worse. Let's have a drink in the press lounge."

We sat at the TV set and ordered Perrier. Chipper Latour, looking bigger than I remembered, smiling grimly, came by. "Congratulations, Bloom," he said. "You pulled it off."

"Ah, a break here, a break there," Bloom said.

On the TV screen, the Arab was battling himself. ". . . this evil . . . this festering evil of Zionism . . . intrusion in our midst . . ." Then he yawned until we almost could see his trembling pink uvula. "This . . . progressive and forward-looking state with whom we seek good relations, whom we welcome into the community of nations . . ."

Chipper Latour rubbed his chin. "Damn that Veg," he said.

Bloom looked up at him. "This time there's something in the cigarette lighter besides fluid."

I sipped my Perrier. On television, Katib was calling for a joint Egyptian-Israeli Space Program. When he yawned again, I yawned with him. I had been there. Or had I?